THE FALL OF FYORLUND
The Second Chronicle of Hawklan

Roger Taylor was born in Heywood, Lancashire and qualified as a civil and structural engineer. He lives with his wife and two daughters in Wirral, Merseyside. He is at present working on the third in The Chronicles of Hawklan.

Also by Roger Taylor

The Call of the Sword
The First Chronicle of Hawklan

The Fall of Fyorlund

The Second Chronicle of Hawklan

Roger Taylor

HEADLINE

First published in 1989
by HEADLINE BOOK PUBLISHING PLC

10 9 8 7 6 5 4 3

ISBN 0 7472 3118 4

Typeset in 10/11 pt Plantin
by Colset Pte Ltd, Singapore

Printed and bound in Great Britain by
Collins, Glasgow

HEADLINE BOOK PUBLISHING PLC
Headline House
79 Great Titchfield Street
London W1P 7FN

To my wife and children

Fragment of an ancient and incomplete map on which certain places mentioned in this history have been marked by an unknown scribe.

NAR

Vakloss

FYORLUND

EIRTHLUND

ORTHLUND

Pedhavin
(Anderras Darion)

'The time of Hawklan is so far in the past that it could be the distant future'

Prologue

Frantically the valleys and peaks sped by. Gone now was even a vestige of pretence at silence and stealth as the brown bird, its ghastly yellow eyes glittering, hurtled over the mountains from Riddin to Orthlund.

Contained within was the news of Hawklan's escape from the trap at the Gretmearc. Within was the news of the destruction of that trap by a strange old man. Within rang the terrible noise of the battle that was even now being fought with that same man for control of the birds' will.

The bird faltered. The battle or the message? All effort to the message, and it would be bound utterly. All effort to the battle, and the message might still be lost.

Then its master's will reached out and touched it. The message must be delivered at whatever cost.

Unsteadily, the bird flew on, its wings a numbing vibration, until suddenly *he* was there. Tall and lank. Alien in the Orthlund sunshine. His eyes, red beacons from another age.

The bird dropped out of the sky towards him . . .

Chapter 1

Jaldaric started suddenly out of his sun-hazed drowsiness. 'What was that?' he said, sitting up and looking round at his friends.

In the distance, one of the horses whinnied uneasily.

There were six Fyordyn High Guard lounging away their off-duty hours in the small glade that they had chosen as a camp site when the Lord Dan-Tor had called an abrupt halt to their journeying through Orthlund.

For a moment Jaldaric thought that a muscular spasm had jerked him back from the twilight fringes of sleep as his body relaxed into the soft turf, but he noticed now that all his men were looking round uncertainly, and an unfamiliar silence filled the clearing. Even the birds were silent.

He repeated his question.

The nearest man to him was Fel-Astian. Fair-haired and strongly built, he was not unlike Jaldaric, though his face was leaner and lacked the seeming innocence of Jaldaric's.

'There was a rumbling sound, then the ground seemed to move,' he said cautiously, as if not believing his own words.

'Did move,' someone corrected, more confidently.

Fel-Astian nodded.

Then, as if signalling a release, a bird began to sing and the uneasy disorientation pervading the clearing faded. The men all began to talk at once, debating this strange phenomenon.

Jaldaric craned his head back to ease a stiffness in his neck. The brightness of the spring sky made him narrow his eyes and he noticed a small brown bird flying just above the tops of the trees. Strange, he thought. It was one of those charmless, drab creatures that the Lord Dan-Tor seemed to be able to tame and bring to his hand. Yet their flight was normally arrow-straight and almost alarmingly purposeful, while this one was bobbing and dipping from side to side, as erratically as a swallow.

A little way from the clearing, Dan-Tor stood on the rocky outcrop that he had made his private domain since he had returned from the village of Pedhavin with his unexpected order to halt and make camp. However, it was not the Lord Dan-Tor that Jaldaric or any of his men would have recognised, even allowing for the fact that his mood had been uncertain of late, and his normal commanding charm had been marred by uncharacteristic bursts of irritation.

His body was rigid and quivering, and his eyes glowed red and baleful with a gaze that no ordinary man could have met and stayed sane. Around his feet the rock was shattered and broken as if wrenched apart from its very heart; innocent victim of his immediate response to the news he had received.

He was consumed with alternate waves of fear and rage. Hawklan had escaped the trap at the Gretmearc leaving his, Dan-Tor's, minion there demented and broken. Worse still, someone had aided Hawklan in his escape and he it was presumably who was now assailing the birds, his messengers, his eyes. Someone with knowledge of the Old Power, and no fear of using it.

Dan-Tor had been locked in tormenting internal debate ever since his decision to lure Hawklan to the Gretmearc to be bound and carried to Narsindal. Now it surged around him in a frenzy like a wind-whipped sea overwhelming a rocky shore.

Grimly he fought off the onslaught, and brought his pounding emotions under control with an icy will that belied the awesome glow in his eyes.

Whatever else had happened at the Gretmearc, Ethriss had not been wakened. He would not be stood debating with himself in this accursed land if that had happened. He would be bound again in the darkness, to wait another eternity, another Coming. He shuddered involuntarily.

His calmer counsels told him that much could be gained from this disaster. *Must* be gained, mocked a voice within him. *Must* be gained, if you are to account to Him for your folly. He grimaced and dismissed the tormentor. *His* anger must be faced in due course, come what may, but actions taken now could perhaps alleviate it, and such actions would not benefit from fretful worrying.

Who or what Hawklan was remained an enigma. And one that spread further mystery in its wake. The message brought to him by the failing bird was scarcely intelligible, but it was clear that Hawklan had played little or no part in his own salvation, and was now fleeing the Gretmearc. And yet his saviour, too, had fled, though by some route unseen, pitting his strength against one of the birds. The thought was comforting. You'll find the bird no easy prey, he thought, maliciously. It has strength beyond your imagining, and when it defeats you, I'll know you, and I'll find you at my leisure.

Standing like a column of rock in the Orthlund sunshine, Dan-Tor's turmoil eased gradually and the unfettered hatred faded from his eyes. Nearby, birds began to sing again. He had been right. Hawklan was a creature of some importance. True, he had not been bound, but his very presence had at once exposed and perhaps immobilised a hitherto unknown enemy capable of wielding the Old Power against Him. And now Hawklan himself was alone and presumably scurrying back to Anderras Darion like a frightened rabbit to his burrow.

Caution seeped into Dan-Tor's momentary ease. The man must still be bound and examined. But how alert was he now? To risk the Old Power again would be unforgivable folly. He sensed a presence approaching.

'Captain,' he said, without turning round.

Jaldaric stopped, surprised as always at the Lord's awareness.

'Lord, we heard rumbling and felt the ground shake. I thought perhaps there might have been a rockfall . . .'

Dan-Tor turned and looked at Jaldaric. At the sight of the Captain's fair hair a memory of long blond hair glinting in the sun came to him, and a device for Hawklan's binding came to him that was truly earthbound and far from the deep powers of older times.

He smiled broadly, a white banner of welcome lighting up his creased brown face. 'That was most thoughtful of you, Jaldaric,' he said, stepping forward appreciatively. 'But I was in no danger. It was a small earth tremor, nothing more. Unusual and most interesting.'

Jaldaric opened his mouth to speak, but Dan-Tor raised a hand and assumed an expression of almost fatherly concern.

'I have to leave unexpectedly, Captain,' he said. 'And I'm afraid I must leave you and your men with a task as difficult and perhaps as distasteful as you've ever had to do.' He looked deeply into Jaldaric's eyes. 'I rely on your loyalty, Captain, as does the King.'

'Ah, Fyordyn are you?' Loman said, looking up from the horse he was tending. The recipient of this remark stood framed in the sunlit doorway of Loman's workshop. He was tall and well-built with fair curly hair and a round face which exuded a worried innocence. Loman judged him to be about twenty-four years old.

Jaldaric and his companions had ridden into Pedhavin down the River Road just after dawn, in search of a smith to reshoe one of their horses.

'How did you know that?' he said in surprise.

Loman smiled and winked. 'No great mystery, young man. It's very characteristic work,' he said, handing him the shoe. 'Quite well made too. Your smithing's improved in the last twenty years.'

'Oh,' came the reply. 'I'm afraid all horseshoes look alike to me. I know very little about smithing.' Then, changing the subject, 'Have you ever been to Fyorlund?'

'No, no,' said Loman quickly. 'But I've seen quite a lot of Fyordyn work in my time. A lot of people have passed through here over the years. Here we are.'

His last remark was spoken to the horse as he moved to the side away from the young man and started busily preparing one of its hooves. The Fyordyn work he had seen had been during the Morlider War and he did not want to become involved in relating sad old tales to sate the inevitable curiosity of this young man and his friends.

He regretted slightly his little demonstration in identifying the shoes, and decided not to ask to which Lord this group were High Guards. They wore no livery, but their whole bearing told what they were as clearly as any uniform to one who had fought by the side of the High Guards. Loman paused in his work and screwed up his face as he forced down the old memories that came to his mind vivid and clear.

The young man walked around the horse to join him. 'My name's Jaldaric,' he said, extending his hand and smiling nervously.

Loman looked up and, returning a reassuring smile, took the hand. 'Are you journeying to the south?' he asked.

Jaldaric shook his head. 'No,' he said. 'We're just spending some leave-time in Orthlund before we go back on duty. We're High Guards.'

Loman nodded understandingly and bent to his work again.

'We're due for the northern borders when we get back, and it's miserable up there at the best of times,' Jaldaric continued.

Loman was surprised to find he was relieved at this voluntary admission, and he reproached himself for harbouring suspicious, albeit unclear, thoughts. He attributed these to 'too many changes going on round here these days'.

'You must be my guests for the day then,' he said, to salve his conscience. 'And tonight you must join in our little celebration.'

Jaldaric seemed a little taken aback by this offer and protested that he and his friends did not wish to be a burden to the smith.

'Nonsense,' said Loman. 'We take a pride in our hospitality in Pedhavin. And, as it's unlikely that you'll come here again for a long time, if ever, you'll need someone to show you round or you'll miss a great many interesting sights.'

In common with most of the other people of the village, Loman felt he was emerging from the dark cloud that the tinker and his tainted wares had cast over the village, and the feeling of lightness, of returning to a welcome normality, had made him quite loquacious. Jaldaric's half-hearted protestations were easily swept aside.

'I've one or two things to do up at the Castle. Join me there in an hour and I'll show you round. Well, I'll show you a little of it anyway. It's a very big place.'

The young men were amazed by the Castle, and plied Loman endlessly with questions, many of which he could not answer.

'I'm a humble castellan and smith, not a warrior Lord – or a builder,' he said eventually.

Jaldaric laughed. 'A child could defend a castle like this,' he said. 'It's the most incredible place I've ever seen. You can see for miles and miles, and you're completely unassailable behind walls like these – and this gate.'

They all expressed surprise that the occupant of such a castle was not a great Lord, but simply a healer, and a healer who had just decided to travel on foot all the way to the Gretmearc. But Loman just laughed.

'We've no Lords in Orthlund,' he said. 'We just tend our crops and practise our simple crafts.'

Jaldaric looked troubled. Loman thought he understood.

'There's a Great Harmony in Orthlund, Jaldaric,' he said, 'which most people from other lands can't understand, even though they might sense it. No one knows why it is. Perhaps we're a special people in some way. We accept Hawklan for what he is. Whatever he might have been once, he is beyond doubt a very special man, and a great healer.'

Jaldaric nodded vaguely.

Loman was spared further questioning by the appearance of Tirilen. Her presence took the young men's minds well away from matters military. Loman smiled to himself as he watched his daughter's light grace draw the satellites away from his own more solid presence. He wondered what her new-found escorts would think if they had seen her in the not-too-distant past when she would crash down the stairs three at a time, or wrestle some village youth to the ground for some slight, real or imagined.

Strangely, Jaldaric did not lead the admiring throng, but kept himself a little aloof, and Loman noticed that he frowned occasionally as if some troublesome thought kept recurring to him.

The celebration that Loman had referred to was not intended to be anything special. The need for it seemed to have been agreed by an unspoken consensus among the villagers, as an attempt to dispel the remaining gloom left by the tinker. However, the presence of strangers struck the powerful chord of hospitality present in all the Orthlundyn, and turned it into a very special occasion indeed.

Jaldaric and his troop found themselves overwhelmed with

food, drink, and merriment, in a bright ringing whirl of dancing and singing and laughter, the predominant feature of which seemed indeed to be Tirilen, flying through the lines of clapping hands and jigging flutes and fiddles.

Eventually Jaldaric had to concede defeat. Flopping down next to Loman, red-faced and panting, he said, 'You dance and sing harder than we do our military exercises. I think your daughter would make an excellent training officer for our cadets.' He took a long drink. 'Not to mention some of the Guards themselves.'

Then they had to leave. In spite of all protests, Jaldaric held his ground valiantly. They had to be back in Fyorlund soon or they would be in serious trouble. They would not forget the friendship of Pedhavin, and would surely return one day when time was pressing less on them. They refused all offers of hospitality for the night, saying that, leave or no, they were bound to certain ways as High Guards, and had to spend their nights in formal camp.

As Jaldaric leaned down from his horse to take Loman's hand, the light from the fire seemed to make his boyish, innocent face look briefly old and troubled and, as he rode away, he seemed ill at ease, not turning to wave as most of the others did.

Too tired to face the long steep climb back to the Castle, Tirilen had begged a bed from Isloman. Now she revelled in the feel of a different room with all its shapes and shadows and smells, familiar, but free of her own personality.

Pausing before a mirror, she raised her chin, pushed her head forward and carefully examined the small scar on her throat. It was noticeably less inflamed and she touched it with a cautious finger. It was healing, but only slowly. How strangely persistent it had been, like the cut on Loman's hand. Then she caught sight of her face in the mirror, incongruous, with lips pursed and chin extended. She put out her tongue and tossed her hair back with a spectacular flourish before setting about it vigorously with a delicate metal comb that her father had made for her many years earlier. It shone and sparkled, sending tiny lights about the room as she swept it repeatedly to and fro, unpicking the dance-swirled tangles.

She jigged about on her seat and sang softly herself as she combed her hair, her head still full of the music that had been playing all evening, and her feet still full of dancing. Impulsively she stood up and swirled round, sending her hair and skirts flying out like canopies. Then, dousing the torchlight, she went over to the window and stepped out on to the balcony.

The sky was bright with moonlight and hardly any stars could be seen. Looking up she could see the Great Gate of Anderras Darion gleaming silver, like a star fallen to earth, while looking down she could see the streets and rooftops of Pedhavin, glistening in the moonlight.

There were still a few people wandering about, talking and laughing, and she acknowledged several friendly calls with a wave. For a few minutes she stood and watched as the moonlight moved across a small carving on the edge of the balcony. The shadows within it made it look like a bud slowly opening into flower. So realistic did it seem that she had an urge to lean forward and sniff its night scent.

'Oh! Too much dancing, girl,' she said to herself, catching the fey thought and, spinning on her heel, she went back inside, continuing her dance across to the bed.

She lay very still for a long time, allowing warm, tired limbs to sink into the bed's sustaining softness as she watched the moonlight's slow march across the room.

Normally she would fall asleep immediately, but the dancing and the pleasant, strange familiarity of the room left her drifting gently in and out of sleep. Each time she opened her eyes, the shadow patterns on the ceiling had changed as the moon continued its journey through the sky. Not for the first time, she wondered why the Orthlundyn were not content simply to make beautiful carvings, but had to fill every carving and every cranny in the village with endlessly shifting shapes in which different scenes appeared with each change of moonlight or sunlight. Sometimes she felt overwhelmed by the massive history that seemed to be wrapped hidden in these carvings, even though it never made a coherent whole. She often felt an ancestral presence reaching far behind her into a strange distant past.

Drifting back into consciousness, with half-opened eyes and

a half-closed mind, she noted the shadow of a man's profile on the wall. It was vaguely familiar, but she could not identify it, and it was already looping in and out of her incipient dreams.

When she opened her eyes again, it was gone.

Instead there was a darker, much more solid shadow there, not lightened by reflected moonlight but cutting it out. It was the figure of a man, standing in the room.

Suddenly she was awake, eyes wide, at first in bewilderment, and then in mounting terror as a powerful hand was clamped over her mouth, and a soft hissing voice exhorted silence.

Chapter 2

In contrast to his leisurely journey from Pedhavin, Hawklan strode away from the Gretmearc as vigorously as he dared without making his progress seem too conspicuous. His long legs carried him easily through the throngs crowding the roads near that bustling, hectic market, but he was troubled and, while he tried to use the steady rhythm of his walking to quieten his thoughts, it was of little avail.

He had journeyed to the Gretmearc seeking answers to a question he had scarcely formulated. Now he came away beset by countless questions that were all too clear. He was a healer, not a warrior and yet, almost effortlessly, he had overcome four of the men who had attacked Andawyr's tent. Then he found himself angry because he had fled, despite his flight being at Andawyr's express command. Fleeing – leaving others to do his fighting. He felt degraded, dishonoured in some way that he could not understand.

Where had these strange fighting skills come from, and from where this feeling of disloyalty at his desertion of the field? And, perhaps even worse, from where the deeper voice within, coldly telling him that this desertion was necessary for a greater good?

Then there was Andawyr himself. The strange little man who had undoubtedly saved his life. Andawyr who had referred to him as Ethriss. 'First among the Guardians,' he had said. Some strange god-like creature from the mythical past. Hawklan wanted to dismiss the idea as a foolish old man's rambling, but Andawyr had radiated a sincerity and demonstrated skills that precluded such an easy escape.

But it must surely be a nonsense? For all his ignorance of his own past, Hawklan certainly did not feel he was anything other than a very frail mortal. Yet Andawyr had seen that too. 'You may be our greatest hope,' he had said. 'But at the moment I'm *your* greatest hope, and you, along with everyone else, are in great danger.' Then, 'Great forces have already been set against you. You need protection until you can be taught to know yourself.' And finally, 'Watch the shadows, your days of peace are ended.' The words were chilling. There was solace in none of them.

And, unbidden, some new awareness had grown in him, making him seek for enmity as well as friendship in strange faces, danger as well as quiet calm where some wooded glade threw the road into dappled shade, treachery as well as hospitality when they passed through some village.

But for all his sombre preoccupations, the journey down through Riddin was uneventful. There seemed to be no pursuit from the Gretmearc, and neither he nor Gavor saw any of the sinister little brown birds following them. None the less, the further they moved from the Gretmearc the easier Hawklan began to feel. It seemed that just as some compulsion had drawn him to the Gretmearc, now something was drawing him back to Anderras Darion. He longed to hear familiar voices talking of mundane matters, and to see familiar faces and surroundings, and he found himself almost elated when they turned from the road and began moving westward along the lesser roads and pathways through the grassy foothills that would lead them back into the mountains and towards Orthlund. Gavor, too, rose high and joyous into the spring sky.

The following day was windy and sunny, with white billowing clouds flying busily across a blue sky. Hawklan had been continuing a relentless pace uphill, and had stopped for a brief rest and a meal. He was lying on a grassy bank at the side of the road, staring idly over the Riddin countryside spread out beneath him and half-listening to the happy babble of a family who were picnicking nearby. The sun was warm on his face and he felt very relaxed, in spite of his dark anxieties.

He had made a small truce with himself – whoever I am, or have been, and whatever I did or have yet to do, and whatever has happened or will happen to me, there is nothing to be gained in endlessly fretting over it, other than confusion and dismay. All will become clear in time . . . probably. Just watch and wait and learn.

Looking up at the moving clouds, he realised that the image of dark and distant clouds lingering peristently at the edges of his mind seemed to have gone. Now, like the real ones above him, they were overhead. But they contained no spring lightness; they were dour and menacing. He knew that what he had been fearing had arrived, but he could not yet see what it was.

Suddenly he realised that the noise of the picnicking family had stopped, and he turned his head to see what had happened. Apparently the father of the group had called for silence and he was slowly rising to his feet and staring up into the sky intently. As he rose, he lifted two of the children to their feet and, with an extended finger, directed their gaze out across the country-side to where he himself was staring. The whole family looking in one direction, Hawklan found his own gaze drawn inexorably the same way.

At first he could see nothing unusual, then a familiar black dot came into view. Surely the group couldn't be staring at Gavor? he thought, resting his cheek on the cool sweet-smelling grass and looking at them again. Then Gavor landed clumsily and hastily by his side in a state of some considerable excitement.

'Look, Hawklan,' he said breathlessly, thrusting his beak forward pointing in the same direction.

'Where?' said Hawklan.

'There,' replied Gavor impatiently. 'There. Where I'm pointing.'

'I can't see anything,' began Hawklan. 'Only clouds and sk –'

He broke off as his gaze, working through the moving tufts of white, had fallen on the cause of all the attention. The sight dispelled his sun-warmed lethargy and drew him first into a sitting position, and then to his feet, though slowly, as if fearful of disturbing the wonder he was looking at. For a moment he felt disorientated and he glanced down briefly at Gavor. The gleaming black iridescence of his friend against the soft green grass reassured him and he looked up again at the large white cloud in the distance.

For a large white cloud is what it appeared to be, one of the great windborne flotilla gliding silently and gracefully over-head. Except that rising from its upper surface were rank upon rank of towers and spires, like a vast and distant echo of Anderras Darion, glinting white and silver in the sunlight.

As he stared, Hawklan saw that the surface was etched with a fine mosaic that could be smaller buildings though it was too distant for him to identify any details.

As the great shape moved, so, like any other cloud, it changed, and Hawklan saw the distant towers slowly, almost imperceptibly, rising and falling in response.

'What is it?' he whispered, unconsciously imitating the hushed awe of the nearby Riddinvolk.

'Viladrien.' Gavor spoke the word at the same time as the man in the group, and the effect, combined with the almost unbelievable sight in front of him, made Hawklan start slightly. Before he could speak again, Gavor said, 'One of the great Cloud Lands.'

Gavor's tone also reflected the awe of the other watchers, and Hawklan himself sensed it was a time for watching and not talking.

'I must go to it,' said Gavor, and without waiting for any comment from Hawklan he stretched his great blue-sheened wings into the breeze and rose up into the spring air.

'It's too far,' Hawklan whispered softly to himself, without understanding why he said it. 'Too far. You'll break your heart.'

As he watched Gavor go, flying straight and purposefully in the direction of the strange and stately Cloud Land, Hawklan thought he caught a faint sound floating softly in the air all around him but, as he strained to hear it, it slipped from him.

For a long, timeless moment, Hawklan and the picnicking Riddinvolk stood on the sunlit hillside in silent communion as the great shape floated by. Less captivated than the adults, the children alternated their attention between the Cloud Land and their silent parents but, sensing their mood, they remained still and quiet.

In the silence, Hawklan seemed to hear again the strange soft singing all around him but, this time, he allowed it to move over him and made no wilful attempt to listen to it. He had never heard such a noise before, nor could he understand it, but he knew it for an ancient song of praise and rejoicing though now it was filled with a strange regretful longing.

Eventually, as the Cloud Land faded into the distance and was lost amongst its neighbours, the children began to tug tentatively at their father and ask questions. The man knelt down and put his arms around his two boys. Hawklan eavesdropped shamelessly, his own immediate sense of wonder being slowly overcome by curiosity.

'It's one of the Viladrien,' the man said, almost reverently. 'Where the Drienvolk live. The sky people. They float in the sky like the Morlider islands float in the sea.'

'Are they bad people like the Morlider?' asked one child anxiously.

The man smiled; rather sadly, Hawklan thought.

'Not all the Morlider are bad,' the man said. 'I've told you that. But no, the Drienvolk are kind and friendly. They've never harmed anyone.'

'Will any of them come down?'

'I wouldn't think so. From what my grandfather used to tell me, they don't like being on the ground. The air's too thick for them. They feel closed in, crushed. They need the space of the skies to be happy.'

Hawklan's curiosity overwhelmed him totally and he walked over to the group and introduced himself. The man welcomed him. He was rubbing his neck and wriggling his shoulders.

'I couldn't keep my eyes off it,' he said with a rueful smile. 'How long have we been watching it?'

Hawklan shrugged. 'Some experiences can't be measured in ordinary time,' he said enigmatically.

The man looked at him thoughtfully and then nodded a slow agreement.

'Did you hear that noise?' Hawklan asked.

The man shook his head. 'No, I heard nothing,' he said. 'I didn't dare to breathe for fear of disturbing the silence. Did you hear anything?' He turned to ask his wife.

'Someone was singing,' volunteered one of the children casually. 'It was all around.' She met Hawklan's green eyes squarely and openly.

'All around?' said Hawklan.

The child opened her arms to encompass the mountains and the plains and the sky. 'All around,' she confirmed. Her father looked at her suspiciously. 'All around, Daddy, as if the mountains were singing to the Vil . . . Vil . . .' She gave up her attempt on the word, but finished her speech. 'But it *was* very soft, Daddy, the music.'

Hawklan intervened gently. 'There *was* a faint singing noise, I'm sure. Maybe it was the wind. Anyway it's stopped now.'

The man smiled. 'It doesn't matter,' he said. 'The appearance of a Viladrien is supposed to be associated with strange happenings. I'm well content just to have seen one. What a sight. What a thing to tell them back home.'

'They'll all have seen it,' said his wife prosaically.

The man refused to allow his spirits to be dampened. 'I don't care. I'll tell them anyway. I'll wager we had the better view up here,' he said excitedly. 'What a sight,' he repeated.

'Indeed,' said Hawklan. 'Can you tell me anything about them? I've never heard of anything like an island in the sky. What kind of people live on them?'

The man laughed. 'You're Orthlundyn aren't you?' he said. 'Don't they teach you the Old Lore in Orthlund?'

Hawklan smiled and shrugged self-deprecatingly. 'A little,' he lied. 'But not all of us listen as we should.'

The man laughed again. 'Well, I can't tell you much,' he said. 'Only old school tales. My great-grandfather was supposed to have met some of the Drienvolk once . . . according to my grandfather, that is. Very high in the mountains, when he was young and had got separated from his parents in the mist. Said they showed him the path. Said they were friendly but a bit strange – shy, in a way. And they floated in the air. I never really believed it, but it's a nice family tale, and the Drienvolk are supposed to be kind and gentle.' The man's manner quietened a little at the mention of his grandfather, and he looked almost longingly after the departed Viladrien.

'And you've never seen one before?' offered Hawklan gently.

The man shook his head. 'Apparently once they were supposed to be quite common, but no, I've never seen one until today. Nor met anyone who has. They say sometimes the odd one has been seen far out to sea, but . . .' His voice tailed off into a shrug.

'I wonder why one should come now?' Hawklan said.

The man looked at him. 'That's a strange question. They're carried on the air like the Morlider Islands are on the sea. They must go where the wind takes them, they must go where Sphaeera wills.' He almost intoned the last part softly as if repeating something he had learned many years earlier by rote.

'Sphaeera?' queried Hawklan.

The man looked at him and smiled knowingly. 'It's a quiet place isn't it, Orthlund?'

Hawklan returned the smile and nodded.

'Sphaeera's our name for the Guardian of the Air,' said the man. 'You've probably got a different one. She's actually supposed to have created the Viladrien. But why one's come now, Ethriss only knows.'

He gave Hawklan a sideways look. 'You've heard of Ethriss, I suppose?' he asked humorously.

'Oh yes, I've heard of Ethriss,' said Hawklan, unconsciously resting his hand on his sword.

The man noted the gesture and laughed again. 'I see you wear a black sword like Ethriss used to. Maybe it's you who attracted the Viladrien.'

It was nearly sunset before an exhausted Gavor returned to Hawklan. The bird sat heavily and silently on his shoulder for a long time before speaking and, when he did speak, his voice was unusually subdued.

'It was much further away and far higher than it looked,' he said. 'And it was large. Very large. I didn't really get anywhere near it at all, I'm afraid, though I thought I caught a glimpse of people flying over it.'

'You seem to have been very impressed,' said Hawklan light-heartedly.

To his surprise, Gavor was almost angry. 'Andawyr was right,' he said crossly. 'You need to study more lore. The Viladrien were Sphaeera's greatest creation. I haven't the words to describe what I felt when that great vision floated into sight. I doubt I'll ever be the same again. I must land on one. I must.'

'I'm sorry, Gavor,' said Hawklan gently. 'I didn't mean to upset you.'

Gavor repented a little. 'It's not your fault, Hawklan. You understand living creatures more than anyone I've ever met, but you're earthbound. You can no more understand what it feels like to be an air creature than I can understand your healing skills or what it's like to have hands.'

Two days later they were deep into the mountains, Hawklan still maintaining a vigorous pace, fuelled by a restless anxiety. He had the feeling that only at Anderras Darion would he be truly safe, and only there could he begin to start learning about what had happened and what was about to happen. He might refuse to fret about what had been, but he realised now that he needed knowledge and would have to search, and learn and learn.

Sitting on the grass and leaning against a tree he watched the distant sky changing through reds and oranges and purples as the sun sank further below the horizon, and the deep hazy blue of the night encroached from the east. Overhead, the odd pink cloud drifted aimlessly, while others, lower, were already turning black and grey. One or two bright points of light hung in the sky, the lights of the vanguard of night.

He had chosen a sheltered spot for the night's camp because tomorrow he would be much higher and would need to pitch his small shelter for the night. This would be his last night in the open for some days.

Although it was not late and he was not particularly comfortable, his hard pace through the day had left him pleasantly weary, and he found himself drifting into sleep, then jerking suddenly awake as his body slid into some improbable position. After the third such awakening he relinquished his viewing of the night sky and, wrapping his cloak around himself, lay down on the soft grass.

Whether it was a quality of the cloak, or whether it was some ancient instinct he was unaware of, he became just another shadow in the rising moonlight, indistinguishable from all the others, as he pulled his face under the hood.

He fell asleep almost immediately but, as the remains of the evening light faded away, he began to be plagued by restless, flitting dreams. Images of the recent past came and went arbitrarily with an insane logic all their own: a horse that could not speak to him; a squat creature that tore off his arm and turned into a group of his friends when he stabbed it; a rushing cheering crowd of horsemen galloping across the sky and a cloud that sang to him a song he understood but did not understand; Dar-volci's stentorian voice roaring profanities in a dark place full of noise and gleaming blades . . . A terrible place. No! he cried out. No! But he could not awaken. He sat up, sweating, but he knew he was still asleep.

A strange expectant silence fell on his mind. Somewhere he sensed a faint, indistinct and shifting light, and a sibilant whisper reached him, like someone shouting very loudly at a great distance.

'Sssss, awaken, awaken . . . ssss . . .'

He tried to find the image of the light. He must see it. But it eluded him.

'Ssss, awaken . . .'

Then, abruptly, three figures were standing in front of him pleading, and a great chorus of sound roared in his ears. 'Awaken!' But before he could react, they were gone, vanished, and he was truly awake, eyes staring up into the moonlit sky and his heart racing.

A noise nearby blew away the remaining memory of the dream like smoke in the wind, and drew his eyes downwards. There, not three, but two hulking figures stood before him dark against the night sky, one with a strange, sinister helm on his head.

Chapter 3

On the morning following the dance, those villagers who had to be were up at dawn as usual and away to their fields; some light-hearted, others lead-footed with reluctance. The remainder, however, were more than content to lie luxuriously abed.

It was thus a quiet Pedhavin, tranquil in the spring sunshine, that Isloman eventually woke to. For a little while he prowled casually around the house in search of Tirilen to offer her good morning but, finding her room empty and her bed in its usual state of monumental disarray, he presumed she had left quietly to avoid waking him. He smiled at the sight, reflecting that Tirilen still had some of the attributes of her more boisterous youth. Then, with a shrug, he left the room and set about his day's tasks.

Some hours later, however, Loman called to see him to borrow a sharpening stone and, imperceptibly, Tirilen's absence began to dominate their conversation, an uneasy shade crying distantly but persistently for attention.

Their concern aroused, it took but a few enquiries around the village for them to learn that no one had seen her all that day. The uneasy shade became a chilling spectre, cold in the heart of each man.

Years before, the two brothers had quarrelled over the favours of the woman who was to become Tirilen's mother. When she had chosen Loman, Isloman had gone to fight against the Morlider in Riddin, taking wounds and pain with him, and leaving pain and wounds behind him. Later, at his pregnant wife's behest, an unwilling Loman had sought Isloman out on the battlefield and the horror of their personal distress had dwindled into insignificance against the horrors of the latter stages of the war. Sharing discomforts, dangers and indignities the two brothers were reconciled, the bond reformed between them, stronger even than it had been before their quarrel.

The joy of their return after a bitter winter journey was completed by the birth of Tirilen and, in this small creature, the two brothers buried the last remnants of their animosity. Now the bond between them encompassed her also and she held them like planets round a sun. Captured, too, like a quiet mysterious comet from the distant stars, was Hawklan. Hawklan, who, within a few weeks of Tirilen's birth, had come out of the snow-clogged mountains with the raven Gavor sheltered under his cloak, to open the Great Gate of Anderras Darion; the ancient Castle that had been sealed and inaccessible since times of legend. Hawklan, who asked for nothing and imposed on none but who drew all to him with his gentle presence. Hawklan, whose quality the Orthlundyn knew was beyond their fathoming and could only be accepted like the other mysterious forces of nature.

When, three years later, Loman's wife slipped beyond even Hawklan's aid and died, tragically young, Tirilen's dominion over the three men became absolute.

Hesitantly, the two brothers pieced together the events of the day to form a picture from which Tirilen was beyond doubt missing. Becoming alternately frantic and practical, each supported the other in turn until both could look clearly, if not steadily, at the realities of what might have happened.

Tirilen was adventurous but not foolhardy and she knew the local hills and mountains well, having often walked them with both, Isloman in search of rocks, and Hawklan in search of herbs and flowers. It seemed unlikely, therefore, that she had had an accident, and the two men found their tense debate dominated by the unreasoned feeling that her disappearance was in some way associated with the visit of the tinker, though how or why was beyond them.

Under normal circumstances, in such pain, they would have turned instinctively to Hawklan for advice, but he was not there. So it came to Loman that they should go after the High Guards and seek their help. With their horses and their military discipline, they would be able to cover larger areas more quickly than any party from the village, and they might even have had news of the tinker. Surely they would not refuse such a request?

Thus, leaving groups of villagers scouring the immediate vicinity of the village, the two men took horse and rode off in the direction the Fyordyn had taken.

Neither were good horsemen but they made adequate, if uncomfortable, progress and soon located the site of the camp that the Fyordyn had used on the previous night. From there a trail of lightly damaged grasses and undergrowth showed that the Fyordyn had ridden towards the Pedhavin Road, before heading north, confirming the High Guard's statement that they were heading back to Fyorlund.

Relieved at noting that the Fyordyn seemed to be making leisurely progress, the two brothers rode through the night as rapidly as they dared, pausing only occasionally to rest the horses and to stretch their own sore limbs.

Early in the morning, they saw the High Guards' camp in the shelter of a small copse and, turning off the road, they trotted towards it, casting long shadows on the dew-chilled grass.

A number of the Guards came forward to greet them and, as the two men dismounted, their horses were courteously taken from them and led away. However, before either could speak they found themselves quietly surrounded and held at knife and sword point. When Loman tried to move, the unequivocal intention of their captors was made quite clear.

'Please don't attempt to escape. We've orders to hold you until Jaldaric can see you,' said one, resting the point of his long sword on Loman's throat.

Isloman reached out gently and rested a restraining hand on his brother's arm. Casting his eyes about significantly into the surrounding trees and bushes and at the group of men holding them Isloman sent the obvious message to his brother.

Although it was unlikely that any of these young men had been in actual combat, they were trained soldiers and as such were not going to commit themselves to violence, where random chance could play too high a part, unless it was absolutely necessary. They had, therefore, ensured the two brothers were totally overwhelmed. Each was restrained by four sharp points, at least two of which, at any one time, were out of sight and were signalled only by the occasional gentle prod in the back. Then there were two bowmen some distance away, weapons at the ready, and clear sounds of movement in the nearby trees.

Isloman looked steadily down into the face of the man opposite him and took some satisfaction in the man's inability to return his gaze. Loman fumed and roared, but did not move.

After a few minutes, Jaldaric came out of one of the tents. Loman smiled and opened his mouth to speak, but Jaldaric waved him to silence. When he spoke, both his manner and voice were formal. 'I regret that it was necessary to abduct your daughter,' he said bluntly to Loman. Both the captive brothers gaped, but found no words. Jaldaric looked down fleetingly then, recovering himself, continued. 'It was done at the direct order of a superior and we had . . . no choice. She's unharmed and is currently being taken to Fyorlund where she'll be given every consideration. Now, unfortunately, you'll have to come as well, but you too will be given every courtesy if you behave correctly.'

Then, with a wave of his hand, he dismissed the two men to the care of their guards and turning on his heel walked quickly back to the tent he had just come from, his shoulders hunched high, showing the inner tension that he had managed to keep from his voice.

Before either man could recover sufficiently to even shout questions after the retreating figure, the surrounding sword points began shepherding them towards another tent.

'Just do as you're told and no harm will come to anyone,' said one of the High Guards. 'This tent's a bit rough, but we weren't expecting you. We'll find you something better tomorrow.'

Loman swore at him roundly, but moved as he was bidden.

Inside the bare tent, Loman spent some considerable time raging after Jaldaric and his companions, but eventually he fell silent and slumped on to the ground with his back against the tent's central pole. As the day wore on, they were given food and drink, which Isloman was just able to prevent being hurled by Loman at the head of the man who brought it. But no one spoke to them, nor offered any answers to their questions, and the entrance to the tent was guarded all the time.

In between fits of rage and frustration, the two men tried to make some sense of their predicament, but their conjectures led them nowhere other than into more frustration. Tirilen's abduction was almost unbelievable in itself, but to learn that it had been done by High Guards of Fyorlund left the two brothers floundering hopelessly. The High Guard were the epitome of Fyorlund chivalry; their action made no sense. Eventually, however, as night came, physical and emotional fatigue took its toll and the two men fell asleep.

Isloman woke up suddenly from a fitful, dream-racked slumber. He shook his brother and gestured silence. Something seemed to be out of place. Cautiously he crawled to the entrance of the tent and peered out. The guards were not there, and there were sounds of merriment coming from one of the other tents.

He found it hard to believe that the High Guards could be so neglectful of their duty but, realising that a similar chance was unlikely to occur again, he gestured frantically to Loman. The full implications of this lapse by the High Guards passed between the two brothers with a mere glance and, after pausing only until a cloud slid in front of the moon, they ran crouching and silent to where their horses were tethered. Fighting down a powerful urge just to mount and flee they led the horses on foot quickly and quietly out of the camp.

After several minutes, Loman stopped. 'What are we doing?' he said. 'We must go back for Tirilen.' His shocked voice was loud in the still darkness.

Spinning round as if struck, Isloman seized him and clamped a huge hand violently over his mouth.

For a moment Loman struggled, but even in the moonlight he could see the desperate plea in Isloman's eyes, and he became still.

'I want to go back too,' Isloman hissed, slowly removing his hand. 'But we don't even know if Tirilen's there, do we? Being taken to Fyorlund, Jaldaric said. And, in any case, what can we do against so many trained soldiers, even if they're a bit the worse for drink at the moment?'

Loman glowered furiously but did not speak. Isloman

nodded. 'Yes, we could do a great deal of damage. But that's all. We'd still end up being killed, and then what would happen to Tirilen?' Loman turned his face away as Isloman continued. 'We have to come back in force. We'll have to go back to the village for help.'

Breathing heavily, but still without speaking, Loman clambered on to his horse and started off at a canter. Isloman glanced back at the camp briefly and then mounted up and rode after his brother. Behind the two men, the sound of carousing and laughter faded into the distance.

They rode back to Pedhavin as they had never ridden before, and reached it in the middle of the morning, stiff and weary, with horses steaming and foaming.

Their noisy arrival brought out many of the villagers and it was barely a matter of minutes before they were pouring out their tale to a gathering of the High Fellows of the Guild. The predominant reaction was one of shock and disbelief. The Orthlundyn regarded the Fyordyn as an honourable people, some of the older men referring to them as the Protectors of Orthlund. This act of treachery was beyond most of them to grasp immediately, and Loman and Isloman had to repeat their tale several times before any semblance of a clear decision was reached.

Ireck summarised it. 'Now you've escaped, they'll assume you'll return with help, so they'll probably make haste northwards. We'll gather such as can be spared and go after them, though I doubt we'll be able to catch them. You two must wait here for Hawklan. He should be on his way back by now. We need his guidance.'

Both Isloman and Loman bridled at this suggestion, but Ireck used the authority of their long friendship and was unequivocal.

'Every one of us around this table loves Tirilen. What's happened defies belief, but we're carvers, we must see things the way they are. You two are too heated and you've been warriors in your day. If you go then there'll be fighting.' He gave Loman a stern look. 'Look at you, Loman. You're clenching your fist even while I'm talking to you.' Loman breathed out heavily and put his hands behind his back awkwardly. Ireck continued. 'If there's fighting, then others than yourselves may be hurt, or worse. Could either of you carry that burden? That Jaldaric struck me as a reasonable and honest young man. If enough of us go to him peacefully they'll not be able to take us captive, and I doubt they'll fight us if we don't attack, so there's a chance we might resolve the matter by talking. Don't you agree?'

Isloman was about to argue, but surprisingly, Loman cut him short. 'You're right, Ireck, it's a good idea. Besides, Tirilen wouldn't want anyone hurt on her account. And we do need Hawklan's advice.'

He looked round at the wooden beams overhead and at the sunlight washing across the floor, then at the ceremonial stone table they were all sitting around. Unlike the rest of the village, but like the remainder of this room, the table was completely undecorated in symbolic homage to the greater carvers yet to come.

'It's a sad tale to relate around our Meeting Table, friends,' he continued. 'But I'm indebted to you, Ireck, for your sound sense. Do what you can. Isloman and I will do our best to wait patiently for Hawklan.'

'When he arrives, give him the horse I bought,' said Jareg. 'Whatever he did to it, he's cured it, and it's a fine animal.'

Loman bowed. 'Thank you, Jareg, but I doubt that Hawklan will ride it. You know what he's like.'

'He'll ride it for Tirilen, Loman,' said Jareg. 'Offer it to him. He'll need it. Times are moving too quickly for walking.'

*

Almost before his mind could register the fact, Hawklan rolled away from the menacing shadows and rose quickly to his feet. As he did so he drew his sword in one singing sweep, though it felt heavy and reluctant in his hand.

In spite of his terror, part of his mind seemed to be watching him: noting with approval his rapid glance around the whole area for other attackers; and commending him for the speed with which he recovered his balance when he caught his foot in his cloak as he stood up.

Taken aback by the quickness of this movement, the two figures seemed to be momentarily paralysed. Then, suddenly, to Hawklan's horror, the strange helm on the taller of the two seemed to come to life. Hawklan crouched low and waited for whatever attack might come from this apparition.

'Dear boy,' said a familiar voice, laden with both alarm and reproach. The helm flapped its great black wings, 'fine way to greet friends,' it said.

Hawklan straightened up and lowered his sword as the faces of Loman and Isloman became clearer in the moonlight. His immediate reaction of delight and relief was, however, stemmed by the appearance of his friends. They were grim-faced and armed.

Before Hawklan could speak, Loman stepped forward, his face fighting for control over some powerful emotion.

'Hawklan,' he said. 'Help us. Tirilen has been taken by strangers.'

It took the two men but moments to tell the tale of Tirilen's disappearance and their ill-fated encounter with the High Guard, and of the decisions made by the Guild.

'We couldn't wait back in the village,' said Loman, almost sheepishly, 'You might have been gone for weeks. We had to try and find you.'

Hawklan nodded silently.

'It's a good job I heard them, dear boy,' said Gavor. 'You disappear without trace when you wear that cloak in the dark. They'd have walked straight past us.'

Even now, Hawklan was difficult to see, wrapped in his cloak and squatting on the shadow-dappled ground, as he listened to his friends' tale. He kept his body very still in an attempt to keep his mind calm, but he felt it was beginning to race out of control. The blows recently struck against him were disturbing and mysterious enough, but this strange and sinister happening seemed to dwarf everything else.

Something within him told him that he was the cause of Tirilen's abduction, and that he was being led towards some destiny whose nature at the moment was beyond his seeing. Both logic and an inner resolve brought him to the same conclusion, namely that he must seek out the person, or thing, that was seeking him, and confront it, or he would be pursued endlessly and his friends would be crushed one by one in the wake of his flight.

'What shall we do?' Loman asked, after a long pause. Hawklan pushed back the hood of his cloak from his face and gazed up into the moonlit sky. A slight signal of concern passed between the two brothers as his pale face shone white in the moonlight. Their friend was changing perceptibly; the healer had wandered off on a strange pilgrimage seemingly transformed into a prince come down from one of Anderras Darion's carvings; now, for an instant, his face looked old and battle-weary. It was a look they had seen in the faces of some of the Muster officers in the Morlider wars. His eyes, however, showed no sign of fatigue, nor his tone.

'When you've rested, we must go straight after Ireck and his party, and hope that his counsels have prevailed,' Hawklan said quietly.

'We need no rest,' said Isloman impatiently. 'We've wasted too much time already.'

'Hawklan looked at him and smiled faintly. 'The horses need rest, Isloman,' he said. 'We'll make no progress at all if we ride them into the ground, will we?'

Isloman slapped his hands on his knees in frustration. Hawklan stood up abruptly and the two brothers echoed his action. He looked at them both in turn.

'We've known one another too long and too well to vie amongst ourselves like silly children about which of us has the greatest affection for Tirilen. We must set aside our selfish pain and think of her. You two must think as you did when you fought side by side before she was born. I'll offer what observations I can.' Hawklan shook his head pensively. 'I seem to be finding many strange skills and ideas within myself these days. I fear I may not be without some experience in battle myself, though I remember none of it.'

Gavor ruffled his feathers noisily in the darkness, and for a moment the group stood in an uneasy silence.

Then, cutting through it, Hawklan said almost jauntily, 'Show me Jareg's horse. I had doubts about whether it would reach Pedhavin alive.'

'It's a fine mount,' said Isloman. 'Jareg knows his horses and he's got a real bargain there. He said it livened up considerably after you'd seen it on the way back.'

Hawklan walked across to the three horses waiting patiently by the path and laid his hand on the animal's nose. It was indeed well again.

The horse spoke to him unexpectedly. 'I am Serian, Hawklan. And your debtor. I'm whole again through your ministrations, and I'm happy to see you returned from the Gretmearc uninjured, if not unchanged.'

Hawklan started. Animals rarely sought to impose themselves on others and it was unusual for one to speak unless spoken to first. However, it did not surprise him that the horse had noticed the changes in him. Certain animals seemed to possess a strange deep vision that hearkened back through many generations.

'Yes,' he replied. 'I'm uninjured, or nearly so.' He held up his bandaged hand. 'Thank you for the warning you gave me. I thought the giving of it would have destroyed you.'

The horse gave the equivalent of a chuckle. 'It was a powerful hand that was laid on me, without a doubt,' he said. 'Even though it was an accident.'

'Accident?' queried Hawklan.

'Oh yes,' said Serian. 'I was only caught by the welt of a restraining curse they were using to disguise their monstrous snare. If they'd realised I'd recognised them I'd be in the pot by now.'

Another innocent harmed by traps set for me, thought Hawklan, but he could not forbear smiling at the horse's remark and he patted his cheek.

'Still, I'm a Muster horse,' Serian continued. 'I don't succumb easily. Now I'm well again, will you allow me to carry you?'

Hawklan stepped back a little. On the rare occasions he had ridden, it had been he who had asked permission of the horse. 'Thank you,' he said uncertainly. 'But I've no wish to burden another animal.'

There was a faint hint of impatience in the horse's reply. 'Hawklan, you'll not catch the Fyordyn on foot, even the way you walk.'

'There I think you're wrong, my friend,' said Hawklan. 'I think I'll catch them however slowly I travel because they wish me to catch them.'

Unexpectedly, the horse reared a little. 'Then you'll need me even more, won't you?' he said. 'If you wish to remain free to release your Tirilen and escape.'

The horse's powerful personality struck Hawklan almost like a physical force.

'And besides,' Serian continued, 'how could you burden me? I could carry thrice your weight until you fell off from exhaustion and I'd know no strain.' Serian bent his head forward and his voice sounded strangely in Hawklan's ears. 'The Sires within me know you, Hawklan, even if I don't, and even if you don't know them. Can you question the destiny that's brought us together? I blighted by ancient and fearful enemies and in need of a healer, and you floundering in the unknown like a cork in a stream and in dire need of a mount.'

Hawklan seemed to hear the distant trumpet call he had heard when first he picked up the Black Sword, and the horse's voice suddenly echoed and thundered in his mind as though they stood in a great chamber.

'Generations have made me, Hawklan. Generations. It's your privilege and your duty to ride me just as it is mine to bear you. Not to do so is to diminish us both.'

Hawklan bowed his head. 'I'm sorry,' he said. 'I didn't understand. We humans forget our place in the world too often. I'll ride you gladly.'

'And I'll carry you willingly and well, Hawklan,' replied the horse quietly, and for a little while the two stood silent in the moonlit stillness.

When he left Serian, Hawklan went to the other horses and spent some time using his hands to ease the fatigue from them. He spoke to them a little, but they were like most animals – shy and reserved. Their very normality highlighted Serian's powerful presence, but Hawklan set aside the strangeness of the horse and of their meeting, placing it with the many other mysteries that were accumulating around him.

'Are they well?' Isloman's deep voice interrupted his reverie.

'Yes,' said Hawklan. 'They'll be well rested by dawn. We can leave then and make good progress. Now, let me have a look at this gashed hand of yours that I've heard so much about.'

Sheepishly, Isloman offered the injured hand. Hawklan

looked at Tirilen's neat and characteristic bandaging and felt a lump come into his throat. Bending forward so that Isloman could not see his face he removed the bandage gently to reveal a livid, inflamed scar.

'It's getting better slowly,' Isloman said apologetically, but Hawklan scarcely heard him. A tremor of savagery passed through him as he looked at the damaged flesh and felt Isloman's inner strength fighting off its evil. He recognised the tremor as a cry for vengeance against the tinker for the damage he had wrought, made almost unbearable by the poignant touch of Tirilen's healing skill emanating from the damaged hand he was holding.

Chapter 4

Gavor turned and twisted high in the cold mountain air. Looking down, he could see the three figures moving along the winding path: Hawklan, tall, straight and relaxed, looking like part of the animal he was riding, constantly having to check himself from riding too far ahead of the others; Loman and Isloman looking anything but part of their animals, struggling awkwardly with the mounting discomfort of having been several days in the saddle, and fretting impatiently at what they saw to be their lack of speed.

Every few hours, Hawklan stopped and made them rest. Ostensibly it was for the benefit of the horses but, in fact, it was to calm and relax his friends with words and occasional massage and manipulation to ease tense and tired muscles and stiffening joints. In this way they made as good progress as such a trio could make.

Gavor straightened his wings to rest on a slow-rising air current and, with the occasional movement of his pinion feathers to keep his balance, soared smoothly around in a great circle. Then he put his head down and, tumbling over in an apparent confusion of feet and wings, he looked again at the gift which Loman had brought for him; if gift it was. A pair of long black, glittering sharp, fighting spurs.

'I'm not sure what they are, but they're the same metal as the sword, Hawklan,' Loman had said, fumbling them cautiously out of a pocket and offering them for inspection. 'I found them near where we found the sword. I don't know why I've never seen them before . . .' He had shrugged in reluctant acceptance of yet another strange chance happening. But all of them had fallen silent when, as if by some ancient instinct, Gavor had picked the spurs up deftly in his beak and snapped one on to each leg.

'Careful, they're very sharp . . .' Loman said hastily, his hand reaching out protectively. Then his eyes had opened wide in a confusion of shock and disbelief. The spurs fitted Gavor's legs perfectly, one even having a special clip to accommodate an irregularity in his wooden leg. Instead of making him look incongruous, however, the spurs made him look formidable, just as the Black Sword had changed Hawklan's appearance.

Loman had turned to Hawklan. 'It can't be possible,' he said.

'But it is,' replied Hawklan simply. 'And I've no more answers than you have.' And he had fingered the pommel of the Black Sword unconsciously.

Even Gavor himself had been at a loss for words, taken aback at his own actions. Now, skimming the air currents, he discovered something else about the spurs. Instead of hindering his flight as he had expected, they improved it. His balance, his manoeuvrability, even his speed, all seemed to be better, and he knew deep inside that few flying creatures could attack him now and depart unscathed.

'I'll be a fearless feathered fighter now, dear boy,' he said, alighting on Hawklan's shoulder. Then, thoughtfully, 'Do you think I should take them off when I go to visit my friends, or leave them on to make a greater impression?'

Hawklan laughed. 'How do you expect me to answer that for you, you fearless feathered lecher? Hawklan the innocent?'

Gavor nodded sagely. 'True, true,' he said. 'I'll have to experiment judiciously. I must admit, this recent protracted period of abstinence could well add a little freshness to the proceedings.'

'Good,' said Hawklan. 'That'll make it easier for you to school yourself to a further period of abstinence, as I doubt we'll be stopping at the Castle for any length of time, if at all.'

'Dear boy,' said Gavor reproachfully. 'I'm finding it hard enough to concentrate as it is.'

Hawklan was unsympathetic. 'Go and roll in the snow for a while, that'll sharpen you up,' he said, nodding towards the more distant, higher peaks.

But it was difficult for them to maintain any spirit of light-heartedness. The reason for their haste and the probable questionable outcome of their journey weighed heavily on them all, nagging like a toothache. As they wound their way down out of the mountains and viewed the wide fertile plains of Orthlund Hawklan thought he could feel even the Great Harmony trembling, as if its very root notes were under assault.

They did not stop at the Castle, and paused only briefly in the village to see if any news had been received from Ireck and his party. But nothing had been heard and the village was strangely quiet. The sound of the horses' hooves and the creak and clatter of their weapons echoed starkly around the three men in the sunny, shadow-strewn streets.

Hawklan stopped and dismounted at the heap of the tinker's wares the villagers had discarded. Metal objects were turning red with rust, wood had lost its sheen, and cloths and silks were already green with decay. He wrinkled his face in distaste and shook his head sadly.

'Why couldn't we see these things for what they were?' he said.

Neither Loman nor Isloman offered an answer.

Loman dismounted and joined Hawklan. Stooping stiffly, he picked up a rusting blade and held it for a moment. He smiled faintly and looked up at his brother. 'The metal's righting itself,' he said. 'Probably the other stuff is as well. But the misuse was great. It'll take a long time.'

Isloman nodded.

Hawklan sensed the lingering aura of Tirilen's protective words, and renewed them with his own. On an impulse he drew his sword and held it over the little pile while he spoke them.

Then the three of them headed north along the Pedhavin Road.

Within half a day, they encountered Ireck's party galloping purposefully towards the village. Sweating horses and stern-faced men milled around as the two groups met, and Hawklan took his horse to Ireck's side to hear his news.

The villagers had met the Fyordyn only a little distance away from the camp where Loman and Isloman had been held. The High Guards were neither pursuing the brothers nor fleeing homewards. Jaldaric had been coldly formal and dismissed the villagers with a casual indifference verging on contempt.

'None of our business, he said. He had his orders and we'd be well advised to stick to our farming if we knew what was good for us.' Ireck's quiet voice was full of rage and frustration. He took Loman's arm. 'I'm sorry, Loman,' he said. 'I've let you down. I tried to talk to him, to reason with him, but he wouldn't listen. He wouldn't even tell us how Tirilen was.' He paused and looked upwards. 'Eventually I threatened him. Told him we'd return, with you, and armed.'

'And?' asked Hawklan.

'He laughed, Hawklan. Just looked at us and laughed.' Ireck clenched his teeth. 'I turned and rode away without any more ado. Some of the younger ones were getting too angry and there'd have been bloodshed there and then. I'm sorry, Loman,' he repeated. 'I don't know if I did the right thing or not. My head says yes, but my stomach says no. We're going back to the village now to get the rest of the men, and arm ourselves.'

Loman shook his head. 'No,' he said. 'Not until we've thought about all this a little more. You were right at the beginning and you were right when you left their camp. If violence is all we're left with, then it mustn't be in the heat of passion. That barrel's not easily plugged once tapped. For our sakes and for theirs, we must overwhelm them completely before they can act. That way there's less chance of death and injury. Hawklan?'

Hawklan nodded in agreement. Then, swinging down slowly from Serian, he led the horse over to a nearby stream, his face thoughtful.

'You didn't see Tirilen?' he asked.

Ireck shook his head in confirmation.

'Did they give you any idea where she was?'

'No,' said Ireck.

Hawklan patted the drinking horse's neck and gazed down into the stream. Quietly, one by one, all the men dismounted and left their horses to graze and drink. The air was full of birdsong and breeze-blown seed, and an atmosphere of unreality and uncertainty seemed to spread over the group as if the spring day would not allow them to sustain their anger once they were free of the pounding urgency of the unfamiliar horse riding.

Loman took Ireck's arm and, together with Isloman, they joined Hawklan on the banks of the stream.

Eventually Hawklan spoke. 'Horsemen, soldiers such as you've described could have outrun you easily if they'd wished. It seems strange to me that you caught them in the first instance and then that you escaped them so easily. And now Ireck's group has found them just as easily. We must presume that they're neither running nor hiding, but waiting.'

'For what?' asked Isloman.

'Not for what, Isloman, but for whom,' replied Hawklan. 'It's me they want, or somebody wants. But who it is, or why, is beyond me. I'm driven across mountains to find an answer to some devilment I can scarcely even define, only to find more devilment and more questions. Then, when I escape that snare, a more earthbound, ordinary trap is laid for me.'

The three men looked at him silently.

'I'm being lured into something, my friends. Someone fears me, or at least fears what I might once have been. Someone evil. I'd be easier in my mind if I knew why I was so precious and why I've to be taken by stealth. But taken I have to be, there can be no doubt about that.' He slapped his hand against his leg and straightened up briskly. 'I weary of defence,' he said. 'Laying traps for me is one thing, using those I love as bait is another. We must move into the attack and lay this villain by the heels before he does something even worse.'

In a nearby tree, Gavor flapped his wings noisily and laughed. The soft spell of the spring sunshine dispersed and the group seemed to take on a purpose again.

'Ireck,' said Hawklan forcefully, 'go back to the village with your men. Arm yourselves and then head for the High Guards' camp. Make no effort at concealment. Look as fierce as you like, but . . .' He raised his hand in a cautionary gesture, 'don't attack them. Keep them at a safe distance, unless Gavor brings you a message expressly to the contrary.'

Ireck seemed inclined to demur.

Hawklan silenced him gently. 'No, Ireck,' he said. 'Do nothing other than as I've said.' He glanced up towards Gavor, who floated silently down and landed on his shoulder. 'We four will go ahead and do what we can by stealth. If we've not achieved anything by the time you arrive, then perhaps your arrival will cause a diversion and give us the opportunity. And, if by some chance we've been hurt or captured, Gavor will at least tell you what our position is.'

Ireck still seemed inclined to argue, as did one or two others in the group, but their erstwhile healer was exuding an authority that would brook no further debate. Nodding reluctantly, Ireck mounted his horse silently and signalled to the others to follow him.

When Ireck and the villagers had ridden into the distance, Hawklan turned to Loman and Isloman, grim-faced. His forced confidence had fallen away from him.

'Now,' he said. 'I'm pinning my faith in you two old soldiers knowing something, preferably a lot, about stealth. I don't think Ireck will be able to control the younger men, if anything happens to us, and I don't want those High Guards massacring half the village.'

Chapter 5

Continuing their northward journey, Hawklan was surprised at the subtle changes he noted in his two friends. It was as if knowledge long dormant were re-awakening. He reminded himself that the two men had travelled widely and fought bitter battles shoulder to shoulder in the past, and that they could not have survived such experiences without developing traits which necessarily would not be apparent in their normal peaceful daily lives.

Both sat easier in their saddles and the anxiety that had lined and furrowed their craggy faces ever since they had met in the mountains gave way periodically to looks of a grim purposefulness that chilled Hawklan, so alien was it to his understanding of the two men.

Worse, however, was the occasional gleam of anticipation he caught in their eyes, though he himself had to admit that his concern for Tirilen was at times forgotten in unexpected moments of exhilaration as Serian carried him steadily forward through the sunlit countryside.

The rhythmic pounding of the horses' hooves, the soft spring breeze blowing in his face, the endless variety of the Orthlund countryside, with its meadows and leas, streams and rivers, forests and arbours, all combined to dispel pain and fretfulness for unmeasured and effortless miles. But to the east were the mountains; white-tipped peaks and heavy shoulders hulking against the blue sky. Their silent, timeless vigil reproached him when unexpectedly he found himself relishing the deeds that were to come.

As the day drew towards evening and the sun dipped beneath a cloud-lined horizon, the three men eased their pace to a steady walk. Gradually, and without debate, both Loman and Isloman slowed down even further, and then eventually stopped and dismounted.

'What's the matter?' asked Hawklan.

'Nothing,' said Isloman. 'But according to Ireck, we're not far from the camp now, and they'll have plenty of sentries looking out for us if your guess is right and it's you they're waiting for. We'll have to leave the road and move very carefully from now on.'

Hawklan nodded. Gavor glided silently out of the darkening sky and landed on his shoulder. Hawklan held out his hand, palm upwards, and Gavor jumped on to it. Speaking softly, as if his voice might carry to the enemy across the still evening, Hawklan said, 'While there's still a little light, go and see if you can find their camp and how many of them there are. We'll stay here and rest until you return.'

Gavor flew off without speaking.

The three men settled themselves down to wait in the shade of a nearby copse, each too preoccupied with his own thoughts to indulge in conversation.

Hawklan felt strange stirrings within him as he lay in the darkness. His stomach felt uneasy and he had difficulty in controlling his breathing, frequently having to stifle a yawn. Then he rested his hand on the hilt of his sword and a quietness came over him. Pre-battle nerves, he thought, without wondering where such a thought could have come from.

At last Gavor returned and the three men sat around him while he recounted his tale. Fifteen men altogether, seven on watch, seven doing nothing in particular, and a leader, Jaldaric presumably. And Tirilen.

Loman started. 'She's there?' he asked breathlessly.

Gavor stepped back a pace. 'Yes,' he replied. 'And she's well,' he added before Loman could ask.

Loman breathed out almost as if he had been holding his breath since his daughter's disappearance. His face wrinkled as if he were going to weep. Isloman placed an arm around his shoulders, but Loman recovered his composure almost immediately.

Hawklan nodded. 'This confirms that they're not interested in Tirilen. She could have been in Fyorlund days ago. She's just being used as bait, I'm sure. Are you sure she's all right, Gavor?'

'Certain, dear boy. She can't get away and she's not happy, but it looks as if she's being treated more like a special guest than as a prisoner.'

After some further discussion, Gavor took off again into the night, Hawklan spoke softly to Serian, and the three men disappeared into the gloaming like three shadowy night predators.

A slow hour later they were at the High Guards' camp.

Gavor flew down and whispered to Hawklan. 'His perimeter guards are constantly moving.'

Isloman nodded. 'They'll have prearranged checkpoints. If we attack one, however quietly, the others will know within the minute.'

Hawklan turned to Loman enquiringly. They had been able to get quite close to the clearing where the Fyordyn had camped, but the trees and foliage that had hidden their approach also prevented their seeing all of the camp clearly. Gavor's information was timely, for without it they would surely have encountered one of the slowly strolling guards.

Loman pursed his lips. 'Shrewd young man, this Jaldaric,' he said. 'Assuming his men are up to scratch, which I imagine they will be, he could destroy a large group of disorganised villagers without even being seen in this terrain, but even so he's taken the trouble to guard his camp like a fortress.' He gave a soft bitter chuckle. 'Someone must have told him *something* about you, Hawklan.'

Hawklan winced slightly at the implications of Loman's comment. 'Indeed,' he said. 'And our second task, after rescuing Tirilen, is to find out who that someone is.'

However, the rescuing of Tirilen would be no easy matter. Even with the element of surprise, Hawklan realised that against such odds they could not fight their way in and out again. And if they were able to rescue Tirilen by stealth, there would be the problem of pursuit, bringing the soldiers down on their backs or into direct conflict with Ireck and the villagers. The matter had to be ended now, Hawklan decided. They must strike at the head of their enemy.

The two brothers took little persuading.

'All the protection is centred on Tirilen. We must seize Jaldaric and then negotiate some peace with them.'

So close to his daughter, Loman was in a mood for cracking heads, not negotiating, but he agreed reluctantly that Hawklan's reasoning was correct.

They skirted around the camp seeking some weakness in Jaldaric's defences, using the breeze rustling through the swaying branches overhead and the occasional scufflings of night creatures to disguise the slight sound of their movements.

'Ah,' sighed Isloman eventually. 'Shrewd he might be, Loman, but he's got no shadow lore. Look.' He pointed out into the clearing.

Hawklan followed his gaze, but could see nothing.

Loman stared intently. Although a smith, he was, like all the Orthlundyn, no mean carver. He glanced up at the moon and then into the clearing again.

'Yes,' he said at last. 'You're right. There'll be a dark path along that edge of the clearing . . .' He looked at the moon again. 'In about ten minutes I'd think.'

'And the rest of the clearing will be brightly lit,' said Isloman. 'Which will make it difficult for the guards to see into the shadow.'

'I can't see what you mean,' said Hawklan.

'Trust me,' said Isloman. 'We'll be able to go straight to the back of Jaldaric's tent in a few minutes. You watch.' He hesitated.

'What's the matter?' Hawklan asked.

'The way they're moving, we might have a guard to deal with,' replied Isloman. 'It'll slow us up and might raise the alarm.'

Hawklan thought for a moment and then spoke quickly to Gavor who flew noiselessly up into the night. Minutes later there was a startled cry from the far side of the clearing as the raven descended on the head of an unsuspecting guard, ruffled his hair a little and then flew off with a great flapping of his wings.

Three guards emerged silently from the shade and ran in the direction of the cry. There were more cries as Gavor repeated his trick. Then came laughter as the guards decided that it must have been a bat or an errant owl. While the laughter and noise continued, the moonlight in the clearing grew brighter and, as Isloman had predicted, one edge of the clearing disappeared into inky darkness.

'Now,' he hissed, and the three men ran low, swift and silent to the rear of Jaldaric's tent. The shadow here was less deep and they had only a little time to act before they would be seen by the guards. Hawklan raised his finger needlessly to his lips and placed his ear against the tent wall. Someone was laughing and describing what had just happened.

Hawklan drew his sword quietly and, signalling his intention to Loman and Isloman, cut a vertical slash in the tent wall with a single silent stroke. The three men burst into the tent simultaneously, Loman moving to the right, Isloman to the left and Hawklan commanding the centre.

The surprise was total. Hawklan found himself unopposed and looking across a simple trestle table at Tirilen and a fair-haired young man with a flat, round, innocent-looking face, who he presumed was Jaldaric.

Out of the corner of his eye he saw Isloman's great hand rise and fall twice rapidly, each movement being followed by a thud, indicating that one of Jaldaric's guests had been excused after-dinner conversation.

To his right he sensed the stocky, more enraged figure of Loman restraining an urge to crush together the skulls of two men he had seized by the neck. Instinctively, the two men offered no resistance to his iron-bending grip.

Hawklan was aware of these actions in an instant, but he also saw Jaldaric knock over his chair and seize Tirilen's wrist as he rose, his face showing fear and surprise, then, almost immediately, anger at his negligence.

It was Jaldaric's brief flash of self-reproach, and the look of concern for the injured men, mingled with the alarm and relief in Tirilen's face, that made Hawklan pause.

It was a pause sufficient for Jaldaric to draw a knife and twist Tirilen's wrist expertly so that she could not move. He offered the knife to her throat and looked at the trio in front of him: two hulking villagers who had dealt with four of his men in no more time than it took him to stand up; and this terrifying man with penetrating green eyes and grim face gaunt in the torchlight. He felt his knees quaking and hoped desperately that it did not show in his face, or sound in his voice.

'Hawklan, I presume,' he said. 'I congratulate you on your

surprise, but I have the advantage, I think, and you can't hope to master my whole patrol. Lay down your arms and surrender peacefully and all this can be forgotten. We want only you. These people can return to the village.'

Hawklan answered quietly. 'And you must be Jaldaric. I'd heard the High Guards of Fyorlund were honourable men, not brigands. Not betrayers of hospitality. Kidnappers of women-folk. What value shall I put on your word, High Guard?'

Jaldaric's jaw tightened angrily. 'Enough,' he said harshly. 'We are High Guards, and we must obey our Lord. I regret what I've had to do but you're an enemy of Fyorlund and I've been ordered to seize you in this way to avoid conflict with the local villagers and the consequent loss of life. Believe me, it's been no pleasure for me to resort to this kind of conduct. The Lady Tirilen will confirm that she's had nothing but courtesy and honourable treatment from us while we've held her captive.'

Hawklan's green eyes searched deeply into the young man and found he was probably telling the truth. Tirilen showed no signs of ill-usage, and her eyes showed alarm rather than real fear, even though Jaldaric's knife was at her throat.

Hawklan spoke quietly. 'Jaldaric. I'm no man's enemy, let alone a country's. You've been deceived. A person who'd give you such orders would be unlikely to stop at lying, would he?'

A doubt flickered across Jaldaric's face, but he tightened his grip on Tirilen's wrist and rested his knife against her throat. 'Release my men and surrender yourself. I'm not here to debate, I'm here to ensure you're taken to Fyorlund to account for your treachery. Surrender now or this girl's blood will be on your heads.'

Hawklan's manner changed imperceptibly, but the tent seemed to fill with a terrible aura of menace. 'No, Jaldaric,' he said. 'I doubt that your loyalty to whatever oath it is you've sworn will enable you to do that. But, even so, you must realise that if you injure Tirilen, your men will die on the instant as will those outside, and nothing could protect you from Loman's wrath.'

Jaldaric glanced at the two unconscious figures sprawled at the feet of Isloman, and at the two with their heads held effortlessly against the table by Loman. He scarcely heard

Hawklan's words, or noticed the look on Loman's face, but the tone of Hawklan's voice and his unwavering green eyes chilled him to his heart. This time he could not keep the fear out of his voice.

'So be it,' he said hoarsely. 'We're High Guards. If we've to die then that's unfortunate. The manner of our dying is rarely ours to choose. Our orders must be obeyed. We've some honour left.'

Hawklan realised, to his horror, that he had driven the young man too far. Now, impulsively, Jaldaric had steeled himself to face death, and his actions would be unpredictable. Hawklan did not allow the uncertainty into his face but an eerie silence descended on the group.

Abruptly an unearthly shriek filled the tent and a black thrashing shape burst through the gash in the tent wall and made straight for Jaldaric's face. Involuntarily he raised his knife hand to protect himself from this screaming apparition.

Isloman took one step forward, seized Jaldaric's wrist and wrested the knife from his grip as if it had been from a child. Then he immobilised him in a great bear hug. Jaldaric was almost the same height as Isloman, but less heavy and far less powerful. He made a token effort to drive the back of his head into Isloman's face, only to find he was suddenly unable to breathe in the huge man's embrace.

Loman casually threw his two captives to the floor, and moved quickly to Tirilen, who had also been deposited on the floor when Jaldaric was seized by Isloman.

Hawklan let out a long breath and put his sword back in its scabbard. Other High Guards appeared in the doorway of the tent, attracted by the noise. Two rushed forward but Hawklan's hands went out like striking snakes and the two men received blows which rendered them so instantly unconscious that they fell to the floor like dropped meal sacks.

The speed and ease of this action stopped the other High Guards in their tracks. Hawklan gazed at the uncertain faces in front of him, as they slowly registered the implications of what they were looking at: their expert defences silently breached, their leader taken and six of their compatriots incapacitated with apparently contemptuous ease, Loman standing protectively in front of Tirilen, his hand on his iron-bound club. The two men Loman had held were massaging their necks and twisting their heads ruefully, but they remained on the floor, loath to make any move that might bring down further punishment on them.

Without taking his eyes off the group in the doorway, Hawklan spoke. 'Loman, explain to these young men that we need to have a little talk.'

Briefly, Loman looked balefully at Jaldaric, then Tirilen touched his arm and his look softened. He put his arm round her again and looked across to his brother, eyebrows raised. Isloman nodded and released Jaldaric who fell, gasping, to the ground. Then Loman spoke to the men in a language that Hawklan had never heard before.

Without exception, surprise suffused the faces of the watching men. Loman, an Orthlundyn, was speaking their Battle Language, the language that was known only to the Fyordyn High Guard. Sometime during his life this Orthlundyn had done service for, or with, the High Guard.

Jaldaric staggered painfully to his feet, his young face riven with confusion. He gestured to his men. 'Lay down your arms,' he said breathlessly. 'We must talk. This has been a sorry affair from the start. We must talk.'

There was some hesitation.

Jaldaric leaned with one hand on the table while the other tenderly rubbed his ribs and stomach. 'Do as you're ordered,' he shouted angrily. He waved his arm towards Loman. 'Didn't you hear him? It was an ill thing to kidnap a woman for whatever reason. Now we find we've made war on the daughter of an Orthlundyn who speaks the Battle Language. We've violated the hearth of one of our own. Lay down your arms *now*. We must talk.'

Chapter 6

While some of the High Guards righted the disarray in the tent, Hawklan busied himself with the injured. With a little massage he very quickly revived the two men he had knocked unconscious, and they seemed none the worse for their experience. The victims of Loman and Isloman, however, had to be advised, after examination, that they could look forward to several days of discomfort.

Briefly, the child still in Tirilen showed itself as she embraced her three rescuers, but it was only they who felt it, and it was a composed young woman that turned away from them and moved her attention to Gavor, now proudly displaying his spurs.

'You look very dashing, Gavor,' she said.

Gavor acknowledged the praise with a toss of the head and a bow and then, jumping on to her head, looked down beadily at Jaldaric who returned the gaze nervously.

'Is that bird safe?' he asked.

'Oh, yes,' said Tirilen. 'Perfectly safe. It's you who's in danger.' Then unexpectedly she laughed and ruffled his hair.

Her laughter lightened the atmosphere and Hawklan could not forbear smiling both at her powers of recovery and at Jaldaric's discomfiture as he stood up and occupied himself with straightening his tunic until he had stopped blushing.

In spite of what this young man had done, Hawklan felt no real evil in him. He was certainly not the instigator of what had been happening. Nor were any of the others, although one or two of them seemed to be of an angry and surly disposition.

However, knowing or unknowing, Jaldaric was a player in this game and was, so far, Hawklan's only contact with whoever was manipulating events.

'Good,' Hawklan said, dismissing his last patient and

dropping into a seat, 'we've reached this point without serious injury or damage to anything other than our peace and our pride. But it's been a near thing. I'd welcome an explanation, Jaldaric, as would Loman and Isloman.'

One of the surly-faced individuals spoke out. 'The Lord Dan-Tor's decreed this man an enemy of Fyorlund, Jaldaric. We shouldn't even be talking to him. Tell him nothing.'

Jaldaric answered him wearily. 'Esselt, sit down. This is a truce. Don't dishonour us further with your foolish talk. I'll be responsible to the Lord Dan-Tor for my decision.'

His attitude seemed to find favour with most of the High Guards present, and Esselt sat down and folded his arms sulkily without further comment. Hawklan was about to ask a question when Jaldaric spoke again.

'Hawklan, are you an enemy of Fyorlund?'

The question was put so positively that Hawklan started.

'Brilliant,' said Esselt sarcastically. 'Such mastery of the subtle techniques of interrogation.'

The men on either side of him eased away slightly, as if to avoid an impending impact.

Jaldaric rounded on him. 'Esselt, keep that wicked tongue of yours to yourself, or you'll find your much vaunted favour with the Lord Dan-Tor won't protect you from severe field punishment, and I'd remind you that we're a long way from home. I'll ask such questions as I see fit and we'll all judge the answers for ourselves.'

Esselt held Jaldaric's gaze for a moment and then lowered his eyes without replying. Jaldaric turned his still angry face back to Hawklan enquiringly.

'I'm an enemy to no thing and no creature as far as I know,' Hawklan said. 'But I see this Lord Dan-Tor of yours imagines I am. I'd like to meet him and ask him why he should think this and why a Lord of Fyorlund should pose as a tinker and bring corrupted wares to our village.'

Esselt looked up but did not speak. Jaldaric looked embarrassed.

'The Lord Dan-Tor has returned alone to Fyorlund, Hawklan,' he said. 'And he doesn't account to us for his actions. He's the King's closest adviser and friend. He's greatly respected and has brought many changes to our land.' Hawklan caught his eye and Jaldaric hesitated. 'Although I think some of them have a price we weren't originally aware of,' he added reluctantly.

Both Loman and Isloman nodded.

'What your Lord brought to our village carried a price in its every fibre,' said Loman. 'It wasn't the work of Fyorlund craftsmen such as I've seen in the past. That had its own rough harmony. These objects were made by evil hands; hands that knew nothing of balance and harmony or, more probably, wilfully destroyed them.'

Hawklan briefly recalled the unreasoned horror he had felt when he looked into the face of the tiny mannequin marching up and down on his hand. A horror that drove him across the mountains to look for its source and, he presumed, was driving him still.

'What do you know about craftsmen, you soil-tilling oaf?' sneered Esselt. 'Nothing can equal the work that comes from the Lord Dan-Tor's workshops.'

Surprisingly, the insult seemed to roll off Loman without effect, and Esselt started as if his own venom had returned and struck him in the face. Hawklan looked straight at him.

'Esselt, you're a foolish young man, but I suspect it's beyond my skill to make you understand why. You seem to be set on an ill course and, if your rash tongue doesn't get you killed by one of your own kind, then I fear much worse lies ahead of you. Be silent and listen carefully.'

Although this was said without any menace, Esselt went white under Hawklan's gaze.

Jaldaric watched the exchange impassively and for a while only the rustling hiss of the wind-blown trees could be heard in the tent. Then he looked at Loman sitting quietly, unperturbed by Esselt's vicious taunt, and then at Hawklan, also sitting patiently, waiting. He made his decision.

'We're escort to the Lord Dan-Tor, Hawklan, but we know nothing of his purpose in being in Orthlund. What he ordered us to do here was contrary to everything that the High Guard should believe in and protect. I should have had no part of it. We betrayed freely and generously given hospitality with foul treachery. I should have spoken up if only for the sake of my men. A High Guard should not obey orders mindlessly.' Then, in reluctant admission, 'But the Lord Dan-Tor has a way of . . .'

His voice faded and there was an angry exclamation of disbelief from Esselt.

'Enough, Jaldaric. You're talking treason. This man's an enemy of Fyorlund. Seize him now. There are enough of us to take them all.'

Jaldaric turned on him furiously. 'I'll not warn you again, Esselt. This is a truce. There's been enough treachery. Besides, if memory serves me correctly, you were in charge of tonight's guard, were you not? These soil-tilling oafs had little difficulty in slipping by your eagle-eyed watch, did they? And we could just as easily have been killed as knocked insensible for all the chance we had to defend ourselves. They've repaid our treachery with mercy, Esselt. You might care to ponder on that.' Esselt glowered at him, but Jaldaric was warming to his work. 'And pray, master of the guard, would you care to stroll out into the woods and see how many more such oafs might be waiting for us right now in these woods – *their* woods? Doubtless the Lord Dan-Tor will be most impressed by your contribution to this evening's work,' he concluded.

Hawklan raised a hand to his mouth to hide a smile.

Esselt fired a parting shot. 'You use his name too lightly, Jaldaric,' he said. 'His sanction justifies all.'

Jaldaric gave him a look of contempt but did not reply. Then massaging his ribs he grimaced a little as he turned again to Hawklan. 'I don't know what to do, Hawklan,' he said. 'Personally, from what I've seen and heard, I can't imagine that you or, for that matter, anything out of Orthlund could be an enemy to Fyorlund, but the Lord Dan-Tor has branded you as such, and this scheme for your capture was of his devising.' He looked down, unable to meet Hawklan's gaze. 'Tirilen was to be used to lure you closer to Fyorlund. We were to move ahead of you so that you would follow until such time as his agents could safely take you prisoner. No one was to be hurt,' he concluded, looking up again.

Jaldaric tapped his fingers pensively on the table. 'I'm sorry,' he said. 'It was an error of judgement on my part to have anything to do with it. I think probably most of my men think so too.'

There were various signals of agreement from the others with the exception of a small group centred around Esselt.

'What will happen to you?' Hawklan asked.

Jaldaric shrugged. 'We'll return to Vakloss, report what's happened and take the consequences. But what will happen to *you?*' he replied. 'I'll be subject to military discipline, but you've no such protection. Dan-Tor will send others for you . . .' He hesitated. 'And rumour has it that he has darker agents than me when need arises.'

Hawklan nodded. 'I think I may have met some already,' he said.

Jaldaric looked at him. 'I don't know what you can do,' he said. 'Other than be on your guard. You seem more than capable of looking after yourself, and you've a friend in every Orthlundyn I've heard speak of you, but . . .'

Hawklan nodded again. He had known his future course of action from the moment that Tirilen's safety had been assured. It was impossible that he should attempt to recapture his old life. Loman's words about hands that wilfully destroyed harmony and balance had crystallised his thoughts. So obvious was it that he wondered how he could not have seen it before.

He used the word evil to describe the creator of these events, but he had used it as a healer, to whom evil is an inadvertent disharmony that needs correction, an accidental movement away from balance and equilibrium. Now, he realised, or perhaps remembered, that evil could be an active force. That some people knew of balance and harmony but chose deliberately to destroy them. People motivated by he knew not what, to take, and to take only. People so tormented that they could not rest while others enjoyed tranquillity.

Such thoughts had not occurred to him in his twenty years in Orthlund and with them came other, darker thoughts. Could he himself contain the seeds of such a creature? Could the strange plateau that Andawyr had shown him imprison an evil that had rightly been locked away by wise hands? However, would Dan-Tor resort to such subterfuge to waken an ally? He felt reassured. But then, evil allies would not lightly trust one another, would they?

A vista of conflicting possibilities opened before him which defied his reason to reach a conclusion. And could he trust his intuition as it cried out 'No. There is no evil in you'?

He had no choice. He must trust it. Both intuition and reason found no evil in Andawyr, and there had been patently much evil in that corner of the Gretmearc and in the wares offered by Dan-Tor.

Then his own words came back to him. Ignorance is a voracious, destructive, shadow-dwelling creature that must always be destroyed. Destroyed by the light of truth, no matter what horrors it exposed.

So be it, he concluded.

A light touch on his arm brought him out of his reverie. It was Tirilen.

'Are you all right?' she asked.

He smiled and put his arm around her shoulder. 'Yes,' he said. 'Just thinking about what to do next.' He looked at Jaldaric's concerned face.

'It would seem that neither of us knows what's happening and that both of us, and my friends, are being used in some way. I'll ride with you to meet this Lord Dan-Tor and seek an explanation from him personally. That way you'll have fulfilled at least part of his instructions, which may lessen your punishment, and I'll find out the truth of what's been happening.'

This pronouncement silenced the onlookers for a moment, then there was a babble of voices. Isloman stepped forward and took him by the arm, his craggy face alive with alarm.

'Hawklan, you can't,' he said in disbelief. 'You might be imprisoned, or even killed.'

Hawklan shook his head. 'Imprisoned? Why? I've offended no law that I know of. And I doubt I'll be killed. I'm sure that could easily have been done many times over by now. This man wants to see me alive. And I'm increasingly anxious to see him. I'm sure these young men will protect me.'

Isloman gazed skywards as if for guidance, and then slapped his hands on the sides of his thighs. 'These young men, as you call them, are soldiers, Hawklan,' he said. 'They'll do as their superior officers tell them. They may argue a little, but ultimately they'll do as they're ordered. And if they don't, then more soldiers will be found who will.'

'That's true, Hawklan,' said Jaldaric. 'If it's your choice, then you may ride under our protection but, once we're in Fyorlund, I can't guarantee your safety. I'm only a humble captain . . . probably less, very shortly.'

Hawklan looked doubtful. He turned to Loman enquiringly. Without moving, Loman looked at his brother and then at his daughter. When he spoke, his voice was strained.

'You'll *have* to go, Hawklan,' he said. 'You're the centre of all this change, if not its cause. You've been chosen in some way, by some power we can't begin to understand. Jaldaric's right. Wherever you go, this Lord . . . tinker . . . will pursue you, and the next time he'll use less scrupulous soldiers.'

Isloman turned angrily on his brother but stopped as he met Loman's desperately sad gaze. Uncharacteristically he swore and struck the table violently with his fist as if such an outburst might destroy all his pain.

'Thank you, Loman,' said Hawklan. 'Go with Tirilen back to the village. When you meet Ireck, tell him what's happened. Whatever happens, Gavor will bring you news.'

There were tears of bewilderment in Tirilen's eyes as she watched and listened. Hawklan took her face between his hands.

'You and I are healers, Tirilen. We have to enter into other people's pain. We have above all to see the truth no matter how painful it is. Your father spoke the truth and you know it. I have to seek out this Dan-Tor for all our sakes.'

Child and woman conflicted in Tirilen's face.

Hawklan continued. 'You've tended your uncle's hand very well. And you did good work on that tortured heap outside the village. You'll be the village healer until I return. Don't be afraid.'

He reached into a pocket for something to dry her eyes with, and drew out the cloth that Andawyr had wrapped around his arm. It was some days now since it had fallen from his arm to reveal it sound and whole again.

'Take this,' he said. 'It has healing powers of some kind. Powers of weave and voice. You might be able to find out more about it in some of the books at the Castle.'

Tirilen took the cloth with a watery sniff, then wiped her eyes boyishly with the back of her hand.

'You'll be all right,' she said, half statement, half question.

Hawklan nodded. 'Tend to the village,' he said.

Jaldaric reached out and, with a slight gesture, gently extinguished the torch that had been illuminating the tent. The change in the lighting was barely perceptible. Fyorlund torches adjusted themselves to the natural light.

'Dawn,' he said.

'You'll find our horses nearby now,' said Hawklan. 'Serian will have led them here as I asked him. Time for you to go.'

He looked at the brooding Isloman and intercepted a brief exchange of looks between the Carver and his brother.

'What are you two up to?' he asked suspiciously.

Isloman's dark look cracked into a smile, increasing Hawklan's suspicion. 'Hawklan,' he said. 'You're too naive to be let out on your own, as is this young man here.' He jerked a thumb towards Jaldaric. 'You're both going into nothing but trouble, and someone's got to look after you. Fortunately I don't have a castle to attend to, and I don't have to take orders from anyone, so I'll come with you. I could do with a change.' He rubbed his damaged hand. 'Besides, I've one or two questions of my own for this Dan-Tor.'

The dawn was flooding the clearing, pink and misty, as the Guards broke camp. Loman and Tirilen turned and gave a final wave before their horse carried them out of sight into the morning haze.

Hawklan and Isloman turned and walked through the dewy grass towards their horses. Gavor, sitting on Hawklan's wrist, flapped his wings restlessly.

Chapter 7

Two days later the patrol was moving briskly and steadily northwards. The sky was pregnant with great swollen clouds waiting to shed their watery burdens and send them cascading down on to the cowering land below. A boisterous west wind shouldered them into towering indignant mounds as it strove to push them eastwards over the mountains.

Jaldaric wrapped his cloak around himself and looked upwards. 'Quite a conflict,' he said. 'I think we're due for a wetting soon.'

Hawklan was gazing into the grey mass accumulating over-head. Since he had seen the Viladrien sailing over Riddin some inner need had constantly drawn his eyes upwards in search of another, and his mind had been filled with a tumbling host of questions. What kind of people could live in such a place? And how? What must it be like to be at the mercy of the winds and to float through great turbulent clouds like those now broiling overhead? How must the world below seem? He had looked down from the tops of high mountains to see patchwork fields and forests, but from the height of these cloud lands . . .? His imagination foundered. But the darker note that had come to taint so many of his thoughts of late would sound. 'Enemy dispositions,' it tolled, 'you would see enemy dispositions.' The sound saddened him, so at odds was it with the haunting beauty of the Viladrien and its barely audible, singing wake.

Jaldaric's comment brought Hawklan's mind back to earth. 'Yes,' he said. 'I think some of that water up there is about to start its long journey back to the sea.'

Jaldaric looked at him, puzzled.

Hawklan smiled. 'Yes,' he said. 'I agree. It's probably going to rain.'

And, as if so commanded, a slow tattoo of great raindrops

started to speckle the dusty road at their feet. Jaldaric turned in his saddle and looked enquiringly at his men. There was much shaking of heads and gestures to continue the journey. Cloaks were fastened and hoods pulled up. The patrol slowed to a walk.

Admitting defeat, the wind dropped and the rain came down triumphantly in a shifting vertical downpour, reducing visibility all around to a few hundred paces. Hawklan stared down, hypnotised by the coronets of spray bouncing off the road, a mobile and patternless web flowing over the almost imperceptible geometry of the ancient stone blocks.

The noise of the rain was sufficient to drown the sound of the horses' hooves, and such conversation as there had been guttered out in the face of this opposition. Each rider withdrew into himself, and the patrol became an indistinct and introverted cortège moving silently through the hissing rain.

Hawklan became aware of Isloman by his side. He raised his eyes from the glistening road and looked ahead into the greyness. Over the past two days he had seen an unexpected change come over his friend.

After the abduction of Tirilen, Loman had discarded the gruff irritation he brought to his daily duties, and had become more voluble and straightforward. Isloman by contrast had become quieter and had discarded in turn much of his bluff heartiness. The two brothers had moved towards one another during the crisis. An understandable reaction, thought Hawklan. Such an event must necessarily blow away the dust that daily routine laid over their real selves.

But now Isloman seemed to be oscillating between elation and troubled concern, as if two parts of him were wrestling for command of the whole.

To Hawklan it seemed that the change began after the High Guards questioned Isloman about his brother's knowledge of the Battle Language, and his own part in the Morlider War had become known.

The Orthlundyn volunteers, though small in number, had made a considerable impression on the High Guards of the day and, by now, had almost entered Fyordyn legend. To be in the presence of one and, for some of them, to have actually been hit by one, brought out an almost boyish excitement in the young men and for a while they plagued Isloman with questions. Even the surly Esselt and his cadre showed an interest.

Now, in the grey rain, Isloman's posture showed that he was troubled again and, even though Hawklan could not see his face under the deep hood, he knew that it was pensive and lined.

'You're riding better,' he said. 'How are your aches and pains?'

Isloman started a little at Hawklan's voice, and then craned forward almost as if to catch the words as they fled into the distance.

'Oh fine,' he said, after a moment. 'I'm remembering how to ride again. And I'm easier in my mind now that Tirilen's safe.'

Hawklan picked on the word. 'I think you're remembering more than how to ride, aren't you?' he offered.

Isloman nodded. 'Yes, I'm afraid so,' he said. 'Talking to these young lads about the old days has brought back things I'd rather had stayed forgotten.'

'They mean no harm,' Hawklan said. Then, in a gently mocking tone, 'You're like something out of a history book to them. A real warrior.'

Isloman did not reply immediately, but turned his head and cast a look full of doubt at Hawklan. 'Even you don't understand, do you?' he said resignedly. 'Not really.'

They rode on in silence for a while.

'It's not your fault, I suppose,' said Isloman eventually. 'No one can understand it who's not actually had to fight for his life – not even these . . . soldiers.' He indicated the following group with an inclination of his head. 'It leaves you with . . . feelings . . . opposite feelings that shouldn't be able to exist at the same time, but do.'

Hawklan looked at his friend intently and almost immediately observed the same phenomenon in himself. The healer in him knew that Isloman must speak his concerns out loud if he was to ease his pain. But at the same time he heard his darker side coldly declaiming that Isloman must deal with this problem now or it would seriously impair his worth as a fighter. He recoiled from the thought but he knew it would not leave him. 'Explain,' he said, flatly.

Again there was a long silence before Isloman spoke, and Hawklan sensed the tension building in his friend.

A small furry animal scuttled its bedraggled way across the road in front of them. The movement seemed to dislodge Isloman's penned-up words.

'Being in a battle is terrifying and degrading,' he said suddenly. 'I *know* that – with both my head and my . . .' He tapped his chest with his fist. 'Everything. It's a thing to be avoided. But a part of me enjoyed it, Hawklan, and, I think, might enjoy it still. It's precious little clearer now than it was then. Part of me enjoying what was obviously wrong. And yet it wasn't wrong, was it? Here was an enemy – people who'd killed and robbed, and worse, people who couldn't be reasoned with and who broke such promises as they made, people who'd kill you and your friends if you didn't stop them. What do you do in those circumstances? When all other alternatives have been unsuccessful?'

He did not wait for an answer. 'And then there's the fear. Horrible. Your heart thumping, your mouth dry and sour, your stomach churning. Until . . .' He reached out and took Hawklan's arm in a powerful grip, 'until you fight. Then ancient forces within you rise and say "This is good". All around is mayhem and destruction, and you don't care. You carry on killing – and revelling in it.' Isloman shuddered as his muscles and sinews recalled long-forgotten deeds. 'And when it's over, when everywhere's full of the sights and sounds of the wounded – crawling and writhing, groaning and screaming – you have to crush your remorse underfoot to stay sane.' He fell silent and gazed down at the bouncing rain. 'Your only solace,' he said after a while, 'is that all other forms of . . . entreaty have failed.'

Hawklan searched for some way to help his friend. Isloman's words had struck a strange chord within him; brought to his mind a dark place full of horror and noise and death. But it was too deep, too distant, and it flitted away from him uneasily when he tried to examine it. None the less it left a faint after-glow of understanding.

'We act to preserve ourselves,' Hawklan said, finally. 'It's the most ancient of laws; written deep into all living things. And who can answer the question that that poses?'

He turned to look at Isloman and a small stream of water cascaded from his hood like a tiny waterfall.

'But there are other things. It's also written in us to avoid violence. It's too arbitrary, too open to chance. Too open to appalling consequences.' He leaned across to his friend. 'But if others strip away that protection from us, then they take the consequences. If it can't flee, then life will fight against all odds and with any means it can, to survive.'

Isloman straightened up. 'Strange,' he said. 'I remember the old Sirshiant I first served with. "Once you're committed to combat," he said, "it's the most violent who'll prevail. You have to be worse than your enemy. Don't think otherwise, or you'll die." Said we shouldn't worry about it. We were good lads and when we'd won we'd "stay our hands from excess".' Isloman shook his head reflectively and smiled slightly. 'Fancy remembering him after all these years.' He turned to Hawklan and nodded. 'And we did too. Stayed our hand from excess. It's something, I suppose.'

'It may well be everything,' Hawklan said.

Isloman seemed lighter in his saddle. His unease was still there, but it had been faced and he saw that time had in fact made it clearer for him. It was not a dilemma after all. It was simply the stern, cruel consequence of life asserting itself against those who would deny its right to be.

Hawklan felt the tension leave his friend but noted again his own ambivalent response. He was happy that Isloman's pain had been eased, but that cold part of his mind was happy also. Isloman's heart would now be uncluttered by hidden doubts should the need arise for him to fight. In the dry shade of his hood, Hawklan scowled to himself.

Gradually the rain eased into a light spring drizzle, and eventually stopped. The clouds receded over the mountains and the sun illuminated their path again, glistening off the wet road and raising clouds of steam in the distant woodlands.

Like enemy camp fires, thought Hawklan.

Hoods were pushed back, horses shook their heads, showering

tiny rainbow-decorated sprays about them, and casual conversation sputtered back into life again.

Jaldaric trotted up to Isloman and Hawklan, screening his eyes against the bright light from the shining road. Then he pointed.

'Riders coming,' he said.

Chapter 8

Jaldaric's expression grew more and more puzzled as the riders approached, but he replaced it with a smile of welcome as the two groups stopped opposite one another.

The visitors were six in number and clad in a black livery. They were grim-faced and had obviously been riding hard. One of them wore insignia which, together with his general demeanour, identified him as their leader. His face was lean and would have been handsome had not narrowed eyes and a curl in his thin mouth given him a cunning and treacherous expression.

Jaldaric saluted, but the gesture was not returned, and an uneasy silence fell between the two groups.

The leader of the new arrivals frowned. 'You're Jaldaric?' he demanded, his voice harsh.

Jaldaric bridled slightly at the man's manner, but replied pleasantly. 'Yes I am. May I ask who you are?'

The man ignored him, and gazed around as if looking for someone. 'Where is the Lord Dan-Tor?' he asked, just as Jaldaric was about to repeat his question. His voice was a little softer, but still unpleasant, and Jaldaric's face flushed at this further incivility.

'The Lord Dan-Tor has returned to Fyorlund,' he said. 'Now, may I ask again, to whom I am speaking and what is your concern with the Lord Dan-Tor?' His voice was harder, and this time it was the visitor who bridled, as if unused to being spoken to thus.

'My name's Urssain,' he said, 'Captain Urssain of the . . . King's High Guard.' Then, before this could be fully registered, 'Did the Lord Dan-Tor receive a messenger from Commander Aelang before he left?'

Jaldaric's innate politeness overcame his immediate surprise.

'We've had no messengers from anyone . . . Captain,' he said. 'But that's hardly of any relevance. What's more to the point is why are you, Fyordyn, marching armed and liveried in Orthlund, enquiring about the Lord Dan-Tor and calling yourselves, of all things, a King's High Guard?'

Urssain seemed disconcerted by the news that Dan-Tor had not received Aelang's message and, for a moment, his face showed his uncertainty. Then, unexpectedly, he leaned forward in his saddle radiating arrogance. 'It's unfortunate that neither we nor our messenger met the Lord Dan-Tor, though it's understandable enough in this benighted country. However, it changes nothing and, in answer to your question, we're here on the King's orders to arrest you. I must therefore ask you to surrender your sword immediately.'

The suddenness of this reply as much as its content made Jaldaric jerk back in his saddle and for a moment he seemed almost inclined to laugh. It was anger, however, that dominated his reply.

'Captain Urssain,' he said. 'Even a child knows that the King can have no High Guard.' He paused, and his eyes narrowed. 'I have no idea from whence you come, or what I'm supposed to make of your rambling – nor have I any intention of wasting my time trying to find out – but your very presence here constitutes a considerable offence in itself, and it's not I who will be surrendering to you, but you to me.'

He made a discreet gesture and his patrol quietly spread itself across the road. Urssain watched the manoeuvre with disdain.

'A larger patrol is close behind us, Jaldaric,' he said. 'Our various messages may have gone astray but I can at least give you the opportunity of surrendering with dignity. If you offer me violence while I'm on the King's business then it'll go much worse for you.'

Jaldaric ignored the comment, but his jawline stiffened. 'Enough, Urssain,' he said angrily. 'Your sword.'

Urssain made no move. 'Jaldaric,' he said, almost conciliatory in tone. 'Understand. We *are* the King's High Guard, whatever you might think about it. We were formed in secret because of the treachery of some of the Lords. You're to be arrested at the King's express command, because your father, the Lord Eldric, was at its heart. He and his co-conspirators are now in prison in Vakloss awaiting trial.'

Jaldaric put his hand to his head. 'This is nonsense,' he said uncertainly.

Hawklan looked round at the faces of Jaldaric's patrol. Esselt's eyes were gleaming, as were those of his friends, but all the others seemed to be as shocked and disorientated as their Captain.

Jaldaric shook his head as if to waken himself. 'No,' he said. 'This isn't nonsense. It's madness. My father's no traitor. With whom would he conspire and for what? He's an old man and a respected member of the Geadrol.'

'The Geadrol was a sink of conspiracy. It no longer exists. The King has suspended it,' said Urssain contemptuously.

A babble of voices broke out at this, and Jaldaric's patrol surged forward almost involuntarily to gather around their leader. Esselt and his friends, however, though also surprised, stayed aloof and watchful. Isloman indicated their response to Hawklan with his eyes, and Hawklan acknowledged with a slight nod.

Jaldaric called out for silence. 'I can make nothing of this. The King cannot have High Guards. The Geadrol cannot be suspended. And how can I be arrested without charge or authority? What crimes have I committed?'

'The King can do all things,' came Urssain's reply, 'and this uniform is authority enough for your arrest. I'm just a Captain obeying orders. I know nothing about your crimes except those you're committing just by arguing with me. I've told you once, surrender now or it'll go much worse for you later.'

For a moment Jaldaric seemed inclined to draw his sword and lay about him, but other counsels prevailed and when he spoke his voice was hard and coldly purposeful.

'The longer we stay away from Fyorlund, the more strange questions accumulate for answering. I'm about to continue my journey to Vakloss, Urssain, together with my guests from Orthlund.' He indicated Hawklan and Isloman. 'You'll accompany us, either peacefully or bound, that choice is yours. When we're there we'll all stand before the Geadrol and, if necessary, the King himself, and you can spin your babbling fancies to your heart's content.'

Urssain cast a quick glance at the two Orthlundyn, then turned away with an insolent shrug. 'As you wish. The rest of my patrol is nearby. I'll complete my orders when they arrive.'

Jaldaric's eyes blazed momentarily, but he walked his horse forward quietly until he was by the side of the black-liveried Captain. Then, turning swiftly, he drew his sword and placed the point against Urssain's throat.

'Listen carefully, Urssain,' he said very softly, 'whoever you are, and whoever's bidding you're doing. You wear a livery unknown to us, you defame the King, you bring arms into Orthlund, then you threaten us, the Lord Dan-Tor's personal escort, and finally you defame both my father and myself. As far as I'm concerned you're just a criminal. I've no doubt you've got friends lurking in ambush somewhere along the road, but be under no illusions as to who'll die first if we're offered violence by anyone.'

Urssain looked uneasily down the length of Jaldaric's sword, and then at the bows the Guards were carrying. His arrogance faltered. Jaldaric smiled grimly.

'We'll dispense with the formalities,' Jaldaric concluded grimly. 'You may keep your sword, for what good it'll do you. I guarantee you'll have no time to draw it.'

Then, without apparent instructions, Jaldaric's patrol moved forward and surrounded Urssain's group. Jaldaric rode across to Hawklan and Isloman.

'I don't know what's happening,' he said, his round face incongruously furrowed. 'Either these people are quite insane or something terrible's happened at home while we've been away.'

Hawklan looked at him without replying.

'I fear it's probably the latter,' continued Jaldaric. 'I can't see six men coming against fifteen of us with that attitude without some resource behind them. We need to get back quickly.'

'I agree with you,' said Hawklan. 'But take care. Whatever's happened in Fyorlund, that man expected his livery alone to command absolute obedience.'

Worry clouded Jaldaric's face. 'Still,' he said, 'it's none of your affair. I can only recommend you head back for home. It looks as if I may not even be able to escort you as far as the border safely, let alone Vakloss. I'm sorry.'

Hawklan stretched his legs lazily and nodded. 'Thank you for your advice, Jaldaric,' he said. 'It's very sound. But Isloman and I are very anxious to speak to your Lord Dan-Tor and we'll be heading for Vakloss no matter what happens. For what it's worth I suspect our questions and whatever political upheavals have been occurring may well be related.'

Jaldaric shrugged. 'If we run into trouble I'll try and talk us through it, but if it comes to a fight I may not be able to protect you,' he said.

Hawklan smiled reassuringly and laid a hand on his shoulder. 'We understand,' he said. 'Don't worry. We'll make our own judgement about when and who to fight. You look to yourself and your men.' He laughed gently. 'We absolve you from your duties as host.'

Jaldaric smiled weakly but could find no reply. Shrugging his shoulders nervously again he turned back to his men. Hawklan signalled to Gavor who was listening in a nearby tree, and the bird took off silently towards the north. Echoing this action, Jaldaric sent two men out into the adjacent fields to scout the road ahead. The remainder of the patrol restarted their leisurely progress.

'You're getting very bold, healer,' said Isloman anxiously, riding alongside Hawklan. 'Smiling and joking in the face of a possible battle against Fyorlund High Guards.'

'Well,' said Hawklan, 'the lad needed reassurance. He really doesn't know whether he's coming or going at the moment. I don't want him worrying about us. Anyway I told him no more than the truth, did I? Whatever happens, you and I go north, don't we?'

Isloman rubbed his hand and nodded.

The patrol moved steadily forward for some time until, passing through a wooded stretch of road, they emerged to find themselves at the top of a rise which gave them a commanding view of the countryside for many miles around. Straight ahead of them, fringing the distant horizon, Hawklan could just make out the white peaks that formed the southern border of Fyorlund.

Jaldaric's face creased in distress when he too saw the mountains. So much had changed since he had been chosen to lead the Lord Dan-Tor's escort into Orthlund and thence to lands further south. Now it seemed that every step they took led them into more and more confusion and difficulty, not to say danger. The sooner he could reach Vakloss and hand this whole mess over to his superiors, the sooner he could see his father and settle back into his ordinary life.

Unnecessarily he stood up in his stirrups and peered into the distance. The road twisted and wound through fields and woods, disappearing from sight for long stretches.

'I see no sign of your patrol, Urssain,' he said.

'You will soon enough,' replied the man, certainty filling his surly reply.

Jaldaric looked at him and then frowned. 'Dismount and rest,' he said. 'We may as well take advantage of the high ground and the trees while we're here. Our Captain here seems convinced his friends will come looking for him.'

Taking their horses with them, the men dispersed skilfully into the surrounding trees and foliage so that they could both rest and watch the countryside ahead of them.

Hawklan caught Isloman's look of approval. The men were well trained, without doubt. He dismounted and Serian wandered off into the trees with Isloman's mount.

Hawklan lowered himself on to a grassy bank and stretched out luxuriously. Isloman sat down heavily beside him, and drew his sword. He looked critically along its gleaming edge and fumbled in his pocket to retrieve a small slab of stone. He twisted the sword round repeatedly and, hefting the stone, offered it to the blade several times indecisively. Then he returned his sword to its scabbard and the stone to his pocket.

'Just nerves,' he said apologetically. 'There's no way a stone crusher like me can improve on an edge that Loman's made.'

Hawklan smiled then sat up suddenly and cocked his head on one side. Abruptly, Gavor was on them. He was jumping up and down with agitation, his eyes wild and distant, and his black spurs twitching and glinting ominously in the sunlight. He was jabbering.

'I can't understand you, Gavor,' said Hawklan frowning. 'Speak normally.'

But Gavor continued with the noise and Hawklan shook his head despairingly. Finally the bird let out a raucous cry and flew off up into the sky, where he circled, crying out strangely every few seconds. Hawklan stood up and watched him.

'What's the matter with him?' Isloman asked.

Hawklan put his hands to his head almost desperately. 'I don't know. He's speaking a language I've never heard him use before. I can't understand it, but it sounds very old.'

He shouted to Jaldaric and the young man ran across to him. Hawklan took him by the arm.

'Prepare your men. Gavor's seen something that's either frightened the wits out of him, or made him angry beyond belief; I can't tell which. But something terrible is coming.'

Jaldaric signalled to his men, and such as could be seen disappeared from view. The six black-liveried men sat dolefully by the side of the road, though Urssain still affected an arrogant indifference. Nervously loosening his sword in its scabbard, Jaldaric took up a position opposite them so that he could see the road ahead and also be seen by anyone travelling along it.

Hawklan cast a glance up at Gavor who was gliding round and round in a wide circle above the scene, crying raucously. Hawklan still could not determine whether the sound was one of rage or fear, but he suspected the former as it was undeniably alarming. Shaking his head and gesturing to Isloman, the two of them faded into the undergrowth.

Then followed an eerie, silent and timeless interval in which everyone seemed to be held in reality only by Gavor's persistent cry growing fainter and fainter as he rose ever higher in a great spiral.

A muffled whisper came out of the undergrowth, and Jaldaric screwed up his eyes to peer into the distance. A long line of men began to emerge from one of the many dips that took the road out of sight. Jaldaric frowned.

'Your patrol's on foot?' he asked Urssain. The man did not reply.

'They're running,' whispered Isloman to Hawklan.

Hawklan nodded. Somewhere from within came the knowledge that they could run for miles and miles and still fight a battle, but who 'they' were was denied him. Again he felt a momentary detachment. A brief flash of another place and another time. Darkness and horror, a vast and malevolent roaring, and a fearful unsteadiness under his feet. Then it was gone, and his gaze focused again on the approaching patrol. It was too far away to make out any detail, but it was large, and travelling quickly. Four horsemen were leading it.

Then it too was gone, hidden behind the green contours of the Orthlund countryside. Hawklan breathed out nervously and leaned back against a tree. The next time the patrol would appear it would be coming round the bend in the road barely a stone's throw ahead of them, and it would be on them.

'Your men will be in no state to do battle when they've climbed this far,' said Jaldaric to Urssain without looking at him.

'They outnumber you, will outrun you, and will outfight you, Jaldaric,' came the reply with a chilling certainty. 'They're used to mountains. This hill is nothing to them. If you surrender now, none of your patrol will be hurt, and you'll be taken safely back to Vakloss for trial. If you fight, you'll all die. Die without note and at little cost.' Then, almost as if by rote, 'As will all Fyorlund's enemies.'

Jaldaric shot him an angry glance. 'If there's fighting it'll be of their starting, not mine,' he said.

Urssain shrugged.

Inexorably the sound of the patrol grew louder; the sound of running feet filling the air like sinister drumbeats underscoring Gavor's grim cries from high above.

Then it appeared. Isloman seized Hawklan's arm, but Hawklan did not respond. His face was strained as if he were trying to remember something. Silently, however, he drew his sword. There was a quality in the action that chilled Isloman more even than the grim sight now slowing to a walk behind its mounted escort.

Here was the Mathidrin's deep penetration patrol so unthinkingly launched by King Rgoric into Orthlund. Isloman was aware of gasps from the concealed High Guards as he took in the long, dog-like snouts, the evil eyes set close in fur-fringed faces, and that most distinctive and terrifying feature from the nightmares of all Fyordyn children – huge curved canine teeth.

Chapter 9

'Mandrocs!' Several of the High Guards involuntarily whispered the word as if for reassurance of the reality of what they were seeing. The word hissed and echoed around the trees.

Jaldaric, however, stood unmoving and apparently unmoved. He was young for a High Guard Captain and in his darker moments wondered if his rank were not due more to his father's affection than his own ability. He was both right and wrong. Lord Eldric was too wise in leadership to subject his son to the burden of a responsibility he could not carry; and too caring of his men also. However, it was indeed his love for his son that had led Eldric to raise Jaldaric to be able to earn the rank he now held; and it was a measure of Jaldaric's worth that his outward appearance now gave no indication of the waves of doubt and fear that were surging over him as he took in the terrible sight scarring the Orthlund tranquillity.

Slowly he drew his sword and raised it in the air. 'Halt,' he shouted.

The approaching patrol stopped and one of the horsemen came forward. His whole posture showed the marks of fretful journeying but, even against the background of the restless Mandroc patrol, he exuded menace. Jaldaric imperceptibly tightened his grip on his sword to prevent his hand shaking.

The rider, however, ignored him and addressed the waiting Urssain.

'Captain Urssain, why do you and your men lounge in the sun when you were ordered to find the Lord Dan-Tor?'

The sound of the words gave Jaldaric the purchase he needed to still his mind. He did not wait for Urssain's reply. 'The Lord Dan-Tor has returned alone to Fyorlund,' he said. 'And your friend lounges in the sun at my suggestion. He found it preferable to lounging in an eternal darkness, which is where his conduct nearly brought him.'

The rider turned and stared at Jaldaric as if only just noticing he was there.

'The Lord Dan-Tor has left, you say?' he said.

'Yes,' said Jaldaric.

'Alone?' The man cast a swift glance at Urssain, who nodded. A brief spasm of irritation passed over the rider's sallow face and he lowered his head thoughtfully. Then, apparently reaching a decision, he turned again to Jaldaric.

'You're Fyordyn, I see,' he said. 'And you've the arrogance of a lordling. You'll be the traitor Jaldaric I presume.'

Jaldaric did not reply, but held the man's grey-eyed stare firmly. For all his menace, he was at least human, and his hostility deflected Jaldaric's mind from the implications of the waiting patrol.

Then the man walked his horse over to Jaldaric and, leaning forward slightly, bared discoloured teeth in a humourless smile. 'My name is Aelang, Jaldaric. Commander Aelang. Mark it well. It's probably the last pleasantry I'll exchange with you.' Without taking his gaze from Jaldaric's face, he levelled a finger at the seated Urssain. 'You've assaulted a Captain of the King's High Guard, and you've drawn your sword against his Commander. These are serious offences and will be added to whatever others you've to face when we get back to Vakloss.'

Gavor's cry floated down between the two men, and Aelang cast a brief irritable glance upwards.

'I presume the rest of your men are skulking in ambush,' he continued in a more conciliatory tone, waving his arm towards the surrounding trees. 'Tell them to come out and lay down their arms – now – and we'll forget this misunderstanding. Don't resist whatever you do.' Conspiratorially he indicated the waiting Mandrocs with his eyes.

Aelang's affectation of comradeship broke Jaldaric's restraint. 'What is this . . . this obscenity, Aelang? Mandrocs, armed and liveried! *Mandrocs!*' He could barely utter the word. 'And pretending to be a King's High Guard no less.' His tone was acid. 'Do you take me for a child? The Mandrocs are to be confined to Narsindal. The Law forbids them even to enter

Fyorlund, and you bring an armed troop of them into Orthlund – Orthlund of all places. If anyone's to stand account in Vakloss, it'll be you, if you're responsible for any part of this nightmare.'

Waiting in the shade, Hawklan felt thoughts coming from deep inside him. Run, Jaldaric. Retreat. Regroup. Don't stand. But he could not speak the words.

Aelang listened to Jaldaric's outburst with an air of waning patience. 'You don't listen, Jaldaric. I've said I'll not bandy words with you. You've been away too long. The King holds all power now. To defy me is to defy the might of the new Fyorlund, a might uncluttered by ancient Lords and their endless prating, a might which can defend Fyorlund against our real enemies.' Then he leaned forward again and spoke more softly. 'Use your sense, man. If you renounce the old order and join with us, there may be hope for you. If you resist . . .' He shrugged his shoulders.

The combination of wild-eyed fanaticisn and self-seeking ambition in the man's tone stunned Jaldaric and he stood for a moment in bewildered silence.

Then he shook his head. 'No,' he said. 'This is madness. You're lying. How could the King seize all power to himself? And what enemies has Fyorlund that would require aid from . . .' He looked at the sinister waiting group. 'The very reason for the existence of High Guards is the restraint of the Mandrocs.'

'And to guard against the Second Coming of Sumeral,' sneered Aelang scornfully. 'You'll believe fairy tales before you'll believe political reality. That's why the King's taken power. Fyorlund can't afford such as you guarding its interests.'

The jibe stung Jaldaric. He seized the horse's bridle. 'If the King's done this, it's because he's a sick man and has probably been coerced by others. Such an act would break not only the Law but the faith of countless generations. But I don't intend to argue the point. Consider yourself under arrest. Disarm these animals now, surrender your sword and prepare yourself to return with me to Vakloss to face the Geadrol and account for this horror.'

Aelang snatched the bridle from Jaldaric's hand, causing the horse to shy and Jaldaric to step back.

'I weary of you, boy, and I'll not be thanked for delaying to remonstrate with the unredeemable. Surrender now or my patrol will root out your companions and slaughter them.'

'Hold,' cried Jaldaric. 'We're no ordinary patrol. We're the Lord Dan-Tor's escort, and I also have archers with me.'

The man steadied his horse and looked uneasily from side to side. Jaldaric followed his thoughts.

'Yes,' he said, 'you're right. We could leave two dozen of your . . . your creatures dead before they even reach us, and that'll improve the odds a little, won't it? And we've allies from Orthlund.'

Aelang cast a glance at Urssain, who nodded again.

Jaldaric continued quietly but purposefully. 'But that's of no concern to you, is it? Your Mandrocs are only here to absorb shot. They fight with crushing numbers and mindless ferocity if my . . . fairy tale books tell me true. More to the point is what you've already worked out. You and the other men will die first if we're attacked.'

Aelang stood motionless in the middle of the road, peering into the trees on both sides in a vain attempt to assess the truth of Jaldaric's words. Only Gavor's persistent cry could be heard, sounding like an ancient funeral knell.

Finally, Aelang narrowed his eyes and swore viciously. Slowly he dismounted. He was a little shorter than Jaldaric, but heavily built and obviously much stronger. Jaldaric stepped back a pace and levelled his sword at the man. Even from his hiding place in the trees, Isloman felt Aelang's physical confidence.

'Jaldaric's in trouble,' he whispered to Hawklan, but Hawklan seemed to be in a trance.

'Hand me your sword . . . carefully,' said Jaldaric. 'Then order your . . . patrol to throw down their weapons.'

Aelang started to draw his sword with his left hand, fearing a hasty response from a nervous archer if he drew with his right. It snagged in his cape and he fumbled with it momentarily.

Jaldaric did not move.

The sword came free awkwardly and Aelang casually tossed back his cloak with a flourish and a friendly smile. As the cloak billowed out behind him, he took a long swift step forward past the side of Jaldaric's sword and, spinning round, struck Jaldaric in the face with his left hand.

The speed and power of the blow, weighted and hardened as it was by the clenched sword hilt, knocked Jaldaric senseless and, without faltering in his step, Aelang bent low underneath him and swung him up effortlessly across his shoulders. Then, with Jaldaric across his back like a great shield, he ran a weaving path back towards his patrol, crying out commands as he ran.

The whole movement was so swift that the arrow destined for him sang through the empty air where he had been standing.

Urssain and the others were less fortunate. All six rose at Aelang's first move. Three died immediately and the other three, one of them Urssain, were wounded.

Then the archers had to turn their attention to the Mandrocs, who, swords and axes drawn, were running forward. For a few seconds the air was full of the hiss of arrows, the sound of bow strings and the thud of arrows striking home through the leather jerkins which were all that protected the Mandrocs.

In those few seconds, Jaldaric's prophecy came true, and the quiet Pedhavin Road was littered with over thirty dead and dying Mandrocs. But the remainder charged on, heedless of their fallen comrades. Mouthing a rhythmic, rumbling battle chant they crashed into the trees in search of the High Guards.

Isloman glanced at Hawklan. To his horror, his friend was swaying unsteadily, eyes glazed and unseeing. Isloman shook him violently and called his name but there was no response. Before he could do anything further there was a crash in the undergrowth behind him and, turning, he found himself facing two gaping Mandrocs. Terror balled up in his throat, but reflexes he had thought long gone saved him as his club and his great fist swung in two murderous arcs to lay them both out almost before they could react. Two more appeared.

Desperately he pushed Hawklan against a tree and, drawing his sword, turned to face them like a wild animal protecting its young. Within minutes, sword and club left five Mandrocs dead or wounded at his feet, but it was all too obvious he could not hold his position for much longer.

'Hawklan,' he shouted over his shoulder as two more Mandrocs closed with him. 'In the name of pity, there are too many for me. Use your sword. Help me. Help me.'

Abruptly he felt Hawklan jerk to life behind him, almost as if his spirit had suddenly returned from some far distant place. At the edge of his vision he sensed a silent Hawklan moving to his side, Black Sword levelled. With an eerie squeal the two Mandrocs turned and fled.

Then, still silent, Hawklan glanced around, his eyes grim and intent, as if he were listening. The trees were full of the terrible sounds of battle, underscored by the rumbling battle chant of the Mandrocs. Then a look of desperate sadness passed over his face.

'These lads are lost,' he said hollowly. 'We can't do anything. This way.'

Three Mandrocs appeared in front of them, jaws gaping wide, eyes elated, bloody swords steaming in their hands. Without a pause, Hawklan hacked down two of them with a single terrible blow and impaled the third almost before Isloman could raise his club. Hawklan shouted for him to follow, and then ran off into the trees.

Isloman hesitated, stunned both by the sight of the appalling and bloody carnage that his friend had wrought with such suddenness and apparent ease, and by fear for Jaldaric and his men. But Hawklan returned and seized him with a powerful grip. 'We can do nothing for them,' he said fiercely. 'Nothing. We run or die.' Then he turned and ran, dragging Isloman behind like a wayward child.

They encountered several Mandrocs as they fled, but these too fell horribly before Hawklan's Black Sword. Scarcely breaking his step, he twisted and turned through them like a mountain stream around rocks, scattering blood and entrails over the sunlit Orthlund woodland. Isloman took in the beauty of his actions and the inexorable horror of their consequences like a helpless spectator.

To the Carver, it seemed they ran for an eternity but, eventually, Hawklan slowed and then staggered to the ground, his head in his hands. Isloman slumped down beside him, breathing heavily.

They lay for a long time until some semblance of normality forced itself upon them. Isloman hesitated to look at his friend, concerned at what he would see, but when he did he found the grim warrior's visage was gone and he had to turn away from the pain that had replaced it.

'All those young men,' Hawklan said. 'Dead. I can't take it in. What's happening?' He did not wait for an answer. 'All of them cut down in a wave of clamouring bloodlust. What were those creatures? They're like something out of a forgotten nightmare.'

Then he looked in horror at the sword in his hand, still red and steaming with gore. 'And where did I learn to use this?'

Isloman shook his head, he could offer no answer to that question, but . . . 'Mandrocs,' he said. 'I've heard of them. They're from Narsindal. Nasty place by all tellings. I think the High Guards were orginally formed to keep them in order, but I doubt any of those lads had ever even seen one.' He stopped and bowed his head. 'It must have seemed like a nightmare come true. That awful chanting mob charging on regardless of how many of them were killed – just charging on.'

Hawklan shuddered as some darker memory flitted round the edges of his mind. He searched for something more prosaic. 'And now they're serving this King . . . Rgoric' he said, half question, half statement.

Isloman shrugged. 'It would appear so.'

The two men fell silent. High in the foliage above, birds sang out to the spring sunshine, and scufflings in the undergrowth marked the activities of countless forest creatures, lives uninterrupted by the grim whirling thoughts preoccupying the two men. A butterfly landed on Hawklan's boot, folded its wings and them spread them out luxuriously. It flew off abruptly as a dark shadow glided silently to land where it had lain.

A rather tattered Gavor put his head on one side and gazed at Hawklan. 'You did well to run when you did, dear boy,' he said, then he bent his head and fiddled with the straps that held his spurs to avoid Hawklan's gaze. 'Very good, these,' he added, proprietorially, though a little uneasily. 'Very good. I killed a dozen or so, but I couldn't save any of the Guards.

There were just too many of those things and they didn't seem to care whether they lived or died.'

Hawklan looked at Gavor, his strange and comical companion – he had killed these creatures too? Then the memory of Gavor's strange cry returned. It was a death song. That's what it was. He recognised it now though he could not say from where or when – an ancient death song – an awful warning of terrible vengeance. He gestured with his head and Gavor jumped up on to his knee. Hawklan smoothed out his iridescent blue-black feathers. A tear ran down his face.

'What's happening, Gavor?' he asked.

'Don't know, dear boy,' the bird replied after a moment. 'But it's happened before. It's all there on the Gate. Evil things are abroad and we have to fight them. The time of peace is ending. Your rest is over. Soon you'll come to yourself.' His voice was distant.

Hawklan looked at him. 'Do you know who I am?' he asked, for the first time in twenty years.

Gavor shook his head. 'Dear boy, I don't even know who I am. My life started with yours, twenty years ago, trapped by the leg in those bitter mountains.'

Hawklan put his hands to his eyes and the memory of the last few days flowed past him. Young men, proud and disciplined. Looking forward to being home and yarning of their exploits in Orthlund, for all the problems they knew they would face. Looking at least towards order and justice. Young men excitedly quizzing Isloman about the Morlider War, and then Hawklan about Anderras Darion. Making plans to visit Pedhavin again in the future. Young men patiently tending their animals, riding jauntily through the spring sunshine and quietly through the grey rain.

All gone. Swept away like dead leaves in autumn. Swept away by their worst nightmare without knowing any part of why. Irrelevant pieces in a greater game.

Hawklan's throat tightened and abruptly, unbidden, his grief burst out. He sobbed uncontrollably for several minutes. Neither Gavor nor Isloman spoke and, when Hawklan finally looked up, Isloman's eyes, too, were damp.

Hawklan wiped his face with a kerchief and then, almost

involuntarily, began to clean his sword with it. Soon the cloth was soiled with the blood from the blade, and Hawklan's hands too were red-streaked. He felt an overwhelming sadness as he looked down at them. Where in all Orthlund can I find a stream that would not be desecrated by washing these hands? he thought. He dragged his mind back to their predicament.

'Where are they now?' he asked Gavor.

'Heading north,' came the reply. 'Taking all the dead with them. They're not as cocky as they were. Between us we took quite a toll.'

'There were no survivors at all?' asked Isloman.

Gavor shook his head. 'Only Jaldaric. I presume he was alive. He was thrown over a saddle and well bound. And those two outriders might be alive somewhere. I don't remember seeing them come back.'

Hawklan wiped his eyes again with the back of his hand, and his face hardened. He stood up wearily. 'Go and look for them, Gavor. Bring them back here if they're alive. And find the horses. I've no idea where they are. We'll stay here.'

Serian, however, needed no guide, and when Gavor returned with the two Guards, he found the great horse standing quietly by as Hawklan calmed Isloman's mount. It was no easy task. Though uninjured, the animal was terrified.

When he had finished Hawklan spoke to Serian. 'You did well,' he said. 'Are you all right? Weren't you frightened?'

'I'm a Muster horse, Hawklan,' replied Serian. 'Of course I was frightened, but I had to look after this, didn't I? I'll be fine. I'm sorry I lost the others. They just scattered.'

Hawklan patted Serian's nose reassuringly and turned away to attend to the newly arrived men, Fel-Astian and Idrace. They were uninjured, but were badly shocked. It took Hawklan some time to piece their story together.

As instructed, they had ridden a wide flanking path to find and observe the approaching patrol. They had, however, overshot it and come back to the road far to its rear. By the time they had realised their mistake and retraced their steps, the battle was virtually finished. From a distance they witnessed the last of their friends disappearing under a wave of chanting Mandrocs. Then both had turned and fled in terror.

It was this last act that haunted them most.

Idrace, dark-haired and stocky, with a hooked nose and powerful deep-set eyes, talked and talked, clenching and unclenching his hands and pacing up and down fretfully.

'All gone. Even that worm Esselt and his cronies. Died fighting while we ran away. Ran away.' Over and over. Then he would stop, drive his nails into his palms and grind his teeth as if he could expunge his shame by slow self-destruction.

Hawklan, however, looked first to Fel-Astian who, though quieter, was probably the more affected of the two. Idrace's remorse would temper into a formidable and unrelenting resolve, but Fel-Astian was of a different mettle.

He was not unlike Jaldaric in appearance, with fair hair and a strong build, though with a harsher, less innocent face. Sitting in the shade of a tree, he shivered continually and wrapped his arms around himself as if for protection against some outward enemy. Hawklan knew that his pain was no less than Idrace's for all its lack of outward raging but, being turned inward, it would destroy him if it found no outlet. It would need care and understanding and all Hawklan's healing skills to draw this man forth relatively unscathed. But it would also need time, and time was not available. Hawklan could form no plan of what he should do next, but he knew that urgency must be its hallmark.

He struck Fel-Astian a stinging blow across the face. The sound stopped Idrace in his tracks and made Isloman look up, startled. Fel-Astian jerked back and looked mildly surprised and reproachful. Hawklan hit him again. This time Fel-Astian sprang to his feet angrily, his fists raised. Hawklan swept down the extended arms effortlessly and thrust a grim face within inches of Fel-Astian's.

'You're one of the Fyorlund High Guard. An elite fighting corps. You set aside your grief and suffering and consider what you must do for your country before all else.' His voice was harsh and commanding. Isloman stared up at him, seeing once again one of the carved figures from Anderras Darion standing in this spring-lit glade.

Fel-Astian's face contorted with conflicting emotions, but Hawklan's countenance defied their outlet.

'Do you understand?' he shouted. 'Your Captain's taken. Your country's undergoing some strange and awful trial, and you, alive, unhurt and armed, sit nursing yourself like a sick infant.' There was a contempt in his voice which outweighed even that in the content of his words. He lifted his hand as if to strike the man again but, this time, Fel-Astian's hand came out and seized his wrist powerfully. Again Fel-Astian's face twisted painfully until, at last, a long, uncontrollable, almost screaming cry came out from him.

'No,' he bellowed into Hawklan's face. 'Sumeral take you. No. I hear you. I understand you. Damn you.'

He pushed Hawklan to one side and striding forward drew his sword and brought it down in a whistling arc into the soft forest turf. Then he leaned forward on to it and slowly sank to his knees as his weight pushed it into the ground. Head bowed, he knelt silent and unmoving.

Idrace stood watching him, his face pale under his dark hair. Fel-Astian's outburst had dwarfed his own loud distress.

Eventually Fel-Astian rose to his feet quietly. He withdrew his sword from the ground and, as Hawklan had done before, took out a kerchief and began cleaning the blade. He gave Hawklan an enigmatic look.

Hawklan's face softened a little and stepping forward he took both of the Guards by the arm. A voice that Isloman recognised now spoke.

'We've no time to dwell on matters. We can't wait for the luxury of time's healing. Listen carefully and remember what I say in your darker hours. You're young and you're strong. Your pain will pass, as does all pain, but you'll not recover from the death of your friends. Still less will you recover from what you've taken to be your failure, your cowardice, in running away from their destruction. But you'll become a little wiser.' His grip tightened in emphasis. 'You must learn from what has happened and what you felt. Learn so that you'll recognise and know it again and know you can accept such things. In that way your friends won't have died in vain.'

Neither man spoke. Hawklan continued, his voice gentle but hypnotic and powerful. 'Your bodies and your emotions accepted the truth of that was happening before your pride and your vanity could interfere. Isloman and I fled the battle as well. With sadness but without qualms. The die was cast. The only thing the patrol could've done was withdraw against those odds – and quickly. But . . .' He shrugged sadly, unable to finish. 'Now other needs call us. Our only way is forward. Let the past arm you for the future and illumine your way. Don't let it obscure your path.'

Later, mounted and ready to part, Hawklan leaned across and grasped first Idrace's wrist and then Fel-Astian's. Then Isloman did the same. They had considered only briefly the possibly of rescuing Jaldaric but, though badly depleted, the Mandroc patrol was too large and, according to Gavor, was making exceptionally rapid progress towards Fyorlund. Their hopes for Jaldaric lay in the efforts that had been taken to keep him alive when the rest of his group were so casually slaughtered.

No further words were spoken as the two couples parted. Idrace and Fel-Astian, grim, but more composed, rode north. It was their intention to enter Fyorlund quietly and find out what had happened in their absence. Hawklan and Isloman turned south, back towards Pedhavin and Anderras Darion, intending to rouse on the way such village elders as they could. The need to seek out Dan-Tor seemed more pressing than ever, but too much had happened for them blithely to enter Fyorlund and leave the Orthlundyn unaware of what had happened on their soil. They would have to return later.

Gavor had flown north again, at Hawklan's request, to observe the Mandroc patrol before himself returning to Pedhavin.

The sun was setting when Hawklan and Isloman emerged from the wood and set off along the ancient road. A slight mist was forming, smothering the land in white anonymity. In places it arched up over the road to form translucent grottos. Through it, the dying sun shone blood red.

Chapter 10

Dan-Tor idly fingered the medallion of office hanging from a slender gold chain around his neck. Then abruptly he released it with a grimace; these lingering traits of his fretful humanity irked him profoundly.

Uncharacteristically he found himself longing bitterly for the day when all pretence could be discarded, when the Old Power could be used, when battle lines could be drawn and he could join with his companions and lead His hordes out of Narsindal to sweep all before them and raise Him, and themselves, to the height that destiny had ordained.

But the road to such a day was hazardous. The past had shown the folly of too lightly dismissing the forces that could be ranged against them. Humans could be endlessly troublesome for all their weakness and inconsistency.

Now, ensconced in his eyrie, in the highest tower of the King's Palace far above Vakloss, unfamiliar doubts pervaded his thoughts.

His encounter with Hawklan – Ethriss? – had made him terminate his journey and go scuttling back to Narsindal with the news. No other could be trusted with that. But He had shown only His cold silent anger at the risks that had been taken in provoking Hawklan. Then, looking into Dan-Tor for a trembling eternity, He had delivered a further blow, a stunning, unexpected blow. 'You have erred twofold. Your King runs amok. Abandon the south, I have others better suited.'

No counsel had been offered, nor aid. Only a brooding silence. Only the weight of that endless dark patience. From this Dan-Tor knew that the consequences of his actions must run their course, however erratic and unforeseeable, and he must bear them.

He closed his eyes and heard again the words of his Master

when He had finally wakened. 'You are my faithful servant and will again be rewarded as my power grows – as grow it will – beyond even its ancient greatness.' Then, the re-affirmation: 'But recall. You are bound to me and by me. You can be expunged at my whim and others made in your image. Serve me well.' It was a statement cold beyond measure and beyond appeal.

'Expunged at my whim,' Dan-Tor mouthed to himself into the silence of his room.

With an effort, he dismissed from his mind the questions that his Master's knowledge about the King had prompted. Who could know what sight He had? What dark envoys?

Then, standing up, he moved to the window and stared out; over the great avenues and parks and proud old buildings that were Vakloss; out over its bustling heart nestling around the Palace walls in a maze of twisting, narrow streets thronged with people. But he saw only the distant mountains to the north, red-tipped and strangely shadowed in the setting sun. Frustration hissed through his clenched teeth and he turned to more immediate problems.

Who could have rescued Hawklan from the Gretmearc and avoided his agents? And what had happened to the birds? A long-forgotten name came into his mind. The Cadwanol. Could they still exist? After such a time? The Cadwanol. Ethriss's ancient allies and repository of most of the knowledge of the First Coming. A constant thorn in His side, but elusive and cunning, hiding in deep and strange places, deep beyond even Oklar's power.

It was a disturbing thought, and it persisted. And yet Ethriss was not awake. The Cadwanol must surely know how to waken their old master? Had not he and his companions learned how to waken theirs after countless aeons bound in darkness? But Hawklan had fled from the Gretmearc; he could not be Ethriss. And yet . . .?

Beyond doubt, he must be captured, Dan-Tor resolved again. But captured with great cunning . . .

A discreet scratching at the door interrupted his reverie. Face twitching irritably, he paused until he could smell the servant's fear leaking through to him.

Was the Lord there? Had he scratched loudly enough? Should he scratch again and risk the Lord's wrath at his impatience?

Dan-Tor could charm the most obdurate of Lords when needed, but the lesser fry of Fyorlund who dealt with him, being both less burdened with office and more perceptive, knew him more truly. He sensed a hand rising hesitantly and on an impulse spared his victim.

'Enter,' he said calmly. The wave of relief sickened him. These humans were contemptible – a small distant voice within him reminded him that he, too, had once been thus.

'His Majesty has asked me to request that you attend him in his rooms, Lord.'

You mean he's told you to tell me, you worm, thought Dan-Tor viciously.

'Please inform His Majesty that I'll attend him immediately,' he said courteously. Another repellent wave of relief, and the servant walked out backwards before fleeing down the Palace's twisting stairs and corridors to safer quarters.

With the King in his present unstable condition, Dan-Tor knew he must not be left alone for long. The damage the King had accomplished in so short a time verged on being a considerable achievement, and nothing could be taken for granted until he was completely under control again. This, however, might prove none too easy. In Dan-Tor's absence, the King had unconsciously turned to his wife, Sylvriss, and her influence, though weak, lay deep. Deeper than Dan-Tor dared risk threatening.

The King lay alone in his chamber, stretched along a wide couch and gazing vacantly up at the ornate painted ceiling. That he was in this room indicated the influence of Sylvriss. It had been their bridal chamber and still carried resonances of happier times.

It made Dan-Tor's flesh crawl.

Large clear crystal doors at the far end of the room looked across a beautifully tended garden of lawns and shrubs and fountains, but, as they faced east, to bring the morning sun into the chamber, they showed now only the mounting evening darkness, as purple mountains merged into the purple sky.

Dan-Tor noted with malicious satisfaction the harsh shadows cast by the light of the globes which had replaced the older, gentler torches. He entered with a discreet amount of noise, and bowed low.

'Majesty,' he said gently and with concern. 'The pain has returned?'

Rgoric made no reply. Dan-Tor did not move, but tried to sense the man's mood. Little ripples of anger still crossed Dan-Tor's mind at what the King had done and at having such inadequate material for the weaving of his Master's design, but he swept them away ruthlessly. Such self-indulgence offered nothing but hindrance and, he thought bitterly, reminded him too much of the King himself.

He moved forward into the King's line of sight, but kept his face slightly in the shade. He was uncertain what might be showing in his eyes and how sensitive the King might be to what he saw there.

'Majesty?'

The King's eyes unfixed themselves from the ceiling and turned to Dan-Tor.

Ah, martyred and misunderstood, read Dan-Tor. Now we know where we are. He moved forward again, the light of a nearby globe falling on his face. And reproachful, too.

'Dan-Tor, you shouldn't go away for so long. In spite of your ministrations, my health is so uncertain. I've burdened myself with too much too soon. My subjects do not – will not – understand. I work ceaselessly for their benefit, for their protection against treachery at home and abroad, but they harry me.' His hands twitched pettishly. 'Where were you?' he said plaintively. Dan-Tor opened his mouth to speak but the King continued. 'I felt so strong, so well when you left. Like the old days. I'll pick up my duties again, I thought. Take the country in a strong grip. Throw out these bleating Lords as we arranged. Lead my country into a new future, make it strong again. Then . . .' He put his hand to his head. 'Then my strength left me – just drained away – and the Lords wouldn't accept my judgement. They defied me. You were away too long.'

Dan-Tor was weary of this monologue, this self-justification. The King had repeated it to him incessantly since his return from Narsindal. Deftly adjusting his long brown robe of office, he knelt down by the couch in an attitude of both subservience and personal concern for his suffering friend. He too must repeat himself.

'Majesty, I accept your rebuke. But you know that I was away so long only because the strength of our enemies grows. A monstrous leader has arisen in Orthlund who rouses the people there to ambition and lust for your land and power. I tried to seize him but, with great cunning, he escaped and I had to leave his capture to my escort and return to you.'

A silence fell and the names of Eldric and Jaldaric floated unspoken between them. The King knew now that his impetuous action against Jaldaric had in some way probably jeopardised Dan-Tor's second plan for the capture of this sinister Orthlundyn leader. Dan-Tor, however, knew that greater benefit would come from his not repeating this complaint, so he let the words remain unspoken, like a sick miasma hanging in the air.

'This coming and going of your strength is the nature of the illness as we know too well, Majesty. You must be patient. You did indeed undertake too much too soon. It'll be many days before you feel well again.' Dan-Tor's voice was forgiving.

The King screwed up his face peevishly. 'Why didn't you kill this . . . this leader, when you had the chance?' he asked suddenly, almost as if he were anxious to receive Dan-Tor's rebuke.

'That wouldn't have been expedient, Majesty. Such an open act would have brought the Orthlundyn down on us like rocks down a mountainside, and . . .' Dan-Tor paused; sow a little more doubt and uncertainty, he thought, it'll always come in useful. He assumed a worried expression. 'To be honest, Majesty, I didn't value him at his full worth immediately. He's subtle and crafty, and has woven himself deep into the hearts of the people over many years. When I realised who he was, and what he was doing, he was almost beyond my reach. It's some measure of his cunning that he avoided my first trap.'

The King scowled at him and gestured dismissively. Then he drew a startled breath and his face contorted with pain. He held out a begging hand to his tall tormentor. Dan-Tor laid his own hand gently on the King's forehead and then looked into his eyes. His manner was soft and reassuring: don't be afraid. I'm here now, it said. All will be well.

He took out a small jewelled box from his robe and, without any apparent movement of his hand, it opened. The King clutched at his wrist feverishly. Dan-Tor delicately picked out a small tablet with his long fingers and, pausing for a cruel moment, placed it in the King's mouth, now opened wide in anticipation like a newly hatched chick.

Almost immediately the King closed his eyes and leaned back with a relieved sigh, the worried lines disappearing from his face. Briefly Dan-Tor was reminded of the young man Rgoric had once been.

'Sleep well, Majesty. When you awake, your pain will have gone and your strength will have returned.'

Dan-Tor sat by the sleeping King for a long time staring enigmatically at the now relaxed face. The fleeting vision of the young King had stirred old memories. It's salutary, he thought, to be reminded from time to time who it is I'm dealing with. Curse this King as he may for being a weak and inconsistent tool in his hands, it would be unwise to forget that he was heir to generations of great leaders. A man to whom others of this independently minded and formidable race had given loyalty without demur. A man who had led a great army to victory. A man of proven courage and skill in personal combat. A power-ful man. And a powerful people. Their complete corruption was essential to His schemes, and could only be achieved slowly. Very slowly.

Dan-Tor longed for His deep, dark patience.

He knew that even now, after so long, his hold on Rgoric, though strong, was deceptive. It was deep, but it did not reach down into the essence of the man; at a level beyond the King's awareness and beyond Dan-Tor's reaching, he knew that the King's old spirit still battled to throw off his domination.

One day, Majesty, he thought. It'll probably kill you before it'll submit any further.

Ironically, the contemplation of the long road ahead eased away the last of Dan-Tor's anger at the King's actions; there is time for many things on a long journey. He knew it would be fruitless to try to find out why the King had done what he had done. Was it some desire to please him? Some desire to be independent of him? Some vainglorious whim? All irrelevant though. the King himself had probably forgotten even the ostensible reason by now, burying it under a great mound of self-pity and recrimination. The play had been made, and no sleight of hand on his part could change it. The game had to be continued from Rgoric's unexpected gambit. Now he must watch daily, hourly even, to see that no irreparable harm came of it.

The suspension of the Geadrol with the inevitable reaction of the Lords and the consequent arrest of four of the most senior; the displacement of the Lords' High Guards by the Mathidrin – both deeds far too premature and both with the potential to tilt the country into civil war. As for calling the Mathidrin his own High Guard . . . Dan-Tor closed his eyes briefly. But, equally, these acts would enable him to gather more power to himself, to claim sedition and treason as excuse for a surreptitiously increased repression of the people. The numbers of the Mathidrin could be covertly increased and those of the Lords' High Guards reduced, and the same reason offered should comment arise.

A faint smile came to his long face. Perhaps a trial of Eldric and the others. That might prove an excellent opportunity for swaying the minds of the people. It would bear careful thought. Much could be salvaged if this were handled correctly. Possibly even progress made.

'And Hawklan – Ethriss?' – came the thought.

The smile faded and his white teeth ground together. The King's use of the Mandroc patrol to vent his spleen against Eldric's family had been folly indeed. Who could tell what effect the Harmony of Orthlund would have on those creatures? The King knew the patrol only as an elite group of the Mathidrin and, while he and the Fyordyn could be persuaded to accept many things, armed and trained Mandrocs in his service would not be one for a long time.

Fortunately, he consoled himself, Aelang, though unable to defy the King, had had the wit to lead them secretly out of Fyorlund, so few, if any, should have seen them; and those few could be dealt with if necessary. But would Jaldaric and his men have responded? And what of Hawklan?

Jaldaric would fight, surely? He would not yield to Mandrocs and strange liveried Guards. Shock alone would probably make him draw his sword. But Hawklan? If Jaldaric had obeyed his orders, then Hawklan would have been some way behind, being drawn by the threads that bound him to the girl. In which case he would have come upon the battle itself, or the remnants of it. And if Hawklan were Ethriss, what in His name would be his reaction to the sight of the Mandrocs or their handiwork? And the girl. She must surely be dead now. That alone might awaken him.

But I'm here yet, thought Dan-Tor. Ethriss isn't awake. The thought offered him little consolation as he remembered the terrible defeat he had suffered so long ago. He shuddered.

The King stirred. Dan-Tor laid his hand against the King's forehead. 'Rest, Rgoric,' he said softly, hypnotically. 'All's well. I'll shoulder your burdens again.'

But forbid it as he might, his mind wandered back out along the Pedhavin Road, teasing through the awesome possibilities that might have been set in train there. So preoccupied was he with this ancient highway that he did not hear the chamber door open and close.

He started abruptly as a hand touched his shoulder.

Chapter 11

Sylvriss, Queen to Rgoric, was the daughter of Urthryn, the Ffyrst of Riddin.

The Riddinvolk had no time for kings and rulers and suchlike, priding themselves on their independence and practicality. But, as befits a practical people, they would always look to one among them for direction and advice from time to time – a first among equals. Such was Urthryn, and had been for many years.

His daughter bore the stamp of the exceptional personality that had placed him in this position. Black-haired, with dark brown eyes, she had an almost tangible presence and was universally loved by the Fyordyn.

Dan-Tor hated her roundly.

'I'm sorry I startled you, Lord,' she said softly, looking down into his alarmed brown face. 'I didn't want to waken the King.' Her voice had the characteristic sing-song lilt of the Riddinvolk. It grated on Dan-Tor's ears.

Angry at his racing pulse, he stood up creakily and bowed. 'I was lost in thought, My Lady. I didn't hear you enter. I was pondering how best I might help His Majesty. His illness is so intractable. Each time I think I'm near success it slips away.'

Sylvriss nodded. She had heard the lie and its variations over many years, but understood all too well the folly of arguing with Dan-Tor or drawing her husband away from his ministrations.

Several times in the early years of their marriage, when she had been more naive and Rgoric more robust, she had persuaded him to abandon Dan-Tor's potions and medicines, seeing they were doing him little good and sensing instinctively that they might even be the cause of his condition. Dan-Tor never objected other than with a light gesture of resignation and a look of sad inevitability on his long face. On each occasion, the King had improved for a little while, then relapsed suddenly into an even more serious condition, leaving Sylvriss no alternative but to seek Dan-Tor's help. It had been a bitter lesson for the young bride to learn, and had cost her many lonely tears.

Over the years she had been forced to stand by almost helplessly as Dan-Tor's influence over her husband and the country grew and grew, like a creeper choking a great tree while apparently giving it an infusion of fresh new life. But she was her father's daughter, a rider in the Muster – had she not ridden as a messenger when only a child in the latter days of the Morlider wars? Such a person could not easily yield the field, but neither could she rail futilely against what was seemingly inevitable. She slowly accepted the reality of her position but resolved to fight Dan-Tor with such weapons as she had. And Dan-Tor knew it, though neither angry words nor deeds ever passed between them.

Riddin lay to the south of Narsindal and was readily accessible from that land only through the bleak and awful Pass of Elewart. If the Riddinvolk could be corrupted and the Muster rendered impotent and ineffective, or better still, if they could be turned into allies, then the Pass could be used and His forces could move down through Fyorlund, Orthlund and Riddin, without fear of attack on their flanks, or threat to their lines of supply as they plunged deeper into the south.

It was for this reason that Dan-Tor had engineered the marriage of Rgoric to the Ffyrst's daughter: it being his hope that this would increase his influence in Riddin and enable him to sow the seed of corruption there, as he had so successfully done in Fyorlund. The marriage of a sixteen-year-old girl and a much older – soon-to-be-ailing – man should have provided ample opportunity for his creative talents. But he had miscalculated seriously. Despite the differences in their ages and backgrounds, Rgoric and Sylvriss fell deeply in love, and formed a bond that would be forever beyond his machinations.

Though the true horror of the man was beyond any mortal's measure, it is probable that even before she came consciously to oppose Dan-Tor, Sylvriss sensed him for what he was at the outset, for subtly she sowed distrust in her father's mind against this 'long streak of smiling cunning'.

Urthryn had been concerned at first by such references in his only child's letters, but had taken due note. He knew, after all, that his daughter was not given either to foolishness or malice, and that having a king rule over a country, fine man though he might be, was a sure way to attract all manner of queer folk. Still, in addition to her soft abuse of Dan-Tor, her letters told also of her love for her husband, so Urthryn contented himself with that in his lonelier hours.

Whenever Dan-Tor visited, which was often at first, Urthryn gave him a rather cloddish courtesy and listened to his advice with a look of bewildered strain on his face before agreeing to 'think on it – when I get time'. When Dan-Tor left, Urthryn consigned the advice to the winds.

Thus, as Sylvriss had had to accept the growing influence of Dan-Tor over her husband, so Dan-Tor had to accept that Riddin was, in some way, being kept beyond his reach by this young woman. More galling, however, and potentially more serious, his underestimation of the love of Sylvriss and Rgoric would mean that his control over Rgoric would need constant vigilance. The corruption of the Fyordyn could not be let slip.

Sylvriss knelt down by her husband and took his hand.

'He'll be asleep for some time,' said Dan-Tor. 'He was in pain and very disturbed.' He gazed down at the black hair of his unspoken antagonist.

As if aware of his scrutiny, Sylvriss turned, and smiling up at him, said, 'Thank you, Lord. I'll sit with him now. You may go. You look tired. I'm afraid Rgoric's blunderings on top of your long journeying may prove too much for you.'

From a lesser person there would have been a sarcasm in such a statement that Dan-Tor could have relished, but there was a genuine compassion in her voice that struck him like a physical blow. It was a constant quality in her and he could not understand it. She opposed him even though she knew she must lose. She must surely hate and fear him. But there was always this . . . this . . . pity? He stepped back involuntarily and then disguised the movement as part of his withdrawal. He bowed, showing gratitude on his face. He intended to thank her for her concern, but the words stuck in his throat. 'You must not stay too long, My Lady,' he said. 'Or you, too, will be exhausted.'

Sylvriss did not reply, but smiled faintly. It was in her smile that the strain of the years told. As she turned her attention to her husband again, Dan-Tor watched her from the doorway, the memory of the smile lingering.

I could expunge you at my whim, woman, he thought, unconsciously echoing his Master. But this way was better. Her suffering would be long and terrible, and made all the worse because it would be for someone else's pain, not her own. You'll carry a burden beyond your imagining before we're finished, woman. So it would be with everyone who opposed His will.

Dan-Tor closed the door behind himself gently and turned to face a twitching Dilrap. He watched coldly as the secretary executed a cadenza of flutters and jerks prior to delivering his message.

'Lord.' Eventually, 'A Captain of the . . . King's High Guard has requested an audience with you. He says it's urgent. Something about a prisoner.'

Dan-Tor's eyes flickered briefly. 'Where is he?' he said.

'He's been put in your ante-chamber. He's been there for some time.'

'Why didn't you find me earlier, Honoured Secretary?' Dan-Tor's voice was quiet but its tone was peculiarly alarming and there was another small spasm which Dilrap could only still by seizing the front of his robe in both hands and holding them firmly against his chest.

'Lord, you weren't in your chambers, Lord, and no one knew where you were.'

Dan-Tor did not reply. 'This Captain has a name?' he asked.

Dilrap's hands fluttered momentarily, like plump butterflies. He did not like these uncouth and arrogant Guards. Dealing with them always upset him. 'Urssain, Lord,' he said finally.

Dan-Tor grunted and nodded dismissively. Dilrap bowed and wobbled off down the high arched corridor, deftly drawing in his robe for the protection of the many ornaments that lined his path. Dan-Tor's still, lank frame stood watching him for a moment and then turned and moved in the other direction.

Urssain. With a prisoner. A faint hope sprang within him, but he quelled it. Soon he would have a real measure of the damage the King had wrought.

Chapter 12

Urssain, travel-stained and with his right arm in a sling, looked round enviously at the luxuriously appointed chamber he had been shown into. Everywhere were objects and furnishings of a quality which indicated the wealth he aspired to. And the power.

The Mathidrin had been trained secretly in Narsindal and in the further reaches of Fyorlund. They were recruited from the malcontents and misfits that any ordered society breeds, however benign its government, though there were a few kindred spirits who had travelled from far distant lands. The darker traits of all had been assiduously cultivated, in the King's name, under the covert direction of Dan-Tor.

The move into Vakloss and the displacement of the traditional High Guards had been the fulfilment of a promise to them and a token that they had joined a winning side. Men began to see new vistas opening before them, and ambition grew apace. Fertile ground for such as Dan-Tor.

But city work was new to them and their harshness and arrogance had not endeared them to the people. Reactions ranged from stony politeness to outright abuse and anger, although a growing taint of fear was beginning to colour almost all responses.

In the Palace, the tension was at its most marked. The many Palace servants and retainers made little effort to disguise their contempt for these loutish newcomers, although one or two might grudgingly concede the quality of their discipline.

Urssain, however, had noted immediately how the attitudes of both servants and officials had changed from surprise to near alarm when he first appeared and produced his special pass bearing the Lord Dan-Tor's mark. It was said that the Lord Dan-Tor was the real force behind the Mathidrin, though those who said it, did so softly and carefully, and with implicit admonitions to secrecy. Undoutedly, however, power lay in this man. Power that would lead to this wealth and, Urssain reasoned, wealth to those who knew and served him well.

He stood up, relishing the soft creak of the expensive upholstery as he did so, and walked over to the window. The carpet too was soft and deep under his feet, feet that had known only rocks, stirrups and barrack-room floors, and its touch drew him further along the path he realised he had begun to tread: the path towards the acquisition of this power and this wealth. His hand clenched in excitement. He looked out of the window, but there was little to be seen other than a courtyard some way below marked out in harsh light and deep shade by the globe lights. Shadows to hide in, he thought. Hide indeed.

He went over his speech again. It would be important with this Lord. He had little illusion about why Aelang had sent him instead of coming himself. Ostensibly it was because he had to accompany the Mandrocs on their clandestine return to their barracks hidden deep in the bleak northern mountains bordering Narsindal. There was some truth in this, as the Mandrocs had been greatly disturbed by what had happened in Orthlund and were proving very difficult to handle. But the reality was that the venture had nearly been a disaster. Finding Dan-Tor unexpectedly absent, Urssain had mishandled his initial approach to Jaldaric and Aelang had done little better. Then those High Guards had fought like fiends, inflicting appalling losses on the Mandrocs. Urssain patted his sling unconsciously. And those Orthlundyn! What a trail they had left. The capture of Jaldaric had been the sole saving grace. His forehead wrinkled as he struggled with the words that he hoped would present him in the most favourable light and, with luck, ensure it was Aelang who bore any odium. Let *him* end up training Mandroc recruits in Narsindal, Urssain thought. He pulled a bitter face at the prospect and pressed his left hand on to the polished and finely worked windowsill as if for comfort. Orthlund might give you the creeps, but the interior of Narsindal . . .

Looking up he saw himself reflected in the night-backed window. He straightened up to examine his image critically.

Not bad, he thought. At one stage he had considered changing into formal uniform to impress this Lord but, on reflection, he had decided that the dust of travel and the rough field bandage would serve him better. It would add just that extra to his account of his heroic actions. Yes, he reflected, he'd done the right thing. This Lord certainly wouldn't be impressed by a parade-ground uniform. He looked down at his tunic and straightened out a crease with his left hand.

When he looked up to examine himself again in the window, he found he was looking into the eyes of Lord Dan-Tor. The man had entered the room unheard and was standing watching him. Urssain spun round, eyes wide and mouth hanging open momentarily. He stammered.

'Lord . . .'

Dan-Tor neither spoke nor moved. He simply continued to stare at Urssain, as if the sudden flurry of movement had never happened. Urssain found his eyes fixed by this tall still figure. Though he had heard much about this strange Lord and seen him distantly on occasions, he had never before met him face to face. Now he felt the awesome force of the man, as he stood impaled on his gaze like a fish on a spear. His carefully rehearsed speech evaporated. To tell this man anything other than the truth would be pointless and foolish, not to say dangerous. Yes, very dangerous. Here was some kind of fountainhead. Urssain could not have found the words for what he wanted out of his life, but he knew beyond doubt that it flowed from this man.

The spear was withdrawn.

'Captain Urssain. You've news of a prisoner I believe.'

'Yes, Lord,' said Urssain, recovering himself somewhat and coming smartly to attention. 'We've taken the man Jaldaric, son of the traitor Eldric.'

Dan-Tor seemed to grow a little smaller, and a look of angry disappointment passed briefly across his long face. He lowered himself into a chair.

'No other prisoner?' he demanded harshly.

Urssain looked a little puzzled. What had he missed? 'No, Lord,' he replied.

Dan-Tor sat in silence for a moment. Urssain became aware of the hiss of the globe lighting the room.

'Make your report, Captain,' Dan-Tor said eventually. His voice was matter-of-fact, but the eyes again impaled Urssain and, not a little to his own surprise, he told his tale truthfully.

When he had finished, Dan-Tor withdrew his gaze and stared thoughtfully downwards, toying idly with the medallion around his neck.

'The two Orthlundyn. Are they among the dead you brought back?'

Orthlundyn? thought Urssain.

'No, Lord,' he said. 'They disappeared into the trees with the others, but they must have run away when the fighting started.' He paused, then added: 'It's as well they did. They must have hacked down a dozen Mandrocs on their way, and left a lot more gibbering – you know the way they do when . . .'

Dan-Tor silenced him with a movement of his hand. 'And was there no woman with them?'

Urssain hesitated. 'No, Lord.'

Dan-Tor fell silent again, pondering the absence of Tirilen and the apparent friendship of Hawklan and Jaldaric.

'Jaldaric is below, you say?'

'Yes, Lord.'

More silence.

Urssain's shoulder started to throb, but he did not dare to move. Dan-Tor looked up.

'Your shoulder is troubling you,' he said. It was a statement not a question. Urssain affected stoicism.

'It's nothing serious, Lord.'

Dan-Tor stood up and walked over to him. Expertly he removed the bandage and exposed the wound. Urssain stayed stiffly to attention.

'Relax, Captain. Stand easy,' said the Lord's soft voice. 'You're right, it isn't serious. But it'll be troublesome and painful for some time, and I can give you something for it.'

He went to a large cupboard behind his chair. The lacquered doors clicked open as he approached, revealing an enormous array of bottles, jars and pieces of equipment whose function Urssain preferred not to guess at. Dan-Tor's long fingers went unerringly into the apparent confusion and retrieved a jar and a roll of bandage.

Urssain rolled his shoulder to ease the pain, but that only made things worse, and the jolt made the blood run from his face. He swayed on his feet.

Without looking at him, Dan-Tor said, 'Don't move.'

The ointment from the jar brought immediate relief to the wound, and Dan-Tor's expert bandaging left Urssain feeling at once freer and more secure. Standing right in front of him, his brown wrinkled face filling Urssain's vision, Dan-Tor smiled. Something predatory in the rows of white teeth chilled Urssain more than any amount of scowling could have done.

'Your arm will be well very soon,' said Dan-Tor. Then, after a long pause, 'I've taken the trouble to repair it for a purpose, Captain. Your meeting with Jaldaric was as ill-judged an affair as I could have imagined. Thanks to it we've lost a large number of fully trained Mandrocs, and landed ourselves with a severe morale problem – those creatures aren't totally stupid you know, not by any means. And worse, we've lost two very important prisoners.' He toyed with the medallion again. 'Putting it bluntly, Urssain, better than you by far have made lesser mistakes and suffered for it more than you could ever imagine.'

Urssain stood very still.

Dan-Tor sat down. 'However, there were forces at work that were beyond you, and . . . I sense qualities in you which are worth developing.'

Urssain breathed out very quietly.

'You're a man who'll learn. And quickly when needs be. You learned immediately that to tell me other than the truth would be not only foolish but dangerous.' There was a dreadful chill in his voice, and the coincidence of the words with his own earlier thoughts shook Urssain profoundly. He remained motionless and involuntarily held his breath again. He wanted to be a long way from here.

'And you have wants, have you not? Desires?' A long bony hand airily encompassed the room. 'Ambitions? For wealth? For power?' Again the coincidence of words. Urssain shrank within himself as if to close off his own thoughts.

'Nothing is hidden from me, Urssain.' Dan-Tor stood up, and placing his hands on Urssain's shoulders, stared deeply into his eyes. Urssain felt himself dwindle into nothingness in the shadow of such power, then he felt himself lifted up and carried somewhere high above his wildest ambitions.

Abruptly the power was withdrawn, leaving only the after image of some attainable goal burning in his mind. Dan-Tor was matter-of-fact again.

'I'll call you when I need you, Captain. Return to your barracks.'

'Lord,' said Urssain as steadily as he could, then he turned to leave the room.

As he reached the door, Dan-Tor spoke again. 'The Mandrocs, Urssain. How did they behave in Orthlund?'

Urssain thought for a moment. 'It upset them, Lord. It's a creepy place. They were very unsettled – anxious to be . . . home . . . somewhere else. I didn't like it very much myself to be honest. But they fought well enough.'

Dan-Tor nodded slowly, then, 'Send word they're to be kept in isolation until I've had an opportunity to study them. Don't let them mix with their own.'

Urssain acknowledged the order and closed the door quietly behind himself.

That at least is one useful piece of salvage from this wreck, thought Dan-Tor when Urssain had left. He had been watching the man for some time, looking for someone suitable to place in charge of the restructuring of the City Garrisons as the Mathidrin were gradually eased into power. Urssain's conduct while making his report had confirmed his worth – the right balance of self-seeking cunning and stark fear, a perceptive man in his own barbarous way. And his ambition! Dan-Tor nodded to himself. You haven't even got your own measure of it yet, Urssain, he thought.

But, despite this, Dan-Tor's thoughts were dominated by Hawklan. Escaped again. Escaped with the knowledge that Fyorlund was under threat from some unknown enemy. Escaped to tell the Orthlundyn that Mandrocs were abroad and had killed on their blessed land – if they didn't feel it already. Not even his Master could foresee how the Orthlundyn would react to such news. And why were Hawklan and that oaf of a Carver riding armed with Jaldaric? And where was the girl? Things were moving too quickly. Dan-Tor had the uneasy feeling that he was watching one pebble dislodge two as it rolled away from him down a hillside.

He dismissed the thought. Whatever the Orthlundyn had been, they were not so now, and in any case they were too few to offer any serious opposition. All the damage that had been done could be repaired with a little thought. Useful experience would have been gained from the Mandrocs' exposure to Orthlund. More traps could be laid for Hawklan. Time was on the Master's side. Tomorrow he would interrogate Jaldaric.

'We'll weave a net to hold you yet, Hawklan,' Dan-Tor muttered softly to himself. 'Weave one from the threads your new-found friend will give us.'

A moth fluttered against the window, futilely rattling its wings against the glass, as the invisible barrier kept it from its goal of light.

Chapter 13

The journey back to Pedhavin was a strange uncomfortable affair. Hawklan and Isloman both wavered in and out of different moods as they tried to adjust to recent events. But no real peace was to be found. Something had been lost forever. Such tranquillity as they could achieve from time to time was only the stillness of the sea between breaking waves. Havoc would descend again on their minds all too quickly and with it came the grim feeling that it would never end.

Gavor returned eventually, exhausted but with news that Hawklan, at least, found heartening. The Mandroc patrol had maintained its rapid progress to the north and, leaving the road, had assiduously avoided all contact with the villages and communities that lay between it and Fyorlund. Jaldaric was alive and mounted, though bound.

'It looked to me as if they were leaving by the same way they came in, judging from the tracks,' he concluded.

'That's a relief,' said Hawklan. 'At least there'll be no more killing.'

Isloman snorted. 'The presence of those creatures in Orthlund is a murder in itself. Wherever they've come from they're a defilement. The very ground they tread on cries out in pain.'

Hawklan looked at him, a puzzled frown on his face at this unexpected vehemence. Isloman met his gaze.

'Can't you feel it?' he said impatiently, as to an obtuse pupil.

'I'm sorr – ' began Hawklan, but Isloman interrupted him with a remorseful gesture.

'Don't apologise, Hawklan. It's my fault. It's hard to remember you weren't born here.' There was regret in his voice, though whether it was at his own impatience or because Hawklan was not an Orthlundyn was not clear. A little further on he spoke again. 'I can't explain, Hawklan, any more than I can explain rock lore to you, but everyone will know that something terrible has happened. You see. The first village we reach – they'll be out, asking, worried.'

And that, thought Hawklan, is all the explanation I'm going to get, judging from the tone of your voice.

Gavor broke the slight uneasiness with a throaty chuckle. 'I'll tell you what those Mandrocs don't like, though.' He fell silent, awaiting a response from one of them. Hawklan looked at him sideways and raised his eyebrows, indicating it would not be from him. After a few moments, Isloman's curiosity got the better of him and, reluctantly, he asked what that might be.

'Ravens,' laughed Gavor. There was a note of malevolent exultation in his voice that made Hawklan turn sharply.

'What have you been doing, Gavor?' he asked, before Isloman could respond.

'Nothing, dear boy,' replied Gavor innocently. 'Just ruffled a few feathers, metaphorically speaking.'

'Never mind the metaphors,' Hawklan said firmly. 'What have you done?'

'Well . . . I just flew round a little.'

'And?'

'Nothing much. Just sang them a little tune I'd remembered.'

Green eyes and black eyes locked. Old friends.

'That little tune, as you call it, is a death cry, isn't it? A warning. Something out of your murky past, you feathered ancient.'

Then Gavor was all devilment. 'Yes it is. Yes it is. I don't know what it means, dear boy, but *they* do. And they don't like it. They became *very* restless. The poor man at the front had a very difficult time with them.' He chuckled again and hopped on to Hawklan's head. 'And less of the ancient, dear boy,' he said, ruffling Hawklan's hair with his wooden leg and hopping nimbly out of the way as a hand came up to dislodge him. 'After all, we're no hatchling ourselves, are we?'

Hawklan ignored the comment. 'Well?' he said.

'Well what?'

'What else did you do?'

'Oh. Nothing special. Just had a closer look at them once or twice.'

'How close?'

Gavor was gone, then . . .

'This close,' he shrieked, flying tumultuously between the two men from behind, and catching their heads with his thrashing wings. Both of them jumped at his sudden appearance and Isloman offered him a clenched fist as he soared high up above them. Gavor laughed raucously and tumbled over in the air.

'*They* didn't like it either,' he cried.

'I'll put you in a pot, you black-hearted crow,' roared Isloman as he struggled to regain control of his startled mount.

'Really, dear boy,' came the reply from above. 'Crow. Tut tut. No need to be personal. Your little brother's influence, I suppose.'

Then he soared in a great circle over their heads laughing to himself. The sound was infectious and Hawklan laughed quietly. 'There's a paradox for you, Isloman. It takes a bird to put our feet back on the ground again.'

Isloman replied with a formidable grunt, and the two men rode on, the silence between them now a little easier and more companiable.

Shortly afterwards, strange noises could be heard overhead. Hawklan's face assumed an expression of mock pain, and Isloman slumped noticeably.

'He's practising his bird impressions again,' said Hawklan plaintively.

Isloman looked up. 'There are times when life seems to be just one burden after another,' he said.

A faint voice came down to them. 'Thank you, thank you, ladies and gentleman. Now – the nightingale . . .'

The first village they came to was Little Hapter.

As Isloman had foreseen, the people came out to meet them. Hawklan knew many of them, and they acknowledged his greetings courteously enough, but there was a general air of preoccupation about them that was unfamiliar, and it was around Isloman that they all gathered.

Hawklan looked at the growing crowd, and for the first time in twenty years felt that he was not one of these people. There was nothing hostile in their attitude, or even unpleasant, but something had disturbed them at a level which heightened his position as an outsider, and drew them to look first to their own kind. Sensing it was a time to listen and learn, he was content to let Isloman answer their questions. He wanted to ask 'How did you know?' but he knew that no answer would be forthcoming.

Their responses to the news of the Mandrocs and the fighting ran the gamut of shock, alarm, and anger, as might be expected. But though these were sincere, Hawklan felt that the deeper shadows in the Orthlundyn were eased by the light of knowledge, however bad, and he felt himself brought back into their circle again.

He was inclined to dismiss the feeling of being an outsider as being over-sensitivity on his part or perhaps even a little residual shock, but he examined it again and found it true. There had been a strange but definite mood in the crowd as they turned initially to Isloman. One that he had never seen before. He set the thought aside for future consideration. It seemed to be important in some way.

Then he was with Isloman, sharing equally the centre of attention, and it was agreed that one of the elders should accompany them to Anderras Darion to discuss the matter thoroughly with elders from other villages.

So it was as they passed through each village on their southward journey – Greater Hapter (the smaller of the two villages), Astli, Perato, Oglin, Halyt Green, Wosod Heath, Lamely Bend and others – the response was always the same. The people knew that something horrific had happened. They knew. And always their darkness eased a little when they learned the truth.

Hawklan had never known the Orthlundyn to be a simple folk. Each year he had lived with them he had learned to respect more and more the sophistication and deep wisdom that lay in their apparently simple life; their natural awareness of balance and order, of freedom within discipline, their respect for each other's freedom. A respect that had made him welcome and left him unquestioned in all his years with them, despite the mystery of his sudden appearance and his acceptance by Anderras Darion. Now, however, a force was at work deep within them that he had never known before, never even suspected.

Abruptly he felt lonely and lost, and woefully inadequate to serve these people who seemed now, in some way, to be looking to him for guidance.

With the passing of each village their little party grew and, as most of the newcomers were old, their progress necessarily became slower. Gavor chuckled to himself from time to time as he looked down on the raggle-taggle parade wending its painstaking way along the old road, through the Orthlund countryside, boisterous with new growth and life.

'A fine strapping army you have here, O mighty Prince,' he gloated, landing with wilful awkwardness on Hawklan's shoulder and steadying himself by sticking his wooden leg in Hawklan's ear. Hawklan glowered at him and Isloman shook with silent laughter.

It was Gavor's irreverent clowning that had prevented the little cavalcade dropping into corrosive introspection and fretfulness, but Isloman found it difficult to equate this Gavor with the one who had filled the sky with an ancient death song and then slit the throats of Mandrocs with his murderous black spurs. Spurs of the same metal as Hawklan's strange sword. Spurs found by his brother near where the sword had fallen. Spurs that fitted his ridiculous wooden leg.

Isloman stared thoughtfully at the pair riding just ahead and to one side of him. Occasionally Gavor would hop on to Hawklan's head and extend his great shining wings in a luxuriant gesture and, to Isloman, the image of his old friend changed briefly from travel-stained and weary healer to a haunted, haggard leader, battle-wearied and a long way from what he loved, a terrible helm on his head and a black slaying sword by his side.

Eventually the distant towers of Anderras Darion came into view and, in spite of himself, Hawklan began to find it increasingly difficult to maintain the leisurely pace that the older people needed.

Gavor found it quite impossible and, as the party prepared to leave Tulhavin, the last village before Pedhavin, he appeared, meticulously groomed and carrying a particularly obnoxious morsel in his beak.

'I'll tell them you're coming,' he spluttered out of the side of his beak, then as if an afterthought, 'Then I'd better see my friends. They'll be missing me.'

Shaking his head as he watched the black shape dwindle urgently into the distance, Hawklan turned to Isloman. 'I'll be glad to see familiar faces around me again,' he said. 'And familiar things.'

Isloman nodded and looked at his hands. 'Yes. I've been too long away from my rock. All this has awakened too many old memories.'

Hawklan looked at him seriously. 'I've no idea what's going to happen, Isloman, but I'm certain that we'll only get a brief respite at the Castle. I fear there's more than old memories being awakened and my heart tells me we're on the verge of journeyings and events that'll offer us no rest in the future.'

Isloman leaned forward and patted his horse's head with his great gentle hand. 'I know,' he said. Then, enigmatically, 'Everyone knows.'

Hawklan did not reply.

'We still have to seek out this Dan-Tor,' continued Isloman. 'And I can't avoid the feeling that when we do it'll only be the beginning of more trouble.'

'*Rrisss awake.*' The voice sounded distant in Hawklan's head, whispering with an unrelenting urgency. He turned sharply to Isloman.

'What did you say?'

Isloman shrugged. 'I said it'll probably be the beginning of more trouble.'

Hawklan shook his head irritably. 'No, no. After that.'

'Nothing,' said Isloman.

'*Thriss . . .*' came the voice again – or voices. There was a quality in the sound that could brook no delay. It was the same sound he had heard in his dream in the mountains and it drew him irresistibly. He stood in his stirrups and looked around desperately.

'There it is again,' he said, steadying Serian, who had become restless under him.

'I heard nothing,' said Isloman. 'It's the trees.'

'*Sssss . . .*' again, but fainter, as if carried away by the wind, or as if the caller were tiring.

'There,' cried Hawklan excitedly. 'Right there.' He pointed. 'Right ahead of us. Over the hill.'

Isloman watched his friend's agitation in amazement. He was about to say that he could hear nothing when Hawklan bent down over his horse's head.

'Now, Muster horse, let me see you gallop,' he said, and with a shake of his proud head, Serian leapt forward.

Momentarily dumbfounded, Isloman stared after the thundering horse now rapidly receding into the distance, with its rider's cloak flying wildly behind him. Then, coming suddenly to his senses, he shouted to the group to wait until he returned, and urging his horse forward, he set off at full gallop after his friend.

Chapter 14

Serian carried Hawklan to the top of the hill effortlessly. There, Hawklan reined him to a halt and looked along the road ahead. In the distance the towers of Anderras Darion shone in the morning light like great jewels crystallised in the ancient mountains, but the road in front of him dipped down into a wooded hollow untouched by the sun, and isolated tree tops protruded through a thick mist like saplings and shrubs in the snow.

Hawklan felt a surging excitement.

'*Ethriss. Awaken,*' came the voice, or was it voices? Strong at first, seeming almost to echo from the distant towers, but fading rapidly.

'No,' roared Hawklan at the top of his voice. 'No.' And driving his knees into the horse he urged him forward at full gallop down into the mist.

As soon as they entered, however, the horse slowed to a cautious walking pace and the dripping silence of the woodland mist folded round them. As the cold dampness struck through him, some impulse made Hawklan draw his sword.

It felt strange in his hand – powerful and alive – as if leading him. He looked at the hilt. The two intertwined strands at its heart seemed to be catching a light from somewhere and were glinting brilliantly, threading an infinite way through the myriad stars that surrounded them.

'*Ethriss, awaken.*' The voice was faint and weak, but a flicker of light seemed to run along the strands in response.

A soft movement in the air thinned the mist briefly, and shimmering in the distance, Hawklan saw four indistinct figures. He leapt down from his horse and ran forward along the road, the sound of his footsteps dying flatly in the greyness. The mist sighed silently back again and the figures were obscured, but Hawklan ran on.

'Wait,' he cried. 'Wait.' Then he halted suddenly as a dark hooded figure emerged through the mist a little way head.

'Wait for what?' it asked in a sharp, cross voice. A woman's voice.

Hawklan ignored the question and ran up to her. 'Where are the others?'

'Others? What others, young man?'

'They were with you. Three of them. They were calling out to me.'

The woman's head tilted to one side quizzically. Hawklan ran a few steps forward into the mist, looking desperately from side to side in a vain attempt to see through it, and swinging his sword wildly as if to cut a pathway. A sense of loss was rising in him. He ran in another direction.

'There's no one here, young man, as you can see. I'm on my own.' The woman's voice showed marked impatience. Hawklan stopped his pacing, his face pained.

'But I saw them,' he said quietly. 'And I heard them. They were here with you. Standing behind you.'

The woman flicked her hood back, revealing a face as cross as her voice. It was an oddly striking face; one that drew the eye, though apparently not beautiful. Its predominant feature was a long pointed nose overhanging a tight-lipped mouth and buttressing a determined forehead. From under the shade of this, two piercing blue eyes peered out. Judging from her stooped posture and the support she took from a stick, she was old, but Hawklan could not have guessed her age. Her gaze was remarkable.

'Three you say?' she said. Hawklan nodded. She made a non-committal grunt and stared at him relentlessly.

'You a bandit?' she demanded after a while. The suddenness of this eccentric question nonplussed Hawklan and his mouth opened and closed vaguely.

'No,' he managed eventually and rather weakly.

'What's that then?' she said, bringing the stick up and pointing to his sword.

'A sword,' he replied helplessly.

She took a purposeful step towards him. 'Do you always address a lady with a sword in your hand?'

Hawklan felt his face redden, and clumsily he put the sword back into its scabbard with a mumbled apology.

'Should think so too,' snorted the woman. 'Charging out of the mist shouting and yelling and waving your sword – looking for people who aren't there. Frighten a defenceless old woman to death you could.'

Hawklan thought this was most unlikely, but he kept his own counsel. He gazed round again, but he knew that the three other figures would not be there. They had been round this woman whether she knew it or not, but they were gone now, that was beyond doubt. A vision of a great glowing answer to the questions that plagued him had opened before him, he knew, but it had slipped away as easily as the mist through the leaves of the trees. Now in place of this vision, he was standing in a dank, foggy dell, talking to a cantankerous old woman he had never seen before and who could quite legitimately reproach him for his conduct.

'May I escort you through the rest of the wood?' he offered tentatively.

Up came the stick again. 'Don't you soft soap me, young man. What would I want with an escort who sees things, hey? Be on your way, or I'll give you a taste of my stick.'

Hawklan was not a man to hold on to an indefensible position indefinitely, and he was about to go back for his horse when a great shape loomed up out of the mist.

'I don't believe it,' came Isloman's voice. 'I thought I recognised those dulcet tones.' He jumped down from his horse. 'Old Memsa Gulda, as I live and breathe. And not changed a jot.'

The woman looked at him ferociously.

'Don't you recognise me, Gulda?'

The woman stepped forward and peered intently up at him. 'I used to know an impudent young whelp called Isloman who had the look of you – snotty-nosed little imp. Quarrelled with his brother over some girl and then went off to the wars as I recall.'

'Not so snotty-nosed by then, Gulda,' said Isloman, slightly subdued.

She was contemptuous. 'You're all snotty-nosed. Men.

Eternally in need of some attention or other or you'll be off creating trouble.' She stepped back a little and looked him up and down as if she were contemplating a purchase. 'You've aged, lad.' Her voice was quieter.

The mist brightened a little as the morning sun skimmed over the hollow.

Isloman stroked his horse. 'Of course I've aged. It's been a long time since you left, Gulda,' he said. 'Probably twenty years or so. Where did you go? Why did you leave so suddenly?'

The stick came up and prodded him in the stomach. 'Cheeky as ever, I see, young Isloman. I go where I go, and for my own reasons.' Then, with a prod for each word, 'Just like you did.' The stick relented. 'A woman needs a little peace now and then, a little time away from people and their noise.'

Isloman was about to speak when the woman released another barrage. 'And it's Memsa to you, my lad,' she added indignantly. 'Gulda indeed. I'll give you Gulda. And a little less of the old if you please. I'd say I've weathered the years better than you have, wouldn't you?'

Isloman seemed uncertain about how to react to this fierce reminder of his youth. He found boyhood fears surprisingly near the surface under the threat of her gaze and her stick.

She spared him further reflection. 'What are you doing here then? Looking after this lunatic?' She continued looking at Isloman, but the stick pointed to Hawklan, standing listening to this exchange with some amusement.

'Gul . . .' Isloman faltered. 'Memsa, this is Hawklan,' he finished formally.

Slowly she turned her head and looked at Hawklan severely. She grunted thoughtfully. 'Hawklan. The healer. The Key Bearer. I've heard a lot about him round and about.'

She walked round him, looking him up and down as she had Isloman.

'Who is she?' Hawklan mouthed silently to Isloman over her head.

Isloman made a tiny movement with his hand to indicate explanations later.

'Stop that,' snapped Gulda without altering her pace. Then suddenly, to Hawklan, 'Perhaps you'd tell me, young man, why the Key Bearer of Anderras Darion should charge about in the mist, sword in hand, chasing shadows?'

Hawklan spoke quietly. 'I'm sorry if I frightened you. I heard someone calling and I saw the figures by you.'

'You've said that once,' said Gulda impatiently. 'And I've told you I'm alone.'

Hawklan shrugged. 'They were there. I saw them. Just behind you.'

'She wrinkled her nose suspiciously. 'What were they calling?'

Hawklan told her.

'Ethriss, eh?' she muttered, again to herself. Then, to Hawklan, 'Is your name Ethriss?' she asked sharply.

'No,' he replied.

'Then why did you gallop into the mist like a madman at the sound of his name?' Gulda pressed.

Hawklan shrugged uncertainly. 'It was me they were calling out to,' he said quietly. Gulda looked at him darkly for a long moment and then pulled up her hood so that her face disappeared into its shade except for the end of her nose which floated white in the darkness.

Abruptly she turned round and headed off down the road. After a few paces she turned. 'Come on,' she said crossly.

Hawklan waved vaguely in both directions. 'I thought you were going . . . that way.'

'Bah,' she snorted and, turning again, stalked off into the mist. Her voice floated back through the greyness. 'I'll see you two at the Castle.'

Isloman swung up on to his horse, a wide grin on his face. 'Loman'll be pleased, I don't think. Get your horse and catch her up. I'll fetch the others.' Then a deep chuckle bubbled out of him. 'But keep out of the way of that stick. And watch your lip, young fella.'

Before Hawklan could speak, Isloman had trotted off into the lightening mist and Hawklan could hear him laughing to himself.

Mounting, he urged Serian gently forward after the woman.

As he reached the top of a small rise and emerged into the sunlight, he was surprised to see how far the woman had travelled.

For all her appearance of age, and her stick and stoop, she had a long purposeful stride and he had to trot Serian forward briskly to catch up with her.

He debated offering her the saddle, but was dubious about the reception of such a suggestion, so he dismounted a little way behind her.

'Come along, young man, don't dawdle,' she said without turning round. 'I've got questions to ask you. Quickly, quickly.'

Hawklan found himself running forward like a schoolboy in response to these instructions. When he reached her he found he needed his long legs to match her unrelenting pace. He cast a sideways look at her, but the hood covered her face and he could see nothing but the end of her nose ploughing steadily forward like the prow of a ship.

A combination of courtesy and amused alarm stopped him asking any questions as they strode on in silence along the old stone road. Occasionally she would mutter to herself as if participating in some internal debate, then, 'Give me your sword, young man,' she said sharply.

Hawklan hesitated. Her right hand stretched out impatiently and the morning birdsong was silenced momentarily by two resounding cracks as she snapped her fingers to indicate that hesitation was not what she had asked for. Hawklan drew the sword and handed it to her gingerly.

'Take care,' he said. 'It's very sharp.'

Gulda grunted and her long fingers closed around the hilt. Hawklan noted the grip. It was not that of a woman examining a dangerous curiosity. It was a swordsman's grip.

'I'm sorry,' he said. 'I didn't realise you were used to weapons.'

Briefly her pace slowed and there was a slight inclination of the head. Then there was another grunt and she strode out again. The sword hilt went to the end of the long nose and was turned round and round, then each part of the sword in turn was similarly scrutinised. Abruptly she stopped walking.

'Well, well, well. Ethriss's sword. His Black Sword.' Her voice had lost its cantankerous quality and was quiet and full of many emotions. 'I thought it might be, but I couldn't be sure in that mist. Then, who'd have expected to see it ever again? How did you come by it, healer?'

'I found it in the Castle Armoury,' Hawklan said. The hooded head turned towards him. With the sun in his eyes he could see nothing of her face, but he could sense those piercing blue eyes, sharp in the blackness of the hood, missing nothing. Then she turned away, and striding out again gave an enigmatic laugh.

'That I doubt, Key Bearer. That I doubt. Ethriss's sword couldn't be found because it was never hidden. *It* found *you*. Have no illusions about that. *It* found *you*.' Then the hilt disappeared into the hood, as if she were listening to it. 'And it's killed Mandrocs recently. I *knew* it.' There was triumph in the voice. 'I knew it. I've not lost all my wits yet.'

Hawklan's eyes widened in surprise. 'How did you know?' he asked.

Her voice was distant. 'Gulda knows Mandrocs. Could smell them. That's why I came back. Couldn't believe my nose after all this time. They've been killing again. Taken life here in Orthlund, haven't they? That's what's upsetting all the Orthlundyn, although they're too sleepy to know it. Running about like ants under a stone instead of feeling what's happened.'

Hawklan shook his head. 'Gulda, I don't understand you. How do you know these things?' Then partly to himself, 'I don't understand any of this. All these strange and awful happenings. What do you know about them?'

The dark hood turned towards him, and there was a long deep watchful silence. Then suddenly, 'Here, catch.' And with a flick of her wrist she sent the sword spinning towards him. Without thinking, his hand went out and caught it solidly. A strange humming vibration came from the blade.

Gulda chuckled then nodded. 'You understand more than you know, healer. I wonder who you are? We'll have to talk later.'

Hawklan put the sword back in its scabbard. He wanted to talk now. He had an accumulation of questions that more than accounted for twenty years of indifference, but she was off, clumping along the road towards the village.

He sighed resignedly. Patience, Hawklan, he thought.

Patience. There'll be plenty of time when we reach the Castle. But, as that very thought came to him, he sensed that time was becoming more scarce, and that the meeting of the elders, and whoever else would be there, would be the last chance he would have to draw on the collected wisdom of Orthlund. After that, he could see only vague images of dispersion and scattering; breaking, even.

Chapter 15

As at all the other villages, the people of Pedhavin came out to meet them in straggling groups, before they reached the village proper. Greetings were genuine and warm, but concern lined almost every face, and Hawklan noted again that everyone gravitated first to Isloman to hear his brief account of what had happened.

Gulda, too, created quite a stir, being obviously acquainted with many of Isloman's generation, and Hawklan was amused to see so many grown men looking sheepish after some encounter with her. Her cross voice echoed through the village and she did a great deal of poking and prodding with her stick, both to carvings and people. A clumping, black, stooped figure stalking around the village, she looked like part of their shadow lore come to life, thought Hawklan.

Tirilen almost charmed her. Hawklan detected a more pervasive quiet in Tirilen's manner, and felt both glad and sorry. The responsibility of being the village's healer in his absence had subtly altered the villagers' attitude towards her, but the new, deeper quietness came mainly from within Tirilen herself. It was like a flower starting a summer-long blooming after the turbulence of spring. Though bewildered and hurt by the news of what had happened, Tirilen also showed the strange relieved acceptance that the other Orthlundyn had shown, and she faced Gulda's scowling inspection with a manner that was at once both pleasant and unyielding and which provoked an entirely new range of grunts from the old woman. Some, to Hawklan's ear, seemed quite complimentary.

Loman, however, fared less well; he appeared considerably less than enthusiastic about Gulda's return. Hawklan gained the distinct impression that the great barrel-chested man was hiding behind his daughter's skirts, but Gulda winkled him out and transfixed him against a wall with both stick and blue-eyed gaze, while her face reflected a memory's journeying through the years. Then her eyes narrowed as a destination was reached. 'Young Loman, isn't it?' she said. Loman coughed slightly, nodded, and went red. Gulda pursed her lips and narrowed her eyes further. The stick tapped him twice on the chest. 'I'll be watching you more carefully this time, young man,' she said.

That was all. Loman cleared his throat and looked vaguely into the distance. Gulda cast another look at Tirilen, who was trying not to smile at her father's discomfiture.

'Hrmph. You take after your mother, child,' said the old woman, turning and walking away.

It was Gulda who led the procession up the steep winding road to the Castle. This time Hawklan did offer her the saddle, although her pace had not slackened. The stick twitched menacingly.

'Are you trying to make a fool of me, young man?' came the unhesitating reply. Hawklan declined to answer, knowing by now when his foot was on quicksand and when a further step would leave him in inextricable distress. He walked quietly by her side, discreetly listening to her mutterings and snorts.

Many of the others continued to ride, but none felt inclined to pass Gulda.

Gavor gazed groggily down at the approaching group from far above in a cosy cranny high in the eaves of one of the towers. The front tip of the distant, shuffling snake gave him trouble. Closing one eye, and concentrating hard, he still failed to make the two black images merge into one. He looked reproachfully at his 'friend' snoring contentedly in the dusty sunlight and muttered something about abstinence, then he wriggled cautiously to try to straighten out some troublesome feathers. His companion's eye opened.

'Gavor,' said a soft voice, carrying a quite unmistakable implication.

Gavor affected to ignore the request and squinted gamely down the dizzying perspective of the tower.

'Gavor.' More urgently.

Gavor debated with himself. Should he fly down and greet Hawklan or should he . . .?

'Gavor . . .?'

Then again, in his present condition he'd probably not remember how to fly before he hit the ground. He looked round.

'You really care for these spurs, do you . . .?'

There were many halls in Anderras Darion that could have accommodated the group which Gulda and Hawklan led in through the Great Gate, but Hawklan chose one of the courtyards. Ostensibly it was because the day was too fine to sit talking inside, even in the airy chambers of Anderras Darion, but in his heart he wanted an open sky and bright daylight to witness what was to be said. Time enough later for confinement and flickering shadows. This matter would not be resolved at one sitting.

Loman used his office as Castellan to make some semblance of a dignified escape from Gulda's scrutiny, and soon apprentices were walking among the visitors with food and drink, galvanised as much by curiosity as by the unusual zealousness of their master.

Gulda dropped herself unceremoniously on to a large stone slab in the middle of the courtyard and, leaning forward until it looked as if she were going to tumble off, dropped her chin on to her two long hands which were folded over the top of her stick.

'I'll be listening,' she said to Hawklan, then her eyes closed.

The Orthlundyn were a patient people, and Hawklan and Isloman had not been plied with questions after they had announced that all would be discussed fully in due course. But now, fed and a little rested, their concern and curiosity started to bubble out like well water. Twice Hawklan raised his arms to try to quell the mounting hubbub, but to no avail. Then he noticed one of Gulda's long fingers start tapping the back of her other hand impatiently. Better I chastise them than you, he thought.

'Enough,' he shouted, his voice ringing round the courtyard and soaring up to the rooftops from where it bounced up into the sky.

High above, a scruffy black bundle tumbled out of a niche in the eaves of one of the taller towers.

'Enough,' shouted Hawklan again, jumping on to the stone slab beside Gulda. 'Sit down, everyone, please, sit down. Isloman and I will tell you what's happened, then we can all decide what to do.'

There was a note in his voice that forbade any remonstrance and the crowd fell silent.

'Sit down, my friends,' he repeated more gently. 'We've bad things to talk about as you know, and I suspect I've as many questions as you.'

A few minutes later, everyone seemed to have found some-where to sit or lie, either on the chairs and benches that the apprentices had brought out, or on the soft lawns around the courtyard. Hawklan jumped to the ground and sat down next to the hunched black form of Gulda. He looked over the waiting faces.

Quietly and simply he told them everything that had hap-pened to himself and the others since the visit of the tinker, omitting only the more unbelievable details of his experiences at the Gretmearc. He concluded with their parting from Idrace and Fel-Astian.

There was a long silence when he had finished as if the mountains themselves were listening. He felt he could almost hear the white clouds moving overhead and he resisted a temp-tation to look up and search for a Viladrien.

A small black disturbance, Gavor landed uncertainly on the stone by Hawklan's side and staggered slightly.

'Have they taken their dead with them?' asked one of the elders eventually, his voice sounding strange after the long silence.

'Yes,' replied Hawklan, slightly puzzled. 'And the bodies of the Fyordyn.'

There was a great deal of what seemed to be relieved head nodding from the crowd.

'I doubt they'll be tending their dead well,' said Hawklan, in a slightly injured tone. 'They've probably only taken them to hide them. To cover their tracks.'

This caused some tolerant amusement.

'Hawklan,' said one man kindly. 'You've been with us for twenty years or so, but in some ways you're still blind. No outlander can hide his passing in Orthlund.'

Hawklan gestured vaguely. 'Even so, that's probably why they've removed the dead. To avoid discovery rather than for respectful burial.'

'The dead return to the earth wherever they fall,' said another elder with a shrug. It seemed to Hawklan to be a peculiarly harsh remark, but it brought no response from the others except some more head nodding.

'But it's better that the murdered lie away from Orthlund,' concluded the man, to further agreement.

Hawklan felt alone again; separated from the deeper lives of these people.

Another spoke. 'The dead sing their new song now. We must look to the living.' The speaker was a frail old man from Wosod Heath. 'There can be no shadows without light.' Then, unexpectedly, 'Hawklan, what shall we do?'

Hawklan started. He had expected to tell his tale and then stand aside while the elders decided what to do – if anything.

'I don't know,' he said after an uncertain delay. 'I'm a healer. I know little of your history and lore, less about Fyorlund, and nothing at all about Mandrocs. Just going to the Gretmearc was an adventure for me. I can't advise you.'

The man from Wosod Heath spoke again. 'No, Hawklan. You're more than a healer. It's a long time since you've been to Wosod and I can see the changes in you. And if the truth's told, you yourself must feel them. You'll pursue this Dan-Tor no matter what we decide, won't you?'

Hawklan remained silent, his head bowed.

The old man continued, 'A horror has been wrought on our land. There's a disease in Fyorlund which will spread ever outwards if it's not checked. You're our healer. Your time has come. Your inner sense of purpose will guide you truly. Tell us what to do. It will be right.'

Hawklan put his hand to his head and swayed slightly. For an instant he was back in the darkness again. A terrible roaring filling his head, darkness everywhere, even the sky flickering black. And under his feet . . .? More than that . . . it was all his fault.

He felt unreasonably angry. He wanted no burden. He

wanted the peace and tranquillity of the last twenty years. These people asked too much. They should not put their hopes in one man.

'No, no, no, no,' he burst out. 'I can't do it. I'm not a leader, you cannot ask it of me. Whatever I am, I'm an outlander. I don't have your wisdom. I can heal most of your ills and hurts, but I don't understand you, not deep inside. I can't advise you. I . . .' His voice faded. 'I can't take this burden. Sometime, somewhere I've betrayed the trust of others.'

The remark brought no response from the quiet crowd. The old man rose shakily to his feet and, leaning on the arm of a young apprentice, he walked slowly forward. Shaking his head, he laid a compassionate hand on Hawklan's arm.

'No, Hawklan. It's not in you to betray. Perhaps, once, you failed. Stumbled under too heavy a load. Maybe you, and others, paid some terrible price. Who can say? But no betrayal. Don't be afraid.'

Hawklan looked from side to side as if for an escape. 'Perhaps nothing else will happen,' he said faintly, but the old man shook his head and smiled sadly.

'Even I can hear this illness crying out, Hawklan,' he said.

Hawklan twined his fingers together. 'It's wrong that you should place such faith in one person,' he said.

'We know that,' replied the old man. 'And no one's going to follow you blindly. But then others *have* followed something or someone blindly and brought death to our land, and we've no choice. We love you. We wouldn't ask this of you if a choice existed.'

'I may stumble and fall again.'

The old man shrugged. 'If you fall, you fall. We share the guilt for having so burdened you.'

'But . . .'

'There *is* no one else, Hawklan.'

'Why? Why me?'

'You've answered that yourself by now I imagine.' It was Gulda's voice, cross and impatient still. 'This Dan-Tor wants you. Why he should is unclear, but he won't rest until he has you, nor scruple to destroy your loved ones. You can't flee – abandon them – you must face him. None of these can do that for you.' Her stick swept the crowd in a broad purposeful arc. 'That's your immediate problem. But if you can't feel deeper things stirring then you're indeed a fool, and the Orthlundyn have been particularly ill-served by fate.'

Hawklan's mouth tightened grimly at Gulda's harsh and definitive delineation of his position.

'Yes,' he said angrily. 'But why me?' Banging his fist on his chest, he used the same words to ask a different question. Why should anyone go to such lengths to capture him?

Somewhere, high above, in one of the many towers, a bell rang out. A single chime. A deep and restful note. The many bells of Anderras Darion rang rarely, and to a rhythm of their own choosing.

All eyes turned upwards as the sound echoed round the towers and spires, spilled over roofs and tiers of ramping walls, surged through empty halls and corridors, and overflowed down into the courtyard to submerge the watching crowd.

Gulda threw up both arms to encompass the whole Castle. 'That answers all your questions, Hawklan – Key Bearer to Anderras Darion. The voice of the Castle itself.'

Chapter 16

As Urssain had remarked, the blatantly illegal appellation, King's High Guard, had caused more adverse reaction from the ordinary people of Vakloss than the suspension of the Geadrol itself and on his re-appearance at the Palace, Dan-Tor had rapidly declared this to be 'an unfortunate bureaucratic error by a junior official'. The new Guards were a 'temporary force' answerable to himself and intended to 'relieve the High Guards of the Lords from routine duties, to leave them better able to meet the difficulties which have led to the suspension of the Geadrol'. This announcement, though vague, was couched in bland apologetic terms and was sufficient to quieten most of the public unease. The new Guards, he said, were known as Mathidrin, from an old Fyordyn word meaning 'Those who walk'. One or two scholars noted that the word meant 'Those who trample underfoot', but its misuse thus was attributed by them to the 'general deterioration in the knowledge of our language these days', and caused no general comment.

Staring out of a high window at the black-liveried men parading below, Sylvriss laid her curse on them, though years of habit prevented her face betraying any emotion. Then she mouthed their name. Riddinvolk to her very heart, she was no student of ancient Fyorlund grammar, but the word Mathidrin had an unpleasant sound to her ears. Her main concern, however, was not the name but the men themselves. Endlessly marching up and down the Palace corridors, the tattoo of their clicking heels announcing their arrival and echoing their departure. Even one alone had to march as if he were with twenty. The High Guard had been formal, but they'd carried out their duties efficiently and without stir. But these creatures . . .

A double gate opened into the courtyard below and a small patrol marched in through the sunny gap.

. . . Nor had the High Guard marched through the streets except for ceremonial parades. But these Guards seemed to thrive on it. Making people move out of their relentless way. Why? It was so unnecessary. But, she knew, Dan-Tor did nothing unnecessarily.

An answer came to her even as she watched the arriving patrol.

The narrow twisting streets that surrounded the Palace were invariably crowded and hectic, and the frequent patrols by the Mathidrin often provoked outbursts from citizens angry at their arrogant attitude. Outbursts that were always put down with some degree of violence. The Mathidrin were beginning to spread fear before them. Again, why?

And Dan-Tor had appointed her their Honorary Commander-in-Chief! She wrinkled her face in distaste at the memory of this unwanted and unrefusable honour.

The leader of the patrol below swung down from his horse. I've seen pigs ride better, Sylvriss thought, then she leaned forward and cast an expert eye over the animal. It was good enough. Certainly good enough for the graceless oaf who had been riding it, but it was no Muster horse; few could match the Muster horses for stamina, strength, speed or intelligence. The thought gave her a twinge of homesickness.

Although she still communicated with her father, she had not seen him for many years and from time to time she missed him deeply. At such times she would recall a childhood memory of riding a fine strong Muster horse by her father's side, mile after tireless mile across the broad open meadows of Riddin, the wind in her face, the rhythmic pounding of hooves, and that exhilarating unity, not only with her steed but with her father and his steed, and all the others riding with them. The memory sustained her powerfully.

The rider had left his mount to the attentions of an underling and was engaged in conversation with one of the other officers. A rider should tend his own, she thought angrily, but at least they're caring for them a little more now. The anger within her faded into satisfaction as she remembered her outburst when she had caught one of them beating a horse.

Drawn to the scene by the cries of both man and horse she

had arrived to find an officer laying into the animal with a leather crop. All sense of queenly decorum had fallen away from her in a haze of fury and, striding forward, she had seized the crop as it swung back, and delivered a mighty whack with it across the man's rump. As he spun round, she had back-handed the crop across his face. The man drew his clenched fist back automatically before he had identified his attacker, and thereby made his second mistake that day. Not that he raised his fist to his Queen, but that he raised it to a Muster-trained woman.

His apparent intention had triggered an old reflex in Sylvriss from her training days and, without a pause, she drove the first two knuckles of her tightly clenched fist into the space between his nose and his upper lip, her entire body behind the blow.

Sitting on the windowsill, Sylvriss smiled one of her rare smiles and flexed her right hand. It had been bruised and sore for several days, but she had found the pain almost delightful. She wished all her other problems could be solved as easily.

The man had staggered back several paces before his legs buckled and left him sitting incongruously in the dust, his eyes wide with shock and his mouth gaping. He placed his hands to the sides of his head and shook it to try to stop the din inside. It was only later that someone told him what had happened. The watching men stood frozen to attention by Sylvriss's icy gaze.

'In future,' she said slowly, 'you will treat your horses correctly. Is that clear?'

Her soft voice had contained more menace in it than the loudest Drill Sirshiant's and, while no official mention was ever made of the incident, the word had spread like fire through bracken, into barracks and staterooms alike, and thereafter there had been a perceptible improvement in the treatment of the Mathidrin's horses.

But everything seemed to be like that these days. Almost every aspect of policy was determined by some unspoken command. Where there had once been clear and open discourse, currents and undercurrents of gossip and intrigue now ran muddy and deep and, she suspected, for less high than herself, dangerous.

It was alien to her nature to dabble in such water, but it was of Dan-Tor's making, and she had no alternative if she were not to be left isolated and ignorant, which, she sensed, was his desire. She knew full well that the affection she was held in by so many had always been a thorn in Dan-Tor's side, but now she had begun using it as a weapon.

Ironically, felling one of the Mathidrin officers aided in this in that it raised her in the esteem of friend and foe alike. More significantly, it delivered a death-blow to Dan-Tor's plans to train the Mathidrin as cavalry.

Traditionally, the High Guards were trained to act as both cavalry and infantry, as well as being competent as individual fighters. High Guards at their best, such as those of Lord Eldric, thus formed a formidable fighting force. Dan-Tor had tried to emulate this in the Mathidrin, but early attempts at co-ordinated horsemanship had indicated a rocky path ahead and no certainty of reaching the destination. He had persisted in a half-hearted fashion, but the Queen's actions had reminded him of the Riddin Muster and the comparison had tilted the final balance.

The loss of a cavalry force did not irk him too much, as the Mandrocs could be developed into a massive and powerful infantry but, although his rejection of the plan had been logical and sound, there niggled a tiny burrowing worm of doubt that he might have been prompted by fear of what would undoubtedly have been the Queen's withering, if unspoken, scorn at such a venture. Didn't she after all twit even the High Guards themselves about their 'gawky horsemanship'? The possibility that such a human trait might still flicker within him sufficiently to influence so serious a decision angered him profoundly.

Sylvriss turned from the window and walked over to the chair in which her husband was sleeping. It was upholstered with tapestries showing scenes from Fyorlund's history and the King's sleeping head was ringed by iron-clad warriors battling the seething hordes of Sumeral's army – men and Mandrocs. The weave was old and skilful, but the pattern had been worn away by the heads of many Kings and much of the finer detail was lost. Even so, the force of the original design was undiminished. The grim resolution of Ethriss's Guards holding back the desperate unfettered savagery of their enemy. The awful, if unseen, presence of Sumeral himself, and the equally awful presence of Ethriss, committing his knowledge and wisdom, his hope and faith, his entire being, to this last terrible battle.

Sylvriss leaned forward and examined the chair carefully, delicately fingering the material. Was it her imagination, or was the pattern fading even more quickly? One or two small areas seemed to have a strained, worn look which she did not recall seeing before.

The King woke suddenly, though without the fearful start that so frequently followed his waking. He looked up into his wife's face and smiled. She kissed him gently and, placing his hand around her head, he held her cheek against his in a soft embrace for a long silent moment.

'I'm sorry I woke you,' she said.

Rgoric smiled. 'It was a nice awakening,' he said. 'Full of quiet and calm. Like when I was a boy and I'd wake up and remember that it was a holiday. No instruction, no regal duties requiring my princely presence.' He was gently ironic. 'Nothing to do. Secure in the arms of a bright summer morning, and the love of my parents, and a world in which everything was right. Perfection. A day ahead in which to play with my friends, or ride with my father, or walk alone in the parks and forests and just daydream.'

Sylvriss's heart cried out to him and for him. He was so rarely in this mood and now she had nothing to say to him, nothing that would bring back to him those lost days when his tread through life was so sure-footed. All she could do was love the man and hope that in some way this would protect him. Soon, she knew, he could slip away from her into a mood of dark foreboding, or manic elation, or haunted persecution. Sadly, it had been these intermittent returns to normality that had drawn the lines of strain across her face. To see him thus, albeit a little lost and fretful, and to hope that it would last yet know it would not, was a bitter burden for her.

All the more reluctant had she been, therefore, to pick up the old standard that had so long ago dropped from her hand, but which had reappeared in front of her once again, ghostly but fluttering faintly.

Rgoric's suspension of the Geadrol and the arrest of the four

Lords had caused considerable political upheaval and was occupying a great deal of Dan-Tor's time. While he was handling the many shuttles of intrigue that would weave the whirling threads of doubt and rumour into the pattern of his design, one small strand parted and fell from his loom unnoticed. He neglected the King.

Almost in spite of herself Sylvriss had seized the standard and held it high in her heart once more.

What attention Dan-Tor had now for the King was confined to keeping him quiet and stable so that he could safely be left. Nothing could accrue but disadvantage to have him bewildered and rambling at present. The King's moods of normality thus became more frequent and it was this that persuaded Sylvriss that the true King, her King, lay still intact under the ravages of his illness; if illness it was, or had ever been. It was like the sight of a shoreline glimpsed between mountainous, shifting waves by a drowning swimmer. It was a re-affirmation. It bred courage and strength.

Slowly and deliberately she had set about reducing the medication that Dan-Tor had prepared for the King. Slowly was the word she said to herself whenever some small change occurred, be it setback or improvement. Past experience had taught her the dangers of both depression and elation. This opportunity must surely be her last, and youthful impatience had nothing to contribute. Now was the time for an experienced hand and a steady nerve if she was to win back her husband.

Relentlessly she lied to Dan-Tor about Rgoric's condition whenever he asked, playing the ignorant stablemaid and wringing her hands at her own helplessness. Sternly she controlled herself when Dan-Tor undid her work with a casual dosage to quell the fretting King. And ruthlessly she set about using her personal esteem to ingratiate herself into the webs of intrigue and gossip being spun throughout the Palace and the City, until few things reached the ears of Dan-Tor that had not passed hers on their journey.

You came into Fyorlund like a silent assassin's blade, she thought, but I'll turn your point from its heart if it kills me. Deeper in her heart, unseen, lay the darker thought that to do this she might probably have to kill *him*.

She smiled at Rgoric. 'I know what you mean,' she said . 'But I think days like that happen just to sustain us later. I think we forget about fathers getting angry because we're slow, and friends quarrelling, and insects and creepy crawlies in the parks and forests.'

Rgoric looked at her. She felt him teetering towards sulky reproach at her reception of his reminiscence, and a small flicker of panic stirred inside her that, from such a small step, he might plunge catastrophically away from her into a dark and deep depression. She had seen it happen too often before.

Impulsively she giggled and put her hands to her face, child-like. Rgoric's expression changed to puzzlement.

'We weren't so fussy about creepy crawlies that afternoon in my father's orchard, were we?' she said, looking at him conspiratorially. Rgoric's face darkened thoughtfully for a moment, then slowly he moved from the self-destructive edge and drifted back into another time. A time of soft springing turf and the scent of ripening fruit, and a beautiful black-haired maid by his side, as besotted with him as he was with her. And she was still here with him. He smiled and then chuckled throatily.

'Wife,' he said with mock severity. 'Calm yourself.'

Then they shared something they had not shared for a long time. They laughed. Ringing laughter that mingled and twined and rose up to fill the room like an incense to older and happier gods, laughter that shone and twinkled. The glittering lethal edge of the dagger that Sylvriss was making for Dan-Tor's dark heart.

Chapter 17

Far below the rare and ringing laughter of Sylvriss and Rgoric was a tiny suite of rooms that had once been servants' quarters. Now it served as prison for the Lords Eldric, Arinndier, Darek and Hreldar, having held them since their arrest.

The garish light of Dan-Tor's globes did not succeed in dispelling the dismal atmosphere that pervaded the crudely decorated rooms, and the confinement of the Lords away from the daylight and fresh air had gradually begun to take its toll.

For a time they demanded to speak before the Geadrol, but their stone-faced Mathidrin guards treated them with an indifference that was more dispiriting than any amount of abuse and rough handling. Over the weeks a sense of impotence began to seep into them like dampness into the walls of an ancient cellar.

Physically, Hreldar seemed to suffer most from their imprisonment. His round face thinned noticeably and his jovial disposition became sober to the point of moroseness. More alarmingly, to his friends, a look came into his eyes that none of them had ever seen before, not even when they had all ridden side by side against the Morlider. It was a grim, almost obsessive, determination.

However, it was Eldric's condition that gave them most cause for concern, for while his physical deterioration was not as severe as Hreldar's, he seemed to have aged visibly, as if he had been destroyed from within. No sooner had the cell door closed behind them than his behaviour began to change. Even his initial thundering and roaring had contained a note of desperate petulance. One morning he lay on his bunk without moving, his face turned to the wall, and from then on it took his friends' every effort to make him attend to even the simple necessities of life.

Arinndier too became worried and fretful, though it was more at the condition of his friends than as a result of his own privation.

Only Darek, thin-faced and wiry, and more given to the pleasures of study than those of the field, seemed to be unaffected by their captivity. His analysis of their conduct was cruel.

'I suppose having behaved like children, we must expect to be treated like children,' he said, sitting on a rough wooden bunk next to a slumped and indifferent Eldric and leaning back against the wall.

Hreldar turned to look at him silently, his face non-committal, but oddly watchful. Arinndier, however, sitting opposite to him, scowled. 'Children?' he said.

Darek looked straight at him, and then began to enumerate points on his thin precise hands. 'Who but children would think the suspension of the Geadrol was anything other than madness or treachery? Who but children would think that four of us with a token guard could either reason with such madness or defeat such treachery? Who but children would see these . . . these Guards marching through the City and hear them called the King's High Guard and think it wasn't beyond all doubt treachery? And who but children would think they could walk into the middle of it and expect to walk out again?'

Arinndier reluctantly conceded the argument, but his reply was impatient. 'Every mourner sees the obvious, Darek. We acted properly. Cautiously and within the Law. We couldn't have foreseen what would happen.'

Darek's finger snapped out accusingly, the sound falling flat in the small dead room. 'We're Lords of Fyorlund, Arin. Trustees of the Law and the people. It's our duty to foresee – to look forward beyond the sight of ordinary people. How big a sign did we need? What could be bigger than the suspension of the Geadrol?'

Arinndier was in no mood for reproaches. 'What else could we have done, for Ethriss's sake?' he snapped.

Darek leaned forward. 'We could have mustered our High Guards, raised the reserves and marched on the City.'

Arinndier's irritation left him and he stared at Darek,

stunned. Of all the people he might have expected to preach rebellion, Darek – lawyer Darek – would have been the last. The two men stared at one another for a long moment.

Eventually Arinndier lowered his head. 'You've been too long in these dismal rooms, Darek,' he said quietly. 'What conceivable justification did we have for such a step? You'd have been the first to cry that force attacked the very basis of the Law.'

A look of anger flashed briefly through Darek's eyes, then it faded and his voice became patient. 'Arin, old friend, listen to me. Force is both the reason for the Law and its very basis. People made the Law to control the use of force because force is a bad way of doing things. It's that simple. You don't need to be a lawyer to understand that. They made it over centuries of bitter learning, to protect themselves – and their descendants – from the darker sides of our own natures. And if you ignore its accumulated wisdom, you'll face that darker nature unarmed, and you'll walk on to the people's naked and pitiless sword.'

Arinndier shifted unhappily on his seat.

Darek spoke again. 'Think about it, Arin. If the Law itself is assailed by those who should sustain it, what else can be done? And, I repeat, what greater attack at the heart of the Law could there have been than the suspension of the Geadrol? And, seeing it, why didn't we act correctly, Arin? Why did we turn away our faces like Eldric's done here and pretend that nothing was happening?' He leaned forward and the movement made Arinndier look up. 'We're the people's sword-bearers, Arin,' he said. 'And we've failed in our duty. Who knows what power blinded us? But now we're penned like cattle and Dan-Tor can do as he pleases. We have to escape. We have to act against him or we'll be condemned forever.'

'Indeed.' The voice was grim and powerful.

Both Darek and Arinndier started, and even Hreldar looked surprised.

The unexpected voice was Eldric's.

Arinndier looked at the old Lord intently. Eldric slowly straightened up and returned the gaze. There was life again in his eyes and it seemed to Arinndier that the aging that confinement had apparently wrought on the man was falling away as he watched. Darek's flint had struck a spark from the iron of the old man's soul. Arinndier felt a lump in his throat.

'Indeed,' Eldric repeated, before any of the others could speak. 'Having failed in our duty once, we mustn't do so again.'

'Eldric,' said Arinndier, his face broken in a confusion of emotions, and his hands reaching out to his friend.

Eldric raised his own hands in a gesture that forbade interrogation. 'I've been away,' he said coldly. 'It won't happen again.'

Arinndier looked at him and remembered the Eldric who never responded well to sympathy; the Eldric who had always preferred to tend his own wounds in private, like an injured animal. Gradually his composure returned and he took up Eldric's first remark as if the second had never been spoken, though he could not keep the relief and joy from his face.

'You may be right,' he said. 'But what can we do? We don't know what's happening outside. We don't even know why we've been arrested. Perhaps the other Lords are . . .'

'The other Lords are dithering, just like we did,' Hreldar interrupted, his voice contemptuous. 'Dan-Tor will be plying them with rumours and lies. Probably telling them that there'll be a trial or some such nonsense – accusing us of treason – of being the reason why the King suspended the Geadrol. He'll pick them off one at a time. They won't even see the blow that's felling them.'

Arinndier winced at Hreldar's harsh tone. 'That's conjecture,' he said feebly.

Hreldar's mouth puckered distastefully. 'Maybe,' he said. 'But do you think it's wrong? Can you see them doing anything other?'

Arinndier did not reply.

Darek gave a grim chuckle. 'What a considerable schemer the man is. If we remain here we can do nothing but serve his ends by our enforced silence. If we escape we must rouse such of the Lords as we can and turn into the very rebels he's probably telling everyone we are.' He nodded a grudging approval. 'It's not without a certain elegance.'

'It's not without a certain horror,' said Eldric angrily. 'Still, warned is armed. In future we'll see a little more clearly and make fewer mistakes for him to profit by.'

'If we have a future,' said Hreldar coldly. 'Besides, Dan-Tor's a man who profits from everything. I don't think we've begun to get the measure of him yet.'

Eldric nodded in agreement. 'True, Hreldar,' he said, standing up and stretching himself expansively. 'True.' Then entwining his fingers, he cracked them methodically, as if freeing the joints of long-accumulated dust. 'But nor does he have the measure of us yet.'

Chapter 18

Sylvriss closed the door quietly behind her and spoke softly to the servant standing outside. 'The King's sleeping. See that he's not disturbed.'

The servant bowed in acknowledgement. 'Majesty.' He watched the Queen walking away from him. Was it his imagination or had he caught a glimpse under the Queen's silken hood, of a face flushed and smiling, triumphant even? No. It must have been a trick of the light. Sadly, loved though she was by so many, the Queen rarely smiled. Ethriss knows, she'd little enough to smile about. The King demented for most of the time; Dan-Tor spreading his pernicious influence over everything; the Geadrol suspended; Lords arrested for treason; these damned Mathidrin terrifying everyone; and even rumours of troubles in Orthlund. So much dreadful change so quickly. None of us have got much to smile about. But the servant's face remained impassive. It was unwise to express thoughts such as these. Rumours abounded about people who had spoken against Dan-Tor or the King and had disappeared mysteriously. Of course, they were only rumours, but . . .? Who could one trust these days?

However, the servant had been correct. The Queen had indeed been smiling when she left her husband sleeping peacefully; smiling radiantly. Now, however, as she walked along to her own quarters, the smile became grim and determined. She pulled her hood closer over her face. Inside herself she could feel an excitement – like the excitement of being First Hearer – picking up the cry, distant and tiny, a faint sound on the very limit of hearing, the warning cry that had to be roared out along the road so that it could be cleared before the riders appeared.

'Muster,' she whispered involuntarily into the still air of the corridor, longing to cry it out loud in defiance of Dan-Tor and his scheming. She had truly seen her long-buried husband again and their morning together had evoked so many old memories that she had seized new hopes and hardened her new resolve. No longer would she accept the defeat that her life had so far offered, its hand so skilfully guided by Dan-Tor. She would not sink any further into helplessness. Nor would she ponder what deep wisdom in the King had made him do what he had done, or what strange folly in Dan-Tor had allowed it. Suffice it that the turbulence it had caused had stirred many long-laid sediments, and now she felt her feet resting on a bedrock. Nothing, not even death itself, would dash these hopes from her now, or deflect her resolution.

A bustling flurry came into view. Dilrap, like a wallowing galleon, emerged from a side passage, his arms full of precariously balanced documents and his round face full of cares. Trying to preserve his burden intact, and maintain some semblance of dignity, he was having a considerable struggle and did not notice the Queen.

'Honoured Secretary,' she said, somewhat regretfully, seeing no way to avoid the almost inevitable outcome. Dilrap started and looked round suddenly. The abrupt movement dislodged a large scroll from the middle of the pile he was carrying.

Slowly it started to unroll. Dilrap's eyes widened and a quiver ran through him preparatory to a reflexive lunge after the escaping document. The quiver ended in a violent twitching as his hand groped blindly underneath his load in a vain attempt to stop the accelerating scroll, while his chin clawed frantically at the top of the pile to steady an ominous sway that had begun to develop in the whole stack.

Sylvriss watched spellbound as the saga unfolded itself in front of her with the predestined order of a classical tragedy. The chin triumphantly trapped the topmost document and stopped the incipient sway, but the middle of the stack bellied forward, intent on explosive self-destruction. Chin clinging valiantly and hand flailing futilely for the lost scroll which was now laying a paper pathway along the corridor, Dilrap took a step forward as if to overtake the swelling bulge. Malevolently, his father's robe chose this time to embrace his feet and, with a woeful cry, Dilrap rolled to the floor amidst the fluttering shower that had been his charge.

Hitching her hood forward again and biting her lip avoid laughing Sylvriss bent forward and picked up some of the nearer scrolls and papers.

'Majesty, Majesty,' cried Dilrap, his alarm intensifying as he scrabbled on all fours to relieve his monarch's consort of this servant's work.

Sylvriss held out a hand to help him, but he affected not to see it and struggled to his feet unaided, only narrowly avoiding pulling down a velvet curtain, and dislodging a carved head from a pedestal.

'Dilrap,' said Sylvriss sympathetically.

'Majesty,' he repeated, looking around at the debris and gesticulating vaguely. Sylvriss tossed back the hood of her robe and smiled gently at him. Dilrap was destroyed. He was so fond of his Queen. He grieved constantly for her suffering, and admired beyond words her steadfast courage. She was one of the few who called him by his name. Most used his title and even made that sound like an insult. She made him feel calm and at ease. And she was so beautiful. So beautiful.

She was fond of him too. He reminded her of a fat old pony she had had as a child, but she sensed other qualities in the man, and quietly grieved for his plight.

'I'm sorry I startled you, Dilrap,' she said. 'But I wanted to speak to you about something.' She gestured to a passing servant and gave orders for the papers to be collected and taken to Dilrap's office then, taking his elbow, she said, 'Come with me.'

There was a brief flurry of hitchings and adjustments before Dilrap fell in with the sauntering pace of his Queen. She walked for some time without speaking. Dilrap cast surreptitious sideways glances at her. It seemed to him that she was changed in some way. Her face was different – less strained – younger, flushed, even. Then, as if on a whim, she turned off the corridor and walking through an elaborate archway, came into the Crystal Hall.

Two Mathidrin standing guard at the archway clicked their heels as she passed, and she acknowledged their salute with a nod and a gracious smile. At every opportunity, in every little way, she was determined to ease herself into the affections and respect of all Dan-Tor's minions, however loutish. It would have been easier for her by far to be cold and distant, but that would have been easier for them too. No, she thought, some affection for me amongst his men can do nothing but hinder him and might prove helpful one day. I'll show you how to train horses, you long streak of evil.

The Crystal Hall was so called because of its strange translucent walls and ceilings. They shifted and shimmered constantly with every imaginable colour. Their smooth surfaces were broken only by thin veins of a golden inlay, curling and sweeping into elaborate leaflike patterns. Somewhere behind each surface could be seen figures and landscapes that seemed to flicker in and out of existence with the slightest movement of the head; sometimes near, sometimes distant.

It was a beautiful place that exuded tranquillity, but no one knew how or when it had been built, or who had built it. In fact no one now knew even the name of this strange craft of inner carving.

Dan-Tor never visited it.

Sylvriss led Dilrap over to a broad seat underneath the pattern of a huge tree etched out in fine golden threads. The threads were flush with the surface of the wall, but the inner work made the trunk seem solid and whole, and the branches shimmered as though sunlight were falling on them through waving leaves. A close examination would reveal countless tiny, multi-coloured insects moving among the crevices of the bark. The leaves, too, flickered and shone as if a breeze were blowing through them, and as different seasons shone their different lights into the hall so the leaves seemed to change and fall.

Sylvriss sat down and gestured Dilrap to do likewise. Dilrap did as he was bidden, and folding his hands in his lap he awaited his Queen's pleasure.

He had neither the stature nor the dignity of his late father, but he had a substantial portion of his considerable intellect and a memory that was superior by far. It was his saving grace as the King's Secretary and prevented life becoming totally intolerable for him. However, this, his real worth, was unknown to most, not least himself, being constantly overshadowed by his circumstances and his excitable and nervous disposition.

In the Queen's company, however, given a little time, he tended to relax and be more at ease, and his truer self would emerge. Perceptively, Sylvriss judged that despite being utterly fearful of Dan-Tor, his loyalty to the King was unquestionable, and his devotion to her total.

He was worth more than her humorous affection, she knew. The very contempt in which many of the Court held him meant that secrets which were jealously guarded from other ears were discussed almost openly in his presence. Often, no more heed was taken of him than of one of the Palace hounds. But, Sylvriss noted, *he* never gossiped. Never sought to protect himself by winning the spurious esteem of others with some display of his knowledge of the intimate details of Palace life. He absorbed all his embarrassment and discomfiture and, presumably, resentment in some inner place. His sole defence was his defencelessness.

The tree shimmered as the sun emerged from behind a cloud and burst into the Hall.

'Dilrap,' she began. 'I need a friend. An ally.'

'Majesty, I'm your most devo –'

She waved him to silence. 'No, Dilrap. I need no Court pleasantries from you. I know what you are.' She stared at him for a moment, then plunged. 'You're a man trapped by circumstances in a public office for which he considers himself totally unsuitable. Circumstances made all the more bitter by the fact that his father ranked as one of the finest Secretaries any King has ever known.'

Dilrap bowed his head. Sylvriss pressed forward. 'But your father didn't have a sick and wayward King to deal with, nor . . .' She paused significantly, watching him carefully, 'nor, Dilrap, did he have to deal with the likes of Lord Dan-Tor.' She offered no embellishment of her description of Dan-Tor. It was not necessary.

Dilrap looked up and caught her gaze. Strange, came a slow thought from deep inside him. Strange that I'd never seen that – that simple, obvious fact. Sylvriss held his gaze and nodded in confirmation of what she had said.

'Your father towers in your life as once he towered in this Palace,' she said. Then slowly and with great deliberation, 'But no man could have contended with the Lord Dan-Tor. No man.'

Dilrap lowered his eyes again. 'Majesty, I don't understand what you're saying. What is it you want of me?'

'I want a friend, Dilrap. An ally.'

Dilrap made no reply.

Sylvriss took a deep breath. She must continue now. 'Dilrap, you underestimate yourself totally. You always have. For anyone who cares to look, there are qualities in you which make you at least as fine a Secretary as your father. The reason your office is burdensome to you, and why you're the butt of so many in the Court, is that Dan-Tor wishes it so. He wants no one around him or the King who might be intelligent enough to interfere with his plans.'

Dilrap looked alarmed and fluttered his hands nervously, like butterflies trying to fly to safety in the glittering tree above them. 'Majesty . . . I don't know . . .'

'Dilrap. I know. I know you're loyal to your office and the King. And to the people of Fyorlund. I know it grieves you constantly that you seem to be eternally impotent to alter the terrible course we're set on.' She seized the dithering hands. Dilrap started. 'Look at me,' she said urgently. 'I tell you again. You must understand. Even your father couldn't have stood against the wiles of Dan-Tor. As sure as fate he'd have been destroyed in the attempt. You must believe that. Somewhere inside you, you know it's true.'

She released the hands and they floated down into his lap again.

'Majesty,' he whispered, 'maybe what you say is true. I know that you above all would play no cruel tricks on me. But what do you want of me?'

Sylvriss placed all on one cast and told him briefly and bluntly. 'The King has no mysterious illness. It was Dan-Tor's treatment that precipitated his condition and it's been Dan-Tor's treatment that has maintained it.' Dilrap's eyes widened in terror, but Sylvriss continued. 'See how well he's been recently, now that it's in Dan-Tor's interests not to have him wandering about demented, further complicating the actions he's accidentally set in motion.'

'Majesty,' ventured Dilrap, 'the King's illness has always been subject to these brief flashes of normality. He may lapse gain at any moment.'

'I know,' said Sylvriss. Then, with some bitterness, 'There's a quality in Dan-Tor's potions that makes the body cry out for them desperately, even though they injure it. I've learned that in the past and suffered for it.'

Dilrap raised his hand as if to comfort the pain that passed over the beautiful face.

'But knowledge is a shield, Dilrap,' Sylvriss continued. 'Dan-Tor quieted the King and then left his tending to me while he occupied himself with political affairs.' Her voice fell. 'Very slowly I've been reducing the strength of the potions I'm supposed to give him.' She raised a finger in emphasis. 'Very slowly he's returning to health.'

Dilrap looked round fearfully. 'Majesty, why do you tell me this? I think the Lord Dan-Tor is capable of anything – anything – I've seen so many . . .' He stopped. 'I shudder to think what his real aims are. But what can I do?'

Sylvriss sat back and nodded slowly. 'You've just done it, Honoured Secretary. You've spoken the truth. You've seen so many things, you said. So many things that shouldn't be. And even the seemingly unimportant things take their toll – lapses in procedure, appointments for personal favours rather than ability, petty deceits and illegalities to avoid the scrutiny of the Geadrol, trivial things. Trivial things that have accumulated over the years to shift power gradually from where it lay, into Dan-Tor's hands. Reluctant but efficient hands, labouring only in the interests of their monarch.'

Then, surprised at her own realisation, '*You've* spoken out about it. You've spoken out and been crushed. Long ago. Crushed with the same meticulous attention to detail that he applies to everything. All the ways a man can be crushed without actually breaking his bones. You fought your battle alone, and you thought it lost.'

The last vestiges of her image of her old pony faded in a tearful mist and this time *she* felt *his* pain. Dilrap sat motionless, a dark expression on his face as countless scores of humiliations and rebuffs marched in mocking triumph before him.

'What can I do?' he said again, simply.

'You must do as I must,' said Sylvriss. 'You must fight again. But with a new resolve, no matter what the odds, if the things you honour – Kingship, the Law, the people, your father's memory – are to survive. You and I have nowhere left to hide. No one will act against Dan-Tor if we don't. He'll twist the rest of the Lords around his finger, and destroy them one at a time. Then he'll destroy the King and everything else of the old way. Including us.'

'Majesty, I'm not a warrior,' Dilrap said faintly.

Sylvriss smiled. 'You're no swordsman, Dilrap, but you're more of a warrior than you know,' she said.

Dilrap tried for the last time to refuse the mantle that was being pressed on him. 'Majesty, if the King is improving in health, he'll surely be able to take control again. He was a powerful and able man.'

Sylvriss shook her head. 'Oh, how I wish that were true,' she said sadly. 'But he's still far from being fully well again. He's quiet and at some semblance of peace with himself, but his condition isn't stable. He teeters constantly on the edge of one extreme or the other. To mention the Geadrol or the Lords would be to push him over the edge.' She sighed. 'Only by keeping his mind on happier times can I keep him calm and give him the time to become stronger.' Her hands twisted in her lap. 'Fortunately we've a fine store of such memories . . .' Her voice faded.

Dilrap looked at the Queen's hands. They were abruptly anxious and fidgety. The hands of a woman who had been too long waiting for ill news, not the powerful hands of the skilled rider that had just seized his own.

'I'm afraid there's no help to be found from the King. Probably there'll be hindrance. I can't always tell how his moods are going to turn.' Her mouth made a little ironic twist. 'You and I'll have to stand around him like the High Guards around Ethriss at the Last Battle.'

Despite himself, Dilrap smiled at the analogy. The imagery appealed to the heroic little boy within him that all life's depredations had not yet totally destroyed.

They did not talk for much longer under the glittering tree. This was no time for detailed plotting and scheming. The essence of their compact had been sealed. Now they were allies against a common foe. Both saw clearly as never before that ahead of them lay degradation and possibly worse if they did nothing.

It might be that this would still be the case even if they acted against Dan-Tor, but it was their only hope for an alternative future and, if they failed utterly, then at least they would have that strange consolation of dying facing an enemy rather than fleeing from him.

Chapter 19

For all their new-found resolve and awareness, the four Lords found their material position unchanged. They did not even know where they were being held except that it was somewhere in the main Palace building and almost certainly underground.

Their journey from the Throne Room following their fateful confrontation with the King had been confused and violent, all four of them shouting and struggling but being relentlessly shepherded by the grim Mathidrin. So unexpected had been the King's action that none of them had had the presence of mind to note where they were going through the maze of corridors and hallways, but their subsequent consensus was that it had been generally downwards. A long way down.

Their food was brought by a series of different guards, and whenever the door was opened, at least two others could be seen standing outside.

'We've set ourselves a fair task, Lords,' said Eldric with a grim smile. 'I for one don't feel inclined to match my muscle against what I've seen of our guards. Wherever they're from, they look fit and tough, and we've no idea how many of them are out there.' Then he catalogued their problems. 'Even if we do get out of this room we don't know where we are, thanks to our dignified journey here, and if we managed to get out of the Palace there's no saying how many friends we'll find in the City to help us back to our estates.' His voice had risen with each statement and finally he smacked his hands on his knees and stood up. 'Good grief, we don't even know whether our estates and High Guards still exist,' he shouted.

'We abandon the idea?' asked Arinndier placidly.

Eldric shot his friend a stern glance. 'Certainly not,' he said fiercely, before catching the humour in Arinndier's eye.

'We just have to move one step at a time that's all,' he concluded, more quietly.

Arinndier smiled. Like all of them, Eldric was paler and thinner as a result of his confinement, but his inner fire seemed to be burning brighter than ever. Occasionally Arinndier felt sparks fly that he had not seen since they fought shoulder to shoulder in the Morlider War. A much younger man had replaced the old one that had so recently been tenanting Eldric's body.

Only once did Eldric refer to his strange decline and recovery. Hreldar and Darek were sleeping and Eldric and Arinndier had fallen into a companionable silence. Arinndier looked at his old friend, pensively tapping a curled finger against his mouth.

'Are you all right?' he enquired tentatively.

Eldric nodded and smiled after a moment. 'Yes. I'm fine now, Arin,' he said. Then, 'I'm afraid age has stiffened me up in more ways than one,' he volunteered.

Arinndier looked at him enquiringly.

Eldric spoke very quietly. 'When the King turned on us like that, I panicked. Not for an instant had I thought that such a thing could happen. And all those guards closing in on us. So many of them . . . so overwhelming. It's a long time since I've been so frightened.'

'We were all frightened,' said Arinndier.

Eldric frowned a little and shook his head. 'No, this wasn't the same. This felt like something breaking inside. Something important that kept me together. Something that would have bent and taken the strain once. It was terrible.' Briefly, his age showed on his face again, but Arinndier did not interrupt.

'Suddenly it was an end, Arin. All the life seemed to go out of me. I felt lost – like a child – all I wanted to do was bolt for cover, hide in my mother's skirts. Then I was in some kind of darkness. I scarcely remember anything until I heard Darek laying down the law about the Law. You know, I seemed to hear my father shouting at me, "Get up". And I did. Whatever had broken came together again. Something dropped back into place.'

He stood up and looked at the slumbering Darek. Sleep had

softened the Lord's lean face and he looked slightly incongruous.

Eldric smiled. 'You remember my father, don't you?'

Arinndier nodded. 'Indeed I do,' he said. 'I always did my best to avoid him.'

Eldric laughed. 'He was all right really. But that's what he used to roar at me if I took a tumble. "Get up. You'll get killed lying there. Get up, or I'll leave you." And he would have done too, if I hadn't made the effort.' He shook his head and chuckled warmly. 'He loved me too much to offer me a hand when it wasn't needed, Arin. I didn't realise how hard that was until I'd a son of my own.'

The mood darkened a little at the mention of his son. None of them had heard anything of their families and estates and, though not much dwelled on, it was a greater strain to bear than the captivity itself.

Eldric moved back to his bunk and his topic. 'I think it was probably the suddenness of the change as much as the violence, Arin. Winded me, as it were. We've been too still too long. Maybe the whole country has. Grown stiff and unresponsive. Perhaps we couldn't have anticipated what might happen, but we should've been able to accept the reality more quickly when it did, instead of . . .' He left the sentence unfinished and shrugged. 'Anyway, we got knocked down for our pains so we must learn our lessons all over again – and that's an old lesson in itself.'

The advantage of moving through life one step at a time is that the worries and doubts of detailed long-term planning are avoided. All that is necessary is a careful probing of the ground immediately ahead, and considerable trust in one's own ability and that of one's companions to move quickly as need arises.

The disadvantage is, of course, that while such probing may prevent a fall into a precipice or a collision with a cliff face, it cannot prevent the return journey that meeting such obstacles entails.

The Lords, however, accepted that they had no alternative, and that their first step was to find out where they were. After some lengthy and fruitless debate about how this was to be achieved, Eldric abruptly gave a frustrated and angry snarl and opted for action. With some truthfulness, but perhaps a little too much bluntness, he gave the first order of his campaign.

'Hreldar, you look the sickest. Get on to your bunk and start moaning – quickly.' Before Hreldar could speak, Eldric took his elbow and escorted him briskly to the bunk.

'Just moan,' Eldric said, sitting the open-mouthed Lord down unceremoniously. Then, striding across the room, he banged his fist on the door.

'What are you doing?' cried Arinndier and Darek simultaneously in alarmed chorus.

Eldric turned impatiently to Hreldar. 'Moan,' he said, authoritatively. Then to the others, equally firmly, 'Follow my lead.' Then he laid into the door powerfully. Fists and feet.

'Open this damned door,' he roared.

Arinndier and Darek looked at one another briefly and shrugged. This was Eldric, their old commander, and they had not seen him for many years.

Eventually they heard the bolts being drawn and the rattle of keys in the lock. Hreldar leaned forward to see what was happening, but Eldric waved him down again. 'Moan,' he mouthed silently.

The door opened slowly and Arinndier quailed inwardly at the sight of the black-clad Mathidrin trooper standing there. He gave the impression of having been carved out of one solid piece of black stone. Tall and heavily built, he exuded a bull-like solidity. Not a man to be tackled lightly, thought Arinndier, or at all, preferably. He also exuded a certain oafish brutality and his fists were clenched at the ends of massive arms that hung in a curve away from his body, indicating that his normal gait was a swagger.

'The Lord Hreldar's ill, guard,' began Eldric. 'We must . . .'

'Less noise, prisoners,' said the guard in a harsh, unfamiliar accent, cutting across Eldric's outburst.

Eldric, however, was riding high. He stood up, straight and relaxed in front of the guard, his very posture making him seem at least as tall as the man.

'Pending the Lord Dan-Tor's review of our case, you'll address us as Lords, guard, and you'll stand to attention when so doing. Is that clear?' His voice was quiet but very deliberate and its tone indicated it would brook no debate.

The guard seemed to swell visibly and, for a moment, it looked as if he were considering knocking Eldric down. But Eldric held the man's gaze with an icy unwavering stare, behind which were all his years as a commander of men. It was a crucial moment, and the three other Lords watched with some trepidation. They were about to have a measure of their worth as prisoners.

After several seconds, Arinndier felt the guard's resolve falter slightly. With impeccable timing, Eldric leaned forward and brought his face close to the guard's. 'Is that clear?' he repeated in a voice that was almost a whisper. 'Or are you deaf as well as improperly dressed?'

Involuntarily, the guard dropped his gaze briefly to examine his uniform.

'Eyes front,' thundered Eldric as if he were in the middle of a large and noisy parade ground. The three Lords jumped as the powerful voice filled the tiny room and the guard snapped reflexively to attention. There's nothing like military reflexes, thought Arinndier, recovering, and casually putting his hand over his mouth to cover a smile. Darek too turned away and, moving to Hreldar, bent over as if tending him. Eldric continued his initiative before the guard had a chance to recover his wits properly.

'The Lord Hreldar's ill. He collapsed without warning. Get a healer immediately.'

The guard dithered. 'I don't know . . .' he stammered.

'Well I do,' shouted Eldric. 'Get a healer. Now.'

The man still hesitated.

'Do you want to answer to Lord Dan-Tor if the Lord Hreldar dies in your care?'

The mention of Dan-Tor galvanised the man, and he turned towards the door. As he did so Hreldar let out a gasping cry and sat up, his hand to his throat as if choking.

'Wait,' cried Darek to the departing guard. 'He's having some kind of a fit. He must have air. He's choking to death.'

Again the man faltered, caught between Eldric and Darek's commands and the apparent distress of Hreldar.

'Quickly, man,' said Arinndier, striding over to help Darek with the gasping Hreldar. Eldric gave the guard an imperative flick of the head to propel him away from the door and over to the struggling trio. 'Hurry, he's heavy. I'll get the other guards.' And before the guard had time to consider what was happening, he stepped out into the passage.

It was no frightened, struggling old man who walked through that door, it was a battle-tried and determined Lord who had clung to old ways and old disciplines when others around him were drifting into idleness and hedonism. He knew he could have only a few minutes' freedom at the most and in that time he had to gather as much information as he could about their location.

The passage was unfamiliar but he allowed himself no time for disappointment. To his right it ended in an old and very solid door. He ran to it and lifting the heavy latch pulled it urgently. The door opened surprisingly easily and almost threw him off balance. He noted that though it was old, the hinges and the latch had all recently been greased. This must have been sealed for years, he thought. Who's opened it now and why? Then he dismissed the question for future consideration and peered through the doorway. A spiralling flight of steps disappeared down into the darkness.

'Guards,' he shouted loudly for the benefit of the guard in the room. His voice sank dully into the dark stairwell in front of him. Faint noises and a dank unpleasant smell rose up to meet him. He wrinkled his nose in distaste and closed the door.

Two figures appeared along the passage. Eldric ran towards them, crying out, 'Guards, guards, come quickly,' before they could speak. Babbling loudly about Hreldar's fit he ushered them urgently towards his cell. Arinndier and the first guard were manoeuvring the now almost dead-weight Hreldar through the door and Darek was flitting around looking concerned.

'He must have air quickly,' said Darek. 'I've seen him in these attacks before. It's the confinement, it happened in . . .'

'No,' interrupted Arinndier angrily, hitching Hreldar's arm around his shoulder. 'This is poison.' And he glowered at the guards. 'We'll find out who's responsible for this, have no fear.'

Good, Arin, thought Eldric. That'll start rumours flying.

'Which way, man?' he snapped at the nearest guard. The man pointed vaguely up the passage. Eldric knew they had only seconds now before the guards took control so, unhooking Hreldar's arm from Arinndier, he unceremoniously thrust Hreldar into the arms of the two guards and starting urging the whole group along the passage towards the first junction.

When they reached it, the first guard found his tongue. 'Pris . . . Lords,' he said. 'We'll look after the Lord Hreldar now. You must return to your . . . rooms.'

Eldric gave Hreldar a concerned look and then reluctantly turned back down the passage. Arinndier caught his quick gesture and turned also. Darek picked up a hand signal. 'Let me go with him,' he said to the guard. 'I've seen these attacks before.'

The guard looked at Eldric as if for guidance, but Eldric, now backing slowly and dutifully towards the cell, shrugged as if to disown responsibility for everything that would happen from hereon.

'Very well,' said the guard, and he nodded to his companions.

Eldric and Arinndier turned and entered their cell quickly, both anxious that the guard should not see the triumph on their faces.

Chapter 20

Hawklan pushed the books away from him and rubbed his eyes with his forefingers. 'Learn your lore,' Gulda had said, in her capacity as self-appointed adviser, and then, in her inimitable manner, 'There's no point in you asking me any questions until you know what you're talking about.' She had marched Hawklan straight to the Castle's massive Library and he had looked in dismay at the endless rows and stacks of books and scrolls. It was not a room he was overly familiar with.

'Where in pity's name do I start?' he had asked plaintively, forgetting the nature of his companion until too late.

'Good grief, man!' had come the explosion. 'Anywhere.' And the stick had banged on a desk prior to being waved round her head at the circular tiers of book-lined balconies looming over them. Then, uncharacteristically showing a little pity, she had gone straight to a shelf and picked out a large red-bound tome. She studied the title pensively and a small spasm of pain passed briefly across her face.

'A fine writer,' she said with a strained casualness. 'This will do to start with.' And she dropped the book on a nearby table with a dull thud. 'Read it carefully.'

It occurred to Hawklan to ask her how she knew her way round the Castle so well, but, before he could speak, she was stumping her way out of the Library with the parting shot, 'Very carefully now. There'll be questions later.'

Now, a week later, Hawklan was more weary and stiff than he had ever been in his entire life. His head whirled with myths and stories, epic sagas, tales of heroism and cowardice, of loves lost and won, of terrible armies and evil warlords, and of the great heroes who conquered them, peoples enslaved and peoples freed, lands cursed and lands blessed. And then the histories, vague and uncertain, so that for most of the time he could not tell whether the myths derived from the histories or the histories from the myths, so alike were they, and so unlikely, so alien to everything he had known – or could remember. More than once, in some despair, he had pushed them all aside and sat glowering at the rows of shelves waiting so patiently. But not too long. Memsa Gulda was well acquainted with the idle and shiftless ways of men, and set him a merciless pace.

'I'll make that tangled string you call a mind work again, young man, have no fear,' she said repeatedly and pitilessly.

He could not help but begin to like her though. On the one occasion when his patience had reached its limit, and to his considerable surprise he had felt sorely tempted to use his fist on the old crone, she was through his guard and into a soft spot like an assassin.

'I know it's hard for you, Hawklan,' she said gently. 'And you must get resentful at times, but these are a fine people, perhaps still the finest in the world. They wouldn't have turned to you even though the Castle has chosen you if they hadn't felt some deeper purpose. We must both persist. They're worth our best efforts.' And that was that. End of rebellion.

Gavor was an amazing help, with a tremendous fund of information drawn from his long study of the Great Gate and the many carvings and pictures that filled the Castle. He shared most of Hawklan's long vigils in the Library, flicking over pages with his wooden leg, and occasionally asking Hawklan to lift down another volume. Never having studied before, Hawklan had found to his own surprise that he was a quick and retentive reader. Gavor, however, was even quicker.

'How did you learn to read so quickly, Gavor?' he asked eventually, after watching him intermittently for several days.

'Dear boy,' was the reply. 'I study the Gate.'

'Well?'

'The well, dear boy,' Gavor began patiently, 'is that I'm not a humming bird. I can't hover. I have to read things on my way past. I can't tell you what a pleasure it is to sit here and read without fear of crash landing.'

Not everything was harmonious, however, a certain tension having developed between Gavor and Gulda. Somewhat injudiciously she referred to Gavor as a 'damn crow', to which Gavor responded by saying that if she shortened her nose by a stride or two, she'd be passing fair – for a pelican.

Fortunately, before this theme could be developed further, others valiantly intervened to patch up a makeshift peace, and now the two maintained a stony truce, generally avoiding each other and eyeing one another suspiciously when circumstances dictated that they co-operate in helping Hawklan.

'It's all too much, Gavor,' said Hawklan, still rubbing his eyes. 'I can't make out truth from fiction, and there's just too much of everything. I feel I'm losing knowledge not gaining it.'

No reply.

Hawklan leaned back in his chair and looked across at his friend. Gavor was sound asleep, his foot clutching the top rail of a chair he had commandeered as his perch, and his wooden leg sticking out horizontally, steadying him against an open book propped up in front of him.

Hawklan smiled. 'Very wise,' he yawned, pushing the books he had been reading to one side. He leaned forward and, cushioning his head on his arms, fell fast asleep without the slightest twinge of conscience.

When he opened his eyes, he found it difficult to focus. Sitting opposite him, next to the sleeping Gavor, was Andawyr, his oval punchbag face looking gaunt and haggard and very old in the soft light of the now darkened Library.

Hawklan smiled and opened his mouth to speak. He wanted to tell Andawyr that his arm was better, but the words would not form properly.

'Listen to me, Hawklan.' The voice was faint and distant. 'I can speak to you only because of my extremity. We've bound the birds . . . I'm held in Narsindal, I may be destroyed at any moment. Go to the Cadwanol . . . in the Caves of Cadwanen at the Pass of Elewart.'

Hawklan felt pain and fear now in the old man's presence, but still could not speak.

'They know of you . . . Tell them I reached out to you when all hope was gone. Tell them the Uhriel are indeed abroad – Oklar, Creost and Dar Hastuin.'

Darkness came into Hawklan's mind from some unknown source. Andawyr's voice became weaker.

'Tell them that they've raised and awakened . . .' The image faltered. 'Raised and awakened their old Master. I've felt His presence and, I fear, He mine.' He looked over his shoulder. 'Hawklan, the Second Coming of Sumeral is upon us. Sphaeera, Theowart and Enartion must be roused.' His hands came in front of his face as if fending off an attack.

Hawklan tried to tell him he was safe; this was only a library. Everything was safe in Anderras Darion. But still he could not speak and his eyes were becoming heavier and heavier. Fading in the distance he heard, 'They need you and you they. Ethriss must be found and awakened, or all will be lost, and Sumeral's power will stretch across the stars. He's wiser by far now . . .'

An ominous chilling blackness rolled over Hawklan as the voice dwindled into nothingness, and Hawklan felt a cold malevolent presence before drifting into forgetfulness.

Slowly, out of the infinite darkness came a tiny bright dancing spark calling his name. Calling it repeatedly, and laughing at him. As it grew, it twinkled and shifted, moving as the sound moved, until finally it burst into a myriad sparks and he opened his eyes to a blaze of light and laughter.

He sat up, bleary-eyed. The Library was bright with daylight carried into the innermost reaches of the Castle by the mirror stones. Tirilen's laughter was ringing in his ears, and the cause of it was dancing up and down frantically in front of him.

'Ah, ah, ah. Ooh, ooh. Do something,' cried Gavor.

'What's the matter?' Hawklan asked sleepily.

'Pins and needles,' Tirilen announced, still laughing.

'Where?' said Hawklan, flexing the stiffness out of his own muscles.

Gavor proffered his wooden leg and Tirilen flopped into a chair, wiping tears from her eyes. Hawklan looked at her reproachfully.

'Not a good attitude for a healer, my girl,' he said, trying not to smile. Gavor, however, continued his plaint until he was suddenly and miraculously cured by the abrupt entrance of Gulda.

'Well, I can see you've slept, young man,' she said. 'I suppose you'll want to eat now will you?'

'Solicitous as ever, dear lady,' muttered Gavor loudly to no one in particular.

Gulda glowered at him. Gavor raised his beak into the air with great dignity and, walking over to a conspicuous patch of sunshine, began to preen himself vigorously, scattering dust and fragments of iridescent feathers into the broad shaft of sunlight that fell on him like a great finger.

Hawklan looked at Gulda and then at Tirilen, who was tossing her shining blonde hair to cut a golden swathe through the sunlight. Suddenly, the memory of Andawyr and the strange horror that had surrounded him, returned with an appalling vividness.

Outside, the sun disappeared behind ragged storm clouds blowing from the east, and the light in the Library took on a gloomier cast.

'Gulda,' he said faintly.

Gulda's eyes narrowed slightly as she caught his tone. Indicating the door with a movement of her head she mouthed 'food' to Tirilen. As the girl left, Gulda sat down by Hawklan and rested her hands on her stick.

'Gulda,' he said, 'I had a dream last night. At least, I thought it was a dream at the time . . . but now I'm not sure.' He shivered slightly. 'It was very strange.'

Gulda did not speak, but she nodded her head slowly. Hawklan's voice made Gavor stop his preening.

'Andawyr was here,' Hawklan continued, pointing to the chair where he had seen the little man.

'Andawyr?' Gulda enquired.

Hawklan gestured apologetically. 'Someone I met at the Gretmearc.' Then, in amplification, 'Strange little man. I owe him a great deal. He and Gavor saved my life. Said he belonged to the Cadwanol, whoever they are.'

Gulda's eyes widened and, for an instant, her fierce expression disappeared into one of profound surprise. For that same instant, Hawklan had a vision of a face that had once been strikingly beautiful.

'The Cadwanol,' she said softly, to herself. 'After all this time. Still watching.' She lifted a hand to cover her face and sat motionless with her head bowed for several minutes. When she looked up, her face was full of self-reproach.

'I haven't asked you what happened at the Gretmearc,

Hawklan,' she said quietly, 'although I could see you were keeping something from the villagers. I'm sorry. I'm becoming as foolish as I'm old. Will you tell me everything now please?'

Gavor cocked his head on one side at Gulda's subdued tone.

'Everything,' she repeated. Some of her old manner returned and leaning forward she prodded Hawklan's knee with her long forefinger. 'Everything since this . . . tinker Lord arrived that you haven't told the others.'

As Hawklan recounted his tale, Gulda folded her hands on top of her stick and rested her head on them, eyes closed and downcast. When finally he finished, she did not move, but Hawklan sensed a tension in her.

'Now tell me of this dream,' she said quietly. Mindful of her earlier admonition, Hawklan recounted Andawyr's words and actions as accurately as he could. It was all still peculiarly vivid in his mind and he shivered a little again.

Though she showed no response, the tension in Gulda seemed to build then, abruptly, her pale face became even paler, the tight mouth quivered and her long powerful hands shook as they clenched the top of the stick. Hawklan became alarmed, thinking she was about to faint. He put out a hand as if to catch her, and she reached out and took hold of it. Her grip was frighteningly powerful, but the hand was cold and shaking.

'I'll be all right in a moment,' she said faintly. Hawklan winced at the pain that radiated from her.

Gavor clunked across the table and looked at her strangely. Gulda caught his deep black eye, and her face softened.

'Ah,' she said softly, almost to herself. 'Faithful bird. Your people did true service in their time.' Then directly to Gavor, 'You'll have to forgive an impatient old woman her sharp tongue and foolishness. There'll be no more. I doubt we've the time.'

Gavor had many qualities but pettiness was not one. 'Dear girl,' he said. 'I'd rather have your abuse than see you wilt like this.'

'What's the matter, Gulda?' Hawklan asked.

She did not answer, but remained with her head lowered for a little while. Then, as though she were a sapling that bowed only while the wind blew, she sat upright. Her face was still white, but was filled with a stern resolution and dignity that stopped Hawklan speaking further.

She relinquished Hawklan's hand and placed her own steadily back on top of her stick. 'Tell me again what he said. Exactly, mind.'

Hawklan repeated his tale.

'Do these names mean anything to you, Hawklan?' she asked.

Hawklan shrugged. 'I keep coming across them in these,' he said, waving his hand over the books scattered across the table. 'And in some of the tales on the Gate. Andawyr talked about Sumeral. Called him the Corruptor, the Great Enemy . . . the Enemy of Life.'

Gulda nodded. 'Didn't he explain?'

Hawklan shook his head. 'A little, but we were attacked before he could finish.' Gulda nodded.

The sound of a door closing quietly made Hawklan look up, and Tirilen came quietly into the room carrying food and drink. She walked over the soft carpeting as gently as if it had been a spring meadow and laid a carved tray at Hawklan's elbow.

Gavor cast his eye approvingly over the wares offered. 'Be enough to spare for a famished avian, won't there?' he whispered.

Tirilen caught the look on Gulda's face. 'Shall I leave?' she said. Gavor looked up in alarm.

'No,' said Gulda. 'Eat. And stay. You're his friend. He'll need you. And to be strong you must also know the truth.'

Gavor began to eat with noisy gusto.

Hawklan picked up a piece of fruit and, toying with it absently, looked at Gulda.

She in turn looked straight into his green eyes. 'You must trust me, Hawklan, like you trusted this . . . Andawyr. It was probably because of your trust that he could reach you in his hour of need and give us his message.'

Hawklan found the piercing blue eyes disconcerting. 'I'll trust you, Gulda. I feel no hurt in you for all your ferocity. And you're a focus for those who're trying to reach me.'

'Yes,' said Gulda. 'Your figures in the mist. I'm afraid they're a mystery to me. I saw nothing . . . but you're a special person and . . . there's a lot I don't know, Hawklan, a lot.' She paused uncertainly. 'However, what I do know, *you* need to know. Your ignorance is pitiful and perhaps even dangerous.'

As it had done in Andawyr's tent, the word ignorance raked through Hawklan like an icy wind stirring long-lain leaves.

'Tell me what you know,' he said flatly. 'Perhaps you can thread these happenings together.'

Gulda's eyes narrowed at his tone, then she looked down for a while as if she had not decided exactly what to say or as if she were trying to recall a tale she had not told for many years.

'Let me speak and then ask your questions, Hawklan,' she said, reluctantly shedding the last obstacle between her tale and its exposition. Hawklan nodded and Gulda began.

'These people here think of me as just a cantankerous old teacher who's come back to persecute them in their middle age like I did when they were children.' A smile flitted across her face, like sunshine off a wave. 'Well,' she admitted, 'I am cantankerous, but only because the old is truer than they can imagine. But I haven't come back to persecute them . . . although I might.' Another brief smile. 'A little, just for old times' sake.' Then the smile vanished utterly. 'No. I've come back because something is stirring. Something dark and evil that once spread its stain over the whole world . . .'

She hesitated, and for some time stared straight ahead with unfocused eyes. Then she grimaced self-consciously. 'I'm sorry,' she said. 'It's so long since I've spoken of these things it's difficult to know where to start and I . . . I didn't know how painful it was going to be.'

'If it distresses you, Gulda . . .' Hawklan began, but she waved him to silence.

'No, no,' she said quickly. And then, in an almost offhand manner, 'Anyway, it's of no consequence why I came here. I should be old enough by now not to put too much store in my own assessment of my motives, eh? Now I'm here I see my task is to instruct you. Then perhaps I can return to my own . . . problem.' Apparently satisfied with this conclusion, she sat up briskly and began like a village storyteller.

Chapter 21

'A long time ago, out of the terrible heat of the Great Searing came four figures. Shining white and brilliant, they walked the cooling world shaping it with their songs and their love into a great celebration of their sheer joy at being.

'Many shapes it took, for great and endlessly varied was their joy. And when the time was due, they formed it as it is now so that their own creations could create in turn and celebrate their own joy at being.

'And these four were called the Guardians: Sphaeera, Guardian of the Air and the winds and the sky; Enartion, Guardian of the Oceans and Lakes and all the rivers and streams; Theowart, Guardian of the Earth, its mountains and flatlands, islands and continents; and then, greatest of all, the First Comer, Ethriss, the Guardian of all Living Things.

'And the Guardians looked at their work and at the Great Harmony of its Song, and were content. And they rested; each fading into his wardship, so that only Ethriss retained his original form, lying atop an unclimbable mountain, hidden from the eyes of men by Sphaeera's mists.

'But a fifth figure had come from the heat of the Great Searing, with lesser figures at his heels. And He shone red and baleful, and carried an ancient corruption with Him from what had gone before. Brooding in His evil, and detesting the work of the Guardians, but daunted by their power and might, He remained still and silent until they rested. Then He came forth, quietly and with great cunning, for He knew that to wake them would be to court His own destruction. For they would know Him. And He walked among men for many generations, sowing His corruption softly and gently, with sweet words and lying truths, slowly souring the Great Harmony that the Guardians had created. And so beautiful was He that none could see the evil in Him . . .'

Gulda stopped her tale abruptly and looked at Hawklan with a strange sad expression on her face. 'And He *was* beautiful, Hawklan, so beautiful.' Hawklan felt a myriad nuances in her voice but they were snatched from him as the momentum of her old tale carried Gulda forward again.

'And so wise was He that some men forgot the sleeping Guardians and took Him for a god and worshipped him, calling Him Sumeral, the Timeless One. And from their worship He drew great power, both in His spirit and in His possession of men's hearts and minds. And men multiplied and spread across the whole world, and as they did, so His power grew until it rivalled that of the Guardians themselves.'

Again, Gulda stopped as if recalling some long-forgotten memory. She raised a cautionary finger and spoke in her normal voice.

'You mustn't think to judge these people, Hawklan. Sumeral wrought His damage always with reasoned and subtle argument. He narrowed men's vision, so that they could see only their own needs and desires. And seeing only these, they became discontented. He blunted their awareness of others – not just people, but plants, animals, everything. He made them forget their deep kinship, their reliance on and their need for all other things that were. He made them forget the joy of being, Hawklan, and knowing they'd lost something, people searched even more desperately for something to fill the emptiness He'd created.'

She leaned forward, and tapped her raised finger into the empty air. 'So more and more He showed them how to satisfy these needs and desires. But each gratification led only to more emptiness and to more desire. And each was always at the cost of some previous treasure for which they now felt nothing. I fancy after twenty years in Orthlund you'll find this hard to imagine, but animals were slaughtered utterly, forests wasted, mountains blasted, great tracts of land destroyed, even the air and the sea became foul with poisons.'

Hawklan lifted his hand to interrupt. At first Gulda had intoned her tale like some village storyteller. Her narrative was similar to many he had read in the past week, and he was prepared to hear old stories retold if that was what she wanted. But what was she saying now? She was right, he could not imagine such extremities, not least because, stripped of her storytelling lilt, the simple words seemed to fall on him like stinging hailstones.

'Gulda, I don't understand,' he said, his perplexity showing on his face. 'You're telling us an old fairy tale as if we were children –' He stopped abruptly as he saw the expression on her face. It was not the angry irritation or stern reproof that such a comment might have been expected to yield, but a terrible lonely sadness, as from an aching pain too deep to be reached by any solace. His eyes opened almost in horror as the healer in him touched on the edge of this torment, and a realisation dawned on him. Gulda saw it, and nodded her head slowly.

'Yes, Hawklan,' she said. 'You see correctly. This is no child's tale. It's the truth. I tell it like an old fireside lay because any other way needs my mind and my heart, and the pain of memory is too much for me.' Tears formed in her eyes but no convulsion shook her mouth or face.

Hawklan's mind washed to and fro like a pebble at the edge of a storm-tossed lake. For a moment he actually became dizzy and he put his hands to his temples to steady himself. Something was shaking his entire being. Here was this silly old woman telling him fairy tales, just as Andawyr had, when he needed answers to his many questions. He cursed himself for his weakness in hoping for so much from this strange creature.

And yet . . . And yet . . . *she* believed what she was saying, that was obvious. And . . . he believed it, too, even though reason railed against it. But . . .?

'How can you know it's true?' he asked at last.

Gulda looked at him and spoke simply and without hesitation. 'That's a tale for another telling, Hawklan. And probably not mine. Do you doubt me?'

Hawklan recoiled from the pain in her look as the bright blue eyes pierced him. This time, they too were filled with doubt, but such doubt that his own fretting of the last few weeks dwindled into insignificance.

Had she placed too much hope in a foolish empty-headed man who had some little skill in healing and who had perhaps stumbled by chance into the possession of an ancient and magical Castle?

For an instant he felt again her appalling despair and loneliness at the realisation that her long, aching journey might after all have to continue, and continue into who knew what distant darkness. Something in his mind shifted, like the dropping of the keystone into an arch, and the doubts and turmoil ceased.

He took her face between his two hand. 'I'm sorry, Gulda,' he said hesitantly. 'I didn't understand.'

She lifted her stick and placed it on the table, then she covered his hands with her own and for a moment closed her eyes.

'And I'm sorry I doubted you, Hawklan. For an instant I thought you were the wrong man and that I'd have to . . . But I see now your doubts were the last throes of your life with the Orthlundyn. It would be a sorry man indeed who wanted to leave what you've had here.'

Hawklan nodded slightly. 'Finish your story – your history,' he said gently.

Gulda smiled sadly and releasing Hawklan's hands recovered her stick. The mutual doubting had been cathartic. She continued her tale.

'Not everyone was seduced by His cunning though. Many remembered the tales of the Guardians handed down through the generations and saw Sumeral for what He was. They resisted Him.' She shook her head. 'There's many a tale there to bring joy and sadness to you. Many a tale.' Then she held up her hands as if she were clasping a sphere. 'Strangely, as those who opposed Him shrank in number, so their resistance hardened. And even among those under His sway, there were murmurs against Him when the degradation of the land and the seas became increasingly obvious.'

She leaned forward, nearing the crux of her tale. 'So, ever the master of originality, He created His most cunning and evil device . . . He taught His people war.'

She stretched out the word war, and it sounded like a death knell.

Gavor cocked his head on one side.

Gulda lapsed into her sonorous storyteller's voice again. 'He delved into the deepest pit of darkness that can be dug in men's minds and drew out wild-eyed, screaming war. "As you worship

Me, so you must worship this, My most mighty creation, for it alone can lead you to crush those who stand between you and the greatness that is yours by right".'

Hawklan looked at one of the window images brought into the Library by the mirror stones. Outside, storm clouds flew overhead, themselves like raging hordes.

Gulda became matter-of-fact again. 'With this He hoped to quell the murmurings of His own people, and destroy those who opposed Him. And for a while He was successful. But He'd overreached himself. The clamour and torment that only war can bring woke the Guardians.'

Gulda rested her head on her hand and shook it bitterly. 'Oh, Hawklan. There are so many terrible "ifs" in this tale. If the Guardians hadn't slept, if they'd wakened earlier or been less drowsy from their long sleep. If, if, if.'

Hawklan waited as the shadows of the clouds marched across the Library.

Gulda continued. 'Sumeral felt their waking, and He was afraid. His power equalled theirs, but He knew that to combat them directly would be to risk His own destruction, even if He were victorious. So it spurred Him to yet another evil deed.' A little of the storyteller's lilt returned. 'He took His three most terrible regents and filled them with secret knowledge so that they became the most powerful of all men, then He gave them immortality and bound them with ties unimaginable to become ever His servants.'

'The Uhriel,' said Hawklan softly. Gulda nodded.

'Creost,' said Hawklan.

'With power over the waters of the earth, to bind Enartion.'

'Dar Hastuin.'

'With power over the air and the sky, to bind Sphaeera.'

'And Oklar.'

Gulda paused. 'The greatest of them all. With power over the land and mountains, to bind Theowart.'

The words hung in the air like a chanted catechism.

'They it was who locked the Guardians in combat and tended to matters of earthly generalship leaving Sumeral to face Ethriss unhindered.'

Into Hawklan's mind came the tales of battles and glory that he had been reading about so recently. He felt a reluctant stir of excitement.

'Tell me about the war,' he said.

Gulda caught a note in his voice and looked at him for a long time without speaking, her eyes seeming to pierce into his very soul. Her face wrinkled into an expression of disgust and resignation, mingled with compassion and understanding.

'Hawklan, Sumeral and Ethriss fought on planes and in ways we can't begin to understand. But amongst *us*, each led mortal armies in human form.' She put her hand to her head. 'Dismiss from your mind all the rhetoric you've read about war – glittering arrays of armoured men, spear points shining in the sun, bronzed helmets, plumes nodding, brave fluttering flags and on and on. Fine poetry, but not truth. Such small good as comes from war is no more than a solitary star shining through the fog to a man lost in a barren wilderness. Heroism, honour, dignity – they happen only because Ethriss's children are infinitely adaptable and will strive eternally to survive, the wiser among them having regard for the needs of others. In the total sum these offerings are outweighed tenfold by the horrors that war works.

'Instead you should feel terror to loosen your bowels, know steel hacking beloved flesh, hooves trampling skulls into the blood-soaked mud. Years of creation gone in seconds. Know great areas of land blighted for generations, rivers choked with mutilated bodies, men suffocating under mounds of their dead and dying friends, men dying of disease and unspeakable wounds, dying without solace or comfort, far away from everything they love. Old people slaughtered, children maimed and wandering. That's war, Hawklan. No glory. No splendour.'

Hawklan bowed his head under this onslaught.

'But the real horror is worse,' Gulda continued. 'Not for nothing did I say war was Sumeral's most cunning and evil device. When Ethriss realised the truth, he wept.'

Hawklan looked at her uncertainly. 'What could be worse than what you've just described?' he asked.

Gulda seized his wrists. Again Hawklan wondered at the overwhelming strength of her grip.

'In any combat, be it between men or nations, only the

strongest and most ruthless can win, and they can win only by inflicting appalling losses on their opponents.' Tears ran down Gulda's face. Not petulant sobbing, but an overflow from some well deep within.

'When Sumeral launched war against His enemies, they scattered and fell in dismay and confusion, like chaff in the wind, totally ignorant of the nature of the terrible thing that was afflicting them. They'd have been swept out of existence had not Ethriss . . .'

'Taught them war,' said Hawklan softly. Andawyr's words at the Gretmearc returned to him: the Guardians had to teach Sumeral's evil to overcome it. Then Isloman's voice in the soft grey rain: you have to be worse than your enemy. Don't think otherwise or you'll die. And his own inexorable conclusion: we act to preserve ourselves. It's the most ancient of laws. Written deep into all living things.

Gulda nodded and released Hawklan's wrists. 'That's why Ethriss wept. He had to complete Sumeral's own work to defeat Him. He had to become a greater teacher of corruption than even Sumeral.'

Hawklan put his face in his hands as if to shut out his own thoughts as the logic of Gulda's tale swept all before it.

'Ethriss's self-reproach at his own sloth and tardiness is a burden none of us can imagine,' continued Gulda. 'The only leavening he could add to the horror of what he had to teach was that men should fight only to preserve what was theirs and not to impose their will on others. And that in victory they . . .'

'Should stay their hands from excess.' Hawklan finished the sentence.

Gulda looked at him, her head tilted slightly as if she had heard a distant sound. 'Yes,' she said. 'They should embrace compassion and eschew vengeance. Lonely and delicate flowers to grow amid such a harrowing. Nor did they always survive.'

The wind outside had dropped and the grey storm clouds hung solid and menacing overhead, like an army awaiting the order to advance, Hawklan thought. He sat up and looked around. Gavor was gazing transfixed at the lowering grey sky, occupied by who knew what thoughts. Gulda, pale and distressed from her long tale, but peculiarly triumphant, was wiping her eyes.

But Tirilen was sitting motionless, with her arms wrapped around herself and her head bowed low. Hawklan felt the fear radiating from her. She was trapped, like a child in a nightmare who, on waking, finds it is no dream.

Hawklan put out his arms and cradled her to him as he had done so many times when she had been a child. Though whether it was to console her or himself, he could not have said.

Chapter 22

'Why are we listening to this, Hawklan?' Tirilen said, looking reproachfully at Gulda. 'It's horrible. I don't believe it. People don't do things like that, nor ever did. It's just an old tale like those on the Gate.'

Hawklan made no reply, but held her close, until the woman in Tirilen could reassert herself over the young girl.

Gulda, woman to woman, was less gentle. 'It was no old tale that cut down your friends from Fyorlund and has brought half the countryside down on us for help, young lady,' she said harshly.

Hawklan winced at the tone, and Tirilen shivered then bridled. She pulled free from Hawklan and thrust her face forward angrily at Gulda. 'No,' she cried out, but her voice cracked with doubt. 'No. I won't believe it. I won't believe in fairy-tale monsters coming to life, and such nonsense. And how could you possibly know such things, you silly old –' She dropped her head abruptly, ashamed at her outburst. Fumbling with her hands in her lap she muttered an apology.

There was a flicker of impatience in Gulda's face, but Hawklan caught her eye and sent a plea for compassion.

'Tirilen,' Gulda said. 'This is hard for you, I know. But you're a healer of sorts, and you know there are times when reason fails. When you have to trust your intuition. To let yourself go. You have to enter into the truth of your charge's pain and accept it. Look at Hawklan and know the truth.'

Tirilen looked up as she was bidden and stared into Hawklan's face. It bore an expression of sad implacability. He had no words for her. She had a step into blackness before her and none could help her take it. She hesitated.

Gulda's voice spoke again. 'Hear the truth, Tirilen. Long ago, the world was once ravaged by a terrible evil. It may be that

that same evil has risen again and if it has then it will ravage the world once more unless we who see it act.'

Tirilen did not move, but continued to stare at Hawklan.

Gulda's tone became sterner. 'As for what and how I know, suffice it that I'm here now because of my folly. With good fortune, the Cadwanol may be here now because of their wisdom. More to the point are these two.' Her eyes passed over Hawklan and Gavor. 'Who can say who *they* are or why they're here now?'

'Hawklan,' said Tirilen softly, desperately, a faint pleading smile imploring him to say it was not true, that all would be as it was.

Still Hawklan had no words for her, though he felt the smile would break his heart.

'Mandrocs killed the High Guards, Tirilen. Then we in our turn killed Mandrocs.'

It was Gavor's voice, simple and clear, like his own black shadow. It broke the last thread restraining the girl and too-long-held tears burst out like a flood. Her hands flew to her face to cover its contortions and her body shook convulsively.

Hawklan knew that Tirilen's tears were not for the massive horrors of a long-dead past, nor the fear of its recurrence. They were for a more immediate loss, that of her erstwhile captors. Young men, full of life, who had been so apologetic and courteous even while holding her prisoner and who had been so cruelly destroyed.

Both he and Gulda breathed out softly. Each had feared that her grief might be restrained too long. Her tears were essential, as had been Hawklan's and Fel-Astian's in the forest. They must run their course freely now, so that Tirilen's natural strength and courage could carry her safely forward.

Hawklan turned towards the window image. Outside, as if in imitation of Tirilen's release, great raindrops were starting to fall out of the leaden sky.

After a while, Tirilen's sobbing stopped and she sat up and began to wipe her eyes with her sleeve in a most unladylike manner. Gavor fluttered up on to her shoulder.

Gulda took up her tale again.

Past its awful heart, she spoke long and easily into the

darkening day, telling of the generations of conflict that surged to and fro across the world as Ethriss and the Guardians sought to stay Sumeral's advance. Telling of Sumeral's continued corruption of men to form His great armies; and of His enslavement of others as workers; of His corruption of the gentle mountain-dwelling Mandreci into the barbarous Mandroc hordes; of Ethriss's formation of the Cadwanol, drawing the wisest men from all nations into a Great Order and giving them such of his wisdom and power as they could use to wage the battle on its many levels; and of the Great Alliance of Kings and Peoples that eventually swept Sumeral and the Uhriel up to their last stronghold in Derras Ustramel, the terrible fortress that rose out of Lake Kedrieth in the bleak fastness of Narsindal; and of the final fall of Sumeral and Derras Ustramel.

'For final they thought it was,' said Gulda. 'Sumeral's spirit was overcome by Ethriss, and His body was slain by Ethriss's guards. And with the fall of their Master, the Uhriel fell lifeless before the might of the Guardians.'

She sat pensive and unmoved by the victory she had just described.

'But the seeds of the Second Coming were sown,' said Hawklan, echoing Andawyr's words.

Gulda nodded. 'It would appear so,' she said. 'Though none had the sight, or perhaps the desire, to see it then. Except perhaps Ethriss. And he was gone.'

'Gone?' said Tirilen.

Gulda nodded again. Her storyteller's lilt returned. 'Ethriss was a great warrior. None could stand against him in combat, save perhaps Sumeral Himself. But he came unarmed to the Last Battle lest the preoccupation with the safety of his body should distract him from his true battle with Sumeral. An Iron Ring of Fyordyn High Guard protected him and Sumeral's hordes beat against them like waves against a cliff while he stood motionless, battling with Sumeral in ways we cannot understand. Then Sumeral, glorious and shining like the sun in His splendid armour, faltered at some unseen assault . . .'

She stopped abruptly as if some old memory had suddenly burst upon her, and her eyes filled with tears and ran freely down her face. For a moment she seemed to be struggling to speak, then she was free again. 'And missiles that had fallen from Him through all that terrible day now found their mark. He crashed from His steed pierced by a score of good Fyordyn arrows. But even as He fell, He loosed one final cast of His spear and struck down the defenceless Ethriss, who fell in the mêlée, unseen, save by one in that ring of defenders.'

Gulda fell silent again for a while and sat motionless.

'When the battle was over, his body was nowhere to be found,' she said eventually. 'There was no sign of him – nor of Sumeral and the Uhriel. There were rumours that the Mandrocs had hidden the bodies of the Uhriel deep in their caves and that the body of Sumeral was lost in Lake Kedrieth when the Guardians exerted their last strength and tumbled Derras Ustramel into ruins, but . . .' She shrugged. 'There was a peace to be made. A terrible price had been paid in the death of Ethriss, but the evil was destroyed, it was believed, and much was to be done. The world was a sorry place.'

Her face softened. 'The Great Alliance became a Great Congress, and pronounced wisely. They remembered Ethriss's injunction to stay their hands from excess in victory. Those nations of men that had been bound or misled by Sumeral were freed and no acts of vengeance were taken, or few, at any rate. Only the poor Mandrocs proved irredeemable. They were sentenced to remain forever in Narsindal. The Fyordyn were given the land you now call Fyorlund, and swore a sacred oath to maintain an eternal vigil over Narsindal and to protect the blessed land of Orthlund to the south. The members of the Cadwanol retired to their caves at the southern end of the Pass of Elewart to study and increase their knowledge, and also to protect the only other exit from Narsindal. And all the other armies returned whence they'd come, to gather up the threads of their old lives.'

Gulda slapped her knees gently and, sitting up straight, smiled. 'It was the start of the Golden Age, Hawklan. Ethriss was gone and the Guardians slept, exhausted from their own dreadful toils against the Uhriel, but the Cadwanol and Ethriss's Kings did due honour to them in their deeds. Fine happy times.'

'But?' Hawklan anticipated.

Gulda smiled ruefully. 'It faded,' she said simply. 'No race on earth had escaped the corruption, taught either by Sumeral or by Ethriss. Slowly it bred ignorance and delight in ignorance, then discontent, until the world is as it is today. Peaceful enough, but a shadow of its former state, and heading steadily towards the darkness. We've all fallen into slothful habits, Hawklan. Telling this old tale again today has made me remember . . .' She stopped and her blue eyes locked Hawklan's gaze again. 'I can see now that Sumeral could well rise a second time. So many "ifs" again. If Ethriss had not been slain; if Sumeral's body hadn't been lost . . . or taken.' She shrugged and fell silent.

Gulda's tale finished, Hawklan stood up quietly and stretched himself. Taking a piece of bread from the tray he sat on the edge of the table next to her.

'All of which leaves us where?' he said softly.

She looked up at him. 'It leaves you a little nearer the truth, which is where you needed to be. It'll help in whatever decisions we have to make.'

'But I still don't know who I am,' said Hawklan. 'Or who I was, or why this Dan-Tor thinks I'm so important. Come to that, who is Dan-Tor?'

Gulda looked at him enigmatically. 'Andawyr said he thought you were Ethriss himself, didn't he?'

Hawklan waved a dismissive hand. 'Andawyr was very disturbed. What happened in that pavilion had shaken him badly.'

Gulda nodded understandingly, but persisted. 'Just as Sumeral slept and has seemingly been wakened, so Ethriss may sleep somewhere in human form. And he too can be wakened. If I judge Sumeral truly, I fear He may have been awake a long time, spreading His corruption silently while His agents searched for Ethriss's sleeping form so that it could be destroyed or bound.'

Hawklan felt momentarily disorientated. 'This is nonsense, Gulda,' he said, his voice suddenly harsh and angry. 'Surely I'd know if I were Ethriss? An all-powerful . . . Guardian from the beginning of Creation.'

Gulda flinched a little, but offered him no resistance. 'Consider, Hawklan. You arrive mysteriously in Orthlund bearing the Key and the Word to open Anderras Darion, Ethriss's greatest fortress. You know the Castle. You have great skill in healing and you know the speech of animals, Ethriss's Black Sword seeks you out.' She paused, still looking at him penetratingly. 'Once the Orthlundyn were a great and noble people. Their sacrifice was appalling, but it sounded the beginning of Sumeral's doom. It's said that as the last of their Princes fell before His army, Ethriss swept him from the field of battle and locked him in a deep sleep, to waken only when the need of Orthlund cried out again.'

Hawklan's eyes narrowed. 'Are you telling me now that I might be such a man?' he said.

Gulda pursed her lips. 'Possibly,' she said, laying a hand on his arm. 'But that Dan-Tor is an agent of Sumeral is beyond doubt, and maybe even . . . well, no matter. But had he thought you just an ancient Prince awakened in some way by the arising of Sumeral, he'd have destroyed you with barely a thought, and precious little effort. But he didn't. He lured you hither and thither with great caution. He used the Old Power very carefully when he tried to bind you at the Gretmearc, and when that failed he didn't risk using it again. Instead he lured you northwards using your simple human affection for Tirilen.'

Hawklan held her gaze.

'Dan-Tor thinks you're Ethriss,' she said quietly.

'But who do *you* think I am?' Hawklan ventured after a moment.

'Gulda eyed him narrowly. 'Ethriss alone knows, my lad,' she said abruptly. 'And it doesn't matter. Whoever you are, I've no power to stir you. You must go to the Cadwanol as Andawyr said. Give them his message and let them decide who you are. He's in great danger.'

She leaned forward. 'In the meantime. You're Hawklan. Hawklan the healer. An ordinary man, heir to all the ills of mortal flesh, and one chosen by the Orthlundyn to advise them.' Then, more urgently, 'From now on you must search for ever more knowledge and you must be forever on your guard. You've already found that your body has resources of which you were unaware. Don't be afraid of them. You'll need them and more. It's a terrible and relentless predator that's hunting you, Hawklan.'

'She hesitated. 'In the end, you'll have to face him in his lair to free yourself.'

Chapter 23

Hawklan was uncertain how the gathered Orthlundyn would respond to the tale that he now had to tell them. He knew they were not a people overly given to studying history and lore, except as it pertained to their particular crafts, and he feared they would laugh him to scorn in their gentle way.

Gulda however had no such qualms. 'Don't be a jackass,' she snapped impatiently. 'Have you learned nothing about them in your twenty years here? Look at their carvings . . . or any of their other work. Look at the way they live, the way they tend the soil, everything. They'll accept anything once they feel it's truth.'

Hawklan still hesitated and Gulda softened a little. 'Hawklan,' she said resignedly, 'they're an exceptional people. Believe me. I've been amongst many races. No amount of fear of me or respect for you would make them accept even the lightest falsehood, but they'll accept *any* truth, however bleak. Tell them. You'll see.'

So, the next day, Hawklan told them, omitting only the conjectures about his own history. Sitting around on the tiered seats of a spacious circular hall, the Orthlundyn listened silently and respectfully. Small torches hidden in the sweeping ceiling brightened the gloom that a leaden-clouded sky brought in through the colonnaded windows, but Hawklan felt another lightening in the atmosphere as his tale unfolded, just as he had when Isloman had told the villagers about the battle with the Mandrocs.

They feel the ill, but it's their ignorance of its cause that disturbs them, he thought. They not only accept the truth, they *need* it. Twenty years is a long time to be so blind.

The old man from Wosod Heath was called Aynthinn and he seemed to have become the spokesman for most of the people there. He shook his head sadly when Hawklan had finished. 'These are dark and fearful things you tell us, Hawklan. The Second Coming of the Creator of Evil; a creature that hitherto we knew only in our children's tales. I doubt any but you could have told us this and I can see it's not been easy for you. Still, the truth of your telling is apparent, and for some of us, the older ones in particular, it answers some long unspoken questions. I remember as a boy, watching my grandfather working.'

Hawklan looked anxiously at Gulda, nervous that the old man was about to ramble off into some protracted reminiscence. Gulda raised her hand slightly to indicate he should be patient.

'I can see him now as clearly as if it were yesterday. Then I look at . . .' he cast around the room for a moment, 'Isloman for example.' He pointed to the Carver, who returned him a gaze of mild suspicion. 'Isloman's the finest carver we have. No one disputes that. What happened to him in Riddin twenty years ago somehow transformed his work and set him above us all. But it's not much better than my grandfather's work, and it's less than most of what our forebears have left us.'

He lapsed briefly into the Carver's argot apparently to explain this remark further, causing both Hawklan and Gulda to lean forward anxiously. Seeing their reaction, the old man apologised.

'I'm sorry, my friends,' he said, 'I forgot myself. However, accept my judgement. Our work has deteriorated through the years. It has become coarser, more impatient, as if we were hurrying towards something. We live in the shadow of those who went before when we should have learnt their lessons and moved forward.'

He paused and looked around the room. 'Ironically, it's been particularly apparent over the last few days. Staying here, among all this.' He pointed to the carvings and pictures covering the ceilings and walls of the circular hall. 'This is something we've all known, but we always seem to avoid talking about it. It's not easy. It's a subtle, elusive thing. But now, let me bring out from the shadow what should be said.'

His voice became strong, belying his frail appearance. 'Consider, my friends. We can't deny our own failings, but doesn't even the land seem to bruise more easily under our feet? Our food grow more reluctantly? Our animals come less close?'

There was an uncomfortable silence in the hall, but no one ventured to disagree with him. Then, very quietly, but very clearly, his words hanging in the waiting air:

'Is not the Great Harmony itself less sure?'

Silence.

'My friends, only a most awesome power could so disturb the Great Harmony.'

With these words the tension in the hall seemed almost to vanish and Hawklan saw many of the listening people nodding their heads in agreement.

Aynthinn turned to Hawklan. 'We've been losing our sight for many years, Hawklan,' he said. 'Now, with your dark news, you bring perhaps a little light to etch out our faults more clearly for us.' He chuckled. 'Subtle shadow lore, yours, outlander. Subtle.' And he looked round the hall, his old face wrinkling into an infectious smile that spread round his audience like a ripple of wind over a cornfield. Chuckling again, he said. 'Forgive us, Hawklan. Carver's humour. Now you must tell us what to do.'

Hawklan's hands came up in a gesture of refusal. 'No, no, Aynthinn,' he said. 'I'll tell no one what to do. We'll all talk and then we'll decide what to do. I'll not be bound by you, nor will I allow you to be bound by me. Whatever's to be faced, we'll face together. None can pass his responsibility to another.' This last remark was said with some sternness, and Aynthinn raised both his hands slightly in acceptance.

As the day wore on, the storm clouds dispersed, though without the redeeming freshness of a downpour the air outside was laden with a lingering sense of regret. It did not, however, linger in the high-ceilinged hall, and with new-found loquaciousness the Orthlundyn talked and talked.

Hawklan found himself hard pressed to get a word in, and he was forced to smile at his fear that they might follow him blindly.

Gulda, though, was silent by choice, her eyes flitting from one speaker to the next in relentless scrutiny. Later, Hawklan learned she was ranking them in order of reliability with judgements that were swift, ruthless and invariably accurate. Tapping her temple with a purposeful finger, she said: 'They're in here. Labelled. "Duffers", "Windbags", "Incompetents", etc.'

The setting sun was throwing its red dusty light through a few remaining black strands of cloud when the meeting finally ended. The gathering had roamed over many topics and through many moods, but for all their trust in Hawklan, implicitly sustained by Gulda's buttressing presence, the Orthlundyn still felt the dearth of information. Rock song as they called it.

'We can't know what to do until we see more clearly what's happening,' they concluded. 'And, as the problem stems from Fyorlund, that's where we must go for information.'

Hawklan realised that this conclusion had been more or less inevitable, but it placed him in a dilemma. On the one hand, he wanted to go to Fyorlund and find this tinker Lord who had hounded him so and wrought such havoc amongst his friends. But, equally, he wanted to seek out the Cadwanol to give them Andawyr's message and perhaps learn his true identity.

Gulda saw the indecision in his face but offered no counsel.

Finally he decided he would ride to Fyorlund for the Orthlundyn. The threat from there was tangible and bloody. He had seen it with his own eyes. The threat mooted by Andawyr was what? No more than a dream? It might be more, he knew, but he would have to live with his unease. Besides, the healer in him *had* to move to where it felt the centre of the ill. He had little real choice.

His decision made, Hawklan spoke out against a formal delegation. 'If all the King's new officers are such as we encountered, then I doubt that reasoned discourse will yield much. In fact I think that a formal delegation might well be in some danger.'

Eventually it was agreed that he and Isloman would retrace their recent journey northwards and continue it cautiously into Fyorlund as 'watchful travellers'. Gavor would act as messenger should they be detained in any way, and horses and riders would be posted along the road for the rapid carrying of the news back to Pedhavin, and thence through the land.

Aynthinn had reservations about such secrecy and prevailed

upon Hawklan to carry with him a document which would enable him to speak for all the Orthlundyn if need arose. Reluctantly, Hawklan agreed.

The Elders departed in a mood almost of excitement, full of promises to take the advice Gulda had given to Hawklan, namely, to learn their history and their lore. Gulda made no comment on this, but her expression was eloquent. Aynthinn, however, conceded everything.

'Gulda. Our lack of curiosity is a willingness to accept ignorance. We see that now. It must end. We must apply ourselves to the knowledge of our past as we apply ourselves to our crafts.'

Gulda's look of withering doubt faltered slightly at Aynthinn's tone and the old man took the advantage with a fleetness that made Hawklan look away to hide a smile. 'You *will* help us, won't you, Gulda?' he asked.

Somewhat dourly, Loman agreed to remain in Anderras Darion to tend to the needs of the Elders and anyone else who came to study. Though Hawklan sensed some relief in the smith that he would thus be able to remain near to his daughter.

Later, however, Hawklan sought him out and, together with Isloman, they strolled idly round the Castle grounds. A soft warm breeze carried the scent of the mountains and a hint of the coming summer heat. High above them, visible in the moonless sky only where they hid the stars, soared the towers and spires of the Castle. To the keen ear, night birds could be heard gliding through the quiet air, but the darkness of Anderras Darion was the darkness of comfort and rest, not menace, and the night was undisturbed by the shrieks of dying prey. Occasionally, clear in the stillness, a dog would bark, or a door close, or a small bud of distant laughter would bloom and fade.

'I appreciate that it's frustrating staying here to look after these people,' said Hawklan to Loman, his voice soft in the darkness. 'But you know the Castle better than anyone, and what the Elders will be doing will be important. However . . .' his voice fell almost to a whisper, 'there's another reason why I want you here.'

Loman looked at him but did not speak.

Hawklan turned to Isloman to ensure he was included in the conversation. 'When the messengers go out tomorrow to tell the villages what's been discussed and decided here, I want you to send private letters to those men who fought with you in the Morlider War. Ask them to come here, quietly, but quickly.'

The starlight caught the glimmer of a smile on Loman's face. He nodded, though still did not speak.

'When you've all finished your reminiscences, I want you to set down everything you can remember about the way the war was fought. Weapons, dispositions of men, tactics, supplies, command structures . . . everything.'

Isloman chuckled, and Loman's smile broadened. Hawklan looked at both of them quizzically.

'I think you must have eaten some of those books, Hawklan,' said Isloman. 'Dispositions, command structures indeed.' His tone was full of mock disparagement and Loman laughed out loud in agreement. For an instant Hawklan felt inclined to be indignant but the mood passed almost immediately and he smiled.

'All right, all right, you two seasoned warriors. Have your fun.' Then poking Loman in the chest with his forefinger, 'But get your old comrades in arms here and get the job done. Then you can take my place in the Library and start looking for all the books you can find on the same subjects. Then see if you feel like laughing.'

His tone became more serious. 'Aynthinn spoke as only the very wise and the very foolish can. He told us the obvious. He showed us what was in front of our faces. We must learn from the experiences of the past. There's no point in relearning bitter old lessons the hard way. It's not a rule confined to carving. I doubt any of those High Guards ever lifted a sword in anger before, but they were trained and disciplined, and they took a considerable toll of those Mandrocs. We've none like that if we should ever need them.'

'You don't seriously think we'll need to defend ourselves like that, do you?' said Isloman anxiously.

Hawklan shrugged. 'I've no idea,' he said. 'But misled though they might have been, those High Guards came deep into Orthlund for no good cause, and those Mandrocs marched in, in armed force, prepared to commit murder. Only through good luck did we stop the one, and we could do nothing about the other. I think it'd be unwise to note those two facts and then imagine it couldn't happen again.'

He started up one of the broad stairways that led up the main wall. The two brothers followed him in silence.

'After the Morlider War, we want nothing to do with fighting, Hawklan,' said Loman unequivocally.

Hawklan stopped and, turning round, looked down at them. 'I know,' he said. 'I understand. But we may not have a choice. Sometimes people's best endeavours can't prevent it. You wouldn't have spent part of your youth in Riddin doing what you did had it been otherwise, would you?'

No answer coming, he turned round again and continued slowly up the stairs.

'Hawklan, you're not thinking about training an army, are you?' said Isloman.

The words seemed to hover in the soft night air, as if fearful of spreading their message.

'I don't know what I'm thinking about, Isloman,' said Hawklan. 'But consider. If they'd wished to, those Mandrocs could've swept through a dozen villages before anyone knew what was happening. And then what resistance could we have made?' He stopped on a landing where the stairway met one of the buttresses to the Great Gate. A sudden surge of anger rose up inside him and with a grimace he drove his fist desperately into the palm of his hand. 'None,' he almost shouted.

Loman and Isloman both started at the unexpected violence of this ejaculation.

Hawklan swung his arm in a horizontal cutting movement. 'None at all. The only thing that would've stopped those Mandrocs sweeping over the entire country in a matter of days is *fatigue*.' He slumped against the wall, frowning.

Neither Loman nor Isloman seemed inclined to argue this statement. There was little point. Hawklan was right, even though his implied conclusion left them uncomfortable. Isloman ran his big hand over the stonework tenderly, seeking solace in its ancient crafting.

'Aynthinn was right,' he said. 'We must have been going

downhill for generations. It's all around us in this Castle. We should be better than our ancestors, not worse. Whether we've lost something or whether it's been stolen doesn't really matter, does it? Somewhere we've betrayed a trust. We've let the old crafts deteriorate to the point where even the Great Harmony suffers. And, now, ill things come in from the outside and we're unprepared.' He sat down slowly on the steps and rested his head against the wall.

The three men remained there for a long time, each absorbed in his own thoughts. Hawklan leaning against the buttress, arms folded and looking moodily downwards; Isloman leaning against the wall; and Loman leaning over the parapet staring out over the Castle grounds in the darkness below.

Somewhere in the distance there was a brief stir of voices and a door was opened and closed.

Hawklan looked up along the stairway, faintly visible in the starlight. Over him the main wall of Anderras Darion loomed protectively. He grimaced again at the unforgiving truth of his reasoning.

'We've no alternative, have we?' he said.

The two brothers shook their heads.

Loman spoke. 'We'll remember and relearn all our old "skills", Hawklan.' There was bitterness in his voice. 'And we'll learn from such others as we can find in the Library, then . . .' he turned round and looked at Hawklan, 'then we'll teach them to . . . to everyone.'

'Hawklan nodded, and echoed their thoughts. 'Yes, I know,' he said. 'There's a wrongness in all this. I can't fault our conclusions in the light of what's happened. There *is* no alternative. But,' he shook his head, 'I can't escape the feeling that the very existence of armed power in Orthlund may in itself destroy the Great Harmony, or that it may somehow attract those it's meant to deter.'

Chapter 24

As Loman stepped out of the maze of ornate columns that guarded the Armoury, he turned round and, with arm extended, snapped his fingers into the maze. It was a childish trick he indulged in occasionally, for the snap of his fingers was deliberately off the path through the maze, and the sounds of its increasing echoes swirled round and round until they surged thunderously against the unseen bounds set by the columns, like an enraged animal crashing against the bars of its cage.

He shook his head at his own whimsy and strode off purposefully down one of the long aisles of the Armoury towards the great mound of weapons. The mysterious appearance of Ethriss's Black Sword had unsettled him more than he was prepared to admit. Had he not known this place intimately for some twenty years? A blade like that could not have lain hidden from him. And yet . . .?

Thus, since his return to the Castle with Tirilen, he had haunted the Armoury, trying to view it with a newer eye and carrying with him a vague compulsion that there was something he should be doing. He had little doubt that the metal was speaking to him but he did not seem to be able to hear it clearly.

His subsequent discovery of the small black blades that became Gavor's fighting spurs unsettled him even further, and the vague compulsion became almost an obsession. Repeatedly now, he cast his eye over the great mound of weapons, wondering what other mysteries it was concealing from him. But everything seemed to be as it had been since he first followed the tall strange outlander into this stronghold twenty or so years ago and stood open-mouthed amid the harvest-field rows of points and edges glittering in a bright summer sun.

Reaching the mound, he stood there once again on an uneasy

vigil all too aware that the familiarity around him still persisted in declaiming itself changed.

'Loman?'

The voice behind him drew his mind from its reverie, and air into his lungs in one heart-jolting blow. He spun round, eyes wide, his mind encompassing uncountable numbers of alternatives and his body incapable of facing any of them.

Gulda raised an eyebrow at this sudden flurry.

Loman finally succeeded in gaining control of his jaw and raised his hand to point in the direction of the distant entrance.

'Memsa,' he demanded, 'how did you get in here? Through the columns . . .'

Gulda brought her stick up and placed the end of it against the smith's stomach. 'I'm looking for Ethriss's bow, young Loman, where is it?'

Loman continued pointing for a moment and then lowered his hand resignedly. So far, Gulda had met questions about her knowledge of Anderras Darion by simply ignoring them. A prod from the stick focused his attention again. Better head for safer ground.

'The bows are over there,' he said brusquely, pointing now to a nearby rack. Gulda clicked her tongue impatiently and levering Loman to one side with her stick walked in the opposite direction.

'Don't clench your fists at me, young man,' she said as she passed. Loman felt a rumbling growl forming inside him and quickly cleared his throat.

Gulda was muttering to herself. 'Now let me see . . . so long ago.' Her hand came to her chin pensively and the great nose twitched as if scenting out quarry. Then she did a brief mime, head bowed, eyes closed and face earnest. Her hands pointed forward, as if marking out some earlier entry she had once made into the Armoury, then they flicked hither and thither, tracing her old route; sometimes decisively, followed by a flick of confirmation; and sometimes hesitantly, followed by a palmy wave to expunge the error. Finally she arrived.

'That's it,' she said, opening her eyes. 'I'll swear to it.' And off she went, Loman trudging behind suspiciously. Eventually they stopped in front of one of the ornately painted wall carvings that decorated those walls of the Armoury that contained no weapon racks.

'Yes,' she said, nodding triumphantly. 'Here it is.'

Loman looked at the picture and then at her. 'It was a picture of the bow you were looking for, was it?' he asked uncertainly, looking at the vivid battle scene portrayed in front of him. A faint smile lit up Gulda's face and she shook her head.

'No, Loman,' she said. 'I wanted this.' And reaching her hand forward into the strange perspective of the carving, she took hold of a black bow held by one of the distant figures, and lifted it out reverently.

Loman was well used to the complexity and distortion of distance inherent in all Orthlundyn carving but, in spite of himself, he found his mouth dropping open. Before he could recover himself fully, Gulda placed the now man-sized bow gently in his hands.

'Hawklan tells me you've turned into a passable smith, young Loman, for all your earlier ways.' She eyed him significantly. 'What do you make of that?' But Loman made no reply. As with the sword, the first touch of the bow had plunged him into another world, and his whole body seemed to be straining to ring out praises for the incredible artifact he was holding, even though such praises could not begin to measure its worth. After a timeless moment, he returned the bow to Gulda.

'It's beyond words,' he said in a hoarse whisper. 'Like the Black Sword. Made by the same hand and in the same manner.' He closed his eyes and swayed slightly. Gulda watched him closely. 'I can't handle work like that too much, it's too . . . daunting.'

Gulda seemed satisfied. 'There's some hope for you then,' she grunted. 'And for the Orthlundyn.'

Loman slowly recovered. 'I've never seen a metal bow before,' he said. 'The bows in here are all of wood.'

'Could you make one?' Gulda asked.

Loman was grateful for the commonplace question. It kept his mind from soaring uncontrollably after the perfection he had just held. 'Not like that,' he said hastily.

'Of course not,' came an unusually sympathetic reply. 'But could you make a metal bow?'

Loman pursed his lips. 'I suppose so,' he said. 'I've never thought about it.'

'Well think about it now,' said Gulda. 'And quickly. I want to see what you can do.' A thought occurred to her. 'But start with some arrows. I've no idea where Ethriss's arrows are, if there were any left, and Hawklan can't go wandering off with a bow and no arrows.'

'Hawklan?' said Loman in surprise. 'What does Hawklan want with a bow? He's never handled one in his life.'

'In the last twenty years you mean,' said Gulda bluntly.

Loman nodded unhappily. That was true of course. Hawklan had never handled a sword either, but Isloman had told him how he had used it against the Mandrocs. And he himself would not soon forget how Hawklan had laid out the two High Guards so effortlessly when they had burst into Jaldaric's tent. Hawklan was an enigma. Loman looked intently at Gulda. So was she.

'I'm no weapons maker,' he said suddenly.

Gulda brandished the bow. 'Neither was the maker of this,' she said fiercely. 'But circumstances gave him no choice, and he learned. As you will.'

Her tone brooked no argument but, in any case, the idea intrigued the craftsman in Loman sufficiently to overcome any qualms he might have about the matter. After all, he had seen men killed with rocks and branches and all manner of innocuous articles seized casually in the heat of battle, just as he had seen works of great beauty engraved on the shafts and blades of swords and axes. And hadn't he seen appalling accidents occur with innocent farm implements that he had made? He knew well enough that the word weapon was vested in an object by the use to which it was put, not by the intention of its maker.

'Very well,' he said. 'But I can't make anything worthy of that bow.'

'Make what you can, Loman,' Gulda replied. 'It will be truer than most, and the bow won't spurn it.'

On their way out of the Armoury, they passed the great mound again. Gulda cast a baleful eye over it. 'And you can start tidying that lot up,' she said, jerking her thumb towards it. 'You're going to need them.'

Loman looked aghast at the towering pile.

Gulda forestalled his protest. 'They're no good in here and

there's precious little point in training people to fight if they've nothing to fight with, is there?'

Hawklan said little about how the Orthlundyn should be prepared and trained.

'They're your people, Loman,' he said. 'And you and your friends know more about practical fighting than I do. With that, and the Library and Gulda, there's nothing I can add.' But he nodded approvingly as he saw Loman supervising the removal of the weapons from the Armoury, and his very presence seemed to sustain their efforts.

Thus the day of Hawklan's departure for Fyorlund dawned darkly for Loman and the others despite the promise it held of bright summer.

Uncertain himself, Hawklan sought solace in repeating what he had already discussed at length with his friends. 'We'll need people strong and flexible in mind and body, Loman,' he said as he made final adjustments to Serian's harness. 'Teach them every skill you know in fighting and surviving, and then teach them they must improve themselves.'

'They're Carvers, Hawklan,' replied Loman patiently. 'They know that already.' A frown clouded his face.

Hawklan looked at him. 'I know,' he said. 'How can any of us find comfort in this, Loman, but what else can we do? At least having a tool on your bench gives you choices.'

The remark brought an unexpected response. 'Yes, but I've never had a tool on my bench that I haven't used eventually.'

Hawklan turned and looked northward. 'I've no answer, Loman, you know that. Having some choice is still better than having none, and all choices, hard or easy, carry responsibility. Having seen what we've seen and learned what we've learned can we do anything other than tell the people the truth and teach them what we can?'

Loman bowed his head. He had not meant to bring his unease to this difficult parting.

Hawklan put his hands on the Smith's solid shoulders. 'Don't worry, Loman. It'll be a far worse day for all of us when we don't concern ourselves with these problems. And worse yet if we ever convince ourselves we've found a simple answer.'

And with that, and brief affectionate farewells to Tirilen and Gulda and the others gathered there, Isloman and Hawklan rode off along the steep winding road leading down from Anderras Darion.

Loman watched them for a long time, until eventually they shimmered and disappeared into the early morning haze. A faint cry high above him drew his attention upwards to a tiny black dot which had just floated from one of the towers. Loman raised a hand in salute, and Gavor dropped and spun over and over in acknowledgement. Knowing Gavor's mischievous temperament, Loman took a judicious pace backwards more into the lee of the Castle wall, but the solemnity of the moment must have infected Gavor, also, for nothing more unsavoury fell to earth than an iridescent black feather. Loman picked it up and examined it thoughtfully before handing it to Tirilen and turning back to the Castle. Tirilen wiped her eyes, sniffed and then, fumbling with a brooch, fixed the feather behind it. Its blackness seemed even darker against her white gown and, satisfied with her work, she turned and followed her father through the wicket gate.

Gulda remained. A tiny black dot dwarfed by the Castle wall and the Great Gate. For a long time she stared into the misty distance as if she could still see Hawklan and Isloman wending their way along the road until, with a grunt, she too turned and stumped resolutely into the Castle.

Strangely, Hawklan had felt impelled to ask Gulda if she wished to accompany them to Fyorlund. She had shown no surprise at the question but had not answered for some time. Instead she questioned Hawklan about Dan-Tor again. Hawklan told her once more what little he knew. 'According to Jaldaric he's some kind of adviser to their King. *The* adviser in fact.'

'Yes, yes, I know all that,' Gulda replied impatiently. 'I want to know what he looks . . .' She paused. 'This King's ill, you say?' Hawklan nodded. 'And has been ever since this Dan-Tor arrived?'

Hawklan nodded again. 'Yes, I'm sure Jaldaric said something like that. The man's not popular with everyone as far as I could gather. He's changed many of their traditional ways, and caused a lot of upheaval. Apparently many people think his influence over the King is excessive and pernicious.'

Gulda digested this in silence for a while. 'And what does he look like?' she said, reverting to her earlier enquiry. Hawklan described the twitching figure of the tinker as well as he could.

'If we stand him upright and still, what would he look like then?' Gulda asked when he had finished.

Hawklan thought for a moment. 'Tall, very tall. Thin. Long brown wrinkled face. Gloomy-looking except when he smiles, then he's got bright white teeth.'

Gulda turned away from him suddenly and pulled her hood forward. Hawklan could hear her breathing nervously. 'Yes,' she said very softly after a while. Her voice was strained.

'Do you know him?' Hawklan asked, incredulous.

'Never mind.' Hawklan started; Gulda's voice was like the closing of a steel trap. Then, more gently, 'I won't come with you, Hawklan. I'm afraid this burden is yours alone. I'm not . . . strong enough yet. Too long doing too little.'

Hawklan tried to pursue the matter further but Gulda waved his questions to silence. 'Just you remember that this man's dangerous,' she said, her face still averted. 'Unbelievably dangerous. He's not what he seems. Be very careful. *Very* careful. You'll need your every resource. There's no limit to his treachery, his cunning, and his knowledge of ancient skills.'

After Hawklan had left, Gulda seemed intent on making up for doing too little for too long and, to Loman, she seemed to fill the Castle as much as all the other visitors put together. She took charge of all the new arrivals, told them in detail what had happened, what was happening, and why. She worked with Loman and the other Morlider veterans on training programmes and co-ordinated their work to minimise duplication of effort. Then, continuing the work she had begun at the first meeting of the Elders, she ruthlessly graded the arrivals to ensure that they received the most appropriate training. Loman was impressed, not only with her tireless efficiency, but with what he considered to be a totally uncharacteristic diplomacy.

For his own part, he found himself studying ancient volumes on military tactics and strategy, his earlier repugnance being grudgingly replaced by satisfaction at the acquisition of new knowledge. He began walking about the Castle, looking at it with a new eye, seeing features in its design and location that added to his appreciation of its original creators. Something he would not have thought possible only weeks earlier. He studied weaponry also, but here with the relentless eye of a Master Craftsman. And he was pleased to the point of smugness when he found that while he could not equal the craftsmanship of most of the weapons from the Armoury, he was satisfied that he could improve their design.

Not that his studying allowed him to escape the rigours of his own training programmes, and in the early days he was frequently to be found discreetly seeking the ministrations of his daughter. Massively strong he might be, but his flexibility and agility left a great deal to be desired, and his striving to attain the standards set by younger and more pliable souls resulted in his acquiring a great many unusual pains.

Tirilen was sympathetic and helpful, but she lacked the detachment she possessed with her other charges.

'You giggling and saying "Poor old soul" isn't helping,' he was obliged to say on more than one occasion. 'Yes, Papa,' she would smirk, driving her fingers into his ribs.

Like everyone else, Tirilen too was kept busy by the changed circumstances in the Castle. Her long blonde hair was invariably swept back and held by a simple ribbon, and her white robe was replaced by a practical grass-green one, though its lapel was still adorned by Gavor's black feather. Bumps, bruises, cuts, scratches, sprains, fractures, aches and pains of every kind paraded in front of her daily, borne with varying degrees of dignity and stoicism, but the more she treated the more she glowed. The worried and the anxious she delegated to Gulda's tender mercies, rightly judging her better suited for dealing with such problems. 'No mithered middle-aged farmer is going to take any notice of me, is he?' she declared.

Not that she was without concerns herself. She knew her father was ever alert in the Armoury for some glittering black relic of Ethriss, and that the absence of the bow and sword in which he had seen such perfection disturbed him in some subtle fashion which was totally beyond her ability to reach.

Following her own advice, she finally confided in Gulda.

'Don't be afraid,' said the old woman. 'You're Orthlundyn. You understand really. Your father's waking, like many others round here. Just the touch of those weapons has taught him so much. Look.' She clumped around her spartan room and returned with a long black arrow which she held up for Tirilen's inspection. 'This was only your father's first attempt. The ones Hawklan took with him were better yet.'

Tirilen knew enough about her father's work to know that the arrow, for all its simplicity, was probably better than anything he had ever made before, but the bright barbed killing points brought confusion to her face.

Gulda put an arm around her shoulder. 'The quality of his craft is a measure of a man's striving for greater understanding. In this understanding, terrible needs are sometimes seen, Tirilen. Needs which will destroy if they aren't faced and answered. Your father's work answers them in his way. This . . .' she tapped the arrow gently, 'is an act of faith by him. Faith in the rightness of the truth he sees. Faith in Hawklan as the man who can use this bitter gift wisely to answer those needs that he alone can see.'

'I don't understand,' said Tirilen.

Gulda embraced her. 'I doubt any of us do,' she said. 'At the end of our reasoning there's only trust and faith.'

Chapter 25

Loman stopped abruptly as he strode out along the broad curving corridor. 'What's the rush, man?' he muttered to himself. 'What's the rush?' There was so much to do these days. But he didn't have to do it all at full tilt, did he?

Satisfied with his own answer he prescribed himself a brief pause in the sun-laden air and, sitting down on a low window-sill, he leaned back against the warm stone and closed his eyes.

Anderras Darion had become the focus of Orthlund. People were coming to it from all over the country. Yet there was ample room for them all. Loman wondered again what kind of people had built such a place, and why, and how many it once might have held. It seemed as though it could hold the entire population of Orthlund and still feel spacious and empty. For all his familiarity with it, Anderras Darion was indeed a mysterious and wonderful place.

In all his years as Castellan, scarcely a day had passed when he did not find some new wonder. Sometimes it would be tiny – a small carving or piece of metalwork, some exquisite miniature. At others it had been unbelievably large. Several times he had found entire chambers, and the feeling was always with him that there were many still to be found. In fact, the feeling was almost that they were hiding from him playfully.

Now, the presence of so many other people seemed to be accelerating this rate of discovery. There was a liveliness about the place that he had never known before. Voices, laughing, earnest, loud and secretive, whispered and rattled along corridors that for many years had known only the occasional soft footstep, until they floated expansively into empty halls and up into hidden crannies and crevices to fade into the Castle's ancient calm. The Castle soaked up the many new sounds like the sands of the parched southlands soaked up rain and, like a great creature waking cell by cell, it seemed to take them as nourishment and transmuted them into a low background harmony note to underscore its song of welcome to the newcomers.

For all the dark purpose of the visitors, the Castle forbade gloom. Time enough for that should the skills they were learning ever be needed, then perhaps memories of the happy sounds of Anderras Darion might carry them through when all else failed.

Loman smiled to himself and opened his eyes. Standing up he stepped up on to the low windowsill and looked out of the tall narrow window down to a courtyard, dotted with lawns and flower beds and the strangely comfortable stone benches that were a characteristic feature of much of the Castle's outdoor furniture.

Two liveried apprentices scurried past, intent on some errand and unaware of his watchful gaze. He was pleased with his apprentices. In his hastier moments he normally categorised them as insensitive little devils, but the new atmosphere seemed to have reached even them now.

He took in the rest of the scene playing before him. Assiduously avoiding the lawns, a small group of younger children were pursuing each other in an elaborate chase game that he remembered vaguely from his own childhood. One or two figures sat isolated on the benches and lawns reading with varying degrees of attentiveness, while an equal number just lay about idly in the sunshine, books discarded. In the far corner, Gulda was holding court to a group of older men and women. He regretted he could not hear what she was saying, because even though he still carried a substantial residue of his childhood terror of the woman, he had come to admire and enjoy her great expositions.

They were liable to happen at any time and anywhere and when she started a small crowd invariably gathered to stand enthralled. He watched her now for several minutes talking apparently without pausing for breath, hands and arms flying expressively from one gesture to the next, an occasional thrust with her stick for emphasis, and her great nose wafting the air like the sail of a tacking yacht as her head moved rapidly from side to side scanning her audience for the telltale signs of blankness in the eyes.

Loman had ceased to ponder on Gulda's nature, as he had Hawklan's many years earlier. Not a topic could be raised but what she knew something of it. And she worked tirelessly. Ferreting through the Library, unearthing the most remarkable old books on military lore, organising the newcomers, organising those leaving, organising him!

And she never seemed to sleep.

Once Loman had met her walking slowly down a long moonlit corridor deep in the dark hours of the night. He had been poring over some old books and, having neglected the time, was hurrying to his quarters to catch a little sleep before rousing his apprentices.

'Memsa, can't you sleep? You'll be exhausted,' he said.

Gulda started a little, then continued her slow pace, acknowledging his concern with a nod that brought her hood forward and threw her face into shade. Loman did not have the skills of his brother but he was Pedhavin-born and shadow lore was in his blood. He saw what she had intended to hide. A look of despairing loneliness that almost made him step back. Instead he stepped forward.

'Gulda,' he said gently. 'You do too much. Perhaps Tirilen can help you. She's no Hawklan, but . . .'

In response to his gentleness, a soft smile appeared in the shade of the hood and she laid a hand on his arm. 'What would I do with sleep, Loman?' she said distantly. 'There's nowhere for Gulda to hide, least of all in sleep, where memories run unfettered.' Then she walked slowly past him.

He had watched the stooped black form retreating down the moon-shadowed corridor. In the glistening light her shape became so black and dense that it looked like the entrance to a long dark tunnel and, for an instant, he had the feeling of long interminable years stretching back endlessly from this brief time of his to times and peoples unimaginable. 'Nowhere for Gulda to hide', had floated back to him as she slowly merged with the distant shadows. He had swayed slightly as if he had woken suddenly to find himself exposed on a great height, his stomach fluttering with vertigo.

The sun now streaming through into the deep embrasure of the window could not illuminate that haunting memory and Loman stepped away from the courtyard scene thoughtfully. There could be no understanding someone like Gulda. Nor anything gained from pondering who she was or why she was now here. Shaking off his reverie he strode out again. He needed to think, but not about this. Hawklan's last message had been the one he had feared most of all.

Such was the impetus given by Gulda, Loman and the Morlider veterans, and such was the natural adaptability of the Orthlundyn, that within weeks of Hawklan's leaving the many vague ideas that had started the enterprise had settled into familiar routines, and offshoots had begun to branch out. Already the more capable trainees were returning to their villages to start preliminary training locally in order to spare the limited time of the Castle's instructors and to minimise the disruption of ordinary village life. They would also survey their own districts to note features of tactical value should conflict develop.

'This is vital,' Gulda emphasised. 'Real strength can only come from firm and tenacious roots. And you,' she swung her stick around the assembled instructors, 'will bring all this information together as soon as possible so that we here will have a complete and detailed picture of the whole country.'

Loman's feet took him upward and outwards until he found himself on the Castle wall looking out across the rolling landscape. He was tired and stiff, though not unpleasantly so. For all her impudence, his daughter had eased the more excruciating pains very effectively.

He stretched massively, drawing the fresh summer air into his barrel chest and closing his eyes to feel the sun on his craggy face. Hawklan had been right. The Orthlundyn, himself included, he realised, strove naturally for perfection and, while it gave them a profound satisfaction to do well, much of it was only because it was a step to something better. Perhaps only an outlander could see that in us, he thought.

In truth though, he could not have imagined that so much could have been achieved so quickly. Few had expressed serious reservations about what was being done. The evil that had come into their land had awakened some long-dormant spirit in the Orthlundyn and, while they regretted the need, they took to their new studies with the same thoroughness that typified all their acts. Their weakness, Loman knew, was that few of them were battle-hardened. Combat was not an extension of training: it was profoundly different. But, for all that, a tool was being formed which could do fine service if the need arose. He frowned anxiously at the thought and patted the stone in front of him with his powerful hand, hoping again that such a need would not arise. Then he turned his eyes northwards towards Fyorlund.

The string of riders established as a message line for Hawklan and Isloman had been used frequently as part of various training exercises and Loman knew that the two men had made steady and uneventful progress, and that they in turn knew of the progress that had been made at the Castle.

Then had come Hawklan's last message before they disappeared into the mountainous approaches to Fyorlund. 'Well done. Now select your finest and train them beyond their limits, for special needs.'

It was a message he had feared Hawklan's reason would lead him to eventually. The formation of an elite corps. He had assiduously avoided mentioning such an idea to Hawklan because in it were enshrined all the painful and unreconcilable paradoxes of the wilful use of violence. Further, he and Isloman had both served with such a group. The Goraidin. The only non-Fyordyn ever to do so. It had been a difficult experience, at once enriching and impoverishing, and he had little desire to relive it.

Even now, so many years later, he would wake occasionally in the night, shivering, full of the nightmare of that first meeting.

Their small unit had been scattered by a surprise night attack and he and Isloman had spent days wandering through the snow-covered terrain trying to find out where they were and what exactly had happened. Then the weather turned and the two brothers found themselves clinging to one another in mortal fear. Everything disappeared into a horrifying glaring whiteness that burned into their eyes. Mountains, forests, even the sky and the very horizon were gone – not as in a mist – not hidden from view but vanished utterly into brightness. Only vaguely could they see one another and their footsteps in the snow. Their main awareness of one another came through touch and, hand in hand, they wandered aimlessly for miles until eventually they stumbled across a fallen tree whose roots offered them some shelter.

They built a rough wall to keep out the wind, and slumped down in the cramped space to contemplate their imminent demise. Even with their Orthlundyn clothing, and the extra garments that the local Riddinvolk, used to such conditions, had given them, the bitter cold struck through and both knew that without food and warmth they would soon die.

Loman was wakened from a fitful half-sleep by his brother clamping a hand over his mouth and whispering in his ear. 'Morlider. Just outside. Listen.'

Nearby voices speaking a strange language drifted into their shelter. Loman craned forward, listening intently, and then raised four fingers to his brother. Isloman nodded. Four men.

'Food,' mouthed Loman silently. Isloman nodded again and raised a clenched fist. This time Loman nodded and cautiously slipped his gloved hand through the straps of his shield. Isloman slowly did the same and, on his brother's signal, the two of them crashed down their snow wall and charged out roaring and shouting at the four men.

Except that there were not four, but six. Without pausing to assess the consequences of their mistaken arithmetic the two brothers pressed on. Strong even in those days, Loman sent two of the men staggering with a single blow of his shield and then swung his club at the head of a third.

But the blow never landed and, instead, Loman found himself sprawling on his back only vaguely aware of where he was and how he got there. There had been no impact, he was sure. He rolled over and tried to regain his balance and then there *was* an impact. A stunning blow came from nowhere and exploded in his head, filling it with white light. Now he was face down in the snow and sufficiently aware to know that he was losing this battle utterly. He was going to die. Somewhere he could hear his brother's voice and the sound of fighting.

'I'm coming, Isloman,' he shouted weakly and, with head still ringing, he struggled to his knees. His shield and club were gone, but he had his fists and his strength. As he moved, he heard a gasp of surprise and the sound of a sword being drawn. Looking up and focusing blearily, he saw a white, fur-clad figure approaching purposefully with a white-bladed sword in his hand. He was not going to be able to move in time.

'Wait,' cried an authoritative voice. 'Wait.' The figure paused. A second figure joined it and, bending forward, spoke to Loman.

'What did you say?' it demanded.

Loman, uncertain at this strange turn in the proceedings, swore at him roundly and tried again to stand.

'Well I'm damned,' said the figure. 'Orthlundyn or I'm a Mandroc. What are you doing here?'

Loman kept his gaze on the drawn sword. 'Wishing I was somewhere else,' he said.

The figure laughed unexpectedly and stepped forward, its hand extended. 'Yes. Orthlundyn without a doubt. Put up your sword, Yatsu, we mustn't slaughter our allies, even if they do ambush us. Take my hand, man.'

Hesitantly Loman grasped the offered hand and struggled to his feet, swaying dizzily. The two men steadied him, and for a moment he leaned on them both while his head cleared.

The second man chuckled again. 'I didn't know Orthlundyn were so hard,' he said. 'One kick from Yatsu is usually sufficient to take a man out of this world and you're only a bit dizzy. Remarkable.' He gestured to an untidy white mound by the roots of the fallen tree. 'Let him up,' he said, and Loman watched the mound break up as four more fur-clad individuals rose to their feet and released his bruised and winded brother.

'Well, Orthlundyn,' said the man, turning back to Loman, 'you gave us quite a surprise. I think we'll talk a little. My name's Dirfrin, and this little group you've assailed is a detachment of King Rgoric's Goraidin.'

The name meant nothing to either of the brothers, and Dirfrin did not seem disposed to elaborate.

After a little wound counting and some awkward introductions, Dirfrin laid a sad hand on Loman's shoulder. 'I'm afraid your unit's been wiped out, Loman,' he said. 'We came across the remains of them earlier. I'm sorry.'

Loman cast his eyes upwards, while Isloman dropped his head into his hands.

After a moment, Dirfrin continued. 'Worse,' he said. 'The Morlider have moved in unexpectedly and now occupy this entire area. If you go off on your own, then the weather, the terrain or the enemy will kill you within a couple of days.'

Loman looked inclined to demur, but Isloman laid a hand on his arm and shook his head.

'Furthermore, I don't want you falling into enemy hands. They're none too kind with prisoners and they'll find out about us for sure, and if that happens we'll be in even more trouble than we are now. It's a matter of urgency that we get back to the army and report where the enemy are and in what strength.'

'What can we do?' asked Isloman.

'You'll have to come with us,' came the reply. There was some muttering in the strange language that the brothers had heard before. Dirfrin looked angry. He drew a long knife and offered it, hilt first, to one of his men.

'Well, kill them here in cold blood if you've the stomach for it, because that's the only alternative we have.' The man lowered his eyes and waved the knife away. Dirfrin returned it to its sheath and Loman and Isloman unclenched their fists.

Dirfrin fixed them with an unwavering stare. 'Listen carefully, both of you. The Goraidin are the finest fighters in all Fyorlund. Our training's so hard that not one in a hundred ordinary High Guard will even aspire to it and only one in three of those who do is likely to complete it. I'm afraid all I can offer you is a slim chance or no chance, but you look fit, you're certainly strong, you're well-clothed and, looking at your shelter, you're not stupid. We've picked up extra supplies from your dead friends so we'll take you with us.' He leaned forward urgently. 'But we can't allow you to delay us. We'll teach you what we can as we go and you'll have to learn as you've never learned before. But understand,' he paused, 'you'll obey any of these men without question, and without hesitation.' His tone was unequivocal. 'Too many people, ours and yours, depend on the information we have for us to be jeopardised by you. If you give us any trouble you'll be killed without compunction. Do you understand?'

Standing on the walls of Anderras Darion, warm in the summer sun, Loman shivered as he recalled Dirfrin's relentless gaze and grim voice. Looking over the sunlit plains of Orthlund, he nodded his head as he had done that bitterly cold day so long ago huddled in a mountain forest in Northern Riddin.

Now Hawklan wants us to train our own Goraidin, he thought. The request still fretted him. He and Isloman *had* travelled successfully with the Goraidin. They *had* learned. They had also taught.

'Well, at least you'll have sharp swords now and know how to use the shadows a little more wisely,' he remembered telling Dirfrin when they had finally parted.

But some of the skills he and his brother had learned disturbed Loman to this day. Countless ways to kill people and to wring information from them. Countless ways to rend and destroy. Yet other things were indisputably fine and made him proud to have been with the Goraidin. Courage, loyalty, sacrifice, the knowledge to survive in the most appalling conditions. He looked northwards pensively. And their actions *did* save many lives in that bitter war.

Loman breathed out noisily and curled his mouth in self-reproach. He was wasting his time debating this. He had no alternative. He had had no alternative ever since he accepted the necessity of the Orthlundyn arming themselves, if for no other reason than the knowledge that any enemy would be doing the same. He needed no trust in Hawklan to tell him that, nor advice from him about what he should do.

He was Orthlundyn. Whatever had been achieved could, and must, be improved.

He walked along the top of the wall towards one of the stairways. As he strode down the steps, two at a time, he went through a list of names that he realised had been forming in his head over the last few weeks. The names of those trainees who would probably be suitable for special training.

Chapter 26

'What do you make of them?' said Isloman discreetly.

'I don't know,' replied Hawklan. 'But we'll be very conspicuous if we try to avoid them now. Keep smiling. If they offer us violence don't resist unless it gets really serious.'

They had been riding openly through the mountainous edges of Fyorlund for some days, avoiding villages and settlements as much as they could without actually appearing to do so. Now, however, they had no alternative but to pass through a large village situated at the mouth of a valley which was effectively the only route available. The cause of their concern was a modest but growing crowd of men in the square ahead of them. No women or children, Hawklan noted, and some of the men were carrying farm implements and other tools. Glancing casually around he took in the few side streets running up the valley sides.

These Fyorlund villages are very pleasant, he thought, in spite of the gathering group. Heavy, squat, wooden buildings, vividly painted and decorated with carvings quite different from those of Orthlund. He had remarked on the difference to Isloman earlier as they had started to come upon outlying farmhouses.

'Wood is wood. Stone is stone,' Isloman had replied. 'They sing a different song.' Then he had laughed and shaken his head affectionately in the way that the Orthlundyn invariably did when Hawklan's rock blindness became apparent.

The houses of this village were scattered apparently at random, over the floor of the narrow valley and up its steep sides, the position of each being determined by some local feature in the rock. Some of the higher buildings seemed to be clinging precariously to sheer rock faces and looked to be completely inaccessible. Presumably they were reached by these side streets, thought Hawklan. No escape there.

'We may have trouble ahead,' Hawklan said to his horse softly. 'Be ready to move quickly on my signal.'

'You *have* trouble ahead,' replied Serian. 'I can smell it from here.' Hawklan patted his head. 'Gently through the middle of them all,' he said to Isloman. 'Make for that building over there.' With a nod he indicated a three-storey building in the centre of one side of the square. It dominated the other buildings in the village and was obviously a meeting hall of some kind. On its roof sat Gavor.

The crowd parted quietly as the two men rode through, and Hawklan took the time to study the upturned faces for signs that might help him decide their mood. It was interesting. There were strong elements of suspicion and fear, and some hostility, but there were some open friendly faces, and a large part of the crowd seemed to be doubtful, or simply curious, though whether curious about them or about what was going to happen, he could not tell. He caught the eye of several members of the crowd and nodded friendly greetings. Tilt the crowd our way, he thought.

Reaching the building he had indicated, he sat back in his saddle with his hands on his thighs and dropped the reins on the horse's neck. It was an open and relaxed gesture that again should impress the crowd favourably.

However, before he could dismount, a burly, ill-favoured man stepped forward and reached up for Serian's bridle. The horse craned his neck forward, teeth bared, and the man stepped back quickly. Hawklan leaned forward and patted the horse's neck as if to calm him.

'Good,' he whispered and then sat up. 'My apologies, sir,' he said pleasantly. 'I'm afraid the horse is a little nervous. He's not used to big crowds.'

As he anticipated, his description of the group as a big crowd caused a little amusement. Some smiles appeared, and the word 'Orthlundyn' whispered into the air from various directions, while at the same time those at the front of the crowd eased a little further away from the great black horse.

The burly man, however, was not so easily daunted. Carefully watching the horse's whitening eye, he came to the side and spoke roughly to Hawklan.

'Who are you, and what do you want?' he demanded.

Hawklan reached out his hand in friendly greeting. 'My name's Hlan,' he said. 'And this is Isman.' Isloman gave the man a friendly nod. 'We'd be greatly obliged if you could tell us where we might buy supplies for the rest of our journey.'

The man ignored the offered hand and the pleasantries bounced off his scowl. 'You're lying,' he said. 'You're Orthlundyn. You're spies.'

Hawklan sensed that while those hostile to them in the crowd were comparatively few, they held a dominance beyond their numbers. He affected a puzzled expression. 'We're Orthlundyn, certainly,' he said. 'But spies? I don't understand.'

'You're enemies of Fyorlund, sneaking in here through the quiet paths hoping not to be seen. We've been told about what's happening in Orthlund and to look out for the likes of you.' Before Hawklan could speak, the man's attitude changed abruptly from unpleasantness to belligerence. He levelled a finger at Hawklan and his face became suffused with anger. 'Well, you'll not get past us. You'll not sneak any further.'

Hawklan raised his hands in a placatory gesture. 'I don't understand you,' he repeated. 'We're just travellers come to look at your country and your great houses and cities. Do we look like spies?'

The answer was swift and unequivocal. 'You're soldiers without doubt,' the man said. 'With the bow and your fancy sword, and that great horse.'

'Ah,' said Hawklan, 'I understand. The horse is from Riddin. It's a Muster horse. I bought it at the Gretmearc. The bow's just for hunting – I'm afraid we haven't enough money to buy food all the time – and, well, I brought the sword in case we ran into bandits in the mountains.'

The man scowled, and Hawklan could see that he was not listening to what was being said. He got the impression of a man who had not been much thought of in the village, despised even, but who had recently been pushed into prominence. His attitude was not one that would naturally command even the mixed support of this present crowd. Such support as there was, therefore, came as a result of some influence which was not immediately apparent. Equally, therefore, Hawklan saw that they might be in greater danger than was immediately apparent. Careful, he thought, and then, as if assuming his explanation had ended the matter, he swung his left leg over the horse's head and dropped down to face the man.

The suddenness of the movement made the man start and there was some laughter in the crowd. He spun round and the laughter faded. One or two stepped away from him.

'That's enough,' he shouted angrily. 'These people sneak in here armed to the teeth, and spin some yarn about hunting and bandits, and you think it's some kind of a joke.' He swung a pointing finger around the crowd. 'Don't think I don't know which of you sympathise with these spies. There'll be a reckoning soon for the traitors in our own camp.'

One or two looked as if they would have liked to disagree, but were too afraid.

Hawklan intervened. 'I assure you. We're not spies . . . or soldiers. We've done no harm and we mean none. If we're not welcome here, we'll leave. But we'd still like to buy supplies to tide us over the next few days.' He addressed this appeal to the crowd and began fumbling in a pouch on his belt. 'We've money enough for that.'

A brief snatch of birdsong floated across the square. Gavor's signal that danger was approaching.

'We don't want your money, spies,' said the man viciously. Before Hawklan could reply, there was a disturbance in the crowd as four men pushed roughly to the front.

'Trouble, Gister?' one of the new arrivals asked the man confronting Hawklan.

'Not now you've managed to get here, Uskal,' said the man. 'Where've you been? This lot's useless.' He flicked a derisory thumb at the crowd. 'I damn near had to whip most of them out on to the street. Left to them these two would've walked right through unhindered.' His voice began to develop a whine of self-justification.

Uskal was almost as tall as Hawklan and powerfully built, with a lowering stupid face enlivened by just enough intelligence to confirm him as being dangerously vicious. He did not seem inclined to explain his late arrival, but immediately directed his attention to Hawklan and Isloman.

'These the two?' he asked.

Gister nodded.

'Right,' said Uskal through clenched teeth, and without further formalities he stepped forward and struck Hawklan in the stomach. To Hawklan, the blow appeared to be lumberingly slow and he was able to absorb its worst effects simply by expanding his stomach muscles and moving back a little to disturb the balance of his attacker. However, he bent forward as if hurt, to see what effect this would have on the crowd. He had no doubt that he and Isloman could deal with Gister and the other four but, if the crowd sided with their own kind, as well they might, then the two of them would probably be overpowered or injured.

Isloman jumped down from his horse and was immediately seized by two of the new arrivals. Hawklan shot him a swift glance as he saw his powerful frame preparing to deal out summary justice. Isloman read the look and struggled in a half-hearted manner until one of the men hit him also.

The third man grabbed Hawklan from behind and Uskal made to hit him again but, pretending to lose his balance, Hawklan staggered sideways, taking his captor with him, so that Uskal's blow fell ineffectually across his face, slightly cutting his bottom lip against his teeth. As if released by the small trickle of blood that ran down his chin, a small evil sprite raised a long-silent voice deep inside Hawklan. 'You'll die for this, you corruption,' it said. Hawklan's eyes opened in horror as he felt the venom within him, and he swept the thought away ruthlessly.

'Had enough, eh?' said Uskal, misreading Hawklan's expression. Then roughly seizing his jaw he brought his leering face close to Hawklan's.

However, a babble of anger from the crowd precluded any reply by Hawklan. One of the older men stepped forward and took Uskal's arm. 'That's not necessary,' he said. 'They weren't causing any trouble. There's no reason to treat them like that.'

Uskal released Hawklan, shook his arm free and, seizing the man by the front of his tunic, pushed him violently backwards. 'That's how we treat weaklings and cowards, Flec.' he said.

Flec, however, was neither weakling nor coward and, recovering his balance, he surged forward at his attacker, seizing him round the waist and carrying him to the ground. For a while they struggled, raising a small cloud of dust, while others tried uncertainly to separate them. But Uskal was the stronger and more vicious of the two and soon had the advantage of the older man. Sitting on his chest, he struck him a savage blow in the face, and then, standing up, prepared to deliver an equally savage kick.

'No.' Hawklan's unexpectedly powerful voice made Uskal stop abruptly and, looking round, the man caught the mood of the crowd. It was a dangerous mixture of fear and anger and it was turning against him for sure. He looked at Hawklan with an expression of intense loathing – a distant trumpet call sounded in Hawklan's memory – the look was familiar, but he had never seen the like in Orthlund.

'Don't shout at me, filth,' Uskal cried, and striding forward he brought his arm back to strike Hawklan full in the face. Unbidden, Hawklan's knees bent and, moving sideways, he hurled the man holding him over his shoulder straight into the approaching Uskal. The two tumbled on to the ground and rolled for some way, such had been the power of Hawklan's throw. The circling crowd widened dramatically. Isloman, still held by the two men, caught Hawklan's eye. Hawklan shook his head.

'Seize him, seize him,' shouted Gister, but nobody seemed inclined to listen. Uskal, downed by this stranger, lost whatever small control he had. He stood up and looked round furiously.

'No more, please,' said Hawklan pleadingly. It was still important to keep the crowd divided in their attitude to him; laying this oaf out might still turn them against him.

But Uskal was beyond listening. He wrenched a sickle off a man standing nearby, sending him staggering with a powerful blow in the chest when he offered some resistance. Then, crouching slightly, he moved towards Hawklan, his face turned into a grinning mask. He twisted the curved, shining blade so that it reflected the sunlight into Hawklan's eyes.

You're a demented, unfettered creature, came the thought to Hawklan, and he felt his right hand preparing to draw his sword. A vision of the Black Sword singing out and severing this abomination in two floated alluring before Hawklan, and he dismissed it only with a considerable conscious effort. Time enough later to consider such thoughts – and the throw that had saved Flec and brought about this predicament, but there was a more pressing problem to be dealt with first.

Uskal was still moving forward, swinging the sickle from side to side. Hawklan retreated slowly, still anxious to play the bewildered traveller.

'No more,' he repeated, to reinforce this, but soon he would have to defend himself in earnest, and he knew that his body would act outside his control when threatened, using skills beyond his knowing. And while this might overcome Uskal, it could turn the crowd against him.

As if sensing Hawklan's dilemma, Isloman started to struggle with the two men holding him, dragging them to and fro. 'Let me go,' he shouted. 'This is madness. There'll be murder done.'

Serian, apparently alarmed by the disturbance, began to jig and prance like a skittish colt, his hooves kicking up a great cloud of dust. But his eyes were firmly fixed on Hawklan, awaiting a command. Hawklan gave it with an almost imperceptible nod and Serian pranced even more wildly.

With a swift step, Hawklan moved across to the horse as though to quieten it, or perhaps hide behind it, away from Uskal's swinging blade. The movement seemed to act like a signal to Uskal who charged towards Hawklan like a wild predator after fleeing prey. Serian reared wildly and his flailing hoof caught Uskal a pitiless and accurate blow on the shoulder, sending him sprawling and screaming in the dust, the sickle bouncing harmlessly towards the feet of its real owner.

Hawklan took his horse's head as if calming it. 'I presume you didn't want him killed,' Serian said softly. Hawklan patted the great head affectionately and then ran across to his fallen assailant who was writhing on the ground and lashing out at anyone who tried to touch him.

'Be still,' he said urgently, kneeling down beside him. 'Be still. I know a little about bone-setting.'

'What's all this noise?' A huge voice boomed out over the crowd and the square became suddenly silent. Even Uskal groaned more softly. Hawklan looked up to see a grey-headed old man standing at the top of the steps of the large building. Bright, penetrating eyes shone out of a stern and powerful face.

Chapter 27

The first citizen of any Fyorlund community, be it village or town, was its Rede. It was an office that fell to many different types of people, though none were young, as all had had some experience of service with the Lords or the King. It was part of the Law of Fyorlund that no man should lead until he had served, though little leadership was generally required of a Rede, the natural temperament of the Fyordyn being generally towards order and discipline. In practice, the office tended to be no more than a form of dignified retirement for some respected member of the community.

It was the intrusion into this retirement of a mounting hubbub that brought a scowl to Rede Berryn's stern face and sent him to a window, and thence to the outer door of his official residence to make his distinctly personal form of enquiry of the crowd.

He had been a senior training officer in the High Guard of a very traditionally minded Lord, and he could make his presence felt and his voice heard over disturbances far greater than that currently raising a dust in his village square.

'Well,' his voice boomed out again, 'what's going on?'

Gister stepped forward to the foot of the steps, his manner a mixture of deference and defiance. He waved an accusing hand towards Hawklan and Isloman.

'These man are spies, Rede. They've been sneaking around for days, they're armed to the teeth, and they've attacked Uskal just because he asked who they were.'

The old man fixed Gister with a look of suspicion and contempt, and then looked at the crowd. Under his gaze, the tiny seeds that Hawklan had sown began to germinate.

'Rubbish,' shouted someone. 'They weren't doing any harm.'

Gister cast a furious eye over the crowd, but apparently could not see his denouncer.

Several others joined in. 'That's right, Rede. They've done nothing. Gister accused them of being spies and Uskal started the fight.'

'But the horse won,' came a delighted laugh, which again had Gister searching the crowd. Many of the others joined in, but several were still quiet and unsure.

'I know you all,' shouted Gister petulantly. 'Don't think I don't see you. You're all traitors, I'll repo – '

'Gister.' The Rede's interruption stopped the man in midsentence. For a moment the two men locked gazes and, although it was Gister who turned away first, Hawklan noticed that the old man was uncomfortable in his authority. He felt again that Gister drew his confidence and power from others, presumably outside the village.

The Rede came down the steps and walked across to Hawklan; he had a slight limp. Hawklan had rendered Uskal unconscious in order to set the bones that Serian's hoof had so casually shattered and, laying the man down gently, he stood up and spoke to the watching Rede.

'I've set the damaged bones, but he'll have to be strapped up and properly nursed,' he said. 'He should be taken to your healer right away.' He looked down at the unconscious figure. 'I'm afraid that arm's never going to be quite right though,' he said.

The Rede grunted non-committally and then gestured in a direction over Hawklan's shoulder. Turning, Hawklan saw a pale-faced, lightly built man moving through the crowd. He wore what Hawklan took to be a robe of office although, from the stains and dust on it, it was obviously also a working robe. Followed by a group of excited children who had obviously summoned him, the man moved straight to the fallen Uskal, confirming Hawklan's first impression that he was the local healer.

Hawklan bowed slightly to the Rede. 'Excuse me, sir,' he said and, kneeling down by the healer, he explained what he had done to ease Uskal's immediate distress. He took the man's hands and moved them over Uskal's arm and shoulder. The healer closed his eyes and then opened them with a start. They were wide with surprise. In an awed whisper he said, 'You must be Hawklan from . . .' But a look in Hawklan's green eyes silenced him.

'Sh, please,' said Hawklan under his breath. 'I gave your friends a false name. You can tell I mean no harm, but it may be difficult with the others. They're in a strange mood. Tend to your charge. I have to speak with your Rede.'

Like a humble acolyte at the feet of a great master, the man nodded and quickly gave orders to some of the men in the crowd for the removal of Uskal to his home. Then, turning to Hawklan, 'Your healing . . . we must speak, sir. Before you leave the village. Please. There's so much I could learn from you.' Then, a little abashed at his forwardness, 'I'd consider it an honour.'

Hawklan smiled at the man. 'If I can,' he said. 'But . . .' He cast a quick glance at the watching people.

Standing, he found that the Rede had moved away and was contending with a now recovered Gister, who was hovering at his shoulder.

'They're spies, Rede. Look at them,' he said, his eyes flicking from the Rede to Hawklan.

The old man waved him to silence irritably but offered him no other rebuke.

'I apologise for your welcome to our village, sir,' he said to Hawklan. 'But times are troubled and there are many strange rumours in the air. I have to confess that your appearance is unusual, with your fine bow and sword, and . . .' he looked at Serian intently, and a note of considerable surprise came into his voice, 'and your Muster horse if I'm not mistaken.'

Hawklan sensed this was a sop being thrown to Gister for some reason.

'But that's no reason for treating you as we have,' the Rede continued. 'Please join me for a meal then we can talk at our leisure and sort out any misunderstandings.'

Hawklan accepted the offer gratefully and with a conspicuous show of relief.

'Go back to your homes,' said the Rede to the crowd. 'I'll find out who these people are, make amends for our discourtesy and do what is necessary.' His remarks however were largely superfluous, as the people were already drifting away, some talking excitedly, some quietly, and others affecting amused tolerance of the children who had now appeared and were running among them mimicking Uskal's crouching advance with the sickle and Serian's mighty kick.

Gister stood alone, fists clenched, irresolute and lowering.

The Rede spoke to him with a barely contained anger. 'Gister, you know what I think of your ranting and your foolish ideas. I'll tolerate a lot, but you go too far. You should have more sense. Uskal's a half-mad dog at best, without you encouraging him.'

Gister burst out '*I* go too far. *I* go too far. It's *you* who go too far. Consorting with enemies of the King. Helping them evade justice . . .'

'Enough,' said the Rede, his anger exploding. 'Or . . .'

'Or what?' said Gister in a tone that amounted to a sneer. 'You'll call a Pentadrol? Talk the enemies of the King to death?'

'The Pentadrol is for restrained and reasoned argument, Gister. If I thought you were amenable to that I'd call one without hesitation,' replied the Rede, but as the old man turned away and beckoned him to follow, Hawklan knew that he had lost his argument with Gister. He presumed that the Pentadrol was some form of village forum whose effectiveness Gister had somehow contrived to undermine. What was happening in this country?

The Rede walked carefully up the steps to his residence. He signalled to a young man standing nearby and asked him to attend to the newcomers' horses.'

Hawklan intervened. 'Thank you, Rede,' he said. 'But we must attend to our own horses.

The old man nodded and smiled knowingly. 'Of course,' he said after a moment. 'Tel-Mindor will show you to the stables.' He raised his hand and a well-built, loose-limbed figure appeared at the top of the steps. Although the man was probably middle-aged, Hawklan was reminded immediately of Jaldaric and the other High Guards. His carriage showed he was active and vigorous, but there was another quality about him which Hawklan could not readily identify. The man returned Hawklan's smile of greeting easily, but Hawklan was intrigued. The young man would have made a perfectly adequate guide to the stables, but the Rede obviously wanted someone of his own to accompany them. To eavesdrop? To restrain? The man's movements were unusually fluid and economical and something deep inside Hawklan began to whisper that he was not a man to be assailed lightly. Protection? Probably the most likely reason. Gister and his following did not look like the type of people who would refrain from ambush on moral grounds. Then again maybe the old man was just protecting his political flank from subsequent accusations. In any event, whatever the reason, it showed him to be a man of some discernment, and one worth cultivating.

A little later the three of them joined the Rede in one of his private rooms where he offered them food and drink. The room was cluttered with papers, documents and all manner of objects which indicated a full, active and acquisitive life. It needed no great powers of observation to see that no woman blessed the Rede's life and that he had once been a military man. The sheer disorder of the place demonstrated the first, while the second was apparent from the quantities of swords, knives, bows, axes, pieces of armour and countless other military relics that littered the place.

Hawklan noticed that those weapons which were obviously decorative and ceremonial were scattered about indiscriminately, lying on chairs, under tables, idling on shelves or standing sentinel-like in corners, while a handful of others, scarred and bruised in real earnest, were solicitously mounted in cabinets around the walls.

Pride of place seemed to go to a battered helm with a great leering dent spreading down from its crown to just over the left eye. Hawklan's gaze flickered to the Rede's forehead in search of a scar, but the man was sitting with his back to the window, and it was difficult to see his face.

'We ran into Mandrocs on one of the Watch Patrols into Narsindal,' said the old man, answering the unspoken question and rubbing his head ruefully. The remark seemed to bring back old memories and the rubbing became pensive. 'It was odd you know. Usually if we saw any at all, they'd keep their distance – disappear into the mist. But this lot came out of nowhere, went straight for us, and then vanished before we could recover fully. Like skirmishers almost . . . organised . . . as if they were practising on us. I've always felt that very strange . . .' He fell silent.

Hawklan watched him for a moment before speaking. 'I thought perhaps you'd been in the Morlider War,' he said

The Rede came out of his reverie abruptly. 'Oh, I was,' he said. 'Later on.' Then tapping his finger on the side of his nose, 'But I was older and wiser then. Never let anyone get that close again, I can assure you, Hawklan.'

Hawklan's eyes widened at the sound of his name and Isloman casually rested his hand on his club. Tel-Mindor, sitting near the door, noted the movement and smiled briefly.

Rede Berryn leaned forward. 'I was a training officer in the High Guards, Hawklan. I can hear a smart-alec whisper from eight ranks back.'

Hawklan shrugged apologetically. 'I don't know what to say,' he managed awkwardly.

The Rede picked up a small fruit from a dish by his arm and chuckled as he began to nibble it fastidiously, his eyes watching Hawklan steadily.

'I think the wisest thing you could say, Hawklan, is "Rede Berryn, I'm the worst spy and the worst actor in the whole world", then perhaps the two of us can talk some sense. Truth for truth.'

Hawklan smiled and nodded his head in acknowledgement. 'I'd prefer it,' he said. 'I don't sit easily with deceit.'

The Rede chuckled. 'No, you certainly don't, Hawklan. You might be a fighter, but you've never been a ranker with an officer to deceive.' Then both he and Tel Mindor laughed loudly but good-naturedly.

As they subsided, Hawklan conceded. 'You're right, Rede, I am indeed a poor actor, and I do owe you an apology. But I'm neither spy nor fighter. I'm just a healer.'

The old man looked at him narrowly for a moment then, stretching his right leg stiffly, he massaged his knee with his hand and rested his foot on a well-worn stool nearby.

'We're very near Orthlund here,' he said. 'There've been tales for years of a great healer, Hawklan, living in some village

by the mountains. Even thought of going to see him myself
. . .' He paused reflectively then shrugged off his digression.
'Anyway, I'm inclined to believe you. You've got a healer's way
about you, and I'll trust our little healer's response to you, he's
a good man, very perceptive.' Then, almost in spite of himself,
he laughed again. 'Poor lad looked as if he'd met one of the
Guardians when you took hold of his hands and he's quite
incapable of anything other than an honest response.' Then,
more seriously, 'As for you being a fighter and a spy, well
you're no ordinary traveller, that's for sure. Nor your silent
friend here.' He indicated the watching Isloman. 'That little
charade with Uskal and Gister wouldn't fool anyone with half
an eye for a warrior. Correct me if I'm wrong, but you were
sorely tempted to use your sword on that oaf's head at one
stage, weren't you?' He did not wait for an answer, but patted
his knee and eased his foot back down on to the floor. 'Anyway,
I'm not too bothered about that. You've got your own reasons
for doing what you're doing and you'd be hard-pressed to hurt
Fyorlund much more than it's hurting itself at the moment.'
His voice was bitter. 'What's more to the point is what we're
going to say to the Mathidrin when they arrive.'

'Mathidrin?' queried Hawklan.

The Rede's face was still in shadow, but the bitterness and
anger in his voice was clear enough. 'They started off calling
them King's High Guard. *King's* High Guard no less. Then
when that provoked a storm they changed the name. That's
a fine way to legalise a crime, don't you think? Change its
name.'

Hawklan offered no comment. 'And these Mathidrin will be
coming for us?' he asked.

The Rede nodded. 'I'm afraid so. Gister will have sent one of
his fellow worms along the valley to their camp.'

'I presume it would be unwise of us to attempt to avoid
them?' Hawklan said.

'Yes,' said the Rede. 'It'd be difficult, even if you knew the
mountains. And Gister's people will be watching for you as
well.' He hesitated.

'And?' offered Hawklan.

'And I'm afraid I'll have to ask you to stay here until they arrive. Gister has a growing following. If I were to release you against orders, that would play right into his hands, and what little authority I still have here would be gone.' His voice was firm, but unhappy.

'Orders, Rede?' Hawklan said in some surprise. 'What orders? What's happening here?'

The Rede turned away from Hawklan's gaze and the sun illuminated an embarrassed and worried profile. 'I'm sorry,' he said. 'I shouldn't talk like this, but . . . seeing you out there, dealing with those louts . . . I don't know what's happening. It's like some kind of madness. Dissension and argument everywhere. The Geadrol suspended. Lords arrested. These . . . Mathidrin arresting and intimidating people. And all seemingly with the King's blessing – or Dan-Tor's. And rumours everywhere, even that the Orthlundyn are preparing to attack us. Have you ever heard such rubbish? Good grief, there's only a handful of them down there . . .' Then the bitterness and anger burst out briefly. 'But it's too much to ask someone from Vakloss to go and look, isn't it? That's far too simple a solution. As for listening to people like me, who live here and could tell them . . .'

Hawklan let the outburst pass unremarked. 'What do these Mathidrin want of us, Rede?' he asked.

The Rede's tone quietened. 'Ethriss knows, Hawklan, but you're strangers from Orthlund, and I've quite unequivocal orders from Vakloss that all strangers are to be detained and handed over to the Mathidrin. I'm sorry.'

Hawklan leaned his head on his hand. 'Detained eh?' he said with a surprising smile. 'I thought there was more to Tel-Mindor than met the eye.'

The Rede shrugged regretfully. 'I'm sorry,' he said again.

Isloman grunted and turned to look at Tel-Mindor sitting casually by the door. The man returned his gaze steadily but pleasantly. Isloman's eyes narrowed slightly as if he were looking for something. Then he made a brief series of small hand movements. Tel-Mindor's composure disappeared and his eyes widened in disbelief. Isloman raised a finger to silence him, then turned back to Hawklan.

'Tell the Rede why we've come, Hawklan,' he said. 'We'll

get an honest hearing and it's going to be difficult to tell friend from foe soon.'

Rede Berryn watched this exchange closely, his fingers idly running around a raised embellishment on the plate by his side. He looked enquiringly at Tel-Mindor.

'Listen,' Tel-Mindor said. The Rede nodded.

Hawklan looked at Isloman. 'Quickly, Hawklan,' said the Carver. 'We may not have much time.'

Hawklan glanced then at Tel-Mindor, who nodded. He turned again to the Rede. 'Rede, I'm sorry about the false names, but I was uncertain about the mood of the crowd and from what's happened to me recently I thought our names – mine in particular – might not be helpful.' He leaned forward. 'We came here to see what's wrong in Fyorlund and to find your Lord Dan-Tor.'

'Why?' asked the Rede.

Hawklan took a deep breath. He had no way of judging this man's loyalties, he would just have to trust Isloman's judgement. Briefly he outlined how Dan-Tor had twice tried to capture him and how his second attempt had resulted in the slaughter of his entire personal guard at the hands of a patrol led by Mathidrin officers. Some inner voice held him silent about the true nature of this patrol.

As he spoke, it occurred to him that even now, sitting in this chaotic room, looking into the face of his jailer host dark against the sunlight, he might still only be following a carefully laid bait. He set the thought aside uneasily.

The mood in the room had changed. Without looking, Hawklan could feel a new intensity in Tel-Mindor, and he knew too that the look in Rede Berryn's shaded eyes had hardened.

'Who was the leader of this personal guard?' the Rede asked coldly.

'Jaldaric,' replied Hawklan. 'As I told you, it was him the patrol came for, and it was only him who survived. The last we saw of him he was tied over a horse and being taken to Fyorlund.'

A long silence weighed heavily in the room.

'Hawklan,' said the Rede eventually. 'I've had it whispered

THE FALL OF FYORLUND 217

to me by a trusted friend in Vakloss that the Lord Dan-Tor was on a friendly mission to Orthlund and that he was driven out by the Orthlundyn. Frankly I didn't believe it. I think my friend has been misinformed, perhaps deliberately so. As I said, we're very close to Orthlund here. But your story verges on the ridiculous. Why in Ethriss's name would anyone want to capture some Orthlundyn healer, however well known, and as for a Mathidrin patrol attacking the Lord Dan-Tor's personal guard . . .' He made a gesture of angry dismissal.

Hawklan looked at Isloman and then back at the Rede. 'Rede, there's something about the patrol I didn't tell you, because even without it I knew my story would be difficult to believe, but . . .'

Isloman interrupted. 'No, Hawklan,' he said firmly, 'he won't believe you, but he might believe me.' And standing up he walked across to the battered helm that had caught Hawklan's eye earlier. He lifted it down respectfully and, holding it in front of him, he spoke to the Rede in the High Guard's Battle Language. Hawklan did not understand it, but twice he caught the word Mandroocai.

The reaction was explosive, as the Rede angrily rose to his feet, grimacing at the pain in his leg as he did so. 'You're lying,' he burst out. 'And you profane our Oath with such a swearing.' Then he stopped, suddenly uncertain. His confusion made him belligerent. 'How do you know our Battle Language and our Oath, Orthlundyn?'

Isloman did not reply, but turned and looked at Tel-Mindor. 'Goraidin,' he said quietly. 'I release you from our Oath of Secrecy. Tell him who I am and whether I would lie.'

Tel-Mindor's easy composure had left him at Isloman's speech. Shock, diagnosed the healer in Hawklan. Fairly massive shock at that. And the Rede too. Tel-Mindor hesitated.

'Tell him, Goraidin,' said Isloman powerfully. 'How can your Rede decide without information?'

Tel-Mindor looked up, his face pale, but his composure returning rapidly. 'Rede,' he said, 'this is Isloman, one of the two brothers who rode with Dirfrin and the Goraidin in Riddin. He is Goraidin. Hawklan has his trust and his sword arm, and his word's beyond reproach. We must accept what he

says. Armed Mandrocs have been led into Orthlund by
Mathidrin officers and have slaughtered the Lord Dan-Tor's
personal guard.'

The Rede leaned forward to speak, but Tel-Mindor raised
his hand abruptly for silence and moved towards the window.
He opened it and the sound of raised voices and the clatter of
horses' hooves washed into the room.

Chapter 28

Patterns, patterns, patterns. Dan-Tor sensed the presence of other minds working contrary to his purpose, but their shape and form, their nucleus, eluded him. He tried to shrug the idea away, but it was reluctant to leave him. The King had started the avalanche, now he, Dan-Tor, had to ride it out through the dust and uproar until all was quiet and the new shape of the land could be surveyed. It was inevitable that opposition would arise and swirl about him from time to time, but while it had no centre, surely it offered no real threat?

These creatures do so look to a leader, he thought. One of their few virtues. They actively seek to be controlled and manipulated. He had debated with himself whether he should allow a leader to arise and then control him, or whether he should extinguish any hopefuls before they became aware of their potential. On balance, he decided, the latter was preferable. Let the crowds spend their energies milling about aimlessly. There were too many risks associated with a leader. No matter how well he might be controlled, one misjudgement and he could be free, and Dan-Tor knew too bitterly what an inspired leader could bring from the people. It was too dangerous. So much easier to douse the tiny sparks before they flared up into what could become an uncontrollable blaze.

Now, however, he found that he could not escape the feeling that a leader had already emerged. One of cunning and experience; one who knew sufficient of the ways of men to keep himself hidden from view while he built up his strength. Working quietly in the shadows until he felt the time was ripe.

Walking to the window, Dan-Tor looked down at the heart of the city nestling around the Palace walls. The pattern of its streets was distorted by long shadows carved out of the bright rays of the setting sun by countless tiny buildings. Even from this height he could see people walking on the sunnier streets, trailing their own great shadows with them. Is it one of them I fear? he thought consolingly. Tiny people with giants' shadows?

But the name Hawklan wandered relentlessly into his mind. The man was loose and was by now aware of danger. All that he heard of him in Orthlund indicated he was just a healer, but a man who commanded so much spontaneous affection was a man to be watched; and a man who saw so clearly and who so evaded his traps, aided or no, was a man who could usefully be feared, be he Ethriss or no. He was at least a flickering spark, and it irked Dan-Tor that it was his impetuosity that might have fanned him into life.

And I'm blind, he thought angrily as he watched a small bird land on the windowsill unaware of the man's brooding presence behind the glass. One of his birds had been bound, and it was the nature of the creature that to bind one part was to bind all. But that required great power, the Old Power. Blind or no, he could now see what that implied. Who could wield the Old Power thus except the Cadwanol? They must indeed still exist. It was a bad omen. Though it seemed they had let Hawklan escape . . .

He shook off the thought, knowing it would lead only to a fretting labyrinth of confusion. His gaze fell again on the preening bird. To release his own birds he would have to use the Old Power himself, and massively, and He had expressly forbidden that. Hawklan even as Hawklan was proving disruptive, but if Hawklan were Ethriss then such a rending use of the Old Power would awaken him for sure, and Hawklan as Ethriss would be doom itself.

Dan-Tor's spies now were human – slow, foolish and unreliable. To use them reminded him too much of his own erstwhile humanity. It was a degradation.

The bird on the sill lifted an elegant black and white wing, and its plumed head bobbed to and fro as it preened and shook itself proudly. Dan-Tor watched it for a moment then narrowed his eyes almost imperceptibly. Without a sound, the bird vanished in a burst of red spray, and a cascade of black and white feathers began a long oscillating journey towards the ground far below. Dan-Tor turned away, a thin smile across his wrinkled brown face. Such a slight use of the Old Power could disturb no one – except the recipient.

Sitting, he stared out of the window again, seeing now only a blank sky paled almost white in the setting sun. His mind was tempted to flit and fret after the missing Hawklan, but a deeper voice forbade it. Even a pack leader must leave tracks, it said. If he seeks you, you'll know of his presence when he has your scent, then who will be hunter and who hunted?

He nodded reflectively, then bent over the papers spread before him. They drew his mind back to his own chains. Confound Dilrap, buzzing endlessly around like a fat bluebottle. It took a considerable effort not to swat him, but he was useful, valuable almost, for all his irritating mannerisms and shrinking temperament. He knew the minutiae of the Law and of the Court procedures that were needed to manipulate events smoothly. Better at this stage to unravel the knots than cut through them. Time enough for that later, and that time would come the sooner if patience were used now.

Strangely, however, Dilrap seemed to be thriving on it. Briefly it occurred to Dan-Tor that, although terrified of him, Dilrap seemed to be deliberately seeking his attention, going out of his way to be helpful. It was out of character surely? Then perhaps Dilrap could feel which way the wind was blowing and was ingratiating himself thoroughly with the leader of the new order that he could see coming.

Still, it was of no matter. He was needed now, and his co-operation was fortuitous whatever its motive. Later, he would not be needed and his motivation would be irrelevant. That the mass of time-consuming paperwork, meetings and petty civic duties – 'For the sake of appearance, Lord', twitch – was being created by Dilrap to distract him, never occurred to Dan-Tor.

Reluctantly he turned to the latest batch of papers that Dilrap had left for him. The first was a thick document concerning the 'Rights and Privileges of Honourable Prisoners'.

'It's a very long time since any Lords have been arrested, Lord,' Dilrap had said. 'But it has happened in the past, and provision has been made within the Law for such a contingency.' Dan-Tor had looked skyward and Dilrap had quailed.

'Lord,' he said, in a great flurry of jerks and twitches, 'if I know of this, then those looking to the Lords' interest will know of it. If not now, then soon.'

'They have no one looking to their interests, Honoured Secretary,' Dan-Tor replied, tight-lipped. 'Save us. They're held by Special Edict. They see only their guards and any of their friends who dare to show their faces see only yourself, or me.'

'This is true, Lord, but . . .' Dan-Tor drew in a loud breath and stood up very straight. Dilrap babbled out his reservations frantically. 'Lord. The Special Edict is an Edict of Examination, it relates only to their detention. A trial must be held eventually. They'll have friends who'll emerge when that happens, and those friends will be looking at the Law *now*, with that end in mind. If we're faulted on small details there's no telling what it might lead to. The people are . . .'

'The people are what?' said Dan-Tor stonily.

Dilrap cast about, becoming progressively more flustered as Dan-Tor's eyes looked through him. 'Uncertain,' he said at last. 'Uncertain.'

Dan-Tor did not speak. Dilrap became confidential, shifty almost. Carefully, not looking at the Lord, he said, 'The four Lords . . . traitors, have many friends and are loved by many of the people, albeit misguidedly. The demand for an early trial will persist; grow, even.' He lifted his eyes and gazed straight at Dan-Tor. 'And *only* a trial will expose the truth of their treachery. We *must* observe the forms of the Law. If we don't, then we undermine our case and it will be doomed from the start. You know what these lawyers are like. If then we detain the Lords, who knows what the people might do. And if the Lords are allowed free . . .' He left the implications unstated.

Dan-Tor felt Dilrap's forked stick pinning him to the ground. The serpent pinned by the worm. But it would be vain to struggle. The Mathidrin could perhaps control rioting within Vakloss and some of the other large towns, but there were too few to control the whole country, and the news of an illegal detention would bring an armed and angry population down on Vakloss like a tidal wave. It was not in his interests to have Fyorlund torn by civil strife. Far better that the people be gradually wooed to him. Let the slow corruption continue. The

King's contribution must be ridden out peacefully.

'We mustn't cede these traitors their victory by tempting the people to rash action or by foolishly ensuring their release,' he said coldly. 'Let me have details of these provisions for the arrest of Lords.'

Dilrap risked a brief knowing smile and, hitching his gown on to his shoulders, bowed and retreated. As he reached the door, Dan-Tor pointed a long brown finger at him.

'Briefly, Dilrap. Briefly,' he said.

Now Dan-Tor stared at the results of this admonition. Sheet upon sheet of closely written script, laden with column annotations, footnotes, cross-references and, at a quick glance, some of the densest legal prose that the Law of Fyorlund could produce. He would have to read it of course. Dilrap's observations had been too accurate for him to ignore. He glanced irritably at the pale light washing in through the window and clicked a globe into life. Its glare dimmed the evening sky outside and cast harsh shadows around his room. Their clarity relaxed him.

Far below, in the darkening streets, a few people noticed the harsh white light appear in the tower wall, like an inhuman eye peering out over the City. Those who knew it for what it was were divided: some saw it as the Lord Dan-Tor working tirelessly to assuage the confusion and disorder that seemed to be sweeping the country; while others, a touch wiser, presumed he was plotting yet more schemes and devilment to undermine the ancient way of life of the Fyordyn. Both camps seemed to find less and less on which they could stand and debate rationally, let alone agree. Both noted a sourness and anger seeping into their lives that they had never known before, and each was inclined to look to the other for the cause.

Further below still, the four Lords indeed plotted and schemed. Their brief foray from their cell, especially that of Hreldar and Darek, had told them where they were, but that knowledge was of limited value. It served mainly to confirm that, to escape their prison, they would need good fortune and more than a little help from the outside.

After their initial euphoria, they lapsed a little into a darker mood as they pondered the problems ahead of them. They found it interesting that there had been no repercussions from their escapade. Hreldar, with Darek's help, had made a slow and convincing recovery once he had reached fresh air, and had shown no further symptoms since, but Arinndier now made a conspicuous point of looking suspiciously at all their food, and of talking to the guards who brought it. After a while the chore devolved on to a single kitchen servant who bore Arinndier's scrutiny with a surly indifference.

Eldric was of the opinion that the incident had not risen very far up the ranks of the Mathidrin. 'They made a mistake, and they don't want Dan-Tor to find out about it, I'm sure,' he said. 'I think we've found an interesting weakness in our jailers with our little piece of theatre.'

Arinndier raised his eyebrows to request an elaboration of this remark.

Eldric obliged. 'These people aren't like our High Guards. They've not entered a service because of duty or tradition. They've entered it for some form of personal gain. Wherever they've been dredged from they've got all the earmarks of ex-prisoners and misfits, and there's more than a few foreigners among them, judging by some of the accents we've heard. I'll wager that such honour as they have is easily purchased.'

'So?' queried Arinndier.

'So they play barrack-room politics, Arin,' continued Eldric. 'They'll form cliques and factions. War amongst themselves for kudos in the eyes of their superiors.'

Arinndier was unimpressed. 'Our own people do that, Eldric,' he said.

Eldric waved a dismissive hand. 'Yes, yes,' he conceded. 'But on the whole they put their service before themselves and, if anything serious happens, they'll come forward and admit it.' He levelled a probing finger. 'Dan-Tor never heard about what we did. We'd have been moved or separated by now if he had. Someone, somewhere, stopped the news going further.'

'So what?' Arinndier maintained his indifference. Eldric scowled and Arinndier looked insincerely apologetic.

'Any soldier with a grain of sense, Arin, would know that what we did should've been reported right up to the top. It was unusual and highly suspicious behaviour.' He sat down by

Arinndier and tapped his arm significantly. 'They didn't even send so much as a horse healer to look at Hreldar after he'd started to look well again.' He paused. 'They don't trust their superiors. They're frightened. Either of punishment or lack of advancement. But whatever the reason, they don't trust them.'

Arinndier sat quiet awhile considering the implications of Eldric's observations. The analysis seemed reasonable. The Mathidrin could well be disciplined by fear, or greed, while the High Guards were disciplined by respect and honour. The Mathidrin would be bound together reluctantly while the High Guards sustained one another willingly.

He nodded. 'So we learn what we can about each one individually. Encourage them in gossip. Bind them with petty corruptions where we can.'

'Exactly,' said Eldric, clapping his hands together. 'Play their own game. We know where we are now. We know our well-being's a matter of some concern to them. Let's find out more about who holds us. Let's start a little more rot growing in the roots of these creations of Dan-Tor's.'

Above them, the City continued its uneasy life in the mellow summer gloaming, until the street globes burst abruptly into life and washed away the soft shadows with their harsh light. It was a regular evening occurrence greeted by some with relief and by others with irritation. But normally, *all* left the streets. It was the wisest thing to do in these troubled times. The light held exposure. The dark shadows, treachery.

Chapter 29

Rede Berryn glanced out of the window at the Mathidrin patrol, then picked up a pen and began writing rapidly.

'Go and bring that Sirshiant up, Tel,' he said, without looking up. 'Don't rush. And look pleasantly surprised,' he added as an afterthought.

Then to Hawklan and Isloman, 'I can't stop them taking you, but I think I can smooth the way a little. This lad's a bit nasty, but he's more ambition than intelligence and I can usually handle him.' He looked at the two men. 'Stay seated until I introduce you.'

There was a discreet knock at the door and Tel-Mindor entered, followed by a sour-faced young Mathidrin officer carrying his helmet under his arm. Hawklan noted immediately that beneath the man's arrogance was an uncertain deference.

'Sirshiant . . .' began the Rede as he rose carefully to greet the newcomer. Then he paused and looked conspicuously at the man's insignia. 'I'm sorry,' he said, smiling broadly. 'Captain, I should say. Congratulations. When did that happen?'

The young man looked down briefly and cleared his throat awkwardly. 'Two days ago, Rede,' he replied. Then, deprecatingly, 'It's only a field commission, it probably won't be confirmed, but . . .'

The Rede waved the disclaimer aside. 'I'm sure it will,' he said heartily. 'Don't worry. Anyway, this may be your big chance. I'm very glad you dropped in.' He proffered the note he had just written. 'I was about to send a messenger to you with this.' He continued speaking while the Captain was reading. 'These two gentlemen are Isloman and the Lord Hawklan, envoy from Orthlund with papers for the Lord Dan-Tor.' At the Rede's discreet signal, Hawklan and Isloman both stood up and bowed to the young officer, who started slightly as he looked up and felt the presence of the two men filling the room. He returned the bow hesitantly, as if unused to such niceties, and his eyes flickered from them to the paper and back to the jovial face of the Rede as if for guidance.

Again, before he could speak, the Rede plunged on, his tone concerned. 'Unfortunately, Gister saw fit to accuse them of being bandits or something, and there's been a bit of an incident – you know what he's like – I'll tell you about it later. Happily, no real harm's been done but, while these gentlemen have very generously accepted my apologies, they're obviously anxious to have some kind of escort for the rest of their journey. Can you help . . . Captain?'

The Captain congratulated himself on not having taken Gister's panic-stricken message too seriously: 'Orthlundyn spies attacking the village'. He'd deal with that blockhead later. Whatever these two were, they were no ordinary travellers, anyone could see that. A rare fool he'd have made of himself if he'd come charging in with his full troop and arrested them. That would have put paid to his promotion beyond doubt, and probably earned him field punishment, if not worse. Interfering with a messenger to the Lord Dan-Tor! The thought of the consequences chilled him.

In his relief, he quickly re-ordered his camp duty rosters. 'Some of the men are due to go back to Vakloss in a day or so, Rede,' he said. 'And I have duty reports to make. I'll escort the envoys personally.' And it'll give me a chance to keep an eye on them, just in case Gister wasn't completely wrong, came a cautionary thought.

When a great branch is lopped from a tree, be it by man or nature, no part escapes the consequences. The weight of the remaining branches leans unbalanced and reaches down the trunk and into even the smallest hair roots. Some are bent and crushed, unable to carry their new burden, while others are stretched skyward and torn from the earth to perish. If the branch lost is large enough, the whole tree may topple almost immediately but, even if it stands, it is irrecoverably weakened.

The very wound exposes the tree to the ravages of disease and predation, while the strained roots will be further damaged with each small gust of wind and fall of rain.

So it was with Fyorlund when its King suspended the Geadrol. With one stroke he severed a huge and proud limb and rocked a nation whose well-rooted stability had sustained it for countless generations. There was not one aspect of Fyordyn life that did not in some degree feel this terrible impact.

Quiet, homely people by their firesides, sharp-eyed street traders, artisans and craftmen, farm labourers out in the countryside, servants, masters, rogues and vagabonds, all the people to whom the Geadrol and the King were distant, remote, irrelevant almost, found themselves affected in some way as the great tree rocked to find a new equilibrium, and fought to heal its wound.

The country creaked with rumour and uncertainty. Dan-Tor sank his knowledge and long-formed plans into the damaged tissues and fought off healing agents and other predators alike. The fear and uncertainty amongst the Lords and the high officials of the Geadrol and Palace leached down corrosively into the populace at large and further undermined the old stability.

Dan-Tor used his Mathidrin to prod and stir where the old order seemed likely to re-establish itself, and they quoted his name and the good of the State rather than the Law, when going about his work, to further erode the worth of the old ways in the people's eyes. But his greatest weapon was distrust.

Clear vision is derived from knowledge and openness, and with clear vision Dan-Tor would be seen for what he was. Rumours of treachery and traitors, of enemies without *and* within, were carefully circulated and sustained, and gradually the Fyordyn lowered their gaze, and began looking at one another furtively and suspiciously. Dan-Tor smiled as he watched his prey mill around in increasingly blind confusion and offered his sympathetic embrace to those who turned to him in their desperation.

His way forward was by no means clear or smooth, however; opposition seemed to spring up spontaneously. But, none the less, it opened up before him inexorably and with each step his strength grew and that of his opponents diminished. He took satisfaction but little joy in what he was doing. This dabbling with the intricate trivia of human society irked him, and the demon bubbling below the surface was never far away, rising to taunt him. 'This game's too long, too slow. Sweep these opponents away, they're but insects in your path. Bind the rest with the Old Power and raise your hands in glorious salute to the Master. Let the New Age begin now.'

He let it have its say, but rarely listened. It was the rambling of the remains of his weak and inconsistent human nature.

'It was your impatience that helped bind *me* in the darkness for long aeons,' he replied. 'You'll not betray me again.' But the demon soothed him with its reminder of his great power and he knew its very presence indicated that the end of the path was much nearer.

Occasionally, however, he would walk the Palace battlements, staring darkly out over the City, and wonder if one of the scurrying dots below him was Hawklan, or if one of the countless rooftops was sheltering him. Then his gaze would wander out to the countryside and the mountains, and his flesh would crawl at the sight of the many hiding places that were available to the man.

You *are* coming to me, Hawklan. I can feel it, he would think, and then abruptly he would teeter away from the fear into a solid confidence. His spies were growing in number. It was only a matter of time before that green-eyed abomination was reported to him. Then here, in his own lair, he would lay such traps as none could avoid. 'I'll bind you silent and unknowing. There'll be no Cadwanwr to help you, or incompetent youths to thwart me with their folly. When you open your eyes, you'll gaze into those of my Master – your Master.' He shuddered a little. 'He has arts now that you can't dream of. He grows stronger daily. Whoever you are, He'll bind you to His service, and you'll be happy to be so bound.'

But these occasions were rare. For the greater part of his time he steered diligently through the troublesome waves that he himself was stirring. Vakloss was full of Lords clamouring to see him about Eldric and the others. He would delay meeting any of them for as long as possible, and then would have them called in individually and unexpectedly.

The escort for the favoured Lord would be Mathidrin; polite but stone-faced. They would lead him through unfamiliar passages whose spartan and militaristic appearance were echoed by the room where he would encounter Dan-Tor. The King's physician would be effusive in his greeting and profuse in his apologies for both the delay and then the suddenness of the appointment. 'The burdens of state impose these discourtesies on me, Lord. I'm afraid the niceties of protocol tend to be roughly used by these troublesome times,' he would say, or some similar palliative. He would also show noticeable signs of strain and concern. The Mathidrin escort would stand close ranked behind the Lord's chair until dismissed by a reassuring gesture. This man is not one of our enemies, he is to be trusted, it would say conspicuously.

By seeing the Lords individually, Dan-Tor was able to consolidate the many rumours he was having spread about the City. He would ensure that the tale he told to each would differ in some detail, and always there would be a point at which he would lean forward and, calling the Lord by his first name, would say, 'I tell you this for yourself alone, because I know you're to be trusted . . .' Or give some other indication of a special relationship between them.

These tactics sowed subtle divisions between the Lords and heightened their growing sense of mutual distrust. The movement for the release of the four Lords and the re-establishment of the Geadrol gradually slowed down.

Accompanying the Lords in Vakloss were many of their High Guards. Etron was one such. A country lad who had recently finished his training with the cadets, he took an innocent pride in strolling through the streets of the City when he was not on duty, pleasantly aware of the quiet stir his elegant uniform caused. Had not his troop, after all, won the Grand Tournament only last year? And had they not received the praise of Lord Dan-Tor personally for their splendid turnout? Apart from one or two grim comments from the older officers about the Watch, the old Narsindal patrols, and how they should be brought back again, he had come to the conclusion that life in the High Guards was both enjoyable and civilised.

One evening he was strolling through the narrow crowded streets near the Palace debating where he might best eat that night, when the sound of raised angry voices reached him, one, a woman's. Curious, he ran towards a small crowd that appeared to be the source of the noise.

A girl, a street trader, was arguing with a Mathidrin trooper. She spoke rapidly and with a strong Vakloss accent, and Etron had some difficulty in understanding her, but it seemed the Mathidrin was accusing her of selling bad fruit and was refusing to pay. Etron saw the Mathidrin was of an age similar to himself, as were his two companions who were laughing nearby.

For a moment he was inclined to intervene, but then thought better of it. Standing orders were to avoid the Mathidrin where possible, and this young man seemed to represent the Mathidrin at their worst: loutish, arrogant and sneering. Etron was about to turn away when the Mathidrin's expression changed at some remark and he knocked the girl to the ground with a savage punch in the face. The crowd stepped back a pace instinctively. One man protested, but the Mathidrin turned on him fiercely and held his clenched fist under the man's nose.

'I know you,' he said menacingly. 'You shouldn't go around speaking up for liars and cheats like this.'

The girl was clambering to her feet, sobbing and bleeding profusely from her nose and mouth. She staggered against the Mathidrin and coughed up a gout of blood and saliva. It splattered on to the trooper's chest and Etron winced as he noticed a white tooth sliding down the black tunic. The man swore and pushed her away violently, sending her sprawling again. Then he turned his attention back to the protester.

'You'd better look to your own affairs. Especially with that nice little shop of yours only just around the corner. I've seen some very suspicious people going in and out of there. Very suspicious.' He looked significantly at his friends who nodded in confirmation.

The man paled a little and his jaw tightened, but he said nothing.

The Mathidrin, however, was not inclined to let the matter drop. Bending down, he took hold of the girl's hair and, staring into the man's face, said, 'This is a liar and a cheat. Shall I show you what we do to to liars and cheats?'

The shopkeeper stared at him icily, frightened to do anything that might bring retribution on himself or make things worse for the girl.

'We do this,' continued the Mathidrin. And, dragging the girl by her hair, he pushed her face brutally into a box of soft fruits standing in front of her stall, much to the amusement of his two friends.

Almost in spite of himself Etron pushed through the crowd and seized the Mathidrin's arm.

'No,' he said. 'That's enough. That's no way to behave. If she's cheated you there's –' He stopped in mid-sentence as the Mathidrin turned slowly to look first at his gripped arm and then at him. Etron released the arm nervously. An unpleasant smile appeared on the Mathidrin's face as he looked up and down Etron's uniform, vivid and ornate compared with his own black tunic.

'There's what, flower?' he said coaxingly.

Etron cleared his throat. He wanted to be somewhere else at that moment, but could not walk away. He wished an officer would appear round the corner. 'Let the girl go,' he said. 'There's the Law or the Chief of Markets if you've a complaint.'

The Mathidrin looked at him in disbelief, and then at his friends, who were smirking. 'Petal here wants us to run and tell tales,' he said. 'Petal doesn't think we can handle our own problems, does it?' And he pinched Etron's cheek between his thumb and forefinger. Angry at the humiliation, Etron struck the hand away. The Mathidrin grimaced, showing his teeth, and with a great push sent Etron staggering into the remains of the girl's fruit stall. 'Down where you belong, flower,' he jeered. 'In with the rest of the fruit.'

Though a High Guard, Etron was not really a fighting man, and certainly not a street brawler, but the tone of the insult and the damage to his uniform was too much. Scrambling to his feet, he flew furiously at the taunting black figure.

For a while, the two wrestled incongruously until they skidded on the slippery ground and crashed to the floor. Somewhat to his surprise, Etron recovered himself first and, standing up, seized his opponent by the scruff of the neck and thrust his face into the same box that the girl had been pushed into. 'See what it feels like, you cockroach,' he said through clenched teeth.

There was some applause and cheering from the crowd.

The Mathidrin got slowly to his feet, his face fruit-splattered and ridiculous. He put his hand on Etron's shoulder, as if for balance, and then hit him in the stomach. It was a stunning and unexpected blow – and worse. Etron realised that more than the wind had gone out of him. Everywhere suddenly felt strange and distant, and his legs wouldn't respond properly. They wouldn't even hold him up. There was a roaring in his ears and, as he slithered to the ground and rolled on to his back, his eye lighted on a brightly painted carved eagle looking down at him from the pinnacle of a nearby building. It was framed in a ring of concerned faces.

Daddy used to carve ridge birds, he thought, and then the roaring overwhelmed him in blackness.

The Mathidrin, pale and nervously defiant, leaned forward and taking hold of Etron's tunic wiped the blood from his dagger. It was an act more repellent in its callousness than the stabbing itself. The crowd seemed to be paralysed. He looked coldly at each one of them in turn as if memorising their faces. 'Go home all of you,' he said. 'This man attacked me and I had to defend myself. Don't forget that.'

Etron's Lord, a simple unaffected man, was beside himself with rage and grief, and a shocked Dan-Tor promised him a full enquiry. But no reliable witnesses could be found, and the Mathidrin, self-assured and smug, left the enquiry to the congratulations of his companions. The older officers of Etron's troop looked at their Lord and saw him impotent and livid. They took the wish in his eyes for their orders.

There was a great deal of rivalry between the High Guards of the different Lords, but not sufficient to divide them against a common foe, and the next few days saw several discreet and cautious meetings in the deep shadows provided by the bright glare of Dan-Tor's globes hovering over the City.

A week after the incident, the Mathidrin trooper was found dead in a park some way away from the Palace. He had a sword in his hand, a wreath of flowers around his neck and a rotting fruit in his gaping mouth. From the footprints in the grass it seemed that the young man had been fighting a duel.

Dan-Tor noted that aspect of the incident and smiled to himself. So you're not quite up to cold-blooded murder yet, are you, you precious guardians of the Lords? But it's a good start.

Then, turning to a servant, he said, 'Have Commander Urssain come to me immediately.'

Chapter 30

Sylvriss had made her main concern the locating of the four imprisoned Lords. Contact with them would, she believed, form an important strand in the rope she was weaving to trip, if not to strangle, Dan-Tor.

The Palace had cells suitable only for the temporary detention of offenders, and she found very quickly that they were not being kept in any of these. Dilrap was not able to help a great deal.

'They're being kept exclusively by the Mathidrin, Majesty,' he said. 'Probably somewhere over in the Westerclave, but nobody seems to know where. And I have to be diffident in my enquiries.'

'I understand, Dilrap,' said Sylvriss. 'Don't jeopardise yourself for this. Your other tasks are more important. However, I can't see our precious Mathidrin cooking and washing for the Lords. Can you find out which servants are working over there? And can we put our own in?'

Dilrap hitched his errant robe on to his shoulders and nodded his head. 'It might be possible, Majesty,' he said. 'At least to find out which servants are in the Westerclave. The Keeper of the Rooms is a bit peculiar about his schedules, but I'm known to be close enough to Dan-Tor now to say it's a spot check ordered personally by the Lord.' He nodded to himself. 'I can always smooth any furrows with a little high praise and a promise that a good report would be made. But as for putting one of our own in there . . .?' Dilrap puffed out his cheeks.

Sylvriss stared at the door for a little while when he had left. He was proving to be a staunch and capable ally, ferreting out information for her and spending hours preparing long and opaque legal arguments to litter Dan-Tor's path while ostensibly clearing it.

But if Dan-Tor began to suspect, what then? Dilrap would be no match for the man and her own part in the proceedings would surely come to light. Then she too would be assailed in some way, and the effort she was now able to put into thwarting her enemy would almost certainly be taken up fully in protecting herself and her treatment of the King. She must not burden Dilrap.

She sighed, and, eyes closed, allowed herself a brief indulgence, taking her mind back to quieter, simpler times. Once, such an action would have distressed and torn her with longing, but she had come to accept that, whatever the present and future held, the past was inviolate. It could not be relived, but equally it could not be destroyed. It would remain a solid and sure foundation to support her at all times, and its rich memories would continue to sustain the slow recovery of her husband.

Rested, she opened her eyes to the harsher present. The Westerclave, she thought. Dilrap's findings confirmed what her other informants had told her. But no one could tell her further. She fidgeted restlessly on the soft upholstered seat as if it had been made of stone. These same informants had also been bringing strange and worrying rumours. The Lords had attempted to escape; they were being poisoned; they were being starved; they had confessed their guilt; and many others, but all too vague and insubstantial. Bubbles from the depths of a dark pool.

She had tried approaching Dan-Tor directly, casually asking after the welfare of the Lords during a lull in a public function they were obliged to attend, but he had merely given her an uninformative answer and then deftly changed the subject. The incident reminded her clearly that she could not hope to lure admissions from such a man, and that to attempt to do so might well prove dangerous.

Abruptly, she made a decision. Her informants could obtain little more, if anything. She could not ask more of Dilrap. Now, perhaps a little blundering might not go amiss, she thought.

Within minutes she was mounted on her favourite horse and trotting around the Palace grounds. It was her normal habit to ride almost daily, and she was unlikely to attract any special comment. On the way to one of the side gates that would lead her into the City, and thence to one of the great parks, she passed the wide stone-arched maw of the Westerclave.

The weather was overcast, a mottled grey sky promising no sign of sun that day. But even in the brightest sunshine, the Westerclave had a gloomy aspect. A strange jumbled building joining two of the Palace towers, it was backed by a huge earth mound and looked as if it had once been built into the side of a hill. Situated where it was, it lay in almost permanent shadow.

That it was older than the rest of the Palace was obvious even to an untutored eye. Its stonework was weathered and crumbling, and lichen and ivy disfigured where they should have enhanced. Also its style of construction was markedly different, harsher and more brutal in its demands of the stone that formed it. Sylvriss always thought of it like a rotten tooth wedged into a healthy jaw, an image in which its gaping entrance became a manifestation of decay.

Legend had it that the Westerclave had been built during the First Coming; that it was the handiwork of the corrupted humans who served Sumeral; that it had been fought over many times, and had been many times won and lost. Over the years it had served many purposes – workshops and storerooms, servants' quarters, temporary barracks for High Guards briefly posted to the City, and now, Headquarters for the Mathidrin.

Sylvriss reined in her horse and looked at the ugly façade. It suited these cockroaches, she thought, using the term of abuse that the locals had discovered for the Mathidrin. Then, following her earlier impulse, she took a deep breath and, swinging down from her horse, walked briskly towards the arch.

Two Mathidrin guards standing stiffly either side of the entrance saluted but looked decidedly uncomfortable as she strode past them into the gloom. They had quite specific orders about allowing anyone into Westerclave, but this was the Queen and their Commander-in-Chief, albeit honorary. Their orders did not cover such a contingency.

She noted with some amusement the frantic footsteps behind her as she headed for a flight of stairs at the end of the broad entrance tunnel, her own footsteps echoing purposefully around the curved stonework. Clattering down the stairs, she tried to recall the layout of the building, but it was a long time since she had been in it, and its maze of corridors and stairways were even more convoluted than those in the main Palace.

The stairs led directly into a broad corridor along which, as she recalled, used to be administrative offices. The only difference between her memory and its present appearance was that now it was brilliantly lit by two rows of globes. Strangely, she found that this was an improvement.

Less of an improvement, however, was the figure seated at a desk which blocked her further progress. He was the most unlikely clerk that Sylvriss had ever seen. His uniform was immaculate, but it could not begin to disguise the bulge of his arm and shoulder muscles. He sat motionless except for his powerful, hairy hands which guided a quailing writing stylus painstakingly but unerringly across a report form. Topped with short-cropped black hair and fronted by a battered and scarred face, an oval head sported the remains of a nose, a full-lipped and vicious mouth, and dark jowls through which beard was fighting a powerful counter-attack after the morning's onslaught.

Sylvriss stood in front of the desk but the head, though clearly aware of a presence, did not stir. The hand moved steadily on. How sweet, she thought maliciously. He wants to play a game.

She cleared her throat discreetly and very deeply. The head, rapt in spurious concentration, slowly looked across to another document and then, satisfied with what it had seen, equally slowly returned to its work.

Time's up, thought Sylvriss. Coming ready or not. And she brought her riding crop smartly down on the desk between the carefully placed hands. With some satisfaction, she saw the eyes widen with disbelief, and the whole frame swell with rage. Then, with calculated anticipation, the eyes followed the riding crop slowly upwards until they met her own steady gaze.

Very professional, she thought, a second later. The man had almost totally recovered his composure by the time he had stood up and saluted.

'My apologies, sir ... ma'am,' he said. 'We weren't expecting you.'

Sylvriss nodded. 'Yes. I noticed,' she said significantly, then, 'At ease, Sirshiant. Perhaps you'd take me to the duty officer.'

'Ma'am.' He saluted again and stiffly bent forward to open a small gate to allow the Queen to pass by his desk. 'If you'd follow me.'

Sylvriss made a wilfully stately progress with her bulky escort, pausing frequently to examine a notice board here, or to peer down a staircase there, or to run a very female finger along a ridge and examine it knowingly. The Sirshiant struggled with this gait, so different from his normal martial stride. Obviously he couldn't march and, equally obviously, he couldn't stroll casually by her side like some courtier. In the end he oscillated between the two, and developed a peculiar twitch of the hands in so doing.

His behaviour told her a great deal about her status within the Mathidrin, as did that of those they passed on the way, all snapping to attention. She acknowledged each with a nod and a direct look in the eyes, marking each face and response for future reference.

I'll rot your corps from its very heart, Dan-Tor, she thought. She was particularly struck by the look of uncertainty clearly visible in every gaze. Fear is the bonding of this structure, she realised suddenly, and, as if on cue, the Sirshiant stopped at a door, and licked his lips before knocking.

The same look was in Commander Urssain's eyes, but briefly it gave way to a ruthless shrewdness, before a calculating blankness hid everything. Without knowing why I'm here, he's already thinking how he can turn my visit to his advantage, the Queen thought, as he came forward and bowed politely.

'Majesty. This is an unexpected surprise. You do us great honour,' he said. 'I'm Commander Urssain.'

'Yes, Commander, I remember you,' Sylvriss replied, 'I recall your promotion ceremony.' And I recall wondering what you'd done to deserve such promotion so quickly, she thought. Nothing pleasant, I'm sure.

Urssain had the confident, arrogant presence that seemed to

be the predominant feature of the Mathidrin, but she could sense he was aware of it and was attempting to control it. The room, too, bore signs of a personality in transition. Spartan and functional, but furnished with a strange mixture of brash cheapness and tasteful elegance. The whole looked incongruous, but she realised that Urssain was learning a new trade. The room represented the first fumbling steps on a ladder of unknown height. One of the rising stars. Would he flare and dazzle for a brief instant, or would he take a permanent place in a constellation that would hover around Dan-Tor?

'I hope I'm not disturbing your routine, Commander,' she continued. 'I'm afraid I've called purely on impulse. It's such a long time since I've been in the Westerclave, and it used to be such a dismal place. It occurred to me as I was passing that as your Commander-in-Chief I really should see how you're all faring here.'

Urssain opened his hands in a gesture of resignation. 'We're all soldiers, ma'am. Any place that keeps out the weather is a good place. I'm afraid we're rather insensitive to our surroundings generally.'

I can see that, you thug, she thought, taking in the room again.

'But I appreciate your concern, ma'am. As will the men also.'

'Perhaps you could spare a little time to show me round,' Sylvriss said.

'Ma'am.' Urssain clicked his heels and bowed deeply to hide the look in his eyes which he knew was beyond his ability to control.

Out in the corridor again, Sylvriss could hear the place buzzing and hissing with news of her unexpected arrival. It'll be interesting to see what Dan-Tor makes of this, she thought. But the very thought made her stomach turn over. This visit's an impulse, she repeated to herself. Somewhere between foolish female curiosity and an equally foolish female wish to do something for the men over whom she was in charge, albeit only nominally. I must act accordingly.

As she toured the building, her memory of the place returned somewhat. Very little had changed, though it was cluttered with all the paraphernalia of a permanent barrack. The main difference was the bright lighting that illuminated every cranny. It *is* an improvement, she thought again. It was the first time she had ever seen Dan-Tor's globes enhance anything. Yet though they clarified, they did not enliven. Rather, they heightened an unpleasant inner bleakness, a harshness in the building. Your lights expose your own soul here, Dan-Tor, she thought. But the discovery chilled her.

She insisted on going down into the cellars to examine the kitchens, this being decidedly a foolish woman's prerogative, and she noted carefully the faces of the servants there. It was the only place in the building where she had seen other than Mathidrin.

'I suppose that big beggar'll complain he's being poisoned again.' The voice came faintly through the rattling din of the kitchen and Sylvriss bent forward hastily to peer into a bubbling, anonymous concoction to hide her interest. Casting round, her eyes lit on a surly-faced individual carefully picking up a tray containing four dishes. Dishes that were more elegant by far than the unadorned metalwork that was hung and stacked about the place.

Straightening up, she allowed her gaze to fall accidentally on the man who was heading towards a nearby doorway. He pushed open the door with his foot and, turning, began down a flight of steps.

'Oh, you've someone sick, Commander?' she said. There was a flicker in Urssain's eyes. 'Surely you don't have your sick bay downstairs? So far below ground?' Before he could answer, she took maternal charge of the situation. 'Sick men, Commander, need fresh air and sunshine. They should be where they can see the Palace gardens and the parks. Where they can stroll and convalesce.' As she spoke, she moved slowly but steadily towards the door which the servant had used, venturing at one stage to take Urssain's elbow with a guiding hand. The look in Urssain's eyes bordered on the frantic, but he kept the rest of his face under control.

At the door, Sylvriss paused, waiting for someone to open it for her. She could almost feel Urssain's mind racing. Then she heard him take a very deep, quiet breath through his nose.

Leaning past her he took the door handle in his squat powerful hand and opened the door without hesitating. He smiled. 'I'm afraid we've no one sick, ma'am. That's to say . . .' He acted out an apologetic little fluster. ' . . . I'm glad we've no one sick. The food on the tray was for prisoners.'

On *those* dishes, she thought. 'Prisoners?' she echoed, stepping back a pace. 'You keep prisoners here? Why not in the Palace cells?'

'They're just military prisoners in transit, ma'am,' Urssain replied, extending his arm down the stairway to indicate he was awaiting her pleasure to show her the offenders in question. 'There are always one or two who have to learn their discipline the hard way. They'll only be here for a few days, and it's easier for us to keep them here than over in the cells.' Then, frankly, 'And to be honest, we prefer to look after our own.'

'Yes,' said Sylvriss uncertainly, backing out of he door and looking as if she wished to change the subject. 'I'm sure I can leave such matters in your capable hands, Commander.'

Urssain was barely aware of the rest of Sylvriss's tour of the building and was almost surprised when he found himself unnecessarily cupping his hands together to offer his Commander-in-Chief a support from which to mount her horse.

'Thank you, Commander,' said Sylvriss, looking down at him. She appreciated the fleeting look of triumph in his eyes. 'I hope my visit hasn't caused too much disruption to your routine.' Then looking at the scarred façade of the Westerclave she said reflectively, 'It isn't the happiest of buildings, Commander, but I think you've made the best you could of it. Please accept my congratulations.'

Urssain saluted briskly and the Queen rode off. He watched her as she headed towards one of the side gates, gently urging her horse into a trot. Women, he thought. She'd come so close to blundering into those damned Lords. Dan-Tor would've had my head pickled in a bottle, or worse, if she'd found them. He congratulated himself on his nerve and his luck, but mainly on his nerve – to have opposed the woman at that door would surely have been to provoke her into going through it. Yes, he'd handled that very well.

*　　*　　*

Sylvriss cantered through the streets towards her favourite park almost oblivious of her surroundings. She had the servant's face, she had the place, and her act had convinced Urssain well enough. It had been a useful and revealing venture, for all her heart was still pounding. But what would Dan-Tor make of it?

Chapter 31

The death of Etron and the subsequent death of his killer was like the start of a fever in the City. The mutual disdain with which the High Guards and the Mathidrin had treated one another slipped easily into almost open warfare.

The more decorative and ornamental Guards were easy prey for the Mathidrin. Outraged by the abuse and scorn levelled at them loudly and publicly, they would eventually respond with some form of ineffectual violence and finish up being soundly trounced for their pains. Beatings and woundings grew daily.

The older Guards, and those whose Lords kept to the old traditions, were, in general, less abused and more able to handle such abuse as did come their way. However, they took the hurts deeply, and slowly and inexorably the Mathidrin found their swaggering domination of the City being resisted by a quiet and grim opposition. The more experienced Guards might be difficult to provoke into street brawling, but they began to ensure that no insult to their own went unanswered.

Apart from the avenging of Etron's death, their reprisals were almost good-humoured, and offending Mathidrin were found wandering in conspicuously public places bound and trouserless, or covered in paint or horse manure, or otherwise bizarrely decorated.

This interlude, however, passed all too quickly, and soon there accumulated a bloody, if covert, record of wounding for wounding and, eventually, killing for killing. The Mathidrin soon found how to provoke the High Guards into open and public combat. They turned their attentions increasingly to the citizens of Vakloss. Anyone who failed to step aside quickly enough, or who did not have a sufficiently respectful look on their face, or who happened to be conveniently available, was liable to be roughly handled, and anyone who offered any protest or resistance would be severely beaten.

Shopkeepers and stallholders had their goods 'commandeered' and could look to have more taken, or their premises wrecked if they demurred. Fear began to spread through the streets of the City and the roads of the countryside like a fen mist – dank and evil-smelling.

Many of the Lords, frustrated by their own impotence, acquiesced in the silent vendettas being pursued by their Guards, but it took no great military experience to smell an organised ambush in the new tactics adopted by the Mathidrin.

'Chew on your sword hilt.' The order went out from Lord right down to cadet in troop after troop. The hope being that no response would cause the Mathidrin to abandon this strategy. All knew that it was only a faint hope, and soon a certain fatalism began to possess the Lords as, rather than ceasing their actions, the Mathidrin increased them.

The Lords appealed to Dan-Tor and again he faced them individually and plied them with inconsistencies. 'I'll look into what you've reported, but there's so much conflicting evidence. The Mathidrin have hard and unpleasant tasks to perform at times, rooting out disaffection and even treachery. They suffer a great deal of abuse and provocation from the people and they may well make mistakes from time to time, but . . .' a small gesture of admonition, ' . . . they don't always get the co-operation from your Guards that they might expect.' Then a dismissive gesture of tolerant understanding. 'However, I appreciate your men may be finding it difficult to adjust to their new roles. Soldiers are usually strong in pride.'

When pressed, he would grow stern, or perhaps confidential, with an affectionate arm placed around the shoulder. 'I fear that difficult times lie ahead of us all. You must understand, there are forces at work that seek our very destruction.' Then the well-established threat would seep into the edges of his reply. 'These enemies are both without *and* within. More will become clear at the accounting of the Lord Eldric and his co-conspirators but, rest assured, there are more guilty parties than the four we have and I want none to escape because the Mathidrin are occupied dealing with the petty rivalries of the Guards.'

Thus the Mathidrin excesses continued and worsened, and the Lords' faint hope fluttered out in the terrible winds that started to blow. From cadet right up to Lord came the message. 'Lord, we can suffer our own humiliation, but the innocent are being trampled. We can no longer stand by.' The Lords' fatalism turned to black hopelessness as Dan-Tor's subtle poisons took their toll and growing suspicion and doubt bound them with unseen shackles.

The High Guards, however, were not privy to such corrosive doubts, nor overly interested in the niceties of the Law. What was happening was manifestly wrong. Their Lords might not be able to act, but it was the sworn duty of the Guards to defend the people of Fyorlund.

So the citizens of Vakloss began to see an increasing number of High Guards casually patrolling their streets. The immediate significance of this did not become apparent until tales began to spread of Mathidrin being subjected to the treatment they themselves had been meting out. The clandestine war broke out openly and in earnest. Initially, clinging to a shred of their Lords' will, the Guards used staves instead of swords but, with the inevitable action and reaction of violence, these were soon discarded and the distinctive sound of sword on sword began to ring through the streets with increasing frequency.

While the Mathidrin were superior in numbers and, as individuals, temperamentally inclined towards bullying and street brawling, the High Guards were better disciplined and better led, and invariably put their black-clad opponents to flight.

For a little while the streets became safe again as the Mathidrin retreated to lick their wounds. But, as if motivated by a sterner resolve than was apparent in their actual fighting, they reappeared in larger and more malevolently inclined groups.

Again their victims were the ordinary citizens of Vakloss whom they now actively terrorised. Again the High Guards responded, but casualties were mounting and the superior numbers of the Mathidrin began to tell.

'They'll wear us down,' became the view of the High Guards organising the resistance. 'There are just too many of them.'

Opinions were divided. Some were for continuing as at present, modifying their tactics to swift running attacks and ambush; others wanted to use their horses to make up for their smaller numbers. Others wanted to 'String our bows. Thin them out at a distance. They're not fit to meet sword to sword anyway'. A faint murmur even began of a large decisive strike against the Mathidrin barracks and a confrontation with Dan-Tor, or even the King.

That *was* beyond the pale, and such talk was squashed with some vigour. But the words had been spoken and were not without tactical relevance. The older heads realised that what had begun as punishment patrols, justifiable, albeit of dubious legality, were, with talk of cavalry tactics and bowmen, sliding tragically close to becoming a major conflict and armed defiance of the King. The Lords would not be able to turn their gaze away from that. And yet, what else could be done? The more astute detected a pattern behind the Mathidrin's behaviour. It was intended to provoke just this impasse. Death by attrition, or destruction through open rebellion. And it was working. Working very well.

The doubts among the officers led inevitably to indecision and a consequent fall in morale amongst the High Guards as their casualties grew and no effective response was ordered. Gradually the streets returned to the Mathidrin, now raucous in their triumph. But their laughter was as strained as it was harsh, and their arbitrary mistreatment of the people lessened as they too felt the atmosphere of the City becoming tense and heavy, full of foreboding, as though a storm were brewing, a storm waiting for that last tiny speck of moisture-laden dust to release the unrestrained fury of its accumulated power.

Dan-Tor stood on a high balcony and looked out over the City. He smiled to himself. True, he was disappointed in Urssain's failure to obtain reliable information from within the High Guards. Their loyalties had proved remarkably resistant to his lures. But then, he shrugged, this was of no great significance. The High Guards' very loyalty told him all he needed to know about them and how best to handle them. A little detailed information from time to time would have spared Urssain some losses and morale problems, but they were unimportant.

Besides, his apparently ready forgiveness of tactical failures by Urssain was another small tie to bind the man with.

Moving along the balcony, he sat down on a carved wooden bench and, resting his head back on the cool stone, looked out towards the haze-obscured northern horizon.

A small movement caught his eye, gliding amongst the trees in the parklands at the edge of the City. Even at this distance he knew it would be Sylvriss. She had been an intractable problem over the years, but persistence conquers all, he thought. Now she was simply grateful to be allowed to nurse her husband after he had stabilised his condition. So grateful. Even taking an interest in 'her' Mathidrin. Stupid stable girl. A doubt floated into his mind as the distant figure disappeared from sight, but he dismissed it. There was no spark left in the ashes of her resistance that could flare up and rekindle the spirit that had been King Rgoric. Closing his eyes Dan-Tor listened to the faint noise of the City floating up to him.

Through the streets a group of Mathidrin were marching. Periodically they stopped and one of them would nail a notice on a door or a tree. Following the eclipse of the High Guards by the Mathidrin, Dan-Tor judged that the notice was unlikely to cause anything more than talk. If perchance the High Guards reacted violently then they would condemn themselves. If they did not, so much the better.

The sun shone on the side of his brown face and made him feel uncomfortable even though the breeze at that height was strong and cold. As he stood up to leave the balcony, he noted again the Queen riding to and fro across the distant park.

An inconspicuous figure studied the notice painstakingly, nodding as he did so. It was a very simple notice. Another Edict. It disbanded the High Guards . . . for their repeated and continuing acts of lawlessness against the King's officers in the execution of their duties . . . In deference to past services, the Guards were to be allowed to return unhindered to their homes, to pursue their civilian occupations, but the wearing of uniforms, congregating or drilling was forbidden on pain of imprisonment, as was failure to report such incidents. Apparently irrelevantly, the notice went on to urge the co-operation of all Fyordyn in these times of threat from enemies both abroad and at home.

The figure moved quietly away from the notice and walked slowly down the street. He had to seek out his old friends. Something had to be done now, definitely.

A Mathidrin patrol came round the corner, but they did not see the figure. He had faded into the shadows and stood now watching them. Although he had been retired from active service for some years, part of his Oath was ever before him. His ears had heard it, his mind had registered it, but his training and experience had merged it into his very nature.

'Yatsu, you will be Goraidin until death and beyond.'

Chapter 32

The guard shifted his feet impatiently while Arinndier performed his daily ritual of suspiciously examining the meal and interrogating the slouching young servant who had just brought it. The delay was irritating but he had learnt from experience that it was pointless to remonstrate as this was liable to start the four of them talking, and prolong the waiting even further. Let them have their games. No point in making trouble.

'You're new here, aren't you?' Arinndier asked the servant.

'Yes, Lord,' said the boy. He was about to continue but a cough from the guard stopped him. Arinndier overruled the cough with a smile. 'What's happened to the other one? Fallen sick after eating our food, has he?'

Eldric chuckled and laid down a book he was reading, to watch the exchange.

'No, Lord,' replied the boy, risking a nervous smile. 'He's been promoted. He's over in . . .'

No cough this time. 'Boy,' said the guard sharply. 'Be silent.'

The boy's mouth dropped open and he looked from Arinndier to the guard and back in bewilderment.

'My fault, guard,' said Arinndier. 'I forgot.' Then, uncertainly, he replaced the last dish cover. 'There now. I suppose it's all right. Would you serve it out for us please?'

'Well,' said Darek when the servant and the guard had gone. 'That lad's not much, but he's an improvement on that surly oaf who used to fetch our food. Fancy him being promoted. The only rise in life I'd ever imagine him getting would be on the toes of someone's boot – preferably mine.' Uncharacteristically he laughed. 'His face was enough to poison most food, Arin. I hope they've not put him in charge of anything perishable.'

Arinndier smiled at Darek's unusual levity, but Eldric seemed preoccupied. 'Something's on the move,' he said thoughtfully, sitting down at the table.

'What do you mean?' Arinndier said.

'I don't know,' replied Eldric, idly pushing a knife to and fro. 'But Darek's given you half of it. Who'd promote that sour-faced lout? Kick him out certainly. But promote?'

Arinndier was unimpressed. 'Eldric, the Geadrol's been suspended. We've been arrested and imprisoned without charge and for no crime. The wrongful promotion of a servant is hardly significant against that background, is it?'

Eldric did not reply, but Darek chuckled. 'Oh, I don't know, Arin. You should study your history more. Kings and Princes come and go, but the servants, the officials, the secretaries – they go on forever. Eldric's got . . .'

Eldric waved a hand gently to silence him. 'Something about that boy,' he said, frowning. 'But I can't pinpoint it.'

Hreldar looked up from his meal and stared at Eldric's worried face. Then he looked at the table. His eyes narrowed. 'Look,' he said, spreading his two hands towards the table. 'Look. That boy lumbered round as if he'd got two left feet, but look at how he's laid this. It's immaculate.' He paused. 'How many times have you seen some little one standing by this kind of handiwork, waiting for your judgement?'

'Of course,' said Eldric. 'Junior cadets and their party pieces.' He leaned back and clapped his hands together. 'It seems such a long time ago. Little shining faces.' Then he laughed. 'Elementary field craft to learn how to survive in the wilds of the mountains, and elementary house craft to learn how to survive in the wilds of society.'

Abruptly his expression became sombre, and a look of determination came into his face, so grim that the others stopped eating and watched him in silence. 'Ask yourselves, Lords,' he said. 'Why would a miserable servant be promoted and replaced by a young lad, a junior cadet who, if I'm any judge, would probably be on the point of entering the Cadets proper?'

Arinndier looked at the table. It seemed a weighty deduction from such flimsy evidence, but the neat array in front of him did indeed look like the grading display of a junior cadet. And the lad had done it with wilful gawkiness. Then, too, he had volunteered the information that his predecessor had been promoted.

The four men sat silent and the low buzz of the globe light filled the room.

'Could he be a spy?' Arinndier offered the suggestion unconvincingly, to break the silence.

Darek shook his head. 'No,' he said. 'Who'd spy on us? Dan-Tor? He knows we wouldn't discuss anything important in front of a servant. Besides, I don't think he gives a night bird's hoot for what we might say.'

Arinndier nodded, and started eating again.

Eldric too started to eat but, almost immediately, he stopped. 'We've no idea what's happening outside,' he said. 'But we must still have friends out there, or Dan-Tor would've disposed of us in some way by now, I'm sure.'

'Maybe,' said Arinndier. 'But we've seen no sign of them so far.'

'Yes,' said Eldric, 'that's true. But think what it means. They'll presumably have tried various legal remedies and met with no success for one reason or another. We know we're in the Westerclave and that it's being used as Headquarters for these Mathidrin, so we can't reasonably expect an armed assault to rescue us. So someone, somewhere, will be tying to contact us. And now this boy comes along. Slouching and acting stupid, but doing this little cadet exercise for us, neat as neat.' He gestured over the table.

Hreldar spoke again, coldly and definitively. 'When he comes back, see if he knows the Hand Language. That'll answer all debate.'

Within the hour, the servant and the guard returned. Arinndier casually tried to engage the guard in conversation, but the man would not be drawn. His eyes followed the boy constantly as he slouched around the table collecting the dishes.

'Careful, boy, you're spilling the wine on my tunic,' Eldric said angrily, standing up suddenly. The boy started and fumbled for a cloth in his belt, nearly dropping his tray in the process.

'Put it *down*, boy,' said Darek testily, waving his hands

emphatically. Flustered, the boy put the tray on the table and, with shaking hands, offered Eldric the cloth. Eldric waved it away with an irritable gesture. The boy fumbled and hesitated, ran the back of his hand across his nose as if about to weep, and then replaced the cloth in his belt.

'I didn't see all that,' said Arinndier when the guard and the servant had left. 'I was busy discreetly obscuring the guard's view.'

The others were looking a little stunned.

Darek spoke. 'I asked him who he was,' he said, repeating the gesture reflexively

'And?' said Arinndier.

'Just two words, Arin,' said Eldric. 'Just two words.'

Arinndier gazed skyward. 'Go on,' he said patiently.

Eldric's hand flicked out the boy's reply. 'Queen's messenger.'

The high hedges threw long shadows across the narrow lane as the Mathidrin patrol rode leisurely back towards the City. For the most part, the six men were silent. The tour had been uneventful and their leader, newly promoted, was peevishly angry that nothing had arisen to provide him with an excuse to demonstrate to his men that his leadership would be worth following.

In the villages that lay on their circuit, they had found the inhabitants remarkably docile. Usually it was possible to provoke the odd individual into some angry response, then enjoy the administration of a little summary justice on the offender. Or some lone soul would be found wandering the fields who could be accused of spying for the Orthlundyn and pursued relentlessly while 'attempting to escape'. But on this tour, nothing. The fields were deserted or the people were present in sufficient numbers to make too blatantly unjust a provocation a little too risky. Now they were heading for Vakloss two days early.

The patrol leader stretched up in his saddle, his muscles aching with the day's riding and the tension of his mounting petulance. If only some yokel would step out of one of these fields, he thought. I'd give these lads something to remember.

Then, as if at the command of his thoughts, a halting figure emerged from a gateway some way along the road from them. It was an old man, the leader noted, and limping. Not much of a chase here, but anything will do after a tour like this.

He loosened his heavy staff in its loop, running his thumb over two small notches cut in the handle. One for each of the 'fugitives' he had killed; struck down at the gallop with a single stylish swinging blow that earned him great praise from his peers when he was just a trooper. Even as he started to spur his horse forward, he was already receiving the plaudits of his fellows back in the barracks that evening. His stomach tightened with pleasure and anticipation.

'You,' he shouted, 'stop!' Somewhat to his surprise, the figure halted and turned to face him. He could not make out the features of the man, as they were hidden under the brim of a large hat and the man was stooping and leaning heavily on a stick. Reaching him, the patrol leader found the bright setting sun shining in his face. He screwed up his eyes and peered down at the figure standing uncertainly in the flickering shadows of the wind-stirred trees and hedges.

'Sir?' said the figure timorously.

'Why were you running away?' the patrol leader asked harshly.

The figure gave a nervous laugh. 'Running, sir? I can't run. I'm lame, you see.' And he lifted his stick a little way off the ground.

But the patrol leader had made his decision. He had to impress his newly acquired patrol and this old fool would have to serve his purpose. He gripped his staff. 'You're lying,' he said. 'You were sneaking about, and when you saw us you tried to run away. Right, men?'

Nodding and grinning expectantly, the members of the patrol concurred.

'He'll have to be taken in for interrogation,' volunteered one. 'There's plenty of room now the old dungeons have been opened up.'

'No, no, no,' said the leader, affecting concern. 'I don't think we need disturb this good man to that extent. After all, we're empowered to attend to these matters as we find them.' Then, leaning forward solicitously, 'You don't want to go to Vakloss and face the Lord Dan-Tor do you, old man?'

The old man was trembling visibly.

Vermin, these creatures, thought the patrol leader. And cowards as well.

'The Lord Dan-Tor's a great Lord, sir,' stammered the old man. 'It would be an honour to meet him. He's done so much for our country.'

'Indeed he has, old man,' said the patrol leader. 'And he'll do more when he's rooted out all the traitorous scum that goes skulking about the lanes spying on his Mathidrin and reporting everything to our country's enemies.' He took out his staff with a luxurious gesture and held it almost touching the old man's face.

'Yes, sir, yes, sir,' said the old man, stepping back a little further into the shade.

'Come on, get on with it,' said one of the patrol. 'It'll be dark before we get back.' The patrol leader shot an angry glance at the complainer. He'd deal with that one later. But this old fool was no use, there'd be no entertainment from him, craven old dolt.

'The young sir's right, sir,' said the old man, reaching out a shaking hand and touching the leader's boot nervously. 'It's going to be a dark night.'

The patrol leader withdrew his foot furiously. 'Don't touch me, old man,' he shouted, almost hysterically. 'This is the only thing belonging to the Mathidrin that traitors are allowed to touch.' The vicious intent that had taken root at the first sight of the old man rose compulsively to its climax even though the route to it lacked the elegance he would have preferred. He stood up in his stirrups, raising the staff high over his head, and brought it whistling down on the old man's head.

But the old man's head was not there. In an almost leisurely manner he stepped to one side at the last moment and the blow missed him completely. Poised for impact, and not finding any, the patrol leader tumbled heavily from his horse. The old man reached out as if to catch him, but his action seemed only to accelerate the man's fall, and there was a skin-crawling crack as the two hit the ground.

The patrol leader subsided into the summer grass, his head at a very strange angle, and his face wearing a surprised, if blank, expression. The old man stood up, remarkably straight now, and looked at the patrol, momentarily stunned and motionless at this unexpected turn of events. The evening birds stopped singing.

'A long dark night ahead, gentlemen,' he said in a voice completely without its previous whine and tremor. Then the evening calm was broken by a sudden rush of wind followed by a sound like the falling of ripe fruit.

With barely a gasp, the remaining five riders fell slowly from their horses, each impaled on an arrow.

Figures appeared silently from the deepening shadows and quietened the nervous horses before moving to the fallen Mathidrin.

The birds started to sing again, and the setting sun flooded the lane red before sinking out of sight.

Yatsu took off his broad-brimmed hat and laid his stick on the ground. 'Careful,' he said to the others. 'Careful how you draw the arrows.'

Sylvriss gazed down at the key lying in front of her. 'This is the key to *their* door?' she asked, eyes wide.

'Yes, Majesty,' said Dilrap, hitching up his robe on to his shoulders.

Sylvriss picked up the key gingerly. 'How did you get it?' she asked, with some awe. She had just returned from riding and, dressed in her riding clothes, with flushed face and shining eyes, she looked magnificent. Dilrap basked in the radiance and beamed rather inanely until he realised what he was doing, then he stammered and fluttered alarmingly.

'The cellars in the Westerclave are only part of the old servants' quarters, Majesty,' he said. 'I think the King surprised more than the Lords when he had them arrested. Apparently nothing was ready, but even the Mathidrin realised that Lords couldn't be kept in the ordinary cells, so they put them in this little suite of rooms temporarily, until the Lord Dan-Tor returned. But like most temporary arrangements it soon became permanent.'

'But the key, Dilrap,' said Sylvriss. 'Where did you get it from?'

'From the locksmith, Majesty,' came the reply.

The Queen's face darkened a little. 'Is he to be trusted?' she asked.

Dilrap's manner was reassuring. 'Majesty, it doesn't . . .'

Sylvriss silenced him abruptly with a sudden but discreet hand movement.

'Honoured Secretary,' she said, quite loudly. 'I assure you, you worry unnecessarily.'

Dilrap looked nervously into those soft brown eyes for confirmation of the presence he felt behind him. The Queen stood up, and, casually placing the key in her pocket, stepped around him and walked towards the tall figure standing silently in the doorway.

'Lord Dan-Tor,' she said. 'This is a pleasant surprise. We see so little of you these days. Perhaps *you* could assure the Honoured Secretary that his concern for me is unnecessary.'

'Majesty?' said Dan-Tor, puzzled.

The Queen levelled a gently accusatory hand at Dilrap, who felt he was now sufficiently composed to turn and face the unexpected visitor. 'He fears I'm too diligent in the nursing of my husband. He fears I may preserve the King's health at the cost of my own.'

'Majesty,' said Dan-Tor. 'The Honoured Secretary's concern does him credit. The healer's burden can be heavy, especially when an illness is as intractable and unpredictable as the King's. I regret that the problems of State have prevented my helping the King as I have in the past, but –'

Sylvriss interrupted him. 'Lord Dan-Tor. It's more important to the King that you continue to carry the burden of State, heavy though it may be. He's quiet now, but far from well, and the merest mention of State affairs unsettles him. Sadly I cannot carry your healer's burden, or I would.' She became confidential and almost childlike. 'But I can nurse him. I carry out your instructions meticulously. I give him his potions and tablets as you've prescribed and soothe him when he's restless; it's little enough but at least I feel that I am helping both him and you.'

Dan-Tor looked at her enigmatically. 'The King is indeed fortunate to have such a Queen, Majesty. But please remember that you must seek me out urgently if his condition deteriorates. No matter where I am. The King is the mainstay of the State. His well-being must override all other considerations.'

'Of course, Lord Dan-Tor,' said Sylvriss. 'But I mustn't burden you with the Honoured Secretary's concerns, must I? What is it you wanted to see me about?'

Dan-Tor affected diffidence. 'At the risk of incurring your displeasure, Majesty, I had hoped to talk to you again about the matter of an escort for you when out riding.'

Sylvriss raised her hand to stop him. 'Now it's you who're too concerned, Lord Dan-Tor. I need no escort.'

'Majesty,' insisted Dan-Tor. 'The times are unsettled. We've rioting and disturbances in our streets now, I can't . . .'

Sylvriss interrupted again. 'Rest assured, Lord Dan-Tor, no one will harm me. Besides, where will you find horsemen in Fyorlund to escort *me*?'

Dan-Tor conceded. 'That's true, Majesty. But I'm still concerned. If the situation becomes worse, I fear even your popularity won't be shield enough.'

'Lord Dan-Tor. I above all don't wish to add to your many difficulties. If indeed the situation in the City worsens, then perhaps we'll discuss this again. In the meantime, I beg of you, rest easy in your mind about my well-being.'

Madam, you can break your stiff Riddin neck for all I care, Dan-Tor thought, but the blame would probably be laid at my feet. 'As you wish, Majesty,' he said reluctantly and, with a deep bow, he was gone.

Sylvriss breathed out a long slow breath and closed her eyes briefly. Then taking out the key from her pocket she waved it at Dilrap. 'The locksmith, Dilrap. Is he to be trusted?'

Dilrap, still fidgety from the sudden intrusion of Dan-Tor, smiled nervously. 'He doesn't need to be trusted, Majesty. The key's of a type that is used for many rooms, he's constantly making the like to replace lost ones. The boy noted the number when a guard dropped it.'

Sylvriss nodded. 'We must get it to the Lords immediately,' she said resolutely.

Dilrap dithered and threw up his hands. 'Majesty, that will serve no purpose. The boy tells me that the door is bolted as well as locked. Besides it couldn't be done. He's constantly watched when he's with them and only able to communicate very cautiously with the Lords, using some secret sign language. We must be careful how we . . .' He paused.

'How we *use* him.' Sylvriss finished his sentence. Dilrap bowed his head. 'It's a shameful word to admit to, Dilrap,' she went on. 'But it's true, for all he's a willing agent. We must be careful what we ask of him, and you did right to remind me. I mustn't let my distance and security make me callous.'

Or careless, she thought. If the boy were exposed, then so also would be Dilrap and herself, and Sylvriss knew that if that happened, Dan-Tor would take delight in destroying her helpers while leaving her untouched. He would relish silently laying their agony at her feet.

She slipped the key into her pocket. 'This is important even if we can't use it immediately,' she said. 'Tell the boy he's done well, and to take great care.'

A group of Mathidrin rode into one of the small squares that were liberally dotted about Vakloss. The brightly decorated houses and shops looked gay in the strong sunshine, and the trees swayed busily in the breeze. The square was littered with stalls and a large crowd was milling around, buying, selling, bartering, arguing, laughing.

The hubbub fell slightly as the Mathidrin entered, a small knot of black intruding into the coloured throng, but it picked up almost immediately, and seemed in fact to rise to a new pitch.

The leader of the Mathidrin looked around bleakly at the happy crowd. Over at the far corner of the square he saw another group of Mathidrin sitting drinking in front of a shop. He sniffed, and his mouth curled in an unpleasant sneer. Then, casually, he raised his right hand and idly rubbed the side of his nose. Nearby stood a stall which glittered and sparkled with mirrors and crystal ornaments. The stallholder looked up at the black rider thoughtfully for a moment and then walked towards him, his face breaking into a broad smile.

'Welcome to our little market, sirs,' he said. The Mathidrin made no response. Unabashed, the man continued, addressing the whole patrol through its leader. 'May I offer you a drink, gentlemen? or perhaps I can find you bargains for your ladies.' He winked.

The leader looked down at him contemptuously, sighed and then, turning away, jerked his horse's reins. The horse moved sideways and bumped into the smiling man. He staggered and muttered something.

The Mathidrin leader spun round, eyes blazing. 'What did you say?' he growled.

The stallholder held his gaze, all smiles gone. He spoke loudly and clearly. 'I said, be careful what you're doing with your nag, cockroach.'

There was a gasp from the crowd in the immediate vicinity and a space opened around him. The two men stared at one another and slowly the square became quiet. Women started to lead their children away urgently. The Mathidrin drinking on the far side of the square stood up to see what was happening and several of them began to move forward expectantly, pushing their way deep into the crowd.

Then, into the silence, came the harsh, rhythmic sound of approaching footsteps. The rider and the stallholder paused and within seconds a Mathidrin foot patrol entered the square.

The insulted leader stood in his stirrups and signalled to it.

Almost immediately it turned towards him urgently, but its formation soon became extended and fragmented as it manoeuvred along the congested aisles between the stalls. The crowd closed silently around it like water round the hull of a passing ship.

The rider watched this disintegration passively then, making a small hand signal to the stallholder, he swung his foot from the stirrup and aimed a seemingly vicious kick at the man's head. The man, however, caught the extended foot easily and with a great heave pushed the Mathidrin out of his saddle.

Yatsu affected a conspicuous attempt to retain his seat before slithering from sight down the far side of his horse with a loud cry. A roar went up from the crowd around him.

The leader of the foot patrol turned to urge his men forward, only to find them scattered and isolated. He started to shout angrily but, even as he did so, hands seized him and the roar of the crowd crashed over him like a great tidal wave.

At the far corner of the square, Yatsu turned briefly to check that the attack on the Mathidrin patrol was well under way then, with a quick signal of thanks to the stallholder and the now silent crowd around him, he and his men slipped quietly away. They had other diversions to set in train that day.

Chapter 33

Since his journey to the Gretmearc Hawklan had ceased to be surprised by his knowledge of places that should have been strange to him. It was intriguing, as were many other aspects of his life, but with so much mystery surrounding him he knew that nothing was to be gained from arbitrary questioning. His approach was pragmatic. The knowledge was there and it was indisputably useful, and that would have to suffice for the time being.

However, as he travelled across Fyorlund with his Mathidrin escort, an uneasiness began to seep into that very knowledge; an uneasiness that deepened profoundly as they neared Vakloss.

The City seeped into view as they travelled across Fyorlund's relatively flat and fertile central plain. At first it was exposed and hidden alternately by minor features in the landscape but, as they drew nearer, it began to dominate the surrounding countryside.

It was built on a great isolated hill and its towers and high buildings, culminating in the towering edifice of the Palace at its central and highest point, topped it like a many-pointed crown. Hawklan realised that he knew the country, but not the City. But even his knowledge of the country was . . . dark? Fearful?

The Palace was no Anderras Darion, but it soared majestically above the City's lesser buildings, although these also were of no mean splendour. Vakloss had been built by craftsmen of some considerable skill. It seemed to Hawklan, however, that the splendour was inappropriate. This place troubled him. It was a focus for something dark inside him.

'You've no cities as fine as this in Orthlund, I'll wager,' said the Mathidrin Captain, riding to his side. Hawklan started out of his reverie and stared about foolishly for a moment. The Captain's tone had an unpleasant edge and reflected his continuing uncertainty about Hawklan, but Hawklan ignored the inflection and took the comment as if it had been a pleasantry.

'No,' he replied, 'we've no cities in Orthlund. Only villages. I've never seen a city before. I can't imagine what it's like to live in one. It seems to be rather a strange idea, but I suppose if you've a great many people in your land, then the ways in which you live together will inevitably be different from ours.'

The Captain smiled uncertainly. Hawklan's constant willingness to accede to his boastful assertions about Fyorlund unsettled him, left him off balance. There was nothing there for him to argue about. He had the feeling that he was both winning and losing at the same time. 'I find it strange to imagine a country that's only farms, countryside and villages,' he said.

Hawklan smiled. 'That probably means we're both victims of our histories,' he said. 'Tell me, how old is Vakloss?'

The Captain frowned slightly. This man asked the strangest questions. 'I've no idea,' he said. 'It's always been there.'

'Always?' said Hawklan, raising his eyebrows humorously, and fixing the Captain with his green-eyed stare. The man avoided the gaze by looking back and rebuking one of his men for some non-existent offence.

'Always?' repeated Hawklan, turning to the front again.

The Captain looked embarrassed. This man had an unnerving way of drawing confidences from people. 'Learning's not encouraged in the Mathidrin,' he said brusquely. 'And too close an interest in the past would be viewed very suspiciously. We're told it's just been one long tale of abuse of the people by the Lords and the Geadrol, and treachery against the Kings. It's our job to put it right, not debate it.'

Hawklan raised a placatory hand. 'Just an innocent question, Captain,' he said. 'It looks such a splendid sight I was naturally interested in who would build such a place.'

Mollified, the Captain volunteered, 'When I was a kid, they used to say it was built after the First Coming. I suppose that just means it's very old and no one really knows.'

Hawklan nodded. 'It's certainly very old, but . . .' his voice tailed off. A dark swirling and roaring surged round him and he heard a distant, failing, trumpet call. A sense of horror over-whelmed him and he felt a cry of unbearable despair forming inside him.

'But?' The Captain's voice brought him back to the day's sunshine.

Hawklan shook his head apologetically. 'Nothing,' he said.

Reining his horse back discreetly, the Captain fell behind Hawklan slightly, so that he could study him again.

Tall and straight, Hawklan rode his splendid black horse with an ease that the Captain had only seen before in Queen Sylvriss. He was relaxed and easy in everything he did and almost always good-humoured and acquiescent. But, neverthe-less, he gave the impression of being very much his own man; unassailable. And, deep inside, the Captain sensed that to pro-voke him to anger – no, that somehow, would be unlikely – but to provoke him to violence, would be to risk a very swift death. That bow. That sword. Those damned green eyes. The man gave him the creeps. It came to him abruptly that he had similar feelings when near the Lord Dan-Tor. He would be glad when he was back in the City. Ambition or no, people like that were best avoided.

The Captain consoled himself with his assessment of Isloman. Big, powerful, easily a match for several men. Super-ficially affable, but with his eyes ever watchful and unable to hide their suspicion. Easier to provoke than his companion if need arose, Isloman was more . . . normal. That was it. He was more *normal* than Hawklan.

On the whole, he thought, he'd done the right thing giving them an escort and coming along himself. He couldn't see how any reproach could be levelled at him for that. If it transpired they were unimportant then he'd been sensibly cautious, while if they were important then his action would be duly noted.

Certainty, however, continued to elude him, and he eased his horse forward to come by Hawklan's side again. On reflection, he thought, the man's not quite like Dan-Tor. He'd helped two of the horses that went lame – and very effectively, too. And he'd pitched in with the work in their overnight camps. Then, of course, he's bound to behave like that if he's looking to make a favourable impression.

'What's that smoke, Captain?' Hawklan's voice broke into his reverie. Screwing up his eyes against the summer glare, he followed Hawklan's extended arm. As if aspiring to join the soaring towers and spires of Vakloss, a single column of dense black smoke was rising from the City.

'A celebration perhaps?' offered Hawklan.

The Captain shook his head. 'No,' he said definitely. 'But I don't know what it is. Probably a house fire.'

'It's a big one, Captain,' said one of the men. 'Look how high it's going.'

The Captain nodded and then shrugged. 'Well, there's nothing we can do.' He laughed harshly. 'I'm sure someone knows it's there.' This shaft of wit seemed to go down well with the men but, as they rode on, the smoke grew more dense and all eyes were fastened on it.

The party became very quiet, disturbing the country stillness only with the sound of lightly treading hooves and the soft creak and clatter of tackle and arms. Abruptly, the rising column of smoke seemed to gather momentum and, disregarding the vagaries of the rooftop breezes, began to billow upwards relentlessly, until it was well above the Palace towers. Soon it was dominating the entire sky in front of them.

'That's no house fire,' someone said hoarsely, mirroring all their thoughts.

Hawklan realised he was craning back his head to see the top of the column. Faintly a distant sound reached him. 'Quiet,' he said, raising his hand and reining his horse to a halt.

Without thinking, the Captain halted the troop as if the order had been passed to him by a senior officer. The group stood motionless and silent as if paying homage to the towering manifestation before them. Across the intervening fields a confused jumble of sounds mingled with the birdsong and the hissing of the gently waving trees. Hawklan's hand remained in the air. Then, quite distinctly, the rapid tolling of a bell reached them. The urgency of its tone galvanised the Captain.

'It's the General Alarm,' he said, almost in disbelief. For an instant he looked flustered. He gave Hawklan and Isloman a worried look then, turning his horse around to face his men, he shouted, 'You three, no, you five, escort the envoys into

Vakloss. Straight to the Palace and notify the Lord Dan-Tor of their arrival. The rest of you come with me at the gallop.' Then, to Hawklan, 'I'm sorry, but if the General Alarm's being sounded, something serious must've happened. We have to ride to it as fast as we can. These men will escort you safely to the Palace.' And then he was gone, together with the rest of his patrol, leaving the seven men staring after them into the dust they were raising.

Hawklan looked round at his reduced entourage. The past few days had taught him a great deal about the Mathidrin, and sadly, this confirmed what he had learned from his encounter with Urssain and Aelang. They were for the most part loutish and brutal, caring little for the animals they rode, nothing for the terrain they lived off, and precious little for the people they had encountered on their journey. Hawklan suspected that it was only his presence that had saved the animals and some of the villagers they had met from casual acts of gratuitous violence – sadism even. Admittedly they were well disciplined, but it was a discipline patently derived from fear. Such glimmers of intelligence as he had espied were heavily larded with cunning and dedicated to self-interested opportunism. It had been hard to keep his feelings to himself. Now, he did not feel disposed to accept the authority of this frayed remnant.

'If that fire's as big as it looks, there'll be a lot of people hurt and needing help. Quickly now,' he said authoritatively, 'you two lead the way. Full gallop.' The men hesitated. Hawklan glared at them. 'Quickly, I said,' he repeated menacingly with a flick of his head in the direction of the City. He could almost see the men's reflexes crushing their doubts. Fear is an important key with these people, Hawklan reminded himself again.

Sylvriss burst into the room unannounced. 'Lord Dan-Tor. What is this? What's happening?'

Dan-Tor, tall and very still, was standing at the window, staring out at the smoke rising high above the City. His gaze was baleful and, as he turned to face his Queen, a lingering residue of malevolence hung in his eyes like morning frost reluctant to obey the sun's bidding. Sylvriss almost started under the impact of this look, but neither her face nor her posture showed any sign of alarm. Resolutely she reminded herself that this was the true nature of the man, and she forgot it at her peril.

'With your permission, Majesty,' he said, indicating Urssain and a group of other senior Mathidrin officers standing stiffly by.

Sylvriss nodded her consent.

'You have your orders,' he said curtly. 'I want the fire and the people under control with maximum dispatch. And I want the ringleaders taken alive if possible. There's more to this than a spontaneous outburst. Dismissed.'

The men saluted and, after bowing to the Queen, left as stiffly as they had stood.

'Lord Dan-Tor, what's happening?' the Queen repeated as the door closed.

'Majesty,' said Dan-Tor, his face now more composed, 'I'm afraid a small number of troublemakers have started a disturbance over in the west of the City. Unfortunately they've also started that.' He indicated the view from the window.

Sylvriss went to the window and stared up at the towering column of smoke. 'The King nearly saw it,' she said anxiously. 'I managed to get him to a room on the other side. He's asleep now.'

Dan-Tor nodded solicitously, his eyes indifferent.

'What is it that's burning?' Sylvriss continued.

'One of my workshops,' Dan-Tor replied.

'But that smoke. So black, so dense, and that awful smell.'

Dan-Tor did not reply.

'Who would do such a thing?' Sylvriss asked, turning away from the window.

Dan-Tor allowed himself a small sigh of resignation, just sufficient to reach but not overstep the bounds of insolence. 'Majesty,' he said. 'The Geadrol was suspended because enemies within were weakening us. We have the leaders of those enemies in our hands, but their followers, those they've deceived, are still at large, working their will.'

'Surely the Lord Eldric and the others wouldn't sanction such . . .' she gestured to the window, 'such destruction?'

Dan-Tor brusquely gathered some documents together. 'Majesty, my evidence tells me so.'

For a moment the Queen considered arguing the point, then changed her mind. Conflict with Dan-Tor at this point would serve no useful purpose, and he was in an odd mood. With a distressed look on her face, she turned back to the window and stared out again at the rising column of smoke. Then, looking down, she saw large numbers of Mathidrin, mounted and on foot, in the courtyard below. A faint spark of an idea formed in her mind. It threw its dim light on plans that she and Dilrap had laid. Plans laid mainly to allay the frustration of their impotence, but thorough for all that.

'What are the Mathidrin doing?' she asked.

Dan-Tor put his hand to his head. 'Majesty, I'm afraid the disturbance is a large one. I suspect that there may be disaffected High Guards involved. It will have to be stamped out quickly and effectively or we may have serious and widespread violence to deal with.'

Before Sylvriss could speak, there was an urgent knocking at the door.

'Enter,' said Dan-Tor. The door opened immediately and a young Mathidrin trooper marched in. His face was blackened and a livid red graze above his right eye glistened painfully. His uniform was scuffed and crumpled, and he was breathing heavily. Saluting, he handed two notes to Dan-Tor whose face darkened as he read them.

Bad news, I trust, thought Sylvriss. Then, aloud, 'Lord Dan-Tor. I can see you've the matter well in hand. I must return to the King. I'll not disturb you further.'

Dan-Tor looked up. 'Majesty,' he said offhandedly.

Sylvriss turned and walked to the door ignoring the slight implicit in his tone. An odd mood indeed. As she passed the young Mathidrin she said, 'Young man, when the Lord Dan-Tor has finished with you, go and have that gash attended to.'

The Mathidrin saluted smartly and there was a brief look of gratitude in his eyes.

Once outside the room, Sylvriss moved quickly to one of the upper rooms of the Palace. Throwing open a window, she leaned out and listened. Alongside the column of dense black smoke, another, equally dense, but of a deathly white hue, was rising. She could both hear and feel muffled concussions in the distance. What in the world has he got in those workshops? she thought. The man pollutes everything he touches.

Faintly, she could hear another sound coming from the same direction. Eventually she identified it as people shouting. Not in fear or alarm, but in anger. A great many people shouting. Dan-Tor's disturbance must be a full-blown riot, she realised, though she found it almost impossible to conceive the Fyordyn, with their painstaking patience, resorting to such indiscriminate violence.

The tainted summer breeze blew her hair across her face and she swept it to one side. At the same time, the spark of the idea she had had flared up brightly, filling her mind with an uneasy mixture of excitement and fear. She craned further out of the window and peered down into the courtyard far below. It was seething black with Mathidrin, as were most of the streets she could see.

She looked intently at a marching column, and then super-imposed the image on those gathered in the courtyard. A quick calculation confirmed her earlier, more subjective impression formed in Dan-Tor's room. Almost the entire City garrison was being committed to deal with this minor disturbance.

Her informants in the City had mentioned nothing of any planned disruption, but she was inclined to agree with Dan-Tor's assessment that this was not a spontaneous outburst.

'It doesn't matter,' she whispered to herself. Any Mathidrin remaining in the Palace would probably be guarding the gate. The Westerclave would be virtually empty.

She took a deep breath to quieten her racing pulse, but it had little effect. Reaching into her pocket, her moist hand closed around the cold key which she had kept with her since it came into her possession. Two images merged in her mind. One, of the Mathidrin officer she had knocked over for maltreating a horse, and the other, that of her father's face smiling anxiously when, unusually for one so young, she had been made a junior messenger towards the end of the Morlider War. 'Nothing worth doing's easy, girl, and some chances only come once.' The memory tipped the scale for her.

She waited a little longer, carefully watching the comings and goings below. The sounds in the distance grew louder, and eventually the courtyard below became still except for a few guards by the gates and the arrival of the occasional messenger.

Now, she thought. Now.

Clattering along corridors and down stairs, it came to her suddenly that even if she were able to release the Lords, they would have difficulty in escaping the Palace. She swept the thought away. There was no time for detailed planning. This was pure risk and dependent on speed above all. Besides, there was havoc out there. Who knew what other opportunities might arise? And the Palace was a big place.

Gently she opened the door of her chamber. Rgoric was still asleep, an open book on his lap. Softly she tiptoed across the room to an alcove where she kept some of her outdoor cloaks.

'Sylvriss.'

She froze. It was the King's voice. Oh no, my love, she sighed inwardly, not now. He would want to talk. Sometimes he needed reassurance when he was awakened suddenly. She screwed her eyes tight shut and bit her lip, torn between his need and the opportunity that fate had placed in her hands. Composing her face into a smile, she turned round and looked at him.

He was still asleep. 'Sylvriss,' he said again, shifting slightly in the chair. The heavy book on his lap started to slide. Without thinking, she strode forward and scooped it up just before it hit the floor. She dared not breathe as she placed the book gently on a nearby table and walked back to the alcove.

Minutes later, she was moving silently along the lower corridors of the Palace towards the Westerclave. Dressed in the plain grey cloak and hood that she sometimes used when she wanted to pass unnoticed in the City, she flitted through the shadows, walking as normally as she could to avoid attracting attention.

Just one of the maids, she repeated to herself. Just one of the maids. But the hiss of her clothes and the muffled pad of her soft shoes sounded like thunder to her.

Eventually she came to a door which would lead into the cellars. For a moment she hesitated with her hand on the latch. The Palace was deafeningly quiet. She had seen no Mathidrin, and such servants and officials as were about seemed for the most part to be gathered in the upper rooms watching the distant fire, but once through this door she would have no excuse for being where she was. Each step forward from now would be a step nearer to exposure. Then, gripping the latch tightly, she pushed the door open and stepped into the cool stillness of the cellar.

She had never been in the Palace's extensive cellars before, but she had studied plans found for her by Dilrap and had frequently travelled this route in her mind, never realising that it might actually come to pass. The difference between the flat sketches and the solid reality, however, gave her a frightening jolt, and it took her a little while to relate the images she had seen to the gloomy array of walls and passages now facing her. With an effort she quietened her racing mind and, after agonising minutes, she reached the door she wanted. The door through into the cellars of the Westerclave.

Now, Dilrap, she thought, let's see if you've kept your promise. The promise that this door, lurking in an unused part of the cellar, would be unlocked against the possibility of this plan being put into operation. Tongue protruding between her teeth, she gently eased the latch and pushed the door.

It did not move. A reproach formed in her mind but she dismissed it guiltily. Please let it open, she prayed, then, grimacing anxiously, she put her shoulder against the door and pushed harder. It moved abruptly and the bright light of the Westerclave burst through the narrow crack. She closed the door quickly and leaned her forehead against it nervously. Spreading out Dilrap's sketches in her mind she went over the final part of her route again. First right, second left, first left, third door on the right. Each step taking her nearer to the more used parts of the cellar.

Then, cautiously opening the door again and screwing up her eyes against the increased brightness, she peered down the long passage in front of her.

It was empty.

She reached into her pocket and felt the two objects there. The key to the Lords' cell and her old Muster knife. Whether either of them would be of any use to her remained to be seen. She had few illusions about her ability to use the knife against a

Mathidrin guard if she were caught and could not talk her way out, but . . .

With a last deep breath, she stepped out of the gloom and into a final commitment.

Heart racing, she walked her memorised route in long, quiet strides. Just one of the maids. Just one of the maids. It kept other thoughts at bay a little but offered little real solace. No maids ever came to the Westerclave cellars.

At each junction she paused and listened before turning the corner. No echoing voices or sounds of movement added to her terror. What can be happening in the City to have emptied this place so totally? she thought.

Then she was at the door to the Lords' cell.

Carefully she eased back the two heavy bolts and, with trembling hands, fumbled the precious key from her pocket. Her hand was shaking so much that she had to seize it with the other to still it sufficiently to insert the key in the lock. The clatter of the key against the keyhole seemed to be deafening.

As she was about to turn the key, a shadow fell across her. She felt the blood drain from her face and instinctively she jerked her hood further forward. Turning round she found herself looking into the cold, grim eyes of three Mathidrin.

Chapter 34

Hawklan and his escort rode at full gallop after the main body of the patrol. The huge column of smoke loomed over the whole City, ominous and bloated, dwarfing even the towers of the Palace. Then, like a sinister giant raising its hoary head, a second column, white in colour, began to rise beside it. Strange sounds drifted towards them and a foul smell began to mar the summer scents. Hawklan reined Serian to a halt, his nose wrinkling.

'What unholy creation could make such a smell?' he said, largely to himself.

Isloman's face was stony. 'It has the feel of that tinker's work,' he said. 'No natural thing would die like that.'

Hawklan turned to the nearest Mathidrin. 'What buildings are burning? Can you tell from here?'

The man looked uncertain and then spoke briefly to his friends. 'It's difficult to say, sir,' he replied. 'But the Lord Dan-Tor has many workshops in that part of the City.'

Hawklan nodded and then spurred his horse forward.

The young officer came alongside him. 'Sir, I'm supposed to take you to the Palace. The Captain ordered . . .'

'I'll explain to your Captain, young man,' Hawklan replied resolutely. 'It seems to me that that,' he pointed ahead to the smoke-filled horizon, 'is somewhat out of the ordinary and very serious. I imagine that most people at the Palace will be too busy to deal with visiting envoys at the moment. Whether we arrive an hour or so late will be of no consequence. On the other hand, I *am* a healer, and healers will be needed at that fire, don't you think?'

The young man hesitated, but Hawklan kept increasing his pace steadily, leaving the man little choice but to follow. He heard Serian chuckle. The other horses were breathing heavily and beginning to sweat, but Serian was taking the long uphill way into the City effortlessly. High above, Gavor flew ahead, spurs unsheathed, maintaining the silent vigil he had kept since they left the village.

When they entered the City proper, Hawklan found himself badly disorientated by the numerous streets. 'Which way – quickly,' became his watchword to keep his escort on the move and prevent their having time to think.

The two great columns of smoke now filled the sky and were spreading out at a great height to cover the sun and throw the City into a premature twilight. The sun drifted in and out of view, round and sickly yellow.

As the group neared the fire, the streets became more crowded and the noise of the blaze could be heard. But it was mingled with another noise: the noise of fighting. Hawklan looked at the crowds milling round. Some seemed to be running away from something, while others seemed to be running purposefully towards it.

He leant down from his horse. 'What's happening?' he shouted to a man running by.

The man, breathless and red-faced, pointed back the way he had just come. 'The Mathidrin,' he said. 'They're attacking the people.' Then with a fearful glance at Hawklan's escort he ran off before Hawklan could speak to him again.

Hawklan looked at the young officer who shrugged off his unspoken enquiry, though he was beginning to look decidedly uneasy.

At the end of the street they came to a large square, and a scene unfolded before them like a waking nightmare. People were running in every direction, shouting and screaming. Faces flickered in front of Hawklan, faces alight with terror, with rage, faces blank and lost with bewilderment and shock. The healer in him reeled at the pain. The jangling of the alarm bell filled the air, echoing from rooftop to rooftop, but above it rose the crackle and roar of the blazing buildings, even though they were still some distance away and could not be seen. The whole was pervaded by a retching smell and a sinister half light formed by the unnatural cloud.

As he surveyed this sight, Hawklan felt the jarring impact of two concussions, and looking up he saw a misshapen ball of yellow flame climbing rapidly up the white column like some fearsome escapee. It bathed the crowd in a shimmering jaundiced hue and for a moment there was silence as everyone turned to watch its scrambling ascent. Then the noise broke out again, louder than ever.

Hawklan was uncertain about what to do. Looking at the milling crowd, he thought he saw some pattern, some order to it, but it was too fluid for him to define. A cry by his side made him turn. One of the Mathidrin was holding a hand to his forehead, blood running between his fingers. Then a stream of missiles engulfed them, and a section of the crowd closed around them roaring and shouting.

'The Lords, girl. Where are they?' The Mathidrin officer's tone was icy. Sylvriss looked up at him, her voice frozen within her by the menacing presence of the three men. The Mathidrin closed his eyes briefly as if looking inwards for patience. Then opening them, he peered into the darkness of her hood. 'The Lords, girl. Where are they?' he repeated slowly and distinctly, as if to a foolish child. 'They're to be moved to safer quarters and no one's bothered to tell us what room they're in.'

Slowly Sylvriss began to gather her wits. Luck was running both for and against her. These men were strangers here. They took her for one of the servants in her grey cloak. She could escape unrecognised. But they were going to remove the Lords and then everything would be lost. A desperate resolve formed in her mind, and nervously she pointed a shaking finger towards the key in the door.

'In here?' asked the man. She nodded. The Mathidrin pushed her to one side and, turning the key, opened the door wide. Two of them walked in, leaving the third in the passage. Sylvriss followed them. The four Lords stood up as the Mathidrin entered.

Before anyone could speak Sylvriss, standing behind the two Mathidrin, threw back her hood so that the Lords could see her, then drawing her knife she cried, 'Lords. Kill these men now. This will be your only chance of escape.' And she lunged with the knife at the back of the nearest Mathidrin.

But the surprise on the Lords' faces betrayed her and the man was turning even as she spoke. He stepped to one side, seized her hand in a pitiless grip and, with a slight twist, brought her down on to her knees. The knife was taken from her effortlessly and levelled at her throat.

Crying out, the four Lords moved forward almost as one, but the first guard struck Arinndier a back-handed punch in the midriff that doubled him up, impeding Darek, then reaching quickly round Eldric's head he gripped the back of his hair and swung him round to block Hreldar's advance. The guard holding the Queen watched, his face concerned. He spoke to them urgently in a language that Sylvriss did not understand and the Lords froze in surprise. Sylvriss found herself released and the hand that had held her so easily on her knees reached out and helped her gently to her feet. She was shaking and bewildered.

'Majesty, forgive me,' said the guard, offering her knife back to her, hilt forward.

'What's happening?' gasped Sylvriss, looking from face to face. 'Who are these men, Lord Eldric?'

'I don't know what's happening, Majesty, but these men are Goraidin,' he replied. 'This man is Yatsu, the others I don't know yet.'

'It would appear you both came to rescue us at the same time,' said Darek.

'Lords, Majesty,' said Yatsu urgently. 'We've no time for debate. The City's in turmoil, but it's only a matter of time before the Mathidrin reserves get here. We blustered our way in through the confusion, but the longer we delay the more likely it is we'll have to fight our way out.'

Eldric raised his hands to his temples as if to shake his bewildered thoughts into order. Then, 'The Queen, Yatsu, what of the Queen?' he asked.

Sylvriss answered before Yatsu could speak. 'I'll return the way I came, Lord Eldric. I'll be quite safe. You go, quickly.'

Eldric looked uncertain.

Sylvriss ignored his doubt. 'Go now, quickly, or we'll all be doomed. You must escape while you can. Dan-Tor must be fought.'

Eldric still hesitated. Abruptly he fell on his knees and took the Queen's hand in both of his. Words formed on his lips but he could not speak them.

Suddenly there was the sound of running feet in the passage and the third guard entered. 'The others are here,' he said urgently. 'Hurry. We've not much time.'

Eldric rose to his feet and after a quick glance around the room signalled the others to follow.

As they hurried out, Sylvriss took Yatsu's arm. 'Goraidin Yatsu. Secretary Dilrap and the young servant are to be trusted,' she said 'But that knowledge is for you and the Lords alone. They're in continual danger.'

'Majesty,' said Yatsu. Then, concerned, 'You're certain you'll be safe?' She nodded confidently and ushered him after the others. He hesitated for a moment, his face anxious, then he bowed and strode off rapidly down the passage.

Sylvriss rubbed her wrist ruefully as she watched him go then, throwing her hood forward, she walked quickly and silently back the way she had come. On the journey she passed two dead Mathidrin.

It was Serian, rather than any decisive horsemanship by Hawklan, that led Hawklan and Isloman from the crowd. He had reared and screamed as if in panic, and then charged straight into the mob, splitting it open before him like wood under a cleaver. Isloman's horse followed suit down the widening cleft, its rider contenting himself with hanging on desperately. Eventually they came to a halt in a narrow and relatively quiet street.

Hawklan leaned forward. 'Thank you, Serian,' he said breathlessly.

The horse chuckled again. 'Great fun, great fun,' he said.

'Don't do that again,' said Isloman, riding to Hawklan's side. 'You frightened me to death.'

Hawklan shrugged. 'It was the horse's idea,' he said. 'Left to our own devices that crowd would've had us down very quickly.'

Isloman grunted at this disclaimer. 'What did they attack us for?' he asked.

'I don't think they were attacking us,' Hawklan replied. 'I

think they were attacking those Mathidrin. Cockroaches, they were calling them.'

'Good name,' said Isloman, who had reached the same conclusion about the Mathidrin as Hawklan during their journey.

'Still,' Hawklan continued, 'we could have been badly hurt in all that confusion. We're well out of it.' He patted Serian's neck.

'What shall we do now?' asked Isloman.

Hawklan stared up and down the street. Figures were flitting here and there, and at both ends he could see crowds milling around. 'I don't know,' he said. 'I'd like to find out what's happened here before we make any decisions.'

That, however, proved to be harder than he had imagined. Those passers-by who were prepared to stop and speak to him left him with more questions than he had started with. The Mathidrin had launched an unprovoked attack on a crowd. The High Guards were attacking the Palace. Malcontents disguised as High Guards – or Mathidrin – were trying to seize the City. Mathidrin – or High Guards – disguised as ordinary citizens, were trying to do the same. Several parties had, of course, started the fires. They had also been started by accident. The fumes had driven the people mad, etc, etc.

Eventually Hawklan stopped trying and sat down on a short flight of steps leading to an upper walkway that ran along the street. Out of the mounting gloom, two stumbling figures emerged. A man, staggering badly and holding his hand to his tunic, and a woman, trying to support him and encouraging him between near hysterical sobs.

Hawklan stood up just as the two slithered to the ground. Instantly the woman disentangled herself and, struggling to her feet, tried to help the man. But he was obviously too weak. He rose to a kneeling position, supporting himself with one hand on the ground, but could do no more. Hawklan and Isloman ran across to the couple and Hawklan knelt down by the man. Gently he took the man's hand. It was clenched in front of his tunic and as Hawklan pulled it away he saw that the man had been holding in part of his intestines. Hawklan grimaced in spite of himself and Isloman, eyes wide, involuntarily raised his hand to his mouth as if to silence himself.

The woman screamed and cradled the man's head desperately. Hawklan drew his hand across his forehead, which was suddenly damp. He knew before he touched the man that he was dead, but to comfort himself in the immediate pain of his discovery, the healer in him had to search for signs of life.

'I'm sorry,' he said to the woman, easing her to her feet. 'I'm sorry.'

The woman fell suddenly silent. Ghastly in the yellowing light, she stood motionless, her eyes and mouth wide, as if all the flailing hysteria had wound itself into a tight, unassailable ball within her. When at last she spoke, her voice carried a harsh calm. 'Why should you be sorry?' she said. 'You didn't kill him did you? The cockroaches did it. We were just trying to get away from the crowds and the fighting.' She was not talking to anyone. She was looking back through the darkness to a brighter, happier life only a few minutes past. 'They chased us, and stabbed him for nothing.'

Hawklan looked at Isloman having no words to speak. Another concussion shook the street and for a few seconds a flickering light filtered down over them. Then the sound of the nearby crowds rose suddenly. Hawklan looked at the woman, now kneeling silent by her dead man, her hunched shadow fading as the light disappeared upwards into the thickening mask. The sight cleared his mind. He took Isloman's arm.

'We go where the sick and injured are, then we find Dan-Tor,' he said.

Isloman looked uncertain. 'What about the woman?' he said.

Hawklan's face twisted, as if the words he had to speak were sour in his mouth. 'There's nothing I can do for the man, and only time can help her now. At least she's not lost. There'll be some of her own nearby ... somewhere.' Isloman seemed about to protest, but the pain in Hawklan's face stopped him. Hawklan closed his eyes to shut out his friend's reproach. 'Right now, people are suffering who I *can* help. I have to do something before the stench of pain and terror overwhelms me.' Isloman looked again at the silent woman, and then nodded reluctantly. Hawklan turned and began walking in the direction the couple had come from. Isloman followed.

The two men were scarcely halfway to the end of the street

when a scream from the woman cut through the gloom. Turning, they could make out several figures moving round the body of the fallen man. The scream rang out again and the movement resolved itself into a struggle. Without hesitation, both Hawklan and Isloman began to run back up the street. As they neared the group, they saw that the figures were Mathidrin. Two of them were holding the woman and a third was threatening her with a knife. Her dress had been ripped wide open. Four other Mathidrin were standing by laughing and shouting encouragement.

Isloman hesitated momentarily. The intent of the Mathidrin was quite obvious and it could well be followed by murder. What action he should take was also quite obvious – but there were seven of them, and all armed. In the brief moment it took him to dispatch this thought, he felt Hawklan surge away from his side like a wild hunting animal and, before he could collect himself, he saw the Mathidrin with the knife fall to the ground senseless. It was the sound of the knife clattering across the patterned stones that brought Isloman's faculties sharply into the present. A distinctly dangerous present. The Mathidrin were drawing their swords. So was Hawklan.

Isloman caught a glimpse of the now discarded woman and then the dead man lying in his own entrails. A spark of vengeance lit up his mind, transforming his fear into an ancient rage. Stepping forward, he drew his iron-bound club. His stone and Loman's metal. A terrible weapon it had once been.

Hawklan faced the two who had been holding the woman. Eyes cold, he swung his sword high and purposefully with his right hand. Instinctively, the two men raised their own swords to block a downward cut but, even as they did so, Hawklan stepped in low, striking one full in the throat with his left hand, to send him choking to the ground. Then bringing his right hand down and across, he smashed the pommel of his sword into the other man's temple.

Facing an opponent of his own, Isloman noted these manoeuvres almost subliminally. The thought occurred to him again. Where had Hawklan learned to fight like that? So sure, so fast. What powers and ancient learning lay hidden in that familiar frame?

But it was no time for pondering. These Mathidrin were not without skill themselves. He felt a blade tear his tunic and cut into his side as he misjudged a feint by his attacker. The pain galvanised him and, before the blade could be withdrawn, he wrapped his arm around his opponent's and with a sudden turn of his body broke it. Continuing the turn he hurled the screaming man into his fellows, knocking two of them down and making a third drop his sword. A few swirling seconds later the skirmish was over, and the Mathidrin were all disarmed and on the ground, either unconscious or nearly so.

Hawklan's eyes were blazing green in the gloom and he seemed to be transfixed, as if wrestling with some appalling urge as he slowly sheathed his sword. Isloman moved over to the woman cowering by the side of the street.

'You're safe now,' he said, holding out his hand to help her to her feet. But she looked up at him with such a strange expression on her face that he withdrew his hand. As he straightened up, a shape moved rapidly towards him out of the gloom. Before he could react, it passed by his head and there was a scuffle and a strangled cry from behind him. Turning he found himself staring into the wild-eyed face of another Mathidrin. In one hand, the man held a knife, but the other was groping at his throat and blood was pouring through his fingers. Isloman stepped aside as the figure staggered dementedly forward to crash headlong on to the ground after a few paces. There was a burst of coughing from above.

'Sorry I was a little late, dear boy.' Cough. 'Difficult to see in all this.'

The incident brought Hawklan to himself again. He glanced down at the dead Mathidrin and then looked upwards. 'Gavor, you shouldn't . . .' he began angrily.

'He saved my life,' interrupted Isloman. 'It was my fault. I was careless.'

Doubt and anger spread over Hawklan's face but, before he could speak, a cry came from one of the fallen Mathidrin. The woman had picked up a dagger and stabbed him. Before Hawklan reached her, she had stabbed a second. None too gently he wrenched the knife from her hand.

'What are you doing?' he shouted, almost beside himself with anger.

The woman met his stare unflinchingly. 'I'm killing these cockroaches just like they killed my husband,' she said savagely.

Hawklan did not reply but, keeping hold of her wrist, he bent briefly over the two men. 'They're dead,' he said.

'So will the others be in a moment,' said the woman, struggling to free herself.

'No,' cried Hawklan.

But with a desperate effort the woman tore her hand from his grip. 'You're foreigners, aren't you?' she said, backing away. Then without waiting for an answer, 'You saved my life and I owe you that debt, but you don't understand what's happening here.' Her face crumpled momentarily, but she controlled it almost immediately. 'You don't understand. Everything's gone. No Geadrol. No Law. No High Guards. Only a sick King, a Warlock Lord and these vermin.' She drove her foot brutally into one of the Mathidrin who was trying to rise to his feet. 'They killed my husband. Now I'm killing them.' She kicked him again repeatedly. Hawklan moved forward and she backed away from the fallen man. 'If no one's going to look after us, then we Fyordyn look after ourselves,' and, bending down suddenly, she scooped up another dagger and drove it into the Mathidrin's stomach before Hawklan could move.

Isloman stepped forward and caught her arm, but she spun round and drove her knee into his groin. He doubled over and she ran off into the gloom.

'Leave her,' Isloman gasped painfully as Hawklan made to run after her. 'Leave her. She's right. She knows what's happening and, as you said, she knows where she is, which is more than we do.'

Hawklan stared uncertainly after the now-vanished woman, and then looked at his friend. 'Are you all right?' he asked.

Isloman scowled and bent forward again. 'Of course I'm not,' he said crossly. 'Just give me a minute or two.'

'I'm not sure we've got that long,' said Hawklan, looking round at the carnage. 'There's nothing we can do here, and there's too much summary justice in the air for us to try explaining this. Come on. Mount up.'

Isloman glowered at him, but straightened up gingerly and hobbled to his horse. Gritting his teeth he accepted Hawklan's support as he heaved himself painfully into the saddle.

No sooner were they both mounted than Gavor flapped between them. 'Run. Quickly,' he croaked, breathlessly.

As they disappeared into the gloom, a large patrol of Mathidrin emerged from the opposite direction and halted by the scattered bodies.

Chapter 35

The nerve centre of Urssain's response to the fighting in the streets was high in one of the Palace towers, where he could supplement the information he was receiving simply by looking out of the window. It was for this reason that the lower floors of the Westerclave were fairly empty.

With the Goraidin setting a stern marching pace, and the Lords looking suitably harassed, the group had little difficulty in making their way through to its arched entrance. Such few Mathidrin as they met stepped smartly out of their way and saluted Yatsu's officer's uniform.

At the entrance, however, they found their horses being scrutinised by an officer. His uniform indicated a high rank, though how high, Yatsu did not know. Two other Mathidrin were standing by talking idly. Yatsu set his face and hoped that his ignorance of Mathidrin ranks and procedures would not betray them.

Maintaining the determined pace, Yatsu steered the group to the far side of the horses from the officer and loudly ordered them to mount, shouting, 'Move, you sluggards, or you'll answer to the Lord Dan-Tor personally.'

Following his lead, the Goraidin and the Lords mounted quickly and prepared to ride off.

'Sirshiant,' came an authoritative and supercilious voice. It was the officer.

Yatsu discreetly allowed his horse to move forward a few paces and then twisted round in his saddle as if seeking the owner of the voice. Finding him, he looked suitably surprised and then saluted smartly. 'Beg pardon, sir. Didn't see you. Watching the prisoners. They're needed urgently.'

The officer's eyes narrowed slightly. Adjusting the grip on his reins, Yatsu sent a danger signal to his men.

'By whose authority have you released these men?' said the officer coldly.

'Lord Dan-Tor's direct command, sir,' Yatsu replied.

The officer's eyebrows rose slowly. 'Direct command,' he echoed, as if testing its soundness. His look of suspicion increased. On the side away from the officer, Yatsu discreetly tapped his horse with his knee, to make it restive. Seeing this, the others did the same and the group fell into a slight but fluid disarray which spread out the watching Mathidrin and made the officer step back a little.

The movement enabled Yatsu to take his eyes off the officer and look around the courtyard. He could see no signs of ambush but his sense of danger was growing by the second. Somewhere a trap was closing, and this officer was playing for time.

As if in confirmation of this the officer waited very deliberately for the horses to quieten down, eyeing Yatsu coldly all the time. A horse jostled Yatsu and as its rider made soothing noises to quieten it Yatsu heard a soft whisper in the Battle Language. 'They've recognised the horses.'

That had always been a risk. They had had to use the horses from the ambushed patrol because the Mathidrin horses were from the north of Fyorlund and were of a build and colour markedly different from local animals. Now some sharp eye had spotted a horse last seen going out on long patrol. Whatever this officer had set in motion, time was against them. Yatsu reached into a belt pouch with his left hand.

'Direct command, sir. I've the orders here.'

Even as his hand left the pouch and swung across him to release his knife in a back-handed flick towards the throat of the watching officer, a flash of realisation passed between the two of them. Ah, Yatsu thought, Mathidrin don't keep orders in that pouch do they? And you spotted it soon enough to avoid my knife – nearly.

The officer's supercilious expression vanished, not into fear, but into resolution as, with unexpected speed, he twisted to one side to avoid the blade which just caught the side of his neck. Yatsu registered the man's reaction and the speed of his responses. We must find out more about these men, he thought, as he drove his horse forward powerfully.

The Lords and the Goraidin followed his move with barely any delay and, crouching low over their horses, they charged towards the nearest gate. As they rode, Yatsu turned to check the disarray back in the entrance to the Westerclave. As he did so, he saw several figures running forward.

'Archers,' he shouted. 'Spread out – weave – and converge on the gate. Close round the Lords as we go through.'

Scarcely had he finished when an arrow narrowly missed his head. The group split up, making themselves into smaller, fast-moving targets, and forcing the Mathidrin archers to concentrate on rate of fire rather than accuracy. The first casualty was Arinndier who, with a cry, slumped forward over his horse's neck with an arrow in his back. Next, one of the horses went down throwing its rider heavily on to the paved courtyard. Eldric seized the bridle of Arinndier's horse, while one of the Goraidin swung low out of his saddle and unceremoniously swept up his dazed companion and threw him across his horse's neck. Then the group came together raggedly for its final dash through the gate, arrows clattering about them.

The officer had obviously sent for the archers as some vague precautionary measure, as the gate still stood open to allow the speedy passage of messengers. An attempt was being made to close it now but the few guards there were milling around in mounting confusion as the riders drew nearer. Their confusion was not helped by the arrows falling among them.

Unused to horses in combat, the Mathidrin's confusion turned rapidly to alarm and then to panic and flight as the group reached them and thundered into the short passage of the gateway, swords glinting through the gloom, and war cries mingling with the deafening clatter of the horses' hooves. Two of the guards were downed and trampled underfoot and those who tried to assail the riders from the side were cut down ruthlessly.

Then, like a sudden summer squall, the riders were gone, swallowed up in the swirling murk.

Minutes later, Yatsu slowed the group down to a walk. 'We'll be less conspicuous walking than galloping now,' he said. 'This . . . fog . . . is unpleasant, but at least it's working to our advantage.'

Eldric and the Lords were looking round in bewilderment at the pervasive evil-smelling gloom, but Eldric confined his questions to the important matters of the moment.

'Where are you taking us, Yatsu?' he asked anxiously. 'The Lord Arinndier's wounded.'

Arinndier was slumped across his horse's neck and though conscious he was barely maintaining his grip on the animal. Yatsu looked at him and nodded thoughtfully. 'Help him keep his seat, Lord,' he said to Eldric, then he cast an enquiring glance back to the rider who had picked up the fallen Goraidin. 'How's Dacu?' he asked.

'Shoulder's broken I think, Commander,' came the answer.

'We've been lucky to get off so lightly,' said Yatsu, returning to Eldric.

'We've been lucky to get away at all, Goraidin. Your planning left a little to be desired didn't it?' Eldric had no sooner spoken than he pulled an angry face at himself for having allowed his anxiety to express itself as such ingratitude.

Yatsu caught the look of repentance in the old Lord's eye and his own dark look softened. After all, he thought, they'd been quite impressive, those four.

'Yes, Lord,' he replied. 'But circumstances left us no alternative. Dan-Tor's wreaking havoc and repressions are growing daily. He's disbanded the High Guards now. We had to do something and information's not easy come by. The Mathidrin have got as many zealots as thugs in their ranks and they all live in fear of one another. They're not as easily corrupted as you'd imagine.'

The party turned into a wider street. It was illuminated by globes which had lit automatically when the light faded. Their garish light shone eerily through the haze and, because several of them had been broken, the street was littered with patches of light, like wet stepping stones catching the sunlight. Acrid fumes from the broken globes added to the already foul atmosphere. A great many people were running about, and the street rang with the sounds of voices raised in both anger and fear.

Eldric thought he saw bodies lying in the shadows but everything was too indistinct. In spite of himself, he spoke out. 'What's happened, Yatsu? What in Ethriss's name's happened?'

Yatsu, however, was looking worried and was glancing round frequently.

Eldric let his question lie. 'Do you think we're being followed?' he said.

Yatsu shook his head. 'No, Lord, but these uniforms will have us in trouble soon unless we're lucky. Damn.'

The oath was provoked by the sight of a crowd gathered at the end of the street. Yatsu reined his horse back and listened. 'Quickly. This way,' he said, and, turning sharply, he cantered off down a narrow alleyway. The others followed. A roar greeted their manoeuvre and the crowd started up the street towards them. Slowly at first, then running. However, by the time the crowd reached the alleyway, the riders were well out of the way, though they could hear the abuse that followed them and the sounds of missiles falling short and rattling along the paved way.

'What's happening?' Eldric demanded of Yatsu again.

'Later, Lord – please,' replied the Goraidin. 'When we're in a safer place. Accountings will be made, but right now we're in danger from both sides.'

'Sides?' Eldric muttered to himself, but he did not pursue his questioning.

'Mind your heads,' Yatsu called out as he led his horse under a low arch into an even narrower alley. 'We're nearly there now.'

The alley was strangely quiet, all the distant sounds of the City being blocked out by the tall buildings between which it was squeezed. When the last horse had clattered through the echoing arch, the hoofbeats became flat and attenuated, and such talking as went on dropped into whispers.

Yatsu began to feel relieved. The day had had consequences far beyond his calculation and who knew what more would follow? Would he indeed be able to face an accounting? But at least the Lords were free. He breathed out and patted his horse's neck gently.

As he looked up, two figures appeared as if from nowhere out of the shade within shade that lined the narrow alley. He started. Why hadn't he seen them? Where had they been hiding? He cursed himself for letting his attention drift so near to their goal. Some old memory flitted uneasily in his mind.

One of the figures lifted his hand and, in a voice well used to command, said, 'Enough, Mathidrin, enough.'

Chapter 36

Hawklan stared up at the rider facing him. The man was nervous, but he had a calm about him which he had not seen before in any of the Mathidrin. It was a relaxed confidence that reminded him of Tel-Mindor. Still, these men were Mathidrin and enough was enough.

'We've seen some of the things you've done this day, Mathidrin, and been pursued through these streets like animals for our pains,' he said. 'We're strangers here, from another country, simply seeking food and shelter from this storm you've stirred up. If you could help us, we'd be grateful. If you pass by us peacefully, we'll offer you no hindrance. But,' he slapped his sword hilt purposely, 'if you seek to harm us as your fellows have, then you'll die.' He felt Isloman's sidelong glance. 'I've used the flat of my blade too much today on people who should have felt its edge.'

Yatsu listened to this speech anxiously, but kept his face as bland as he could manage. Instinctively he tried to assess the danger from these two men. A faint memory stirred as he looked at the hefty one, standing there like a rock outcrop and gently swinging that strange club. Obviously strong and powerful and, Yatsu felt, perhaps faster than his size might indicate. Not a man to be tackled lightly, least of all in a narrow alleyway. But the other one, the speaker. He was different. He offered no gratuitous menace in either his tone or his manner, but Yatsu felt fear rising such as he had never known and for an instant he felt as though he were not really there, but looking through someone else's eyes. Shock, he noted uneasily. Trained to listen to his instincts where reason was inadequate, they were unequivocal in their message. To assail this man would be to die.

Isloman swung his club in a lazy circle and smacked it into the palm of his hand. 'My friend's too good-natured,' he said.

'After what I've seen today, I'm ready to kill you no matter what you do, and then discuss it with your Lord Dan-Tor in like manner.'

Hawklan laid a restraining hand on his arm.

Oddly, the overt threat and Hawklan's reaction made Yatsu feel easier. It had substance. It was something to work on. He smiled. 'Orthlundyn aren't you? By your speech. You've picked a bad time for visiting our country.' There was much he would have liked to ask of these men, but time was against them. 'We mean you no harm. In fact, I'd not have seen you if you hadn't moved. We're not what we seem, Orthlundyn, but we *are* in a hurry, and we have two sick men in need of urgent help. Will you allow us to pass?'

Hawklan was uncertain. The rider's manner, as well as his posture, was decidedly unlike any of the Mathidrin they had encountered so far. 'Sick, you say?' he said.

This time it was Isloman's hand that did the restraining. 'Take care,' he said. 'There's something odd about this lot.'

Eldric, unable to bring his horse by the side of Yatsu in the narrow alley, dismounted and came forward. Hawklan watched him without expression.

'Stranger,' said Eldric, 'I give you my word as a Lord of Fyorlund that we mean you no harm. But our business *is* urgent, and we *do* have two wounded men who need immediate attention. Please let us pass.'

Hawklan glanced at Isloman. The Carver was blunt. 'What's a Lord doing riding with these . . . cockroaches?' he said.

Arinndier groaned softly. Eldric looked back at his friend and then at Yatsu. Yatsu's hands flickered casually – we'll charge through if necessary, but it'll be dangerous, they said.

'Very,' said Isloman stepping forward menacingly, 'and you'll be the first to go if you do.'

Yatsu started as if he had been stung. An Orthlundyn understanding their hand language?

Eldric shook his head. 'I think you, too, are not what you seem. I'll risk the truth with you. I'm the Lord Eldric and with me are the Lords Arinndier, Darek and Hreldar. These riders are not Mathidrin, but High Guards in disguise. They've rescued us from Dan-Tor's custody but the Lord Arinndier and one of their number have been hurt. That's information enough for you to collect a sizeable reward from the Lord Dan-Tor if you wish.'

'Not quite the truth, Lord,' said Isloman. 'These men aren't High Guards, they're Goraidin or I'm a wood carver.' He placed his club back in its belt strap. 'But you're friends. We need help ourselves. Please let us accompany you.'

This time it was Eldric who stared at Isloman's unexpected knowledge, but he recovered himself quickly and turned to return to his horse.

'There's no need to mount, Lord,' said Yatsu. 'We're only paces away. Come.'

The group moved forward slowly, and Hawklan and Isloman faded back into the shade to allow them past before following.

'You're a considerable healer, Hawklan,' said Arinndier weakly. Hawklan did not reply, but laid a hand gently over Arinndier's eyes. Standing up, he turned to Eldric who was standing by the window looking out into the globe-lit murk and scowling. 'He'll sleep for a little while now,' he said. 'He was very lucky.'

Eldric did not hear him. Thoughts were tumbling through his mind, defying his every effort to stem their flow and introduce some order. The Goraidin fulfilling their ancient role, dressed as the enemy and venturing into the heart of their territory; the Queen appearing from nowhere, like the Muster itself, eyes ablaze and wielding a dagger; Arinndier wounded; the City as he had never known it; a nightmare of choking fumes, mayhem and chaos. Then these two strangers – Orthlundyn, of all things – an odd pair to say the least. Hawklan exuding an awesome presence, first like a dark presager of death in that gloomy alley and then a giver of life. And Isloman, who knew the hand language and who knew of the Goraidin. He closed his eyes irritably. A hand touched his shoulder, gently and temporarily stilling the turmoil. Turning, he found himself looking into Hawklan's face.

'Lord Eldric,' Hawklan said quietly, 'from what I can gather, a great deal has happened, very quickly. You and your friends must rest.'

Eldric waved his hand dismissively. 'No . . . Hawklan. You don't understand. We must get to our estates as soon as possible. Find out what's happened to our families, our High Guards, our lands . . . everything.'

Hawklan raised a single finger for silence. 'Yatsu tells me his plans for moving you from the City have proved to be impractical at the moment. The disruption in the streets is far worse than they envisaged. He feels it's too dangerous for you to go out.' Eldric made to interrupt, but Hawklan was implacable. 'I'm a stranger here, Lord Eldric, and I know nothing of your City or your people, but I do know the streets *are* dangerous, and I think it'd be unwise to ignore the advice of one of your Goraidin, don't you?'

Eldric fidgeted with his beard for a moment, and Hawklan's tone became a little more conciliatory. 'Yatsu says this house is safe, and Isloman and I will make two useful extra defenders if the need arises.'

But Eldric's turmoil merely flowed into this softening by his opponent. 'No, no,' he said. 'This is no time for rest. We can fight our way out of the City if necessary.'

Hawklan stood up very straight. 'You'll rest,' he said, in a tone that Eldric had not heard for many, many years. 'And your friends will rest. You're no use to yourself, to your families, to the country, anything, while you're in this state. When you've rested we'll talk. Answer all the questions we have of one another, and then decide what to do. That's the way of your Geadrol, isn't it?'

Eldric clenched his fist and his jaw. Hawklan raised an eyebrow. 'Lord,' he said, 'you were just prepared to ignore the advice of your Goraidin. Now you'd offer me violence? Is that the act of a wise leader?' He paused, locking Eldric's gaze with his own. 'But perhaps there's a flaw in my logic. I'm not used to your ways.'

Eldric surrendered totally, though with a commendable degree of dignity, and soon Hawklan had placed the three Lords into a deep and restful sleep. He smiled as he watched the strain ease from their faces, then he stood up and went over to the window, as if to continue the vigil that Eldric had abandoned.

* * *

After leaving Hawklan at the house to attend to the wounded men, Yatsu and the others had taken the horses to a nearby stable and attended to their needs. Yatsu had then made a brief excursion alone into the nearby streets to try to form some impression of the mayhem that had followed the diversionary riot he and his fellows had planned. As he returned to the house, he felt he was being observed, and once or twice thought he heard someone coughing nearby. Above him? You're getting old and tired, he thought.

Closing the door behind him, he leaned against it, took off the black Mathidrin helmet and puffed out his cheeks in some relief. Almost immediately, his nose picked up a savoury trail and he followed it down a short red-flagged passage towards a lighted doorway. It opened on to a small room lit by the thoughtful glow of an old torch. His men were sitting round a narrow table eating hungrily and talking noisily, while the man and the wife of the house busied around them, constantly filling their bowls and plates. The smallness of the room made it seem very full.

'This'll get you started,' the woman was saying. 'Big lads like you should eat plenty. Keep your strength up.'

Yatsu smiled. 'Anything for a little lad then, mother?' he said.

She bustled him to a seat at the end of the table and thrust a large bowl in front of him. 'Less of the mother,' she said with a playful slap. 'You're no sapling yourself, young Yatsu. Just put yourself outside that.'

Yatsu took the admonishing hand in both of his and pressed it to his face affectionately.

'Go on with you, you daft thing,' she said as she retrieved her hand and scuttled off to attend to some culinary chore.

Yatsu looked distastefully at the helmet he was carrying, then laid it down on the floor by his chair. When he looked up he found himself staring along the table at Isloman. The man was more familiar than ever, but the memory still would not click into place. He saw, however, that Isloman recognised him.

'Well I'm damned,' said Isloman. 'I thought my shadow-lore was deceiving me out in that murk, with you hiding in that black . . . soup bowl, but it is you. Yatsu.'

Yatsu half rose. Pieces of memory juddered together. 'Is-lo-man,' he articulated slowly. 'Of course. That rock for a head. And that club. Who else could it have been? How could I have forgotten?'

'You forgot because you were once young and stupid, and now you've grown old and stupid,' said Isloman. 'As opposed to me who was young and wise, and am even wiser now.'

Yatsu walked round the table and, seizing Isloman by his short cropped hair, shook his head from side to side, laughing. Isloman wrapped his arms around him and lifted him well clear of the floor.

'Enough, enough,' cried Yatsu almost at once. 'Never let it be said that I didn't know when to surrender.'

Isloman lowered him effortlessly and the two men stared at one another affectionately.

'It was no wise thing to come to Vakloss in the middle of a riot . . . old man,' said Yatsu eventually. Then, before Isloman could reply, Yatsu turned to his men who were open-mouthed at the bizarre spectacle they had just witnessed.

'Men,' he said, 'stand up.' One or two pushed their chairs back hesitantly. 'Up, up, up,' Yatsu repeated, gesturing. Then, placing an arm around Isloman's shoulders, 'Men. Raise your . . .' no glasses, 'raise your mugs. A toast to Isloman here. *The* Isloman. With his brother Loman, the only outlanders ever to ride – and fight – with the Goraidin.'

There was a stunned silence for a moment, and then the room was alive with applause and the babble of countless questions. For a while Yatsu and Isloman both found themselves recalling and recounting many long-hidden memories – sad, funny, bewildering – all the personal paraphernalia that combat leaves in its wake. Their discourse was interrupted only by the insistence of the woman of the house that they attend to the really important business of eating the considerable quantities of food she was steadily placing in front of them.

Suddenly Yatsu slapped his forehead angrily and swore. 'I was so engrossed, I forgot,' he said. 'What's happened to the Lord Arinndier and Dacu?'

'Your friend has a broken shoulder bone, some lacerations and some bad bruising.' It was Hawklan's voice. He had been standing quietly in the doorway for some time listening to the hubbub of reminiscences filling the room. 'I've set the one and bound it up, and given him something to soothe the others. He'll be all right if you do as I say, as will the Lord Arinndier. Right now, they and the three other Lords are sleeping. I think we'd all better do the same as soon as possible. I suspect the next few days are going to make heavy demands of us.'

The room had fallen suddenly silent at Hawklan's entry and all eyes were on him.

Isloman cut through the uneasiness jovially. 'Men,' he said, 'this is my friend Hawklan. A healer by inclination, but quite useful in a fight if sufficiently provoked.' Then, a little more seriously, to emphasise the point, 'I consider it a great honour and privilege to ride with him.'

Yatsu, who had faced Hawklan directly in the alley, leaned back in his chair and nodded quietly to himself. He was watching the response of the others. The Goraidin was a close-knit group, its strength lying not least in the knowledge of the severe training that each member had undertaken. They would accept Isloman on his recommendation and because he and his brother had their own special niche in Goraidin lore. But this man was different, even though he had faced down their Commander, done service to Lord Arinndier and one of their own, and had Isloman's loyalty. Courtesy he would certainly be given, but acceptance? That was another matter.

One of the men stood up and offered his chair. 'Lord Hawklan,' he said, 'please join us. You must be hungry yourself after your unusual welcome to Vakloss.'

Hawklan thanked the man, but declined the seat. 'I'm no Lord,' he said. 'There are no Lords in Orthlund. I'm just a healer, as Isloman said.'

'Well, healer,' said another with a laugh. 'You still need to eat. Put down your sword and any other tools of your healing trade, and join us in the meal the good lady has prepared.'

Hawklan conceded and, leaning his sword against the wall, he pulled up an empty seat and helped himself to a large portion of bread from a great brown loaf in the centre of the table. Yatsu watched carefully to see what his men would do next. He knew that in spite of his approval of the man they would test him in some small way, even if they were not aware that they were doing it.

Isloman watched also, sensing the same, and as the conversation picked up again various remarks headed Hawklan's way which might have provoked a more defensive spirit. He knew that Hawklan would not lose his temper, but he was far from sure how the Goraidin would interpret his apparently placid acceptance of their wilful probing.

Then, to the considerable surprise of both Isloman and Yatsu, Hawklan started to laugh. Not laughter clanging with hollow defiance, but open and full of genuine amusement.

He's going to test *them*, Yatsu realised, and he could not forbear smiling to himself a little.

'Gentlemen,' said Hawklan, 'we're all too old for this cadet's game, aren't we? You're uncertain because I'm not one of you. I've shared neither your training nor your experiences. I'm not one of the spiritual decendants of the men who guarded Ethriss at the Last Battle. And it worries you that your Commander didn't just ride right over me in that alley, doesn't it?'

An uncomfortable silence filled the room at this sudden declaration.

Hawklan pointed to Isloman and continued. 'We came to Fyorlund because of certain evil deeds done by your Lord Dan-Tor in Orthlund. Now we find a sickness in your land that will spread and corrode far beyond your borders if it's not stopped.' He stood up. 'What I need to know is what kind of men you are. Are you good enough to help us fight against this ill?'

Some of the men were beginning to scowl angrily, but Hawklan's voice had a power that commanded their attention.

'I'm prepared to accept Isloman's word as to your worth as fighters, but time is against us and I'm *not* prepared to wait for all of you to come to the same conclusion about me.'

What's he doing? thought Yatsu, in mounting alarm.

'Look at me, each of you,' continued Hawklan. 'You value truth and openness. Speak your minds, *now*. Look into your hearts and form your conclusions *now*, for there'll be precious little time later and I want no doubters around me when I have to seek out Dan-Tor and hold him to account for what he's done.'

Reaching out, he picked up his sword, drew it and held it out along the table. It gleamed jet black in the torchlight. Slowly he looked from one man to the next. None spoke, but each stood up as his gaze met theirs.

'This is an ancient sword,' he said. 'Let the resolves in your heart be sealed by the sight of it. It's an enemy to the enemies of life. It will serve you if you will serve it. I will serve you if you will serve me. The threat to Fyorlund is not to Fyorlund alone, and lies deeper by far than the machinations of one evil Lord. Its destruction may be the work of many generations.' Then, looking round again at each of the standing men, 'If this work, this service, is beyond you, speak now and go in peace, without reproach.'

The atmosphere in the room heightened perceptibly. Unknowingly, Hawklan had used the very words spoken to each Goraidin after his successful training and before his acceptance into the corps. No one moved or spoke and the distant comings and goings of the householders filtered into the room.

Yatsu stood up and looked at his men, his friends, standing in two uncertain ranks either side of the extended sword.

'My apologies, Commander Yatsu,' Hawklan said. 'But time is not with us. I don't know whether I chose this road, or whether I was chosen for it, but I am here, and I must set the pace, not follow it.'

Yatsu looked straight at him. 'Hawklan, we're Goraidin. No slavish followers of any man. But you fit no mould – neither Goraidin nor Lord, nor anything I've ever met. You leave us at a loss.' He looked again at his men and seemed to receive some subtle acquiescence. Gently he laid his hand on the black blade, and bowed. 'Until time shows otherwise we'll trust you to guard our backs,' he said.

Hawklan bowed in reply. The Goraidin had given him the highest accolade they could. He returned it. 'And I'll trust you to guard mine, Commander – men.'

Chapter 37

It was a baleful sight that greeted those who looked across their City the following day. Early morning mist often swathed the plains around Vakloss, lapping like an idle tide at the foot of the great hill which bore the City, but today it had seeped up into the very streets and above, curling around the rooftops, its normal soft whiteness now a pale infected yellow. A single mottled plume of smoke rose straight into the air like a slender column supporting the hazy sky.

The sun shone a feeble and watery light over the scene as if the previous day had prematurely aged it into winter. No street traders jostled the morning quiet with their ritual contests for the most favourable places. No craftsmen or servants purpose-fully marched the streets to start their daily tasks. The streets were empty and quiet except for an occasional flitting shadow scurrying for safety, and the rhythmic tramp of Mathidrin patrols seeking out such stragglers, and inexorably binding the City in a web of black intent.

Dan-Tor smiled, his teeth predatory white. The sight beneath him reminded him of Narsindal, with its creeping mists and its long waiting silences. It was a good omen and fed his soul. Today was going to be a good day, the first of many. Today he would begin to seize the power which he had been patiently edging towards for so long. His enemies had thrust it into his hands.

A movement disturbed him, like a mote in his eye. His fore-head creased a little and the smile froze as his gaze flicked from side to side to seek out the offender. Then he saw it: sharp, black and clear-cut, a great black bird gliding over the City – his City – offending its portentous stillness. The black scar of clarity and its smooth harmonious movements jarred his pleasure at the sight of the exhausted, blurred City, unfocussed under its gauzy blanket, and without thinking he reached out his hand to destroy the creature.

Hawklan, came the thought, and drawing in his breath, Dan-Tor withdrew also his intent. The bird disappeared behind a nearby tower and Dan-Tor leaned forward in anticipation of its gliding reappearance, but it did not emerge and he felt a wave of irritation at this further, if petty, unfulfilment.

Straightening up, he scowled angrily. That had been a serious mistake. He had used the rioting well for his own ends, but the cause must surely have been Hawklan. Hawklan, elusive and enigmatic, must now be here, playing the hunter, seeking him out in his own lair. Briefly, he felt a twinge of fear, but he crushed it. That is *your* mistake, Hawklan, he thought. Your successes have made you over-confident. Now you've given me Fyorlund and I'll draw *you* in like a fish in a net. And on a mere whimsy he might have dashed the cup from his own lips. To send the Old Power winging across the City, the City where Hawklan lay, just do destroy a bird! He closed his eyes in silent rage at his near folly.

Another figure stood looking out of a window, meditating on the same events.

'Keep away from the window, Hawklan,' said Yatsu, entering the room quietly. 'There are Mathidrin patrols everywhere and they need only the slightest excuse to arrest people. Just watching them is more than enough.'

Hawklan nodded and moved across to a low comfortable chair that had housed him for most of the night. 'You look tired,' he said as Yatsu flopped into the chair's partner opposite.

Yatsu blew a noisy breath and rubbed his face with his hands. 'Yes,' he said. 'I am. And worried. I've been prowling the City all night trying to find out what's happened.'

'Can the Lords leave today?' Hawklan said.

Yatsu shook his head. 'No,' he said. 'We'll not even be able to move about the streets today. They're already posting edicts up to that effect.' He frowned. 'They've been so fast. They seem to have recovered from the disturbance almost immediately. I was counting on at least one clear day of general confusion in which we could slip away, but . . .' His voice tailed off and he sat silent for a moment. 'It's all gone wrong,' he concluded bitterly. 'But I can't begin to see where or why.'

'Not all, Yatsu, not by any means,' said Hawklan. 'The Lords are free and at comparatively little cost. You've found two allies – for what they're worth. And you know your Queen is with you, and perhaps thus your King.'

Yatsu looked at Hawklan. So the men had told him about their escapade. That was an interesting sign. 'But . . .' he began.

Hawklan waved the word aside. 'No buts, Yatsu. The game proved to be bigger than you thought. Probably more players than you realised. Still, if we can't leave, then we must make the most of the time we have in talking and planning. But first, you must rest.'

Yatsu smiled wearily. 'Needing to rest and being able to are not the same, healer. I'm battle-weary I know, and there are too many moves and counter-moves flowing through my head. But I can't lay them to rest like I used to. I'm not the man I was twenty years ago. Can't take the pace any more.'

Hawklan felt the man's doubts and regrets. 'You misjudge yourself,' he said. 'But I'll help you.'

Yatsu shook his head and made as if to rise. 'No,' he said, 'I haven't the time.'

Hawklan reached across and put a hand on his shoulder and gently restrained him. 'Yes you have, Commander,' he said, his voice low and reassuring. 'You've just admitted it.' Yatsu felt the hand heavy and immovable on his shoulder. 'You must rest quietly now,' continued the low voice. 'Just for a little while. Your friends are all rested and will watch for you. You know you can trust them. Soon we'll talk and plan . . . talk and plan . . . when you're rested . . . rested.'

Hawklan's voice faded into the distance and, taking his hand from the now sleeping man's shoulder, gently he placed a cushion under his head. Then sitting down again, he said, 'Come in, Lord Eldric.'

Rather sheepishly Eldric stepped into the room. 'I can't make you out, Hawklan,' he said softly to avoid disturbing Yatsu. 'Or your friend for that matter. The two of you faced down a Goraidin patrol, then, from what I can gather, you virtually took charge of them. Your every move marks you out as a warrior and yet you look after our wounded and weary like . . .' The sentence faded away. He looked down at the sleeping Yatsu and shuffled awkwardly. 'I wasn't spying out there, you know, I . . . I just didn't want to disturb you.' Hawklan smiled broadly and Eldric looked upwards, a mixture of annoyance and confusion on his face. 'Why am I justifying myself to you?' he said, then he leaned forward and asked the inevitable question. 'Hawklan, who are you?'

Hawklan looked into the old man's face. Through the scars of his recent captivity he could read a splendid mixture of compassion and wisdom though they were only barely containing an almost youthful impatience.

'Lord Eldric,' he said. 'I'm Hawklan. A healer from Pedhavin in Orthlund.' Eldric began a gesture of rebuttal, but Hawklan continued without pause. 'Events over the last few months have shown me that that's not all I am, but little else. I have more questions about myself than you have, Lord. When I know who I am, I'll tell you. But for now, the question can't be answered. Certainly not by me nor any I've met, including your Lord Dan-Tor.'

Eldric looked at him his eyes narrow. 'Then I must judge you by your deeds,' he said.

Hawklan sat back and folded his arms across his chest. 'If you must judge, then my deeds will suffice as evidence, and I'll abide by your verdict,' he said.

Eldric raised his hands and lowered his head. 'I'm sorry,' he said. 'It was an ill-chosen word. I'm already in your debt for your help to Lord Arinndier and Dacu. How can I repay you?'

'There's no question of payment, Lord Eldric,' Hawklan said. 'We're all under siege here, and in desperate straits, I imagine, for all the comfort of our immediate surroundings. Isloman and I came to Fyorlund to find out what was happening here and to seek out this Dan-Tor. That's still our aim. You and the others will be looking to leave the City as soon as possible, I presume, to flee from him, for your own sakes and for the sake of these people sheltering us.' Eldric nodded and Hawklan leaned forward. 'Dan-Tor's machinations are common to us both. The greatest service we can do one another, therefore, is to share our knowledge, then we can define our intentions and plan our actions. As a military man I think you might say – intelligence, strategy and tactics.'

Eldric nodded again. 'Indeed, healer,' he said, with a soft irony. 'Indeed.'

Through the day, Dan-Tor also gathered in his intelligence, sitting still and silent at the centre of the web his Mathidrin were weaving over the City. Occasionally he would walk over to the window and stare out at the slender strand of smoke still rising in the distance. Like incense from a votive offering, he thought.

A light breeze had risen with the sun, bending and dispersing the column, and the jaundiced haze of the dawn was being gradually swept aside by air that brought with it the fresh scents of the fertile plains which surrounded the City. The sight was much less to his taste, but little could alloy his satisfaction at what had been achieved. On the whole, it was a substantial achievement.

True, the Lords had been released; that was not good, but had presumably been the reason for the start of the disturbance. Two of his workshops had been destroyed; that was unfortunate. Several Mathidrin had been killed; that was of little concern. And several citizens had been killed; that was of even less concern. But the greatest gain came from his being able to lay the blame for all the havoc squarely at the feet of the four Lords, and their more active supporters, even though he sensed Hawklan was the true originator. 'Didn't I tell you? There's treachery all around us,' he could say. ' Look what these people have wrought with their greed and ambition. And these are our own kind. What then can we expect from the Orthlundyn?'

On the pretext of rooting out the traitor Lords and their helpers, he could increase the power of his Mathidrin, and with the terror that they would spread he could gradually dispense with the irritating forms of law behind which he was still obliged to shelter.

Idly he pushed a writing stylus along a book in front of him. For a while it overhung the edge then, at his least touch, it tilted down on to the desk top. The balance swings my way, he thought. But it will not swing back. Fyorlund will go ever downwards under the weight of my Master's heel. A substantial achievement indeed.

Nevertheless, Hawklan and the Lords weighed too heavily in this balance. At liberty, they could dispute this version of events, could rouse many of the people, particularly away from the City, where the Mathidrin had less influence. They could cause endless trouble.

And Hawklan? Still an enigma. It *must* be he who started this, but why? And how?

His mind went back to the green at Pedhavin. What demon had made him think he could sell his corruption to the Orthlundyn, of all people? That remnant of the ancient race. He should have followed his original intention and moved quietly through Orthlund and out into a world that was ripe for him. But he had *had* to stop. *Had* to try their mettle. And what demon had made him play the clown at the foot of that accursed Castle, and brought him face to face with the man who might house the greatest of all enemies? But, above all, what demon had prompted him to try to enslave the man without His aid?

Was it that old buffoon, Chance? Was it some dark test by his Master? Was it even some plot by Ethriss himself? If the devil were awake, might not he too have the infinite patience and cunning of Him? Searching and learning in his mortal frame, not wasting his power on lesser fry, until he knew the strength of his long-silent enemy. The thought was as sharp and clear as the black bird that had soared through the morning murk and it unsettled Dan-Tor profoundly. A powerful servant to an infinitely cruel and subtle master, he knew he was. But a puppet? One whose strings could be seen and pulled by those who had the sight, to make him jerk and twist unaware of their will? He glanced uneasily from side to side as if listening for distant and mocking laughter.

Then, rolling in the wake of these doubts came the most terrible of all. That even the deeds of Ethriss and Him might be determined by a force beyond them all.

With a grim effort, he shook the convoluting thoughts from his mind. None have the vision for that, he thought. You seek that which must be forever from you. Deal with matters of immediate moment. You'll gain scant reward for doing anything else. Hawklan must be in the City. The Lords could still be. They must be found and taken before the balance of his progress did indeed slip away from him.

He walked over to the door and stepped through into a small ante-room. An immaculate Mathidrin officer stood smartly to attention as he entered. 'Lord?' he said.

'Have Commander Urssain join me on the north battlements immediately he returns.'

As the day progressed, an ordinary upstairs room in an ordinary Vakloss house saw Hawklan's suggestion put into practice, as the Lords and their rescuers and finally Hawklan himself told their respective tales.

The room was lit only by such daylight as could percolate through the thin curtains that had been left drawn since the house awoke. The movement of people in an upstairs room might possibly attract the attention of the patrolling Mathidrin, but torchlight shining through curtains certainly would.

Eldric spoke for the Lords. His telling was simple, precise, and short, if a little formal. Hawklan noted some of the Goraidin winking at one another as he rose and began as though he were in the Geadrol. He told of their arrest and imprisonment and of their unexpected and tenuous link with the Queen, but he made no observations on the motivation of the King or Dan-Tor.

Yatsu's telling, however, was longer and more anguished. The patterned curtains threw uneven shadows across his face like an imprisoning mask. He told of his decision to mobilise his old Goraidin companions when he read of the disbanding of the High Guards. 'Without the Geadrol, everything is mist and fog. The course of the country's affairs can't be seen, nor who steers it. Appeals by the other Lords for your release or trial were met with endless and wilful prevarication. The Mathidrin ignored and abused both the Law and the people. I saw no alternative but to attempt to release you so that some light could be shone into the gloom.'

Eldric nodded, but when he spoke, his tone was stern. 'Hawklan has told us, and you've confirmed yourself, some of the things that have happened because of your actions. The City ravaged, with rapine, murder, looting. That's an appalling price to pay just for our freedom. How can you justify it, Goraidin?'

Hawklan watched Yatsu closely. Eldric's blunt question forced the man's pain to the surface, and for all his control, he could not keep it from his face. 'I can neither justify it, nor account for it, Lord,' he said. 'We planned carefully. We studied the City patrols. We chose reliable High Guards officers.' He emphasised reliable. 'The older ones. We arranged an extensive series of diversionary riots and the firing of one of Dan-Tor's workshops to draw out the garrison from the Palace. We knew there was a risk that we wouldn't succeed. We knew there was a risk that . . . some civilians would be hurt. That I would have laid to my accounting. But what's happened . . .' He shook his head and clenched his hands together. 'I don't understand. The Mathidrin seemed to have run amok and, vicious though they are, they're not undisciplined. it makes no sense. Why should they do that?'

'I'm afraid that's obvious.' Hreldar's voice was cold. 'Dan-Tor ordered it.'

'Your Gathering's premature, Lord,' said Eldric quickly.

Hreldar waved the comment aside. 'No,' he said, shaking his head, 'Dan-Tor intends to seize all power to himself – that, we've decided, even if not why. The Law and its many manifestations in our society are his greatest obstacles. Anything that disturbs them is to his advantage. He merely played the pieces that Goraidin Yatsu and his companions laid out.'

'I agree,' said Darek. 'We have much rumour and gossip here today, but the speed with which events appear to have moved can only be because Dan-Tor has had such a blow long planned. He was never short of an alternative in debate, if you recall, Lords.'

Eldric rested his forehead in his hand. Then he nodded. 'I fear you're right,' he said. 'Goraidin Yatsu, I know I can't lift the burden of these events from you, but my own feeling concurs with that of my friends. You can't accept responsibility for what someone else has done with *your* sword.'

Finally came Hawklan. The strange Orthlundyn. The healer?

The man who held the loyalty of the outland Goraidin, Isloman. The man whose very presence had virtually commanded their loyalty. Following Yatsu's grim distress, the atmosphere in the room became jagged with attention when Eldric motioned him to speak.

He told of Dan-Tor's strange incursion into Orthlund and of its tragic conclusion. The group listened quietly and patiently until at the end he mentioned the name of Jaldaric and revealed the true nature of the patrol that had attacked them. For a moment there was a stunned silence and then uproar broke out, and Hawklan found himself assailed by disbelief and anger on all sides.

Eventually Eldric calmed the din. Shaking his head as if to silence the babble of his own thoughts, he leaned forward urgently, his face a mixture of many emotions. 'Hawklan, this is madness. Mandrocs armed . . . and liveried . . . marching into Orthlund! Killing! Madness! And my son, my son, what . . .'

He stopped, unable to continue. Hawklan caught his gaze and held it. 'Lord Eldric. I've told you the truth. I've little comfort for you if that Jaldaric was indeed your son. When I saw him last he was captive but alive, and the man Aelang seemed anxious that he remained so.' He looked round at the other Lords and the Goraidin, their questions restrained only by Eldric's will. Hreldar alone seemed unmoved. 'You have only my word for this, and that of Isloman. But we saw what we saw, and we're here because of it. Of your own kind only Fel-Astian and Idrace survived and they left us to return here. I don't know where they are now.'

Under his gaze, the anger and disbelief in the watchers began to fade. The enormity of his tale seemed to sound like a deep underscoring note that transformed the chaos of recent events into an even more sinister discord. In its wake came only uncertainty and bewilderment, hanging stagnant in the air.

Eldric's voice cut through the eerie silence. 'We're a logical people, Hawklan, but over the past months we've had to come to terms with many happenings apparently beyond logic. When we spoke together earlier I said I'd judge you by your deeds, and that judgement tells me you're our friend and ally;

my heart tells me that also. Lords? Gentlemen?' He looked enquiringly around the room.

There was no dissent.

He continued. 'But, Hawklan, you tell us an appalling tale. We must decide . . .'

'Hush.' The sound came from one of the Goraidin standing by the window. Carefully he eased back the edge of the curtain and peered out. Then equally carefully he replaced it. The others noted the signs. Sudden movements attract attention. They fell silent. Those who were seated, stood up quietly and reflexively checked their weapons.

'Mathidrin,' the man whispered. 'Probably a couple of hundred. It looks as if they've closed the street and are searching each house in turn.'

Chapter 38

Hreldar and Darek were correct in their assessment of the
reason why such horror had arisen so apparently spontaneously
from the tight-knit diversionary tactics devised by the
Goraidin. The Mathidrin did indeed have orders to aggravate
any large-scale disorders in the City. Dan-Tor adjusted the
details as the day developed, but the overall plan was one of
many he had prepared against different contingencies.

Now the men gathered in the upstairs room overlooking a
Vakloss street saw another plan being implemented: the
systematic and thorough searching of all parts of the City. It
was a massive operation, and Mathidrin had been brought in
from many of the nearby towns and villages to implement it.

Yatsu looked at the speaker. 'Archers or horsemen?' he asked.

The man shook his head. 'I didn't see any bows. And only
one or two officers are on horseback,' he said.

'Two hundred?' continued Yatsu.

'Thereabouts,' came the confirmation.

'Commander,' said Eldric to Yatsu, confirming the man's
status. 'Do you have any plan for an escape from this house?'

Yatsu shook his head. 'Not under these circumstances,' he
said. 'We should have been away from the City early last night,
but it wasn't possible.'

Eldric nodded. 'You have groups waiting outside the City?'
he asked.

'Yes,' replied Yatsu. 'And more friends inside the City. But
that's all they'll be doing – waiting. They've no way of knowing where we are or how they can help us.'

Yatsu signalled one of his men to check the back of the house.
Within seconds he returned saying this was guarded also. 'As
far as I can see. The alley's narrow. It's hard to get a clear view.'

There was an intake of breath from the man by the window.

'They've found the horses,' he hissed. 'They'll be on us in minutes.'

An anxious scurrying in the doorway announced the woman of the house. She was flushed and agitated.

Yatsu raised his hand before she spoke. 'Yes, we know,' he said, walking over to her and laying a hand reassuringly on her shoulder. 'Is there any way we can get into the houses on either side?'

The woman fluttered her hands helplessly.

'Yatsu,' said one of the men. 'These houses are old. They might have common roof spaces.'

The woman nodded her head. 'Yes, they have, and there's a trapdoor . . .' She stepped backwards out of the room and pointed to a panel in the carved ceiling.

Unbidden, one of the Goraidin clambered on to the shoulders of a companion and pushed back the carved trapdoor. Small flurries of dust floated unhurriedly down on to the heads of the watchers below.

'Yatsu,' said Hawklan, 'Dacu and Lord Arinndier can't go scrabbling through that.'

Yatsu ignored him. 'Gag the wounded,' he said to one of his men.

Hawklan's eyes opened in horror, and his fist tightened. Isloman laid a hand on him. 'Eldric's accepted him as Commander,' he said. 'If you don't trust his judgement, trust mine. I know Yatsu, and I know these people. Do as he says without question. If anyone can get us out of here, he can.'

Before Hawklan could answer, Isloman received a nodded command from the Commander. 'You next,' said the Carver with a grin and, enfolding Hawklan in his powerful embrace, he lifted him effortlessly up towards the trapdoor, where four hands seized him and dragged him into the dark warmth of the roof space. Amid the buffeting he heard a hammering from down below.

He had scarcely recovered his balance before the rest of the group appeared, including the gagged figures of Dacu and Arinndier. He took charge of them immediately and led them after the others who were disappearing into the dust-laden gloom ahead.

A figure came alongside him and thrust a small torch into his hand. It had a comfortable, solid feel to it, and gave a good steady light. Ahead he could see other torches bobbing in and out between the moving shapes of the running men, and the motionless shapes of the intricate tracery of rafters and spars that supported the complicated roof. As they moved, black bands of shadow swept swiftly and silently about the roof space, adding ghostly lines to those already etched out by the roof timbers. The air was full of whispered scufflings.

Occasionally the floor swelled up in front of them, marking some elaborate ceiling below, and in places the roof dipped low so that they to crouch almost on all fours as they moved forward.

Hawklan watched Arinndier and Dacu closely. They were moving well but both were obviously weak and in pain. He felt a momentary anger at Yatsu but Isloman's words reminded him of the stern reality of their position. At the same time it occurred to him that both Arinndier and Dacu would probably tolerate almost any pain rather than hamper the group. At least their pain will pass, he thought. My role here is to follow, help and learn.

Abruptly the light in the roof space dimmed a little as the trapdoor was dropped back into place. Yatsu caught up with him. 'We haven't too long,' he said. 'The door's barricaded and they'll have to find the man and the woman before they can find out where we've gone.'

In a flash of self-reproach, Hawklan suddenly realised he did not even know their names or how they came to be involved in such danger. 'What will happen to them?' he asked.

Yatsu shrugged fretfully. 'We bound and gagged them. Apart from saying that we forced our way in, they'll tell the truth about us. That's their best protection. But, I don't know . . .'

Hawklan looked at him sideways without altering his forward pace. Yatsu's face was strained. Yes, thought Hawklan, asking others to face danger on your behalf isn't easy, is it? He could sense the man's mind moving back to the sound of screams and cries echoing through streets choked with fumes and ravening crowds. Not your fault, he thought, though you'll never really accept it. Just another scar to bear. More despair. Yatsu was an old soldier. All he could offer the maimed innocents was vengeance but, as an old soldier, he knew it wasn't enough.

Suddenly the group stopped. The way ahead was blocked by a stone wall.

'Is it the end of the row?' Hawklan asked.

Several of the men shook their heads irritably. 'No,' said one, 'there should be as far again if my pacing's right.'

Hawklan decided to stay silent.

Yatsu had not allowed himself the luxury of a single oath at the sight of the obstruction, but his face was as blank and hard as the wall itself.

Hawklan heard no order, but three of the men ran back the way they had come, and as their torches suddenly blinked out, he knew that the first Mathidrin to enter the roof space would die before they even realised they were under attack. Turning back to the others he saw knives scratching at the wide joints in the wall. The mortar was soft, but the wall looked very solid and the task seemed impossible. It was hard to imagine even these resourceful men overcoming this obstacle.

He turned to his charges. Gently he made Arinndier and Dacu lie down and, with a soft murmur and an almost imperceptible pressure of his hand, he sent both of them to sleep. Yatsu eyes widened in a mixture of concern and anger. Hawklan gestured him to the wall. 'I'll keep them on their feet,' he said. 'Sleeping like that will husband energies they'd otherwise squander in waiting and fretting.' Yatsu looked at him and then nodded.

'Give me light.' Isloman was standing in comparative darkness a little way from the others. Yatsu directed his torch towards him. There was an exclamation of satisfaction.

'Here we are,' Isloman said. 'I thought I saw it.' He ran his finger along a dog-legged crack running through the stonework. Without a pause he drew his knife and, using his clenched fist like a hammer, quickly and expertly removed much of the mortar surrounding one stone. Hawklan had often seen Isloman work like this when carving fine details, and gave it no thought, but in the circling torchlight, the Goraidin and the Lords formed a necklace of amazed faces about the spectacle.

'Poor workmanship this,' Isloman muttered, sheathing his

knife. Then closing his eyes he thrust his fingers into the open joint and even Hawklan was amazed as he saw the power of the Master Rock Worker surge down into his hands and slowly ease the damaged block from the wall. Several willing hands took it from him and he thrust his arm into the gap he had made. He looked pleased.

'That's lucky,' he said. 'Just one skin. These others will be easier.'

But, for all his confidence and skill, it took him several minutes to pull free sufficient blocks to make a gap large enough for a man to pass through and sweat was running down his face when he had finished.

Hawklan had Arinndier and Dacu lifted through the gap before he roused them, and then the silent race was on again. As Isloman replaced some of the blocks, he caught a glimpse of lights in the distance. 'They're here,' he whispered urgently to Yatsu.

Yatsu nodded. The Mathidrin had obviously moved through the house slowly, as he had hoped, fearing ambush after finding the bound householders. With luck they would continue to do so through the dark and complex roof space. Then Isloman's replaced blocks would be no slight obstacle. Each one had made two of Yatsu's men stagger. But time was still against them, and he could not begin to assess what deployment would be happening down in the street. They could simply be running towards disaster. He dismissed the thought. It served no useful purpose even if it were true.

All too soon, however, the thought presented itself again as another wall blocked their path. This was indeed the end of the long row of houses and once again three of the men disappeared into the blackness behind them.

Yatsu looked at the wall then, beckoning Isloman, moved to one side until they were both crouching in the eaves. Hawklan saw Isloman nodding and abruptly, over the sibilant cautious breathing of the waiting group, there was a sharp, brittle crack, and a bright jagged splash of light fell into the gloom, dimming the torchlight and illuminating a myriad scurrying dust motes.

The whole group stood motionless in this new twilight. Yatsu's hand went up, unnecessarily, for silence and his head turned slightly as he listened to the sounds that were entering through the gap at a more leisurely pace than the sunlight.

Apparently satisfied, he nodded to Isloman, who quietly removed more tiles. Yatsu picked up several pieces and put them in his pouch. 'There might be archers out there.' Hawklan heard him say. Cautiously, and a little incongruously, Yatsu stood up and peered out of the opening. As he reappeared, a crash sounded flatly through the roof space, followed rapidly by another and another, each more distant than the last. Isloman's blocks had been located and were being prised aside. Then came a brief frantic scuffling.

Three figures came running silently out of the darkness. Yatsu raised his eyebrows in enquiry.

'We let three get through before we killed them, then we killed two in the gap,' said one. 'Left them all skewered on their own swords and wedged there. That'll slow them down.'

Yatsu nodded and turned his attention back to the others. 'Quickly, form a ladder. I can't see the alley, but we'll have to go over the top.'

Two men disappeared through the gap in the roof and Isloman followed them.

Yatsu beckoned Hawklan urgently. 'Get Arinndier and Dacu across first,' he said. 'We'll fetch the other Lords.'

Hawklan looked out through the gap and felt his knees start to buckle. He deduced they were above the archway at the end of the alley, but he could not see it, or the storeys above it. He could see only the pitched roof that topped it. It was not too long, spanning the narrow alley as it did, but it was some distance below where he was standing and it fell away very steeply from its pointed ridge down into the alley. A chasm whose base he could not see.

'Quickly, man,' said Yatsu, as he hesitated in the gap.

The two Goraidin had clambered down on to the roof and, with one sitting on the shoulders of the other, they leant against the wall to form a human ladder down on to the ridge. Isloman was standing slightly bow-legged, straddling the ridge at the far side, where it continued past the high wall of the opposite building to form a valley in which they could move in comparative safety, and unseen from below.

Without allowing himself the luxury of any further thought, Hawklan levered himself through the opening and gingerly slithered backwards down the roof and down the two men until his feet touched the narrow ridge. Cautiously he looked up and saw Dacu being lowered down the same route. He reached up and caught the man's belt as he was released. But Dacu was a Goraidin and, injured though he was, needed little help. He twisted round Hawklan and scuttled along the ridge almost before Hawklan realised what he was doing.

Arinndier, however, proved more of a problem. Fit as he was for his age, he was no Goraidin, and he was a big man. Hawklan heard the two men breathing heavily as they took his weight, and saw feet shifting on the sloping tiles, and hands gripping the wall as they struggled for a better hold to accommodate the unbalanced fumblings of the injured man.

As he touched the roof, he lurched backwards and, staggering into Hawklan, fell heavily across the ridge. A substantial groan escaped his gagged mouth, and his eyes closed in pain, but he was safe enough. Hawklan was less fortunate. As he staggered to regain his own balance, one foot skidded from under him and sent him sprawling forward. His left hand reached out for the ridge, but fell short.

As he watched his hand sliding over the tiles, he felt the narrow alleyway at his back luring him down with a dark siren song. A fearful screeching filled his ears as his fingernails dug into the hard tiles seeking purchase in their tiny blemishes to slow his slide. He saw Arinndier's eyes opening in horror and Isloman starting forward with appalling slowness.

Abruptly he felt his feet slide over into nothingness and an eerie calmness came over him. Now will come all my answers, he thought, but reflexively the fingers of his right hand found an open joint between two tiles and drove themselves into it ferociously. For a fraction of a second this stayed his slide, then his left wrist was seized in a powerful grip to stop it completely.

Seeing Hawklan fall, Isloman had seized the ridge with one hand and flung himself after his friend. Now he dragged him up the slope and unceremoniously draped him over the ridge next to Arinndier before pulling himself back up. 'Stay there,' he whispered unnecessarily.

In the few seconds that he lay there, gathering his wits, Hawklan realised the Goraidin were retrieving Arinndier and shepherding the Lords over him. As he tried to stand up, two pairs of hands gripped him and dragged him the remaining short distance to the comparative safety of the valley gutter on the far side of the alley.

'Are you all right?' asked Yatsu casually, as he stood looking alternately after the rest of the party departing along the roof and at the hole in the roof they had just left.

Hawklan glared at him balefully. 'No, you . . .' he began, but was checked partly by the flicker of a smile on the Goraidin's face and partly by a cry from behind. Turning he saw a Mathidrin emerging from the hole. He was calling to attract the attention of others, presumably below.

'After the rest, quickly,' said Yatsu, ushering Hawklan in the direction the others had taken, and at the same time reaching into his pouch. Looking round after a few paces, Hawklan saw the Mathidrin ducking from sight, then he saw Yatsu's arm swinging forward and a large piece of tile go flying through the hole. The second one, he presumed.

'Every second counts,' said Yatsu, by way of explanation as he came up to him. 'We've got a good chance if they don't spot our first few turns. These roofs spread a long way.'

'I'll gain us some more then,' said Hawklan and, putting his fingers into his mouth, he gave a long penetrating whistle that echoed round the surrounding rooftops and down into the street that fronted the houses they had just left.

It seemed to the trooper who was guarding the horses there that the large black stallion they had found bowed its head as if listening and then spoke to the others. But he did not survive to tell of his impression: a blow from Serian's flailing hoof dispatched him instantly, and the Mathidrin troopers scattered in panic as the horses galloped screaming from the street.

Chapter 39

Dan-Tor's satisfaction grew apace. So, Hawklan, he thought, you'd hunt me? Me of all creatures. And hunt me to my own lair. He smiled as he arranged the recent events into their new pattern. With Urssain's report of the rooftop escape it was clear beyond doubt now that Hawklan had used disaffected High Guards to start the rioting and effect the release of the four Lords from the Westerclave.

He felt almost jovial. True, Hawklan had eluded him yet again, and the High Guards had shown themselves to be resourceful and terrible fighters, but a bloodied nose would do the Mathidrin no harm, and the benefits that would accrue from Hawklan's error would be considerable.

Only one solitary stain of unease marred his grim rejoicing. Hawklan's reach was far longer than he had imagined. Had not a survivor of a border guard patrol caught in the rioting reported escorting Hawklan from the border to the City in the guise of an envoy from Orthlund? With a message for Lord Dan-Tor? Before the rioting?

The stain spread and clouded his thoughts. Hawklan had moved subtly, silently, and with great cunning in his preparations, and had erred in his plan only because he, Dan-Tor, had seen the play and joined the game. Indeed, Hawklan's strategy in attacking what he saw as the source of his troubles, and his tactical skill in planning and launching the attack while seemingly absent, showed him to be a dangerous enemy.

Safe from the use of the Old Power because of my own doubts about your true nature, healer, he thought, and now increasingly alert to your peril as a man – how deep have you penetrated unfelt into my side, you green-eyed thorn . . .?

Dan-Tor set the thought aside. No matter how difficult the

task Hawklan would have to be brought down and bound. Well bound.

But still softly. Very softly.

'Urssain.' Dan-Tor ended his musings abruptly as the spectre of his own Mathidrin patrols rose in front of him.

The waiting Commander snapped to attention.

'This man, Hawklan – the Orthlundyn – I know him. He's dangerous and very able. While he guides the Lords they'll be difficult to find and, once found, their taking will be expensive. We've too much to do with out City force, consolidating the success of the last few days, to have them wasted in a futile search for these renegades which could only end in conflict.'

He stood up and levelled a baleful gaze at Urssain. 'There are reasons why the man Hawklan must *not* be assailed. We'll lay a lure to draw back the Lords, and if perchance they're discovered they can be taken, but . . .' Dan-Tor's cold eyes flickered suddenly red and it seemed to Urssain that they filled his entire soul. He caught his breath as if fearful what his least movement might unleash. 'Understand,' said a voice through Urssain's terror. 'And make sure that every last one of your men understands. If found, Hawklan is to be offered courtesy and respect. If he is offered violence or even threat of violence, the perpetrator can look to a death longer and more awful than his wildest nightmares – as can those with him.'

When a wide-eyed and fearful Urssain had left, Dan-Tor sat down and closed his eyes leisurely. Now he was satisfied. Now began the real fall of Fyorlund. Now it passed the point beyond which it could not recover by its own resource. Years of careful corrosion had done their work. As he tightened his web of fear over the country, the weak, the craven, the appeasers, all those in whom the darker side of humanity dominated, would be squeezed to the surface as out of some weeping sore, to spread the infection even further. Soon Fyorlund would crash down like a great tree, leaving a carcase as host and home for the scavengers who would overrun it. The death knell of Fyorlund would be the birth cry of the new order. And all sooner than had been planned.

Although the presence of Hawklan disturbed this flow, there was an irony in the balance of events. A longer delay, and

Fyorlund would have been weaker, but Ethriss, wherever he lay, might have been nearer waking.

Dan-Tor nodded to himself. There was always a price to be paid. It would differ from one time to another, but paid it would have to be. And when all was finished it would be measured in time only. A mere blinking of the eye to the eternities that were to come.

Beyond the houses from which Hawklan and the others had escaped lay a rambling patchwork roofscape of plains, peaks and valleys as elaborate and varied as any ice-broken mountain range. The group scurried and scrambled across this strange terrain, invisible to the street watchers and overlooked only by a black dot circling high in the summer sky above them. Eventually they were able to drop down into the disused upper storey of one of the many public buildings that littered Vakloss.

The presence of so many Mathidrin on the streets and the shock of the previous days' events kept many people to their houses. But daily needs and the innate and massive momentum of normal commercial activity had brought many others out automatically and, moving cautiously down through the building, Hawklan and Yatsu found themselves looking down from an internal balcony on to a busy trading hall that by its very activity seemed to be trying to scour away the recent horrors.

Hawklan shook his head as he looked down. 'I don't know whether to be happy or sad to see such a sight so soon after what's happened,' he said.

'Think about it later,' Yatsu said. 'We've still got to find a way out of the City.' He cast his mind over his charges. The Lords were sufficiently unkempt to pass perhaps for labourers or craftsmen, although Arinndier and Dacu were wilting noticeably. However, the Mathidrin uniforms that he and the other Goraidin were wearing were soiled and scuffed and would inevitably attract attention, as would the foreign clothes worn by Hawklan and Isloman. 'It's too dangerous,' he said. 'We're too conspicuous. We can't risk the Lords being recognised in the streets, or running into any patrols. We'll have to wait for darkness. There are plenty of empty rooms upstairs.' Hawklan did not seem disposed to argue with Yatsu's conclusion.

'Twilight will be the time to move. Before the globes come on.'

For the few remaining hours of daylight, they rested in an empty storeroom high in the building.

'Not too palatial, Lords, I'm afraid,' said Yatsu. 'Nor too fitting for an Envoy from Orthlund.'

Hreldar flopped on to a pile of sacks. 'It has a door that opens, Commander Yatsu. That's all the palace we need.'

Darek and Eldric nodded their agreement with this sentiment, but Arinndier was asleep. He was lying on the wooden floor next to Dacu, both their heads resting on makeshift sackcloth pillows. Hawklan was sitting by them, leaning on a rough wooden pillar. He looked pensive.

'Are they all right?' asked Yatsu.

Hawklan nodded, then smiled. 'Yes,' he said. 'Dacu's body has a resilience that would be the envy of many a man half his age, and the Lord Arinndier's strong and fit for his years. But they'll need rest and careful attention to recover quickly.'

Yatsu looked up at the faded and cracked ceiling. 'There'll be precious little rest, and only such attention as you can give them, healer,' he said. 'I'm sorry.'

'*I'm* sorry, Yatsu,' Hawklan replied. 'I understand. I didn't mean to burden you further.'

They lapsed into an easy silence, and Hawklan looked round at the others.

Once they had decided to wait, the urgency that had been driving them evaporated. Routinely, the Goraidin had examined the escape routes from the building, agreed watches, and then settled themselves down in various postures about the storeroom. To a man they were now asleep.

Yatsu caught the look on Hawklan's face and smiled. 'Goraidin see clearly and accept what they see for what it is, Hawklan. They cling to nothing. Not place, object, person nor time. That way lies turmoil, and in turmoil lies fruitless death. Death of the spirit, death of the body, death of love. Only by letting go of what we value can we retain it. I'm sure *you* understand that, whoever you are.'

Hawklan laid his hand on Yatsu's arm by way of reply. The man's words seemed like a timeless thread of hope and wisdom stretching back through countless generations.

The sinking sun shone in through a small, high window. Looking at the sleeping figures around him, misty in the half light, Hawklan felt he might be in some Orthlund barn, tired and satisfied after a hard day's harvesting. He focused on the silent motes hoving in the sun's yellow beam and allowed himself to sink into the deep calm pervading the room. The countless tiny lights reminded him of the stars deep in the handle of his sword.

He did not sleep. Instead he seemed to float among the myriad lights, just another speck amongst the uncountable. Strange images and sounds floated by him. Calm at first, a forgotten memory of a time when all was radiance and song, an eternity of time, an endless unfolding into richer and more beautiful patterns. Then a wave of unease, slight and distant, rippled the patterns. A faint clarion call sounded and, with an appalling suddenness, horror and darkness engulfed him as he battled, weary in every fibre of his soul and body, against the endless waves of an unseen enemy that must inevitably triumph. He was choking on his despair and guilt.

Hawklan jerked upright, his eyes wide and sweat slicking his forehead. The sudden movement caused a flurry of eddies in the watching motes and they twisted and darted in the now-reddening light as if trying to escape. Through their dance, Hawklan saw the figure of Andawyr, transparent yet strangely solid in the softly swirling air, and radiating that same embattled weariness and despair. His head was bowed but, as if hearing an unexpected sound, he looked up suddenly and gazed directly at Hawklan. For a moment he stared in disbelief, then a faint hope flickered in his eyes.

'How did you come here, Hawklan?' he said, his voice strained and distant. 'Help me.' His faint hands reached out in supplication. Unhesitatingly, Hawklan leaned forward and took them. He felt the healing spirit flow through into the figure as if into some terrible wound.

'Ah,' came Andawyr's voice again. 'You're here and not here, just as I'm bound and not bound. We've hope yet . . . Seek out the Cadwanol and the Guardians . . . His power holds me in thrall . . . Waken Eth . . .' The figure vanished abruptly and for an instant Hawklan felt a terrible chill seize his hands.

'What are you doing?' a voice hissed in his ear. Turning he saw Yatsu's alarmed face staring at him. It seemed to be at once very close and very distant. 'What are you doing?' Yatsu repeated.

Hawklan turned to indicate Andawyr, puzzled by Yatsu's question. But the figure was no longer there, although he could still feel the healing flowing from his hands. He blinked in surprise and, as he did so, his head suddenly cleared and he was alone with Yatsu in the storeroom again.

He was half inclined to ask Yatsu if he had seen Andawyr, but he knew it would be to no avail. Whether it was dream or vision, he did not know but, whatever it was, it was for him only to see. He lowered his outstretched arms.

'Just dreaming,' he said apologetically, with a faint smile. 'Just dreaming.'

Yatsu's face, however, indicated that something more urgent than his strange companion's eccentricities was troubling him.

'What's the matter?' Hawklan asked.

'I've been out,' Yatsu replied. 'The Mathidrin are posting Dan-Tor's response to our escapade everywhere.'

'Well?' said Hawklan.

Yatsu looked quickly at the others still lying asleep, then he whispered in Hawklan's ear.

Hawklan's eyes opened wide in horror. 'That's beyond me to advise,' he said after a moment. 'You know your own country and the value of these people to it. What will you do?'

Yatsu, however, had clearly made up his mind. 'The Lords mustn't know. Especially Eldric. I'll take the consequences. We must get them out of the City immediately and away to their estates to start raising some real opposition to this man.'

Hawklan looked at him, unable to ease his burden. It had been no error on Eldric's part to accept this man as Commander.

'It's a choice of evils,' Yatsu said. 'No choice really.'

'What about Dacu and Lord Arinndier?' said Hawklan.

Yatsu looked at the two figures on the floor. 'Also no choice,' he said. 'They can't stay here. I can't leave them with any of our friends here, it's too dangerous. They'll have to travel with us. It'll be easier, the further we get from the City. Will you come with us?'

'How long's the journey?' Hawklan asked.

Yatsu shrugged unhappily. 'Anything from one to two weeks, it just depends. Conditions are changing so quickly.'

Hawklan was torn. He was loath to leave the two sick men to face such a journey, but he was loath also to become involved in what was surely to be a protracted and bloody dispute between Dan-Tor and the Lords. He had come here to confront Dan-Tor for his own reasons, which, though still ill-defined, seemed more urgent than ever now. Then, there was the renewed urgency of Andawyr's appeal. Go to the Cadwanol. Waken Ethriss.

A cold calculation came into his head. Let the Fyordyn fight. What better protection for Orthlund than their neighbours torn with civil strife? He crushed it angrily. Orthlund would not be served well by neighbours who had fallen into corruption, and he sensed that Fyorlund now stood precariously balanced. The least movement could have consequences that would spread forever.

'I'll come with you, Yatsu,' he said simply. 'Isloman and I must face Dan-Tor at some other time, when he is weaker, or we stronger. I need to know more about you and your people. Fyorlund is perhaps Orthlund's only defence against Dan-Tor's corruption and, at the moment, you are Fyorlund's. I'll help you all I can.'

There was open, honest relief on Yatsu's face. Hawklan's heart went out to him. Here indeed was a man who would be more cruel than his enemy, but who would seek no violence and would stay his hand in victory.

Chapter 40

Dan-Tor pursued his leisurely walk around the Palace grounds. It was a rare moment for him. A pivotal moment. It had the stillness of a pendulum at the height of its sweep. For a little while there was nothing he could do. For a little while he must sit and wait on the actions, the responses, of others.

It was not a circumstance he relished. To sit too long was to release thoughts that should be forever bound. Constrained as he was against the use of the Old Power, the True Power, it was better by far to be scheming, manipulating, subtly betraying, weaving his own patterns into the Great Design that was His, each tiny stitch imperceptibly bringing nearer the whole, as a wind carves its will into a rock over the centuries.

Dan-Tor consoled himself with the knowledge that masks and cunning could soon be dispensed with, at least in part, and knives could be sharpened and used. Now was a time of harsh and sudden reality.

As if echoing his thoughts, the setting sun emerged from behind a cloud and glared across the expansive gardens, dazzling the eyes and throwing long dark shadows which melted down the solidity of the trees and ornaments and cast a strange new landscape of their own.

But mine will be more permanent, he thought. Neither passing cloud nor turn of the planet will change it.

A towering figure loomed ahead of him in the yellow-white glare, and he had to move into its shadow to see more clearly. It was the Queen, sitting motionless on her favourite horse and staring into the distance. Even in stillness she had a harmony with the animal that irked him.

He walked forward and stood silently by the carved stone balustrade that edged the raised area they were on and curved down a broad flight of shallow steps into a garden laid out with innumerable paths and elaborate shrubberies and flower beds. The glaring sunlight had leached all the colour from the scene transforming it into an unrecognisable patchwork of light and shadow which stretched out towards the two watchers as if trying to escape the sun's mockery.

'Lord Dan-Tor,' said Sylvriss, acknowledging him with a slight nod.

'Majesty,' he bowed. 'I didn't mean to disturb you. I was taking a stroll to clear my mind of the turmoil of these past days.'

'Terrible events, Lord Dan-Tor,' Sylvriss replied. 'I'm afraid I've had to tell the King something of them. It's made him very restless.'

The King, thought Dan-Tor. It was the first time he had thought of him since the riot started. Now Rgoric figured even less in future plans than before, but he would still be needed for some time, and could still prove a considerable nuisance if handled wrongly.

Dan-Tor nodded sympathetically. 'Forgive me, Majesty,' he said. 'I've been so occupied, I'm afraid my duties as Chief Adviser have displaced my duties as Physician. I'll come to him immediately.'

Sylvriss looked at him and smiled sadly. 'No, no,' she said. 'He's quiet again now, and sleeping. It eased him to know you were looking after his affairs. It may unsettle him if he felt you were neglecting State duties to attend to him.'

Dan-Tor feigned doubtfulness.

'Have no fear, Lord,' Sylvriss continued reassuringly, 'I'll seek you out if his illness worsens.'

'Perhaps you'd care to tell him that I've plans afoot that will bring the four Lords to heel very shortly,' Dan-Tor volunteered. 'And further plans to root out the other traitors in our midst.'

Sylvriss's heart froze, but she gave no outward sign of her fear. What did this . . . creature know? How many of her informants would be, had been, discovered? And Dilrap? Her horse shifted uneasily, aware of its rider's distress. She reached forward and stroked its cheek. Dan-Tor edged away a little. He had no love for animals, nor they for him.

'That will be a comfort indeed should he ask,' Sylvriss said, with mild indifference. Then, gently backing her horse, 'Your burdens have been greater by far than mine, Lord. I'll not disturb you further. Enjoy the solace of the sunset.'

Dan-Tor bowed again, and watched her as the horse trod slowly down the narrow steps into the gardens. Soon she had disappeared into the glaring sun.

Later, Sylvriss discreetly sought out Dilrap. She studied him as he sat opposite her. Being constantly in the presence of Dan-Tor had, over the months, taken its toll on the Secretary. She remembered her entry into the Lords' cell and the sudden shock of seeing them all so changed, so grim-faced and lean. Now Dilrap was wearing the same expression. She asked him about the plans to which Dan-Tor had referred.

'I don't know, Majesty,' Dilrap replied. 'But it wouldn't matter if I did. I don't think any of us will be able to do anything now.'

'What's happened?' she said in a mixture of fear and concern.

'Majesty,' replied Dilrap, 'Dan-Tor's declared himself Ffyrst.'

The news made no impression on Sylvriss. 'My father's title is Ffyrst,' she said. 'What's significant about that?'

'Majesty,' said Dilrap, 'the position of Ffyrst in Fyorlund is very different from that in Riddin. It's a legacy from the distant past. In times of grave national danger the Geadrol would appoint someone as Ffyrst to govern the country until the danger was past. Usually it was the King, and he would select a small group of senior Lords as advisers. But it was a temporary appointment and was constantly reviewed by the Geadrol.'

'And Dan-Tor has appointed himself to this position, using the riots as an excuse?' said Sylvriss.

'I'm afraid so, Majesty,' said Dilrap. 'He's used the Law to destroy the Law. The Geadrol is suspended. The Lords are in disarray, divided by conflicting loyalties and confused by rumour. The Mathidrin hold the streets in Vakloss and many other villages and towns. He has a substantial veneer of legality in the title that will satisfy many ordinary people . . .' He waved his hands in angry despair.

'What of you then?' Sylvriss asked.

'I was of use to him only for dealing with the minutiae of the Law, Majesty. His word's the Law now. He needs no guide there. All my tangling and twisting has counted for nothing in the end. The Goraidin's bold stroke cut through them all. And the Law. And probably my neck.' The comment sounded oddly flat, without bitterness or reproach.

Sylvriss looked away from him. 'At least the Lords are free,' she said eventually. 'Dan-Tor may not be the gainer after all. He's only changed the name of what he already had.'

Though what she said was true, she could not sound convinced. Dan-Tor's power would undoubtedly grow the faster for being uncluttered by the trappings of the Law, and the direction of his achievements boded ill not only for the Honoured Secretary but for herself and the King if unchecked.

Dilrap looked at her. 'How is the King's health, Majesty?' he asked unexpectedly.

Ruthlessly she cut his last thread. 'Better, Dilrap, but he's still weak. We can look to no help from him, I'm afraid.'

In desperation he clutched again. 'Majesty. I'm ill-fitted for the role Fate's cast me in, but the man's destroyed everything I valued, and will eventually destroy everything . . . everything I love.' He pulled an ornate dagger from the folds of his robe. 'For a little while I should still be able to get close to him. Physically close. One swift stroke and it would be done with.'

Sylvriss reached forward and took his wrists gently. She remembered vividly her own futile attempt to stab Yatsu and the contemptuous ease with which she had been disarmed and almost killed for her pains. And *she* was Muster-trained.

'No, Dilrap,' she said. 'That would be a useless gesture. You'd die achieving nothing. You and I have no choices now. I shall continue to nurse my husband. Playing the foolish stable girl until times swing our way. Your task is harder. You've been useful to him of late and his very contempt for you may be your saving. You must become his lackey. Law or no Law, he'll need men to administer his . . . stewardship. You've learned to dissemble. Continue. Make yourself of value to this . . . new order. For your sake, and all our sakes, Dilrap, allow no other underling to interpose himself between you and this demon.'

Then slowly, 'As you love me, Dilrap, be as ruthless as he.

No one must stand in your way. Our nearness to him is our only protection, maybe even Fyorlund's only protection.'

When Dilrap had left, Sylvriss went over to the window and, drawing back the tapestried curtain, looked out into the night sky. It was ablaze with stars. Beautiful, but cold and distant. A spartan solace for her. She stood there for a long time.

Chapter 41

The Lord Evison's estate was in the north of Fyorlund, its borders disappearing vaguely into the mountains that lay between Fyorlund and Narsindal.

Occasionally, Mandroc raiding parties would venture down into the bleak northerly stretches of the estate to steal cattle and sheep. It was a perennial problem for most of the northern Lords but not usually a serious one, as the parties tended to be small and disorganised and would invariably scatter as soon as the villagers started unearthing their old swords and spears. On the rare occasions that raids became too frequent or the parties too large, the High Guards would be sent to deal with them. However, there being no benefit to be gained from capturing or killing Mandrocs, they were normally allowed to escape back into the mountains.

Then, abruptly, the pattern changed. The raids grew in intensity. The Mandrocs became more persistent and even started to stand their ground and fight.

Following a bitter year in which both villagers and High Guards were killed, Lord Evison requested from the King permission to extend his High Guard in order to patrol his northern border more effectively.

Such a request was considered to be only a courtesy which the King could not reasonably refuse, but the King *had* refused it. Like most of the northern Lords, Evison was a traditionalist in the mould of Eldric, though somewhat more blunt. In his immediate anger, therefore, his reply to the King's refusal was less than diplomatic. The King, in turn, cited some ancient statute and declared Evison a rebel, along with several other Lords who had made the same request.

This caused some stir but, knowing of the King's illness, the offending Lords let the matter lie in the fairly certain knowledge that they would eventually be able to sort it out in the Geadrol. No harm would come of it. In the meantime, they had a more pressing problem to deal with that required men, so they levied their full High Guards and increased the number of reserves.

Despite the extra patrols, however, the raiding parties continued with increasing frequency and violence, and reluctantly Evison decided that he must mount a major operation against the Mandrocs, pursuing them back into the mountains so that he could find, and perhaps even treat with their leaders or, if necessary, destroy their bases. Accordingly, he consolidated his High Guards and, on a bright summer day, set forth at the head of several thousand men to resolve the problem once and for all.

Commander Ordan, Lord Evison's Second-in-Command, walked fitfully up and down the battlements of his Lord's castle. His frustration at being ordered to remain behind in charge of the castle had gradually been displaced by concern. It had been too long since any message had come back from the troop. The last one had said they were entering the mountains following the trail of a large raiding party, but had contacted no Mandrocs so far. Since then, silence.

'Riders.' The look-out's cry cut into his dark reverie like a ray of sunlight. Jumping up on to the wall, he looked northwards, following the look-out's pointing hand. He felt a great relief as he saw the distant riders approaching and there was some cheering from others who had been keeping informal watch on the battlements.

Within minutes, however, all elation was gone, and Ordan found himself running wide-eyed and alarmed out of the main gate to greet his Lord. Bloodied by battle, and fouled with a desperate journey, Lord Evison slithered from his mount only seconds before it collapsed, foaming and steaming. The riders following him were in no better condition.

Urgently shouting orders for the care of the returning men and beasts, Ordan bent forward and swung his Lord's arm around his shoulder for support.

'My Lord,' he said. 'What happened?'

The old man did not answer, but for a moment leaned heavily on his Second-in-Command. 'Who'll believe us?' he said after a moment.

Ordan looked at him. 'My Lord?' But Evison's eyes showed he was in some other place. 'My Lord,' Ordan said again, more urgently, above the mounting clatter of activity that was filling the courtyard.

Abruptly, Evison jerked upright and stared at him, a distant look of recognition in his eyes. Then he seized Ordan's arm and, limping slightly, dragged him into the castle.

Unable to resist his Lord's urgent grasp, Ordan was pulled through familiar rooms and passageways in a strange, almost nightmare silence. Their journey ended in the Hall of the Four Guardians.

Evison walked purposefully over to an ornate cabinet housing his family's Festival Shrine. He stared at it for a moment, his face riven with conflicting emotions, then without warning he smashed the glass with his mailed fist. Before Ordan could speak, a second blow smashed into the shrine itself, splintering its delicate painted woodwork and sending its simple contents scattering.

Ordan stood aghast as Evison groped through the wreckage and, with an almost touching carefulness in his awkward gloved hand, picked up one of the fallen figures.

Ordan's first thought was that his Lord had gone insane, but when he looked into his eyes, he saw cold reason underpinning pain and horror.

'Commander,' said the Lord, wrapping the figure in a blood-stained kerchief, 'you understand what this is?' He held out the small bundle. Ordan nodded and opened his mouth to speak but Evison cut him short with a wave of his hand, then taking hold of his arm began to manoeuvre him powerfully out of the hall. 'Ask no questions, Ordan,' he said, striding relentlessly, his face pained with the effort. 'This is my last order to you. Every second means death for someone. Take this to Lord Eldric. He'll believe me.'

'My Lord . . .' Ordan protested, but Evison's pace allowed him no pause.

'No questions, Commander. Obey my order. Ride as you've never ridden. Destroy anything that stands in your way. Tell Eldric we have captives by way of proof, but . . . they . . . they're coming after us.' His voice faltered, and a look of disbelief washed momentarily into his eyes. 'We'll hold if we can,' he said softly.

When they reached the courtyard it was choked with wounded and exhausted men, and more were straggling in through the open gate. Ordan hesitated, unable to accept what he was seeing, but Evison's momentum propelled him forward irresistibly towards a fresh courier mount.

'Go,' Evison said. 'Lord Eldric and none other.'

Still under the impetus of his Lord's driving urgency, Ordan mounted the horse. For a moment he paused and looked down at Evison, hoping for some explanation, however brief. But the despair on the old man's face would bear no interrogation. Very softly, he said, 'My blessings will be with you, Ordan, but as you love and have served me, go, now.'

Then he was galloping frantically through the gates and along the dusty road lined with bright sunlit flowers, and filled with buzzing insects, his vision stained with the sight of the returning remnants of his companions, and his ears filled with the sound of his Lord calling his quiet, ordered castle to Battle Stations.

On Yatsu's command, the group filtered casually into the darkening streets in twos and threes. No sooner were they all out of the building, however, than there was a clatter of horses' hooves behind them. Yatsu spun round in disbelief. He had checked the area only minutes earlier, and there were no patrols about.

The horses, however, were their own.

'Not a bad bunch of nags,' Serian declared to Hawklan rather patronisingly. 'They'll knock into shape. At least they do as they're told.'

Hawklan looked at the powerful animal and then at the smaller mounts the Goraidin had stolen. I'll wager they do, he thought, when *you* tell them. However, he kept his peace, knowing from past experience that it was unwise to become involved in debates with animals about their hierarchies.

'Good,' he replied. 'Look after them, Serian. We need them.'

Yatsu was impressed and heartened. Being mounted from the start could make all the difference to their chances. 'Have you any more surprises for us, healer?' he said.

Hawklan could not forbear a smile. 'I've a friend in high places,' he said, and raising his hand he signalled to Gavor circling high above. The raven glided down silently and landed on his shoulder. Yatsu started.

'This is Yatsu, Gavor,' said Hawklan. 'You've seen what he's done for us. I've accepted him as Commander, will you do the same?'

Gavor put his head on one side. 'Very martial, aren't we, dear boy?' he said. 'But whatever you say.' Then, after pausing to give Yatsu a beady and unnerving look, he launched himself at the unsuspecting Goraidin. Yatsu raised his hand instinctively, but Gavor avoided the manoeuvre and landed with wilful awkwardness on his shoulder.

That, though, was the end of his clowning. Soon he was flying high above them and looking for patrols, floating down occasionally to alight on a post or low eaves from which he could speak to Yatsu without being conspicuous.

At Yatsu's orders, some of the fragmented group were walking by their horses, some riding slowly, so that they could mingle more easily with the other traffic in the street. Such people as were abroad, however, were, for the most part, making for their homes after their day's work, and were oblivious to other travellers. In addition, the Mathidrin uniforms, soiled though they were, tended to make passers-by avert their gaze and hurry past as quickly as they dared.

Gavor's high-flying observations of the real Mathidrin patrols sent the group scurrying into byways several times but, on the whole, their journey was uneventful. It was not, however, easy. They had a long way to go and the strain of maintaining a slow pace fatigued them almost as much as if they had been running.

'This is loathsome,' said Eldric. 'Sneaking through Vakloss like thieves.'

'Be quiet, Lord,' said the Goraidin accompanying him, sharply. 'Keep your eyes on the Commander.'

'I'm sorry,' Eldric said, genuinely. 'An old man's impatience.'

The Goraidin looked at him significantly. 'Stay calm and watch, Lord,' he said slowly and firmly.

Eventually they reached the far side of one of the great parks, and the tension eased a little.

'There's nothing near,' Gavor said to Yatsu. 'I think you should make some speed now. I'll keep on looking.'

Yatsu nodded, and swung up into his saddle. 'Mount up,' he said. 'Let's take our scout's advice. There's only one small group of houses to pass through and we'll be in open country.'

He spurred his horse to a trot, glad to be rid of their slow progress. It was important that they be as far away as possible by dawn. Vakloss had a commanding and far-reaching view of the surrounding plain.

As they neared the houses, Gavor floated down out of the growing darkness and landed on Yatsu's head. Bending forward he tapped his beak irreverently on the Mathidrin helmet.

'Slow down a little, Commander,' he said. 'There are two cockroaches putting up a notice. They'll be gone in a moment.'

Yatsu nodded. Gavor flapped his wings to regain his balance.

A small crowd had gathered when the group arrived. They were examining the notice to which Gavor had referred. Yatsu slowed his horse to an easy walk and led the riders quietly forward. Hawklan noticed that the light was different. Looking round, he saw the ubiquitous globes had been broken, and that the light was being provided by newly rigged torches similar to those he had seen in the house in Vakloss and, so long ago it seemed now, in Jaldaric's tent. The light they emitted was less bright than that of the globes, but under it, details were more clearly visible and shadows less harsh. They enhance the darkness, he realised. He noted Isloman nodding to himself.

Yatsu followed Hawklan's gaze. 'Yes,' he said, 'Dan-Tor may have power but there's been a lot of opposition in the past to many of his . . . improvements.' He curled his lip in distaste as he said the word. 'I think more will surface after the mess those burning workshops made.'

Suddenly there was an angry noise from the crowd and Hawklan looked down to see several of its members approaching purposefully towards them. Their leader, a tall rangy man, seized Yatsu's bridle. He had the mien of a scholar rather than a warrior and, to Hawklan, his actions indicated he had been considerably provoked. Yatsu, too, was surprised but, before he could speak, this man burst out angrily.

'Get out. Get out. Get away from here. You're not wanted, nor any of your kind. Clear off.'

His cry was taken up by several others. Hawklan looked at the growing crowd. It was different from that which had greeted him in the border village. That had been hostile, but calm and quite curious. These people, however, were in the first flush of anger and a powerful animal sense of threat surged over him. He realised it would take very little to make them push aside the normal social restraints that controlled their dealings with others.

To his relief, however, Yatsu's response was conciliatory.

'Come now, sir,' the Goraidin said, leaning forward slightly to stroke his horse and at the same time nudging it gently into restlessness, 'you're frightening my horse. We'll be gone as soon as you let us through.'

The tall man hesitated at Yatsu's quiet response but Hawklan sensed his rage uncoiling. Something had released a long-felt anger in the man and, unleashed, it would run its course like an overflowing river, sweeping aside anything that stood in its way.

The man shook the bridle violently and the horse reared its head up in alarm. 'Curse you and all your kind,' he said through clenched teeth. The small act of misdirected violence seemed to calm him a little and, still glowering at Yatsu, he stroked the horse's cheek, regretful of any small hurt he might have done the animal. 'Damn you all. You make us all like yourselves,' he muttered.

Yatsu waited uncertainly. Like Hawklan, he too understood the nature of the man's anger and knew that it was neither fully expended nor yet controlled. There was no saying what he might do next. He looked like a teacher; a man unused to violence and, as such, unused to its control. That made him unpredictable and very dangerous, both to himself and to anyone else who got in the way. Yatsu wished he were somewhere else.

He let out a long low breath. 'Please let go of my horse,' he said gently, bending forward and looking directly into the man's eyes. 'We're off duty. Look, some of us aren't in uniform. We just want to get back to our billets. And I've two injured men here. Let us pass. We mean you no harm.'

For a moment the two stared at one another. Yatsu's quiet reason and his unseen but implacable will stood like a cliff face before the surge of the man's anger. Subtly it offered both unmoving resistance and a way out.

The flood abated and the man released the bridle. 'Get out,' he said again, quietly and viciously, striking his clenched fist impotently against his own leg. 'Get out.'

'No,' cried another voice as Yatsu prepared to urge his horse forward. 'No, wait. Keep hold of him, Mendar.'

A figure pushed determinedly through the crowd until it was by Lord Eldric's horse. Eldric looked down into the round earnest face of a middle-aged man. It was familiar, and his memory immediately started tracking back and forth to identify it.

'By Ethriss, it *is*,' said the man. 'The Lord Eldric. I thought my eyes were deceiving me. Too long under that brown streak's globes.' Then he stepped back and saluted smartly.

Eldric's memory arrived at the face, not without some pride. 'At ease, Sirshiant Astrom,' he said, returning the salute and then leaning forward, hand extended. 'Good to see you again, Astrom,' he said, smiling. 'It's some years since we last met, isn't it? Not as trim as you used to be, I see, but just as unforgettable.'

Impressive, thought the cold part of Hawklan's mind.

'Indeed, Lord,' said the man, beaming and patting his stomach in mock regret. Then, urgently, 'My Lord. I don't know what's going on, but we none of us believe those rumours about you. Just give me the signal and we'll have these cockroaches down and we'll march with you to the Palace to free your son.'

Yatsu interrupted quickly. 'Lord, if this man's known to you, have him ask these people to let us through. Time's against us.'

Eldric raised his hand to silence him and leaned further forward towards Astrom. 'Free my son, Astrom. What do you mean?' he said.

Yatsu looked at Hawklan almost desperately. 'Lord,' he said urgently.

'A moment, Commander,' Eldric said firmly. 'My son, Astrom?'

Someone thrust a crumpled paper into Astrom's hand and he handed it to the Lord. Eldric pressed out the creases and held up the paper to read it. He became very still.

When he had finished, he handed it to Darek and turned to Yatsu. 'You knew of this, Commander?' he said stonily.

Yatsu met his gaze unwaveringly. 'Yes, Lord,' he replied.

'And you'd have led me from the City without telling me?'

'Yes, Lord.'

'You took a heavy responsibility on your shoulders. Did you think I didn't know my duty?'

Yatsu's eyes narrowed slightly. 'That's unjust, Lord,' he said. 'You're human. I took the decision, as I've taken all the others. You were rescued because of your value to the people and I put that value before your feelings for your son, and before your son's life. I took nothing but pain in doing it, but it was right, and I'd have accounted for it to you in due course, as you know.'

Eldric seemed to shrink a little. He looked at Hawklan. 'And you. Did you know?' he said.

'Yes,' replied Hawklan quietly.

'And you've met my son?'

Hawklan lowered his eyes. 'Yes,' he said. 'I'm sorry. I liked him. But Yatsu was Commander. He knew you, and the people, and all your needs far better than I.'

Eldric sat up stiffly and gazed into the sky. Hawklan could feel the struggle within him. An old conflict. That between duty to the people who looked to him for leadership and duty to his family.

Finally Eldric let out a deep breath. 'Yatsu, I and my family absolve you from blame,' he said. 'And I apologise for my reproach. It was just an old man's reaction to sudden pain. You were, and still are, Commander here. You've done well.'

Yatsu bowed.

Eldric reached out for the notice, which had been passed around his companions. He read through it again, lips pursed.

'The Lord Dan-Tor's demanding that we four return to the Palace and throw ourselves on the mercy of the King. Not the Law, you'll note.' He looked at Darek. 'But the King's mercy. Which means, of course, Dan-Tor's. The nature of which can be determined from the statement that my son, *my* son,' he emphasised, ' "having been found an enemy of Fyorlund by the King's Special Court sitting in closed session", will be publicly executed if we don't return within two days.'

He paused for a moment and bowed his head to hide his face from the watching people. Unconsciously he screwed up the notice. 'This is an abomination,' he said unsteadily, almost to himself. 'Secret trials. Public executions, for Ethriss's sake. I begin to dread the very passing of time. Each second seems to sink our poor country further and further into some bottomless mire.'

He was silent for some time, his hands fidgeting idly with the crumpled paper. Then he looked up and raised and lowered his shoulders as if he were adjusting a great burden.

'Still,' he said, his voice almost matter-of-fact. 'It's good to know the lad's alive.' Then, very purposefully, 'Commander Yatsu, here are your orders. Go with the Lords to my stronghold in the hills as fast as you can. Commander Varak's in charge there. Find out what's happened to the estates and High Guards of the Lords Arinndier, Hreldar and Darek. Then raise the old hands, the veterans, and start work on recruitment and training. We have to forge a weapon large and strong enough to face Dan-Tor and his Mathidrin and . . .' he caught Hawklan's eye, and the terrible image of the armed Mandroc patrol and all it implied appeared before him. ' . . . and whatever other forces he may have.'

Turning to his friends, he held up the crumpled notice. 'This alone shows the rightness of Commander Yatsu's actions, and of the conclusions we ourselves have reached. No further debate is necessary except on the strategy and tactics of how we rid ourselves of Dan-Tor. Do you agree?' The three Lords nodded without speaking.

Then Eldric turned to Hawklan and Isloman. 'You're bound to neither me nor my country by any oath or tie, but will you help us further?'

'We've a common foe, Lord Eldric,' Hawklan replied, taking his hand. 'You'll have our help and probably that of all Orthlund should the need arise, though in what manner time alone will tell.' He looked at the old man. 'But what are you going to do?'

Eldric, satisfied, nodded, then turned to the crowd. He held up the notice again and addressed them all. 'According to this, my son's to be executed if we four don't surrender. Executed! After a *secret* trial! No man's been executed in Fyorlund for three generations.' He paused and looked intently at the crowd momentarily silenced by his passion. Then he continued more quietly, 'I can't begin to understand what Dan-Tor wants of us. However, it behoves us to remember that he's a man of great cunning and deviousness. A man who turns all eventualities to his own ends. A man capable of anything. I can only imagine that he wants the City rent by riots again, for surely few Fyordyn could let such infamy pass unhindered.'

Some of the crowd shouted their approval, but Eldric waved them to silence, and then pointed to Yatsu and the others. 'These men are not what they seem. They're High Guards and it's due to their courage that we four are free today. You all heard the orders I gave them. Publicly and openly announced, in the Fyordyn manner, for all to hear. I'll offer no one violence but I fear that superior force will be the only way this man's hand can be stayed.'

More shouts of agreement came from the crowd.

Eldric continued. 'But there must be no rioting. No random, ill-judged violence. We must not hand this man weapons to strike us down with. While my one hand arms itself, I'll offer the other in peace, if not friendship. Two days hence, on the day set for my son's . . . execution, I shall present myself before the Palace and demand a public Accounting of my accuser, according to the Law. I ask you all to accompany me to witness this.'

The crowd fell suddenly silent, and then began to shout and applaud.

Hawklan looked at Darek in puzzlement. 'What does this mean?' he asked.

The lean-faced Lord seemed to be deeply moved. Quietly, he

said, 'Under the Law, any accused person has the right to demand a public Accounting of his accuser. It's the very heart of our Law, Hawklan.'

Hawklan nodded. 'But surely if he appears in public he'll simply be taken by the Mathidrin?'

'Not now,' said Darek. 'The word will fly around the City. His very openness will protect him until the Accounting. More than any other act, if Dan-Tor were to breach his right of Accounting it would unite the City against him to a man. It's not merely deep in the Law, it's deep in the people.'

Hawklan frowned. 'And after this Accounting?' he asked.

Darek looked at him, his face unusually pale. 'Who can say?' he replied. 'Eldric's fulfilled his duty to the country by publicly ordering us to unite and arm, presumably he sees the Accounting as his duty to his family.'

'The Accounting's his duty to everyone.' It was Hreldar. 'It'll expose Dan-Tor to the real scrutiny of the people for the first time. They'll start realising they must choose. He's providing himself as a focus for the people. He's trying to lance the boil that's been festering in our society ever since that . . . man arrived.' He looked at Eldric, now in earnest conversation with Astrom. 'He's also bought us time,' he said slowly.

Later the party rested some way outside the City so that Hawklan could tend to Arinndier and Dacu. Everyone sat motionless in the starry darkness. Eldric's decision dominated all their thoughts, but no one spoke of it. Time enough later.

Hawklan stood leaning against a tree looking back at the City. Streaked with the bright lights of the globes lining its streets, it looked like some great phosphorescent animal that at any time might waken and come seeking them in the night.

Free now of the immediate dangers of the last few days he felt again the strange unease he had noticed when he first approached Vakloss. It was like a low rumbling note deep within him. What was this place when I was last here? he asked himself.

'You'll ruin your shadow vision staring at those lights.' Isloman's voice interrupted his reverie.

Hawklan nodded. 'I'd not have thought it possible that anyone could use light so destructively,' he said.

'Consider yourself fortunate to be as shadow blind as you are rock blind, Hawklan,' Isloman replied, his voice strangely solemn. 'Those lights of Dan-Tor's are the stuff of nightmares. More corrupt by far than anything he brought to Pedhavin. He has some terrible, fascinating knowledge.'

Hawklan looked at his friend. Fascinating? 'Take care, Carver,' he said.

Isloman nodded. 'I understand,' he said. 'Dan-Tor's a man of deep and subtle traps. I wonder how many good men have unwrapped his evil, layer by layer, only to be trapped at its heart by those very wrappings?'

'Does it frighten you?' Hawklan asked.

'A little,' said Isloman after a moment's pause. Then, 'No. It frightens me a lot. He's powerful beyond my understanding, old friend. I think he could destroy us with the blink of an eye if he so wished. Still, perhaps I've known that ever since we left the village. It doesn't alter the fact that we have to face him and all he offers. If we don't, we'll die with him at our backs.'

Hawklan laid his hand on Isloman's shoulder, and turned away from the City to rest his eyes in the deep purple distance.

'Mount up, gentlemen.' Yatsu's soft order came out of the darkness. 'We've some hard riding ahead.'

Chapter 42

On the day appointed for Jaldaric's execution, the very elements themselves seemed to reflect the new turmoil within the City. An unseasonable wind whipped and buffeted the streets, flapping through the market stalls, blowing petals from the innumerable floral displays that still decorated the colourful houses, and shaking the milling crowds.

Only in the darkest corners of the City did there linger any of the stench that had emanated from the funeral pyre of Dan-Tor's workshops.

Overhead, tattered streams of clouds blew relentlessly from the north as if pursued by some demon, though higher still, the sky was blue and calm and the sun shone warm.

The crowds, too, were unusual: restless and noisy, roaming the streets, then becoming quiet and patient, hovering expectantly near the Palace. They lacked the busy purposefulness of the normal City crowds.

Dan-Tor looked out over the City and scowled as he watched the shadows of the clouds scrambling over the rooftops below. Their innocent movement and the strange, quixotic behaviour of the crowds disturbed him.

Standing behind him in the comparative shade of the centre of the room were Urssain and Dilrap. Urssain watched Dan-Tor carefully. Emotion on the man's face was a rarity. I must learn to read him better, he thought. Urssain's ambition and his fear of Dan-Tor were like badly matched horses in a chariot. First one would pull ahead and then the other. His ride was always uneasy.

'Tell me again,' said Dan-Tor without turning round.

'The rumour came in from all over the City,' Urssain said. 'Eldric has ordered the three Lords and their rescuers to return to their estates and begin organising the High Guards against you.'

'Against *me*?' Dan-Tor said. 'Not the King?'

'Against you, Lord . . . Ffyrst,' Urssain confirmed. 'And he announced that he'd come to the Palace today to demand a public Accounting of you as his accuser.'

'And nothing else?'

'No, Ffyrst. It was always the same story.'

'Did you succeed in following this rumour back to its source, Commander?'

Urssain shifted uneasily. 'No, Ffyrst. It proved to be rather . . .'

Dan-Tor turned slightly and fixed him with a sidelong gaze.

'It was impossible, Ffyrst,' Urssain said defensively. 'We interrogated a few people, but the trail invariably led back to some public gathering place of one kind or another. It was obviously started in several places at once.'

'And what do you deduce from this, Commander?' Dan-Tor turned round, his face bright with an open smile. Urssain's stomach went leaden. He had learned that this smile meant his Master was at his most devious. The inviting smile was like soft grass covering an iron-toothed trap. He had learned also that this was no time to try intellectual games with him. Let the fear dominate. Simple honesty was the best protection.

'Very little, Ffyrst,' he said. 'Except that he still has many loyal friends in the City. This rumour could be to cover his escape from the City, or it could be to mislead us into thinking he's left the City when he's planning another assault on the Palace to rescue his son, or . . .'

Dan-Tor raised his hand. 'Commander,' he said, 'Palace life is making you too devious. I'll tell you what all this is.' He waved his hand towards the window. 'It's not a rumour. It's a simple announcement. Lord Eldric's torn between his country and his family, so he's left the country to his friends and is hoping to save his son by this futile gesture. It's a solution to his dilemma that I had thought probable, though I hadn't anticipated his flair for theatre. I presume he's hoping to avoid clandestine arrest by making himself so visible to so many people.'

The smile again.

'His hopes may be fulfilled, Ffyrst,' Urssain said, cowering inwardly. Dan-Tor's head tilted like a curious schoolgirl's. Urssain's mouth dried. 'The crowd's in a strange mood,' he continued. 'Expectant, uncertain. In my opinion it would be dangerous to provoke them needlessly.'

Silence.

'They're talking about the Law, and the Accounting. Everyone seems to have become a juror. All the fear we've instilled into them over the months seems to have evaporated. At least for now.' He hesitated. 'The threat to Jaldaric pushed many of the waverers their way. If we do something imprudent such as seizing Eldric before he speaks we could bring the whole City down on us.'

The white smile vanished and Dan-Tor turned again to the window. Urssain released the muscles he had been holding tense and breathed out carefully. He kept his eyes fixed on the lank, motionless silhouette, vertical against the horizontal clouds streaming past in the sky beyond.

'Are you saying, Commander, that you'd be unable to control this civilian rabble?' said the silhouette eventually.

'If those crowds turn against us, united? Yes. Quite unable. Besides there may be disaffected High Guards amongst them waiting to take advantage of any violence that breaks out.'

'Dilrap?'

Dilrap hitched up his robe on to his shoulders and twitched back a sleeve. 'I fear that Commander Urssain's right, Ffyrst,' he said. 'The Fyordyn are a legalistic people. They'll dismiss rumour and conjecture once appeal has been made to the Law or the Geadrol. It's an old habit. Those people down there will expect to hear cases argued, especially the way Lord Eldric's gone about it. It's like a piece of folklore come true. A shrewd act. There'll be trouble beyond doubt if he's obstructed in any way.'

He walked over to the window and joined Dan-Tor in his surveillance of the City. 'If Eldric appears and demands an Accounting, then we've a serious problem. He's perfectly entitled to do so under the Law and, if he names you personally, then Ffyrst or no, you must reply.'

'Must?' There was an evil edge to Dan-Tor's voice,

Dilrap flinched, but stood his ground. '*Must*, Ffyrst, with all those people there. We can dispense with legal niceties here and there, but not the overall form of the Law. It's too well-known and respected for all the recent changes. If you don't answer, you'll be judged guilty of malicious accusation . . .'

'And?' Dan-Tor picked up the hesitation.

Dilrap spoke more softly. 'I fear the resentment that's accumulated since the suspension of the Geadrol will manifest itself in considerable violence.'

'Damn the Law,' said Dan-Tor contemptuously. Dilrap made a gesture of agreement. 'But the Law's deep in every Fyordyn, Ffyrst. Every child knows the adage "Who destroys the Law destroys his sword and shield". For all the simplification that your new office allows, it would be unwise to do anything that can't be given at least a veneer of justification within the Law. And with respect, Ffyrst,' he lowered his voice, 'Commander Urssain's correct. The threat to Jaldaric was ill-judged.'

Dan-Tor looked down at Dilrap. The man was still an irritation, but he'd been undeniably useful over the months. Now he seemed to be developing a reassuring self-interest; ambition even. He was harder to fathom than Urssain but he could still be useful. An interesting and unexpected development. The Secretary twitched under the gaze but kept his eyes fixed on the shifting crowds below.

'So your advice is?' Dan-Tor asked.

Dilrap turned to Urssain. 'Can you find him and seize him quietly?' he asked.

Urssain shook his head. 'Not without time and a great deal of good luck,' he said.

Dilrap turned back to Dan-Tor. 'There's your answer, Ffyrst. You don't need my advice. If Eldric appears, you must meet him in debate and defeat him. It would be useful, however, if you announced that Jaldaric's sentence is being reviewed. That will make the crowd a little less partisan.'

'You say must, again, Secretary,' said Dan-Tor quietly but angrily, a red fire flashing momentarily in his eyes.

Dilrap staggered back as if he has been struck. Steadying himself against the chair he had backed into, he gasped for breath, then frantically and needlessly adjusting his robe he stepped to the window again. 'It's not I who say must, Ffyrst,' he said, unashamedly fearful. 'It's *they* who say it.' And he prodded a desperate finger down towards the throngs choking the streets below. 'If Eldric appears and you assail him by force, then they – those people – in that mood will bring us all down. With or without the help of High Guards.'

'Bring *us* down, Dan-Tor noted, looking at the quaking figure in front of him, still desperately trying to advise him in spite of his mortal terror. Slowly he turned his gaze back to the window. 'What of the Orthlundyn, Urssain? The man Hawklan?'

'The same rumour says he left with the others, tending their sick,' replied Urssain.

Ah, Hawklan, Dan-Tor thought, I'd not expected to catch you today, but I continue to learn about you. You're an arrogant player to give me such a piece as Eldric, albeit I have to cut my way through this farce. You attack too recklessly, far too recklessly.

However, came a cautionary thought, I must not be lured into the same folly.

He nodded slowly. 'Your advice is sound, gentlemen. We mustn't lose what we've so carefully gained, for want of a little more patience, must we? When Eldric appears, I'll confront him. It'll be interesting to see how he defends the riots his men started, and his links with the Orthlundyn. Stay near, Dilrap. Your agile knowledge of the Law could prove useful.'

Dilrap bowed.

'In the meantime, Urssain. If your men happen upon Eldric and can take him discreetly – very discreetly – do so. It'll save complications. But if they encounter him on his way here, publicly, they're to escort him with every courtesy. If we have to play this farce, and it seems we have, then that will doubtless make a favourable impression on the . . .' he waved a dismissive hand towards the crowds '. . . on the jury.'

The sun was high in the sky and the streaming clouds white and triumphant as they surged overhead in the strengthening wind, when a perceptible change was noted in the crowds thronging the City streets.

It became apparent first to curious observers high in the Palace towers, and the bustle in the streets was reflected by a bustle in the Palace corridors as the news hissed rapidly from room to room. Soon all the windows and balconies were filled with excited faces, and the battlements themselves began to fill with servants and officials jostling for position between the rigid Mathidrin Guard.

Seeing the activity in the Palace, the crowds by the gate received the message sooner than did those who were much nearer to the approaching Eldric, and the atmosphere became almost unbearably tense. Not for nothing was Eldric one of the most loved and respected Lords of the Geadrol. He had a natural gift of leadership, and years of experience had honed and hardened it into a formidable weapon which he could use with very little effort. But what planted him deep in the hearts of the people was his honest open nature. He had asked two things of Astrom and his neighbours. Shelter, until he could ride through the City to the Palace, and their help in spreading the truth.

When Yatsu and the others had said their uneasy farewells, he had spoken to the gathered crowd. 'Go to as many of your friends as you safely can, and tell them everything you've heard this evening. Tell them it's my wish that they in turn tell as many as they can of what's happened.'

Astrom looked alarmed. 'Everything, Lord? What you've ordered the other Lords to do? Are you sure?'

'Yes, Astrom,' Eldric replied. 'I can account for the truth to the people and accept their verdict. Let Dan-Tor weave his web of lies. It'll bind him soon enough, and I've no desire to be caught out in some petty deceit that will taint my whole story.' He took Astrom's arm. 'Besides, this . . . gossiping . . . may be dangerous for you. If you're questioned by these Mathidrin, you'll have nothing to hide from them. Tell them the truth. Hide nothing. And tell them it's my specific order that you should do so.'

It had been a wise judgement, he thought now, as he walked his horse slowly through the quiet crowds. It was the most useful thing that Astrom and his enthusiastic friends could have done, and it was the best protection he could have given them. The truth had added a quality to the consequent rumours that had cut through the murky innuendoes being spread routinely by Dan-Tor's aides.

He had to admit to no small pride when he saw the crowds waiting for him, but he knew it for the treacherous bloom it was. He had spoken long and earnestly to Astrom's wife when her husband was out spreading his tale, and she had confirmed and amplified all that the Goraidin had told him of the events that had occurred since his arrest. It had been a sad and sobering experience.

Be careful, he reminded himself. You know you're innocent, but these people have been ravaged in many ways since you last walked among them. They'll need to have the obvious proved to them. And looking into the faces around him, he felt the responsibility of his position more keenly than for many years. Yes, he thought, I've failed. We've all failed; we Lords of the Geadrol. We lowered a guard which was not for our protection, but yours. We didn't maintain our vigilance, and it's you who suffer the most as a result. Perhaps we can start rooting out the evil that our negligence had allowed to seed here.

Quite suddenly he realised his pulse was racing. It puzzled him at first. His ride through the crowd was leisurely, and the crowd's mood was full of friendly welcome. There was nothing to excite or alarm him. Then an old memory returned to him and he identified the sensation. Battle fever, you old fool, he thought. Many a time he'd ridden through his High Guards before doing battle against the Morlider willing them to take that fear and weld it into anger. He smiled to himself and several people in the crowd cheered.

But there was a darker quality to his thoughts that eluded him for some while. He recognised it only as he passed by the Warrior, a statue of an armed man leaning exhausted on his battered shield, a hacked and blunted sword in his hand. It was a haunting sight, almost certainly the work of some ancient Orthlundyn Carver. Its original purpose was unknown, but it had been rededicated to the memory of those men who died in the Morlider War. As Eldric drew near, he turned to face it and bowed, as was the tradition. When he looked up he found he was staring directly into the statue's eyes. A trick of the light, he thought as he turned away from what he had seen, but the sight had chilled him. The ancient stone eyes were alive with torment and doubt, with unresolved conflict. Then he recognised the unfamiliar shape in his own thoughts. The dark figure shepherding his pride and battle fever was vengeance, the spirit that tapped deep into the ancient darkness of the mind, and bound both madness and sanity with chains of self-justification.

Laying in ambush for me were you? he thought. I recognise you, you old fiend. I've seen too many good men go down to your blandishments. Well, you may watch and take what relish you can, but you'll not guide me further.

Then, as if echoing his inner declaration, the sun blazed out from behind the cloud that had hidden it for several minutes, and bright warm light flooded over the crowd. On an impulse, Eldric reined in his horse and gazed around at the crowd.

'My friends,' he shouted. 'I thank you for your welcome. Many things have happened of late that shouldn't have happened. I'm going to the Palace to seek an Accounting of the Lord Dan-Tor. Your presence would honour us both. I beg of you, attend on us. I'm in need of your verdict and your judgement.'

'They're cheering,' said Urssain, turning to looked at the seated figure of Dan-Tor. 'He's stopped to make a speech. We could have an angry crowd on our hands when he arrives.'

'No, no,' said Dan-Tor, 'that's not his way. He'll wait until he's here before he lays out any recriminations. Right now he's just trying to "sway the jury" a little, that's all. it'll present no problem. I can play this game as well as he, I'm sure.'

'Game?' queried Urssain.

Dan-Tor said nothing. It's as well you don't know how small a pawn you are, Commander, he thought. Nor the nature of the Master who plays with you. The very thought of him would shrivel your vaulting ambition out of its feeble existence.

Urssain did not press his question, but turned again to look at the now visible Eldric approaching the Palace gates below.

'He's a splendid sight,' he said involuntarily.

Dan-Tor rose and joined him at the window. 'Indeed,' he said after a moment's contemplation. 'Indeed he is. Most picturesque. A relic of days long gone, like something out of an old picture. It's quite fitting that such a figure should attend the death of the old order and the birth of the new.'

But the sight irritated him, bringing back ancient and bitter memories of the time when many, dressed thus, had unjustly brought down his Master and sent him into the long darkness. For Eldric was in battledress. Not the formal battledress he would have worn for the Geadrol, but the full battledress worn by the High Guards at the time of the First Coming. A light, close-knit mailcoat that would turn almost any edge or point, and a rounded helm that would deflect them. A white surcoat with the symbol of the Iron Ring emblazoned on it, and a red cloak to denote his rank and make him conspicuous in combat – an invitation to the enemy and a focus of courage and leadership for his own men. At his left side hung a sword in a decorated scabbard, and at his right swung a double-headed axe that glinted bright in the sunlight.

Dan-Tor looked at the glittering axe. Developed from a much cruder Mandroc weapon, he remembered. Ethriss was always learning and improving. Suddenly a great swell of primordial rage rose up through him, as if these old memories had opened some long-closed door. Closing his eyes, he struggled to fight it down. Had Urssain chosen that moment to turn around, he would have seen his master strangely and evilly transfigured, but Dan-Tor's restraint prevailed and the moment passed.

'A brief word of advice for your men, Commander,' he said.

'Ffyrst?'

'Patience,' replied Dan-Tor. 'Move only on my *express* command. I intend to make this a long and tedious day, and I want no acts of "initiative" from any of your more foolish young men, do you understand? Behaviour to Eldric and to the crowd is to be both impeccable and friendly.'

'Yes, Ffyrst,' Urssain acknowledged.

'Besides,' continued Dan-Tor, 'he may be an old relic, but he's a dangerous one, and he's come dressed for close-quarter fighting. Armed like that, he'd slaughter dozens before you could bring him down.'

Urssain offered no comment on this judgement of his men.

He still carried the memories of how the High Guards had fought in Orthlund, and he would not make the mistake of underestimating them again.

Below, an expectant semi-circle formed in the crowd and Eldric rode slowly forward into the open space.

'Ah,' said Dan-Tor. 'We're here. Let's attend the honourable Lord, Commander, and make ourselves available for the Accounting.'

Chapter 43

As they left the outskirts of Vakloss, Hawklan advised Yatsu to allow Serian to set the pace. 'He's a better judge of horses than either of us, and time's important.' The Goraidin acceded, but was uncertain for some time until he saw the progress they were making and how fresh the horses remained after following Serian's unseen commands to walk or trot or gallop.

On a few occasions Hawklan asked Serian to stop for the sake of the men, but the horse remonstrated with him. 'No,' he said. 'We're going well. We're in harmony. Our spirits are flowing. You look to your own, Hawklan, I'll look to mine.' And Hawklan had to content himself with tending Dacu and Arinndier and encouraging the others while in the saddle, until Serian deemed it fitting to stop.

A combination of Serian's will and Isloman's shadow lore sped them through the night, and Gavor's high circling watch kept them clear of Mathidrin patrols during the day.

'They're not looking for anyone,' he concluded eventually. 'We've been too fast for them. They don't know what's happened.'

A further, lengthy sortie by Gavor yielded the information that they were apparently not being pursued at all. Yatsu was uneasy.

'It could be for many reasons,' Hawklan said. 'Perhaps Eldric's giving Dan-Tor severe cause for thought. Perhaps he's uncertain of your support in the country and is frightened of over-extending himself.'

Yatsu shook his head. 'No. He has enough Mathidrin in the country to deal with us. He must know where we're going and why by now. If he's not pursuing us with everything he has, then he doesn't care that we'll raise an army against him, which means . . .'

'He's got greater forces at his command somewhere than we've seen so far.' Hawklan finished his conclusion.

Yatsu nodded. 'We must execute Lord Eldric's orders as quickly as possible.'

On the third day out from Vakloss Gavor swooped down unexpectedly out of the windy sky. 'Rider coming,' he said. 'Very fast.'

'Mathidrin?' asked Yatsu.

'No,' said Gavor. 'But he's liveried, armed and riding as if his life depended on it.'

Yatsu spoke a few soft orders and four of the Goraidin melted into the adjacent fields and hedgerows. Within minutes, the rider thundered round a bend in the road ahead. Seeing the waiting group blocking the road he brought his sweating mount to a precipitate halt. Hawklan could see the mixture of emotions that illuminated the man's face as he looked at them. Then, reluctantly he turned his horse as if to flee, and Yatsu's Goraidin appeared out of the fields to seal his retreat.

The rider spun his horse round several times indecisively, then abruptly he lifted a double-headed axe from his saddle and held it high and menacingly in the air. The gesture and the man's attitude radiated an unequivocal intention. Hawklan heard Yatsu draw in a sharp breath.

'He's battle crazy,' he shouted. 'Defend yourselves.'

The man's horse reared violently, and with a terrible roaring cry he urged it forward straight at Yatsu's group.

The force of the man's desperate passion hit Hawklan like a breaking wave, and he felt a strange stirring deep within him.

'Stop,' he shouted. Not to the charging figure, but to the Goraidin by him, who were drawing back bows to end this threat at a safe distance. Before anyone could argue, Serian leapt forward into a full gallop seeming to read Hawklan's will without words being spoken.

The group watched, stunned, as Serian gathered speed and headed straight for the oncoming rider. But Isloman's eyes opened wide, almost in terror, as once again his old friend had disappeared, and in front of him was some ancient figure sprung alive from the walls of Anderras Darion.

At the sight of Hawklan approaching, both the man's cry and

his horse faltered slightly, but not sufficiently to stem either the physical or the emotional momentum that had been built up. The axe swung around his head in a lethal hissing circle, and his cry became more shrill, but Yatsu screwed up his eyes in a sympathetic grimace as he heard the fear in it.

As the two horses closed, Serian swerved suddenly to the right and Hawklan leaned to the left, bringing his hand up in front of the man's face. The move was so rapid and unexpected that the man rose up out of his saddle and crashed backwards on to the ground even though Hawklan had barely touched him.

Hawklan dismounted quickly and walked over to the fallen man, the grim aura that had surrounded him during his charge falling from him like an unwanted cloak. He knelt down by the man's side and began gently and swiftly checking for injury. Isloman watched uncertainly, two images lingering in his mind: Hawklan the healer he had known for so many years; and Hawklan the terrible warrior who appeared in times of physical trial.

As Hawklan's hands moved across the man's face, his eyes flickered open and gazed upward, unfocused and bewildered.

'You're badly winded, but uninjured,' said Hawklan. 'You were lucky. I'm sorry I had to be so rough, but you were about to be killed.'

Memory returned to the man's face and he tried to rise.

Hawklan restrained him with a gentle hand on his chest. 'Just rest for a moment,' he said. 'You're safe now.'

The Goraidin gathered round and the man struggled for a moment unavailingly against Hawklan's hand. Then his head dropped back despairingly. 'Damn you,' he said weakly. 'Damn you and all your kind.'

Hawklan smiled. 'I don't think there are a great many like me, and you're misjudging the others, they're not what they seem.'

The man glowered at Hawklan, but Hawklan returned the look with another smile. 'You're alive, aren't you?' he said. Then, flicking his thumb towards the watching Goraidin, 'These men would've killed you in another pace if I hadn't stopped you. They had quite specific, if hasty, orders about it, and every personal inclination, the way you were swinging that axe.'

The man's expression did not change. 'What did you hit me with?' he asked. 'All of a sudden you weren't there and then . . .'

Hawklan laughed and stood up. 'You hit yourself in a manner of speaking,' he replied. 'But don't bother about it. Just consider yourself lucky you weren't badly hurt. Lie still for a little while until you're fully recovered.'

But the man eased himself gingerly into a sitting position as the rest of the group joined them. 'That's the remains of a High Guard livery he's wearing,' said one of the men.

'Lord Evison's livery,' came a voice from behind them. It was Arinndier, carefully dismounting from his horse. 'And ill-used at that. Explain your condition and your conduct, Guard.'

'Lord Arinndier?' said the man in surprise. He accepted the hands held out to fetch him to his feet. 'Lord . . . I . . .' He looked round in confusion. 'What are you doing with these . . . these . . . people? A group of these tried to stop me and I had to kill three of them.'

'Answer *my* questions, Guard, before I answer yours,' Arinndier replied. 'Suffice it that these people, as you call them, aren't Mathidrin, despite their uniform, but High Guards such as yourself. You've fallen among friends . . . literally. And you owe the Lord Hawklan here your life.'

The man swayed a little and Hawklan took his arm. 'He's very weak, Lord Arinndier,' he said, then looking closely at the man's face, 'and exhausted. When did you last sleep or eat?' he asked.

The man shrugged vaguely. 'I've to find Lord Eldric urgently,' he said. 'Lord Evison's message . . .'

Hawklan's tone was gentle but unequivocal. 'The Lord Eldric's in Vakloss and, I suspect, in no position to receive messages at the moment. The Lords Arinndier, Darek and Hreldar will accept it, I'm sure, but only when you've rested.'

The man became agitated. 'No, you don't understand,' he said angrily. 'I've lost too much time already. The country's gone mad.' He shook himself free of Hawklan's hand and immediately staggered uncontrollably around the small circle formed by the gathered men. As each tried to help him, he pushed them away until finally he collapsed on to his knees.

Hawklan bent down and passed his hand over the man's face. The agitation left it and he slithered gently to the ground.

'That was a little premature, Hawklan,' said Darek. 'I'd say from his condition that his message was one of some urgency.'

'Undoubtedly,' said Hawklan. 'But he'll tell you precious little in that condition. He's on the verge of total collapse. I'd judge he's been riding for several days without food or sleep. However urgent his message I don't think an hour or two would make much difference.' He looked at Yatsu. 'Can we spare this man a little time?' he asked.

Yatsu raised an eyebrow. 'Ask your horse,' he said ironically. The comment provoked a little more laughter than it merited as it carried the group's residual battle tension into the breeze.

As if following it, Gavor extended his shining wings and rose leisurely into the air. 'I'll keep watch for you, Commander,' he said. 'It's a good day for resting on the air.'

Yatsu acknowledged with a nod of thanks, but posted sentries anyway. Only Hawklan heard Gavor's distant chuckle.

Hawklan made the newcomer comfortable and then joined the three Lords and Yatsu, who were sitting on a grassy embankment at the side of the road.

'Let me look at your wound,' he said to Arinndier. The Lord smiled to himself. He had already learned that this green-eyed healer was not to be stayed by any form of protest. As Hawklan's hands examined the wound and manipulated his neck and shoulders, Arinndier felt a deep relaxation seep through him.

'You've magic in your hands, Hawklan,' he said. 'The only person I've met who could do the same was Dan-Tor.' He paused thoughtfully. 'No, that's not quite right. He treated my wrist once when I sprained it. He cured it very quickly, but it felt more as if the injury was being . . . torn out almost, by a great power.'

The hands on his shoulders stopped moving and he turned his head to look at Hawklan. 'I suppose that sounds rather foolish to you, doesn't it? Healing's healing, isn't it?'

Hawklan smiled and, placing his hand on top of Arinndier's head, turned it to the front again. 'No, not at all,' he said. 'Far from it. You've just told me a great deal about the man. I'll have to think about it, it may be important. Now, be quiet and relax.'

But Arinndier was not so easily stopped. 'And where in this world did you learn that trick you used on our messenger?'

'I'd like an answer to that,' said Yatsu. 'What possessed you to tackle someone in that state? I take some pride in my fighting skill, but that was a textbook case of when to retreat. I've seen men like that take a score of arrows and still kill a dozen before they fell.'

Hawklan did not answer immediately. He looked down at his hands seeking out the damage in Arinndier's back. Though he knew no others could see it – even Tirilen would see it only faintly – it was written there quite clearly for him to read. The arrow wound, centring a vivid mosaic of tensions and strains brought about by the man's posture generally and his anxious response to the injury in particular. A mass of tiny interlinked wounds leading deep down into the very heart of the man. His hands would gradually release them, but he knew the body would partly re-establish some of them in spite of itself. These people were always the same – these people, the phrase made him scowl slightly – always a part of them dedicated to self-destruction.

'The man had to be protected from the consequences of his actions,' he said.

'*He* had to be protected?' exclaimed Arinndier. 'What about us? He was the one with the axe and the frenzy – ouch.'

'Be still,' Hawklan said, firmly. 'How many times do I have to tell you to relax? Stop fighting your body's attempts to heal itself.'

Yatsu casually lifted his hand to his mouth to hide a smile.

'Anyway, you were in no danger,' Hawklan continued. 'Your Goraidin would've killed his horse and then him before he'd travelled half a dozen paces. Isn't that so, Yatsu?'

Yatsu nodded. 'There's no other way with people like that if you can't run away. At least I've never seen one until today.' He rolled a grass stalk between his thumb and finger and then launched it gently like a tiny spear. The breeze caught it and tumbled it along the road.

Hawklan sensed that Yatsu was recalling memories he would have preferred stayed forgotten. He looked again at Arinndier's back. 'That's all the answer I have for you, I'm afraid,' he said. 'I saw a path and followed it. It was different to yours.'

Yatsu looked at him. 'You took an incredible risk,' he said.

Hawklan shook his head. 'No,' he said. 'The path was there to be followed. The only danger lay in my leaving it.'

'I don't understand,' said Yatsu.

Hawklan laughed and slapped Arinndier's arm. 'That should do for now,' he said. 'Remember, relax into the pain when it troubles you. Stop fighting it.' He turned to Yatsu, still laughing. '*You* don't understand it?' He bounced his finger ends off his chest in emphasis. '*I* don't understand it. Now where's Dacu?'

Ordan emerged from a warm, comforting darkness into a warm, comforting summer light. He stared up at the sky picture his father had carved and painted on his bedroom ceiling. The breeze on his face must be coming from an open window. Soon the house would start to bustle awake, and a sunlit day would spread before him.

Then he realised the cloud pictures were moving, and a small black dot was sweeping a wide watchful circle high above him. With an appalling jolt, his memory returned. His message. Lord Eldric. More Mathidrin attacking him. He tried to sit up, but a gentle hand restrained him.

'Not yet,' said a voice. 'You're with friends. Rest while you can. We haven't much time, but you must eat, and tell us your tale before we decide what to do.'

Ordan turned his head towards the voice. The speaker had a lean carved face with high cheekbones and bright green eyes. Ordan remembered a haze of weariness and mounting frenzy, and a great force that had torn it from him effortlessly. The words 'You're alive aren't you?' came back to him. This green-eyed man had saved him in some way when he could just as easily have killed him.

'What's happening?' he said. 'Who are you? Who are these . . .'

'My name is Hawklan,' came the reply. 'These other men are High Guards, of a kind, despite their uniforms. As for what's happening, that's a complicated tale which will have to keep. Come on, sit up.'

But the momentum of Ordan's long journey reasserted itself and swept away most of his new-found quiet. He struggled unsteadily to his feet and looked round at the groups of resting men and grazing horses. Lord Evison's order had been unequivocal. Give the message to Lord Eldric only. But he had lost so much time. Lord Eldric's Castle had been sealed and his household reputedly fled to the mountains. Then he'd had to fight his way through black-liveried guards he'd never seen before. Now, this strange green-eyed man – Orthlundyn by the sound of him. High Guards in black livery? Lords? Arinndier, Darek, and was that grim-faced one Hreldar?

He put his hand to his head. He knew he was too tired from his relentless journey to think clearly. But these were Eldric's close friends. They would advise him. He walked over to them and saluted. 'Lords. Ordan Fainson. Commander of the Lord Evison's High Guard. May I speak?'

Arinndier returned his salute without rising, and motioned him to sit down.

Ordan told his tale quickly and simply and the Lords listened intently and without interruption, though Hawklan could feel their mounting alarm. At the end, Ordan took the bundle from his tunic and gave it to Arinndier without comment.

Hawklan looked at the figure resting on the bloodstained kerchief. It meant nothing to him but, glancing around, he saw it meant a great deal to the Fyordyn.

Hreldar's face had become harder. The face of a man confirming and confronting his worst fears. Darek's face was torn between belief and disbelief, while Arinndier simply scowled and shifted his injured shoulder. The movement was unnecessary and painful and Hawklan watched him closely, waiting for him to emerge from behind the shield of self-inflicted pain that he found more acceptable than the truth of what he was looking at. When he did so, his face was contorted with anger.

'Commander, are you insane?' he shouted. 'You know what this is?'

Ordan bridled a little but stood his ground. 'Yes, Lord,' he replied. 'I know what it is. It's my Lord's message to the Lord Eldric, sent to ask for help in extremity.'

Arinndier muttered to himself.

'What does it mean?' ventured Hawklan.

Darek started a little and then turned to him. His face was pale and his manner uneasy. He looked faintly embarrassed as he spoke. 'It's the fourth figure from a Festival Shrine. The figure of Ethriss.' He seemed reluctant to continue. 'It should never be visible. The appearance of the fourth figure is a portent of the Second Coming of . . . Sumeral.'

'Madness,' muttered Arinndier, nursing his injured shoulder again. 'Evison's stirring up trouble because the King declared him a rebel.' But his tone carried no conviction.

'Nonsense,' Darek said impatiently. 'Evison's been badly treated by the King, but he's neither rebel nor troublemaker. I'll ask you to recall our discussion before we went to meet the King.' He gave a soft mirthless laugh. 'Our last night of innocence.'

Arinndier blustered. 'Eldric was unwell. I formalised things to avoid embarrassing him.'

'No,' said Darek. 'He was perfectly well and perfectly rational and he said nothing that wasn't fit for Gathering. You'll perhaps recall also that we agreed first face proof for what he submitted.' He became heated. 'Everything that's happened since has been like a waking nightmare. That first face proof has been enhanced with time and you know it.'

Arinndier turned his face away angrily with a contemptuous oath.

'Enough,' said Darek coldly. 'Have you been so long away from the Geadrol, Lord, that you forget its ways so totally? I'll put your indiscipline down to your wound and your fatigue.'

Arinndier stepped towards him, eyes blazing.

Darek's jawline tightened angrily and snatching the figure from his friend he held it up close to his face. 'In Ethriss's name, Arin, *think*. You know Evison. He's got even less imagination than Eldric. Do you think he'd have done this for no reason?'

Under the impact of Darek's uncharacteristic passion, the resentment and anger suddenly drained out of Arinndier like water from a shattered bowl. He bowed his head. Sympathy replaced Darek's anger.

Hawklan took Arinndier's arm, and looked at the anguished

Lords and the Goraidin, standing bewildered at this outburst. 'Lords,' he said, 'Isloman and I are here because we believe this, too. Sumeral is risen again, and Dan-Tor is His agent. He'll unleash His corruption on the whole world if we don't oppose him. Even now, this very division among you here is a small victory for Him.' Before he could be questioned, he splashed practicalities in their faces. 'But our immediate problems are simpler,' he said. 'You have a known foe in Dan-Tor. You must obey Lord Eldric's orders and continue to his estate as quickly as possible and prepare to face him.' He took the figure gently from Darek and looked at it closely. It was beautifully and intricately carved. Its slightly raised right arm seemed to point to yet another new direction for him.

'Isloman and I will return with Commander Ordan to find out what happened to Lord Evison to prompt him to send this . . . ancient message. We'll meet you at Lord Eldric's stronghold as soon as we are able.'

Chapter 44

At the Palace gate, Eldric paused to compose himself. The wind tugged at his red cloak and, looking down at his shadow, he congratulated himself on the armour he had chosen from the many that Astrom and his friends had offered him. It would impress the crowd with its classical imagery and it would enable him to defend himself very effectively if Dan-Tor chose to offer violence.

Slowly, he unhooked a large horn from the horse's saddle and with half an eye on a passing cloud, he blew a great blast on it just as the sunlight flooded into the square. The effect was electric. When the echoes died away, the whole crowd stood expectant, motionless and silent, awaiting Dan-Tor's response. The challenge had been issued.

Dan-Tor himself, however, was no mean manipulator of crowds, and be delayed his appearance until the effect of Eldric's entrance had begun to ebb away, and a wisp of restlessness was beginning to rustle through the waiting people.

Slowly the great double gates of the Palace opened and, equally slowly, Dan-Tor walked through the widening gap, out into the bright sunshine. He wore a simple undecorated brown robe of office and carried no visible weapons. The high cowl of his robe threw his face partly into shade and Eldric was unable to see his eyes. Some way behind him came Dilrap and Urssain. The former twitching a little less than usual, the latter also apparently unarmed but exuding the menace that his uniform had come to mean in the City.

Eldric glanced at Dilrap. The Queen says he's to be trusted, Yatsu had told him, but Eldric knew he could expect no aid from him this day. To survive, Dilrap would have to help bring him down.

'Stay,' said Eldric in a commanding tone. 'That's near

enough. The people are gathered here to listen to your Accounting, Lord Dan-Tor. We must needs keep our distance, for their sakes.'

Dan-Tor bowed slightly and raised his hands in acquiescence. 'Lord Eldric,' he said pleasantly and clearly, so that his voice projected well across the square. 'It's in deference to your past service to the King that I come to meet you in this . . .' he waved his hand searchingly, 'in this strange fashion. You're a fugitive from custody. Your co-conspirators ravaged the City to release you. I should order the Mathidrin to arrest you immediately, but I can see that would only cause more bloodshed, you've so deceived the people.'

'Enough,' said Eldric. 'You draw conclusions prematurely. Don't insult me or the people by such contempt for the Law. This is no strange meeting as you know full well. It's the meeting of accuser and accused, as demanded by the Law. The time and the place are unusual, but they are also irrelevant. The form is *not*. We will hear and test each other's evidence freely and openly. If you chose not to do this you risk the immediate verdict of this jury here.'

There were some cries of encouragement from the crowd but, keeping his gaze on Dan-Tor, Eldric held up his hand to silence them. He wished he could see the man's eyes more clearly. His face seemed affable and relaxed, but his eyes? He reached up and adjusted his helm slightly to throw his own eyes more into the shade.

Dan-Tor shrugged regretfully. 'Unlike you, Lord Eldric, I'll do nothing which might endanger these people. I've only the best interests of the people and Fyorlund at heart in these times of treachery and danger, when trusted Lords . . .'

'Enough,' thundered Eldric, resting his hand on his axe. 'You try the patience of the people, Lord Dan-Tor. If you abuse the form again I'll slay you where you stand, unarmed or no.'

An awesome silence fell on the crowd such was the weight of his anger and, for an instant, Eldric saw Dan-Tor's eyes flash red in the gloom beneath his cowl. For a brief instant the sight filled Eldric with an appalling and unreasoning fear and it was only with great effort that he did not turn and flee. Yes, he thought, whoever you are, let's see if this day can bring your true nature before the people. 'Now hear me in silence, as I in turn will listen to your Accounting.'

Then came his charges: suspension of the Geadrol; formation of a King's High Guard; disbandment of the Lords' High Guards; armed expeditions into Orthlund and attacks upon its people; arbitrary arrest and imprisonment of the Lords; threatened execution of Jaldaric after secret trial; appointment of himself as Ffyrst. Then came the final charge: the training, arming and use of Mandrocs against Fyordyn.

The mounting murmur of approval from the crowd that had accompanied each charge stopped suddenly with a noise like the hiss of a descending sword blade.

Dan-Tor felt the impact of the crowd's reaction. A serious problem, Dilrap had said. The words came back to Dan-Tor with a dark irony. Ah, Hawklan, he thought, I misjudged you again. It was a cast well worth the sacrifice of your Eldric. For an instant he felt the edifice of his years of scheming totter and shake. Such an announcement as Eldric had made could bring the stunned crowd on to him like wolves on to a downed prey. That would leave him only the Old Power. And where are you, Hawklan . . . Ethriss? Did you truly leave the City? Or are you awaiting nearby for the touch of my folly to awaken you? Trapped. Dan-Tor swayed slightly as aeons of darkness opened before him.

'Your answer, Lord.' Eldric's voice reached through to him.

Patience, came a thought from deep within.

Dan-Tor brought his mind sharply to the present and, under the shade of his cowl, he scanned the waiting crowd. Another irony began to unfold itself. Eldric was to be his unwitting saviour. The man's majestic presence as a protector of the Law was tempering the crowd's baser nature. They had not fallen on him immediately. The form would be observed. They would stand and listen. Dan-Tor felt the darkness move imperceptibly from him. Patience. Time would be everything.

Slowly, he began to reply to the charges. First in broad and general terms, and then working repeatedly over each in turn, in ever-increasing detail. The crisis passed.

In the crowd were two Goraidin, Yengar and Olvric, sent by

Yatsu, unbeknown to Eldric, to report on the Accounting. After a while they exchanged glances. Dan-Tor's tactics were becoming clear. Having survived the first and most serious part of the confrontation, he would weary the crowd and wear Eldric down with interminable argument, until exhaustion determined the outcome.

It was an effective tactic. As the day progressed the crowd thinned gradually, and Eldric himself began to feel very weary. His concentration wandered. He wished Darek could have been by his side to bolster him against the bombardment of petty items that Dan-Tor assailed him with. He longed for the comfortable debating chambers of the Geadrol. Then Dan-Tor would be off on another tack. Stretching out explanations and precedents until they became lost in a cloud of detail.

It came to Eldric slowly that he had misjudged his opponent. He was appallingly formidable. He had chosen this Accounting almost on impulse, hoping that his oratory and the blatant justice of his case would see him through. But Dan-Tor picked away relentlessly; confusing, obfuscating, corroding his arguments.

Eldric looked down at the lengthening afternoon shadows and realised abruptly that he was going to lose. The Fyordyn had listened patiently, as he knew they would. And they were judging, as he knew they must. But this form of debate was ancient and, at heart, crude. From it had grown the Geadrol and the Law with their elaborate and sophisticated ways, but it was a meagre parent to such fine children, and now he realised the obvious. In this simple arena the people could only judge the matter on the skill of the advocates, not on its merits painstakingly and objectively examined.

He felt that he had betrayed the people again, and it was only a momumental effort of will that kept the self-reproach from his face.

Dan-Tor, however, sensed him failing. 'Lord Eldric,' he said. 'I've shown you every courtesy, but I'm wearying of this endless picking over trivia. I *am* Ffyrst, and I've given you the reasons for this as determined by the Law and by the necessity of circumstances. I've answered each of your baseless accusations fully, in front of all the people here, when I should have had you arrested.' He paused to feel the mood of the crowd.

Slowly it had changed. Now doubts, bewilderment and fatigue mixed liberally with the partisanship that had initially been almost totally Eldric's. And there was increasing support for himself among the more foolish elements, aided by some calculated noisiness and irresponsibility emanating, he judged, from men that Urssain had placed in the crowd earlier.

In the tone of an affectionate parent whose patience had been tried too far by an erring child, he said, 'You mock the Law you pretend to defend, Lord Eldric. Had you any real regard for it, you'd not have taken such pains to escape lawful detention before a trial could be arranged and, given that the aberration mightn't have been totally of your own making, you would now lay down your weapons and return to the King's custody in peace and await his will.'

After so many hours of debate and argument, Eldric was in no mood to countenance such a device. 'You ignore the form again, Lord Dan-Tor, as you did at the beginning. You've answered *none* of my charges. Not one. At best you've thrown up a cloud of trivialities to obscure the real nature of your crimes. Your sole object has been to confuse and mislead. If my own inadequate advocacy hasn't served me well, it's at least shown the people here that while I strive towards the truth for them, you wish them to remain in confused ignorance.'

There was a mixture of cheering and jeering from the crowd and Eldric winced inwardly as he felt the rightness of his case fading into the darkness cast by Dan-Tor.

'If you believe that, Lord Eldric, then let the people judge us both *now*,' shouted Dan-Tor, sweeping his long left arm across the crowd. This provoked more noise.

'No,' roared Eldric above the clamour. 'No. How can the people judge when so much has yet to be presented? You weave fifty lies for every one you affect to refute.' He stood up in his saddle, his blazing eyes peering relentlessly into the gloom of Dan-Tor's cowl.

Dan-Tor started. It was a look he had not seen since he battled by the side of his Master, wielding world-shattering power against the Demons of the Great Alliance and all their forces.

The line still runs then, he thought. Through all this time. 'I'm not to be assailed, Lord Eldric.' His voice rumbled ominously.

The crowd fell suddenly silent, but Eldric did not yield. 'I don't assail you, Lord Dan-Tor,' he said. 'It's the weight of your crimes that assails you. The weight which will crush you when the people learn of them fully.' A tension began to build in the square. 'And they *shall* know, Lord Dan-Tor. I'll shine a light into every cranny of your dark Narsindal-misted soul. I'll untangle your every lie in front of these people, if I've to stay here on this horse until the Second Coming.'

Urssain shifted his feet wearily and fidgeted with his hands. Abruptly, there was uproar in the crowd. Seeing the hand signal, Urssain's men in the crowd began shouting noisily.

'It appears the people wish to make their judgement now, Lord Eldric,' Dan-Tor said.

Eldric's expression changed to an angry scowl as he turned to look at the crowd. 'Your Mathidrin agitators wish to make a judgement you mean,' he said.

Dan-Tor shrugged innocently. '*My* agitators, Lord? More accusations. Doesn't the form dictate that all accusations be stated at the commencement of the Accounting?' His white teeth shone a malevolent sneer at Eldric.

Despite himself, Eldric laid his hand on his axe, but released it immediately as a triumphant red glare flashed from Dan-Tor's eyes.

The crowd, however, had not heard Dan-Tor's provocation and saw only Eldric's angry movement. Urged on by Urssain's men the localised shouting and scuffling spread through them like a wind-blown fire in grass. The frustration and confusions of the day polarised the crowd and, as Dan-Tor had intended, brought them rapidly to the edge of riot.

As Eldric turned again to the crowd, Dan-Tor walked over to him quickly. 'We must stop this,' he said urgently. 'There'll be bloodshed again. The people are still unsettled after the riots. There's no saying where it might end.'

Eldric spun round, startled to find his enemy so close. He glowered down at him. 'This is your doing, Dan-Tor. Your men have been stirring this crowd all day. Do you think I'm so blind? And Urssain might as well have used a flag for all the subtlety of his hand signals.'

'I know nothing of this, Lord, I swear,' Dan-Tor replied, his tone sincere and concerned. 'If Urssain's arranged this I'll see he's punished, have no fear. But we must stop it *now*.'

Eldric's expression did not change.

Dan-Tor scowled as if looking for a solution as the noise of the crowd rose. 'Lord Eldric,' he said anxiously. 'Accept voluntary custody at the house of . . .' he cast about. '. . . Lord Oremson. You surely trust him? And we'll continue this . . .' his voice became angry, as if he were being reluctantly obliged to yield something against his better judgement, 'this matter tomorrow. And for as many days as needs be.'

Eldric thought for a moment. He realised he had been outmanoeuvred in some way; that Dan-Tor had reached some decision from the crowd's reactions. But the suggestion was reasonable and the crowd was becoming unmanageable. Oremson was an old friend and a staunch Geadrol Lord. It was unlikely he would countenance any treachery whatever he thought of recent happenings. Eldric nodded brusquely.

Reluctantly he found himself joining with his foe to quieten the crowd by urging on them Dan-Tor's suggestion as if it were his own.

During the confusion, Yengar and Olvric, having identified Urssain's men in the crowd, took the opportunity to down four or five of them discreetly.

Through Astrom, Eldric had asked those Lords remaining in Vakloss not to attend the Accounting. 'When the Geadrol meets again, I'll give you my own Accounting and accept your judgement,' read his message to them. 'For the time being, I beg your indulgence.'

Lord Oremson was thus most happy to welcome his unexpected and battle-clad guest. He himself had much to discuss. He welcomed also the large number of people who had accompanied Eldric, determined to see that the Accounting would not be foreshortened by some act of treachery on Dan-Tor's part.

'I can't offer you beds, my friends,' he told them. 'Although I can give you some food and drink after your long day. And the hardy among you are welcome to rest on my lawns if you wish.'

For a little while, there was an almost carnival atmosphere as the people ate and drank Lord Oremson's fare and talked about the day's events. Gradually the late afternoon faded through a soft evening into a purple, star-strewn night and, as the wind fell and the last clouds drifted overhead, a silence descended on the tree-lined gardens and the people settled to their night vigil.

Yengar vanished into the shade guarding an old oak tree, from where he could see both entrances to the grounds. He settled into a deep state of relaxation so that his body could rest and recover from the day's activities while his mind would watch and wait.

As the night deepened, the torches in Oremson's house went out one by one, and the low background of conversation from the waiting people gradually faded as they drifted into sleep. Yengar's eyes and ears adjusted to the shadows and the myriad tiny movements of the night. Occasionally there was a cry, a laugh, or a snatch of incoherent conversation as some portion of a dream emerged briefly into reality like the tip of a great iceberg. Yengar sank deeper into his own quietness.

At the darkest part of the night, Yengar's eyes picked out a flitting shadow entering the grounds. He knew it for Olvric; only a Goraidin could move like that. He made a low soft nightbird signal to guide his friend. As Olvric neared Yengar sensed his agitation. A hand signal brought him to his feet and the two of them moved noiselessly and quickly out of the grounds.

Within minutes of their leaving, a large Mathidrin patrol moved quietly into the gardens.

Chapter 45

Yatsu, though reluctant to lose Serian and Gavor, did not feel inclined to oppose Hawklan in his declaration that he and Isloman should ride with Ordan to Lord Evison's castle. He did, however, insist that two of his own men, Lorac and Tel-Odrel, ride with them.

'They'll gather information that's appropriate to the way the High Guards fight, Hawklan, that's what the Goraidin are for. And they'll be able to bring you to Eldric's estate through the mountains – save you days of exposed travel.'

Maintaining a steady pace, the five riders came within sight of the northern mountains that separated Fyorlund from Narsindal within two days. Ordan pointed to them. 'That's the northern boundary of Lord Evison's estate,' he said. 'If we ride hard we can reach the castle before evening.'

The two Goraidin looked at Hawklan. Waiting.

'No, Ordan,' said Hawklan, definitely but gently. 'If your Lord's under siege we'll be no help arriving exhausted at nightfall. Besides, five of us aren't going to be able to relieve him. We need to be able to approach cautiously and leave quickly. We'll keep on steadily and then camp so that we can come to the castle early in the morning.' Then, turning, he intercepted a brief exchange of significant looks between the two Goraidin. 'Is that acceptable, gentlemen?'

Caught thus in their judgement, both men nodded, half apologetically. Isloman smiled to himself.

The rest of the day was spent for the most part in companionable silence as the group rode on through the rolling lands which marked the southern edge of the Lord Evison's estate. They avoided such few villages as they saw, uncertain of the reception that they would receive, particularly as the Goraidin were still wearing Mathidrin livery. Their night, however, was restless with even Gavor and the horses fretful and anxious. Hawklan, too, found himself frowning as he lay awake, listening to their disturbed and spasmodic slumbering.

As if wilfully belying their unease, the following day arrived with a soft misty dawn that promised a bright summer's warmth. It did little, however, to lift their spirits as they mounted and continued their journey. Then, as if in confirmation of their concern, a thin column of smoke came into view, rising over the horizon like an admonitory finger. The group halted and Hawklan nodded to Gavor. Without comment, the bird rose into the sunny air, circled a few times, as if reluctant to leave them, then unhurriedly turned towards the rising smoke.

'That's from a dying fire,' said Lorac quietly, glancing anxiously at Ordan. Hawklan nodded and urged Serian forward into a trot. 'Gavor will warn us if there's trouble ahead,' he said.

As they topped a small rise, the Lord Evison's castle came into view. It was broken and devastated. The column of smoke that had guided them rose fitfully up from the ruin to be dissipated in the rising morning breeze.

As Serian carried him forward, Hawklan tensed his stomach as if to prepare for a powerful impact.

Gutted by fire, the castle stood like a jagged black crystal mounted in a setting of unpolished granite. But the rock on which the Lord Evison's castle was founded was far below ground. Fertile fields fringed its feet; fertile fields now churned brown, and mottled white and carmine with hacked bodies. The summer breeze carried a sweet, appalling confirmation of the vision to the riders' nostrils.

His own sensations suddenly numbed, Hawklan felt Serian quivering beneath him. 'There are horses dying there, Hawklan,' said the horse. 'Can't you hear them? The humans have been dispatched, but the horses are still dying. Help them, Hawklan.'

The five men dismounted in silence. Round the castle were hundreds of bodies; bodies that had been stripped and mutilated in an orgy of violence. Hawklan felt the blood pounding in his ears, and steadied himself against Serian. For a moment he was overwhelmed by a roaring surge of old memories smashing through whatever had been holding them back to inundate him, like a raging sea storming through ancient sand dunes. But, like the sea, they ebbed as quickly as they had come and left Hawklan only with the knowledge that he had seen this and worse many times before; and would again.

As he recovered, this cruel knowledge contended with the pain of the healer rising within him in a futile howl, but gradually some deeper knowledge told him to harness the two in a grim alliance. Truth was truth, however fearful, and healing had inevitable limitations. Equally, his healing skills in all their forms must strive forward, accepting the pain of knowledge and refusing to become calloused by repeated impact.

Ordan vomited. The sound brought Hawklan to himself. He looked at the others. Their faces were grey with disbelief and horror. Then he became aware that among the bodies there were murmurings and scufflings.

Suddenly Gavor dropped from the sky and swooped low over the dreadful field with a terrible cry. For a brief instant, the scene was alive with birds and small mammals fleeing; fear of this vengeful shadow overwhelming their greed. Where they scurried a black smoky cloud rose up briefly.

Flies, Hawklan mouthed to himself, and then he shuddered.

Unbidden, Serian moved forward, stepping delicately between the strewn bodies and severed limbs. Hawklan drew his sword and followed. There were no live humans left here, he could sense that, but he could meet Serian's plea and perform a last healing act for any of the horses that were still alive.

There were only a few and they had already passed the worst of their suffering. Hawklan could make nothing of such mutterings as he heard, but Serian bent low over each one and listened intently.

'You're fearful creatures, you humans,' he said when the task was finished. 'Fearful.'

Hawklan had no answer for him. 'Did any of them say what had happened?' he asked.

Serian's tone was one of barely restrained anger. 'No,' he said. 'They were too near the portals to recall such matters without great pain. It's not for you or I to demand such a price. They've played their parts, they must rest now. I commend your skill in easing them over, healer.' Then he walked away to join the other horses.

Hawklan turned his attention to his companions. He could not see Ordan, but Isloman and the two Goraidin were wandering among the bodies. Hawklan picked an uneasy path through to them, his boots clogging with bloodstained mud. Enter the pain, he reminded himself as he neared them.

Lorac looked up as he approached. His eyes were tormented, but his voice was firm and almost formal. Goraidin see clearly and accept what they see for what it is. Yatsu's words came back to Hawklan. But you must cling to some things at times like this, mustn't you? he thought. Even if it's only the reassurance of your own voice.

'Never seen anything like this,' said Lorac. 'Never. There were some bad things in the Morlider War, but nothing . . .' His voice faltered. 'I keep hoping I'll wake up. Who'd do this to dead men?'

Hawklan looked at him. 'A foe we don't want to meet unprepared,' he said. 'We'll have to close our hearts to the horror of this until another time, Lorac. We must find out everything we can and take it back to the others. Then perhaps these men won't have died in vain.'

Lorac looked at him enigmatically. 'Yes, I know. It's what we're trained to do.' He clenched his teeth. 'It's just . . . I never thought it could be so hard. All I keep thinking of is what I'd like to do to whoever did this.'

Hawklan's voice became harsh. 'It's not as hard for us as it was for these.' He waved his hand over the scene. 'But we and others will end the same way if we don't put our every resource into finding out what's happened. You'll take no easy vengeance on whoever wrought this. Direct your rage towards that, Goraidin.'

Lorac's eyes blazed angrily and his fist tightened. Hawklan knew that if the man hit him now, he would be unable to defend himself. But Lorac's rage faded almost immediately. Nothing could flare bright in the stultifying aura of death that hung over the field.

He bowed his head. 'You're right,' he said. 'Our training's all we've got left. We can't do anything for these except learn from them and hope we'll be more fortunate when our time comes.'

A cry interrupted their uneasy conversation. It was Ordan, standing in the shattered gateway of the castle and beckoning them. As they approached he turned and passed through a doorway, again gesturing that they should follow. Reaching the door, Hawklan peered into the gloomy interior until his eyes adjusted to the reduced light. A little way ahead, through a mist of smoke and fine floating ash, he could see Ordan cautiously working his way through a maze of fallen and burnt beams. He moved after him, followed by the others.

For several minutes they moved slowly through the remains of a decorated corridor, treading underfoot the charred remains of its ornate ceiling and its fallen wall carvings. The air became increasingly unpleasant, heavy with smoke from the still-smouldering debris, and clingingly warm from its stored heat.

Hawklan looked at the others in some concern. 'This is dangerous,' he said. 'These fumes will overcome us if we stay too long.'

When they reached Ordan, he was standing in front of a closed door. His eyes were still wide with shock, but his voice was steady, if hoarse. 'The Lord Evison said he had captives,' he said. 'If they're anywhere, they're here.' Then, drawing his sword, he touched two of the ornamental bosses that studded the door. There was the sound of bolts being drawn and, unaided, the door swung open.

Drawing his own sword, Hawklan moved to Ordan's side, but all that could be seen through the doorway was a flight of stairs leading down into darkness.

Slowly, Ordan lowered his sword and bowed his head. 'I'd hoped to see torchlight and trouble,' he said sadly. 'But there's no one alive here. No light, no life.' Sheathing his sword he stepped forward and started down the stairs. Torches flared gently into life as he entered, to reveal a large, stone-arched cellar. The air was cool and strangely pleasant after the stench outside and the choking air in the corridor, but lying sprawled headlong at the foot of the stairs was a body.

Hesitantly, Ordan knelt down by it. When Hawklan reached him, he looked up, his face distraught. 'It's Lord Evison,' he said. 'He's dead.'

Hawklan bent down and examined the body. The Lord's wounds showed that he had obviously died in combat, but he had not been mutilated like the others outside. His hand was clenched tightly around a heavy fighting axe.

'Look, there's someone else.' Tel-Odrel's voice interrupted Hawklan's thoughts. The Goraidin pushed past and ran over to a second body lying some way away. When he reached it, he stopped suddenly. 'Hawklan,' he said softly, beckoning without taking his eyes from the body at his feet.

Hawklan and the others joined him around the second body. It was a large Mandroc, its huge canine teeth gleaming in the torchlight in a malevolent death rictus. It wore battledress: an iron cap with curved cheek pieces and a heavy leather jerkin reinforced with metal plates secured about its muscular body by heavy buckled straps. All this, however, had proved ineffective against the axe blow that had hacked a great wound from the creature's neck to its stomach.

'Only small, but Lord Evison was a powerful man,' said Tel-Odrel. 'Not one to face in extremity.'

No one spoke.

'Mandrocs armed and armoured,' said Lorac softly at last. His voice a mixture of awe and disbelief. Then, seeking refuge in his training, 'We'll have to strip its armour. It should tell us a lot.'

Back outside in the sunlight, Ordan's grief abruptly overwhelmed him. Rather to Hawklan's surprise, the two Goraidin were sensitive and sympathetic with the man. He found it reassuring that for all their harsh and brutal skills, they still kept some contact with those qualities that they had sworn to protect. Something in their training leavened its own brutalising effect. Truth, perhaps?

And yet the very existence of this caring betokened an even greater ruthlessness. They were not allowed the numbing that brutalisation brought with it. And the greater the caring, the harder – the more brutally – they would fight when it was threatened, either in themselves or others. Hawklan's thoughts started to circle mockingly as he began to see images of himself within himself. Lorac's voice broke into his thoughts. He was talking to Ordan.

'We all knew some of your friends, Ordan,' he was saying. He put his hands on the man's shoulders and looked at him earnestly. 'But there was nothing you could have done. You obeyed your Lord faithfully and well. You know that. This happened days ago, probably within hours of your leaving, and your being here would have made no difference. It's not much consolation, but . . .' He left his sentence unfinished.

Turning round, he looked at the gutted castle, and spoke to the others. 'They must have been overwhelmed before they were ready. From what Ordan's told us, Evison's force must have been spread out for miles. Either that or he completely underestimated the speed at which his enemy could move. It looks as if they fought their way in to release the captives but Evison locked himself in with that one.'

Hawklan looked around the battlefield, still alive with flies and now slowly being repopulated by the scavengers that Gavor had frightened away. No weapons, he thought suddenly. Not a dagger, not a sword, not even a broken spear shaft. And no Mandroc dead. All had been removed.

Lorac seemed to read his thoughts. 'Apart from that one body, they've left no sign of who or what they were. They just came after him to make sure that no one who had seen them would survive to spread the news.' He wrapped his arms tightly around himself. 'I'm frightened,' he said, unexpectedly.

'You're wise to be,' said Hawklan. 'Soldiers that would do this are not lightly defeated. Evison found that to his cost, and we'll pay the same price if we don't learn.'

'What can we do?' Lorac said.

Hawklan looked at Gavor.

'Whoever did this is long away,' said the raven. 'There's no one about for miles. No one alive, that is,' he added.

Hawklan nodded then spoke without hesitation. 'Ordan, you go to Eldric's mountain stronghold with that Mandroc's armour. Tell them what you've seen. The rest of us will go north, to see what Evison saw.'

*   *   *

As the four men rode steadily northwards, none of them spoke a great deal and at night they made a dark and silent camp, each taking turns to stand guard.

Hawklan opened his eyes as Tel-Odrel approached to wake him for his watch period. The Goraidin crouched down beside him as he sat up. 'Something's wrong with Isloman, Hawklan,' he said softly. 'He's restless and he's been muttering to himself on and off all night.'

Hawklan frowned slightly. He had never known Isloman suffer any illness. Moving over to him he laid a hand gently on his forehead. There was no sign of fever, but he could feel a turmoil rising in the man. He frowned again. 'It's probably shock. And grief,' he said quietly. 'We'll all be suffering from it to some degree. I can hardly close my own eyes without seeing those hacked bodies fringing that black castle.'

Tel-Odrel nodded, but he noted an uncertainty in Hawklan which worried him a little.

The following day, Isloman seemed well enough, but he was uncharacteristically sullen, and took no food when he woke. Hawklan looked at him anxiously, but he saddled up and mounted without demur, and maintained the pace that was set without complaint.

Even after passing the destroyed remains of Evison's troop, it needed no tracking skills to follow the trail of the departed attackers.

'This is how the Mandrocs left Orthlund,' said Gavor. 'As if they were crushing something to death with every footstep.'

Gradually the countryside yielded to the mountains proper and soon they found themselves moving between dark lowering crags. The two Goraidin were uneasy about their vulnerability in such terrain, but Gavor's high-flying vigil enabled them to maintain their pace without any real fear of ambush.

Eventually the route they were following became too rocky and awkward for rapid progress and, feeling that time was against them, Hawklan sent Gavor ahead to see if they were near to any kind of settlement or encampment, or anything else that might be worthy of examination.

It was dusk when he returned, a shadow sweeping out of the

shadows. 'Leave your horses and climb that peak there,' he said, and was gone.

Without speaking Isloman stood up wearily, and began walking in the direction Gavor had indicated. Hawklan ran after him. 'What are you doing?' he asked anxiously. 'Where are you going? We can't walk up there now, it'll be pitch dark soon.'

But Isloman kept on walking.

Hawklan moved in front of him and held out a hand to stop the Carver. 'Isloman, what's the matter with you?' he demanded.

Isloman stopped and looked at Hawklan as if puzzled by this enquiry. 'I *have* to see, Hawklan,' he said. 'Stay with me, you'll be all right.'

Hawklan still sensed the great turmoil in his friend, but no sickness. He gave a small resigned shrug and, stepping aside, signalled the others to follow.

The peak, however, was no easy walk, especially in the meagre light offered by the stars and a thin moon. Isloman seemed to have little trouble, but several times the others had to call out softly to him to slow down a little as they carefully negotiated extensive areas of shattered rock and steep rubble-strewn slopes. At last, after several hours of leg-aching trudging they reached the summit.

Unusually it was not the rounded grass dome that character-ised most of the smaller mountains, but a jumbled mass of jagged rock. This, however, did not deter Hawklan and the two Goraidin from flopping down gratefully when they reached it.

Isloman had not seemed to be hurrying, but he had set a relentless pace. As they rested, he wandered fitfully over the summit, turning round and round repeatedly, like a weather vane in a gusting breeze. Finally he stopped and stared straight ahead. Then slowly he raised his hand and pointed out into the night. 'There,' he whispered, as if fearful of being overheard.

Hawklan stood up and carefully walked over to him across the uneven rocks. 'What?' he asked, following Isloman's gaze. 'What is it?'

But Isloman did not reply. Instead, he wrapped his arms around himself and slowly sat down.

Hawklan bent down to him. 'Isloman, what's the matter?' he said. 'What's happened? What's out there?'

'Leave me alone,' came the faint reply through the darkness. 'Leave me alone.'

Instinctively Hawklan reached out to his friend, but he felt the man's agony before he touched him. Abruptly, Isloman's powerful arms swept up as if to dash Hawklan aside but, just as suddenly, they slowed and gently pushed him away. Hawklan stood up and looked down at him, puzzled and uncertain.

'Is he sick?' It was Lorac at his elbow. 'He could have picked something up around those bodies. They'd been there some time.' His enquiry tailed off.

Hawklan shook his head. 'No. It's nothing like that. It's something deeper. Don't worry. I'll stay with him.' He turned round and looked out into the night in the direction Isloman was staring. 'You rest. We'll see what the daylight shows us.'

Isloman did not move all night but, long before Hawklan noticed a change in the light, he said, 'Dawn,' and stood up. The slow softening of the darkness that followed this announcement reminded Hawklan of the many times he had stood on one of the high towers of Anderras Darion and watched the dawn break over the mountains. It was like a reaffirmation of some intangible but vital quality, and he felt an inner ease which he realised he had not known for some time. For a while his mind left the bewildering cascade of events that had occurred since the day Tirilen had led him down the steep road from the Castle to look at the strange tinker on the village green.

He stood up and joined Isloman. 'Show me now, shadow sage,' he said, hoping that a touch of humour might help his friend, but Isloman just pointed. 'There,' he said.

As the light grew, Hawklan found he was looking between two mountains into a far-distant valley. He could make out what looked like white scars and gashes running down the sides of the valley, and a longer, more even line that twisted and turned sinuously before it disappeared from sight.

'A road?' he said, after a moment. 'And quarries?' The scene meant nothing to him. Before he could question Isloman, Gavor fluttered down to join them. His manner was agitated. 'You've seen it, then?' he said.

'The road? Yes. And are those quarries?' Hawklan asked. 'But I don't understand what I'm looking at, Gavor.'

Gavor's tone was strained. 'You're looking at a new, very large road, heading north into . . . there. And yes, they are quarries. And there are more on the other side. And mines. The road's taking . . . I don't know . . . whatever's coming out of them.'

No one spoke. Gavor continued. 'Those streaks that you can see are great mounds of waste that have been spewed down into the valley. It's unbelievably foul. And there's worse.' He paused. 'The work's being done by slaves.' All three men turned and looked at him. 'Men, women, even children . . . and Mandrocs,' he said slowly. 'And all under the none-too-tender supervision of those cockroaches.'

There was an uneasy silence.

'That's not possible,' Lorac burst out suddenly. 'You've made a mistake, bird.' His voice was vicious and angry, but layered with fear and uncertainty.

Gavor's eyes blazed and he spread his wings menacingly. 'Don't doubt me, human,' he hissed, his black mouth gaping wide. 'I tell what I see. Your brothers are torturing your brothers over there. They've poisoned the land with their filth. And the rivers. Even the air I flew through was tainted.' He craned forward and beat his wings savagely. 'It's not for nothing that above all the other creatures in this world, He's assumed *your* shape for His work here.'

Lorac quailed under Gavor's appalling assault and lifted his hands as if expecting to be physically attacked.

Hawklan held out his hand to Gavor. 'Gently, Gavor, gently,' he said. Then to the chastened Lorac, 'You can trust Gavor totally, Goraidin, totally. We mustn't take our pains out on one another. We've got real enemies to fight. Gavor, can we come any closer?'

'No,' said the bird, still eyeing Lorac. 'That valley's two days away for you, and half a day will bring you in sight of their look-outs. You won't even reach the remains of Lord Evison's troop.'

Hawklan nodded and thought for a moment. 'Well, if we've seen all we can see, then we must take the knowledge back to the others as quickly as we can.'

'Hawklan.' It was Isloman. 'Help me. Get me away from here . . .' His voice was hoarse and distant, and it tailed off into a long failing breath as his knees bent and he fell to the ground.

Chapter 46

Hawklan bent over his fallen friend and examined him urgently. But his hands and his healing told him nothing. Whatever had brought Isloman low was beyond his knowledge. All that remained was Isloman's own judgement: 'Get me away from here.'

The journey back to the horses, however, was a waking nightmare as the three of them struggled desperately with Isloman's limp bulk, while the brightening summer sun and the splendour of the emerging mountain scenery seemed to mock them.

Driven by his concern for his friend and his own feeling of impotence, Hawklan found the inevitable slowness of the descent unbearable. Twice he slipped in his haste. Once slithering incongruously down a damp grassy slope and, another time, more seriously, missing his footing on moss-slimed rock.

Tel-Odrel caught him and with a friendly grin supported him while he recovered his balance, but Lorac rounded on him furiously. 'In Ethriss's name, Hawklan, look what you're doing. You could have injured yourself and Tel, and how long would it have taken us to get back to the others then?'

Part of Hawklan rose up in anger at this rebuke, but another quieted him. The Goraidin's right, healer. Concern yourself with your friend. He deserves better than your self-indulgence.

It took them several hours to reach the horses, and they were exhausted when they did. Hawklan examined Isloman again but his condition was unchanged.

'Let me carry him,' said Serian and, with an effort, they lifted him into the great horse's saddle and tied him there firmly.

The journey back to Eldric's mountain stronghold was no less arduous and unpleasant, and Hawklan, unused to his new mount and unable fully to relax because of his concern for his friend, felt as if he had been in the saddle for his entire life.

However, he had repeated cause to be grateful for Yatsu's insistence that Lorac and Tel-Odrel accompany him. Their knowledge of the country and the mountains shortened the journey considerably and, amongst other things, spared them the need to pass by the carnage around Lord Evison's castle.

Isloman improved a little as they moved further away from the blighted valleys. He regained consciousness for increasingly longer periods but still did not speak, and Hawklan felt that the Carver was fighting to hold something at bay rather than recovering from it.

On the night before they were due to reach their destination, Hawklan, as usual, spent some time in making Isloman comfortable and in easing the aches of Lorac and Tel-Odrel that Serian's unrelenting pace had brought about. But there was a restlessness in himself that he could not still and eventually he wandered away from the camp, sensing that, while sleep might restore his body, something else was needed to quieten his mind.

Alone in the dying light, he sat down on a grassy knoll that overlooked the long valley they had spent the day negotiating. Suddenly he was overwhelmed by a longing for Anderras Darion and the calm and harmony of its encompassing mountains and rolling countryside; for Pedhavin and the silver river that ran through it; and for all his many friends there.

Without thinking he drew his sword and, pressing its cold black hilt against his face, closed his eyes. Thoughts suddenly burst in on him as if they had been penned by some great dam. Thoughts of a tiny mannequin full of corruption; of the huge, bustling Gretmearc and the sinister trap that was laid for him there; of the malign presence of Dan-Tor seeking him out, spreading corruption into his life and through him into the lives of all the Orthlundyn; of Andawyr, that strange scruffy little man, filled with light, who searched into his mind and came to him mysteriously with terrible needs; of Mandrocs and of the slaughtered guards; of a fume-choked Vakloss and of the vengeance of a lone, lost woman against her persecutors; of appalling carnage fringing a blackened castle, and of mines and quarries, the very sight of which had brought down his friend.

These and many others surged and tumbled through his head beyond all control, swirling like a frenzied maelstrom seeking a path down into a cold, dark stillness.

For a moment he floundered then, abruptly, he let them go. They were beyond resolution. They were the myriad tiny ills that he had seen so often emanating from wounds and disease. Some could be eased for the comfort of the sufferer, but always the source should be sought and its influence assuaged.

But was *this* healing in *his* gift? Or was he only a humble part of a greater healer's work? Again, no resolution. Only a healer's faith. Whoever or whatever he was he would oppose this corruption where he found it and seek towards its centre when he could. He had no choice.

Gradually the clattering thoughts faded and went their way unhindered, and he sat for a long time in silence and stillness until he became aware of the cold mountain air blowing around him.

Opening his eyes, he held out the hilt of the Black Sword and looked at it. The stars inside it glittered and twinkled like reflections of the sky above him, and the intertwined strands pursued their journey into an endless distance. He felt a lightness again that he had not realised he had lost.

They reached Eldric's stronghold late the following day. Yatsu took one look at the four travellers and immediately postponed the questions that had been building in his mind since the return of Ordan with the Mandroc armour and his tale of horror. 'We'll hold an Officers' Council tomorrow,' he said. 'Now you must eat and rest properly.'

Hawklan sat pensively in a high-winged chair. It was ornately carved, though its arms and rails had been worn smooth by countless years of use. It was also extremely comfortable. Just above his left shoulder, Gavor slumbered, his claw closed around the top of the chair. He was muttering incomprehensibly in his sleep. Opposite Hawklan, in an identical chair, was Isloman. He was sitting upright, but his eyes were half shut and it needed no healer's touch to tell he was oblivious to everything around him.

Hawklan gazed at him, as he had been doing for the past

hour. Wilfully he avoided fretting about his friend's condition, hoping that some inspiration would drift into his mind.

What came, however, was not what he had either expected or hoped for. This man's a liability in this condition, it said. He's too good a soldier to lose, he must be brought back into fighting fettle. The thought was so cold and callous that Hawklan slammed his hands into the arms of his chair as if the noise would prevent his hearing it, or as if to punish himself for it.

'Damn it, Isloman,' he said fiercely. 'Don't leave me like this. Other people depend on us. Speak, man.'

The outburst woke Gavor, who fell off the chair and only just managed to regain his balance before hitting the floor. He glided up on to the mantelshelf that topped the large open fireplace separating the two men and, ruffled, looked down at Hawklan indignantly.

Before he could speak, however, Isloman stirred. He opened his mouth as if to speak but no sound came. Then his great hands tightened around the arms of his chair and he swayed back and forth, racked by some inner conflict.

Hawklan leaned forward intently. Faintly he heard, 'The words don't exist, Hawk . . .' He caught the phrase and held it; a precious jewel glinting in the barren earth. It was a phrase common among the Orthlundyn whenever he asked about their crafts, and he himself used it when asked about his healing. 'The words don't exist.' He repeated them to himself.

Around their sharp focus formed the realisation that Isloman's illness was associated with his craft. It was obvious, he saw now, and he should have seen it from the start. But he refused to be lured astray by self-reproach. Isloman was still struggling. Hawklan knelt down in front of him and, taking his hands, looked into his eyes. The blankness had gone, but it had been replaced by pain.

'I understand,' he said. 'I understand. It's the song, isn't it? The rock song.'

A low distant note sounded in Isloman's throat and swelled rapidly into an almost inhuman roar. 'There was no song,' he cried. 'No song. Only a great cry of horror and pain.' He clasped his arms about himself and rocked to and fro again, as if nursing some terrible internal wound.

'Why?' persisted Hawklan. 'What's happened?'

'No words, no words,' muttered Isloman. Then his powerful hands broke free from Hawklan's grip and shot out to seize his arms. 'Worse than all those bodies, Hawklan. Far worse,' he whispered hoarsely. 'So deep. Deep beyond any reaching. It's infected me, Hawklan, I can't hold on. Even to think about an obscenity like that would . . . But to feel it . . .' His voice tailed away and, releasing Hawklan, he wrapped his hands around his bowed head and curled up like an unborn child.

Hawklan reeled back under the impact of his friend's distress. He had hoped that the trickle of words might presage a deluge and with its passing so would pass Isloman's pain. But it had not. Instead, his friend was slipping further away as if his brief contact with the present had loosed his weakened grip.

Guilt and doubt swept into Hawklan's mind and his head jerked desperately from side to side as if looking for help from the pictures and statues that decorated the room. A jabbering crowd of voices seemed to fill his head, raucous and clamouring.

'Let go, Hawklan,' said one. It was Gavor. Hawklan looked at him, perched on the mantelshelf. 'I felt the taint, but I haven't Isloman's vision and I can fly high above and soar in the clear air which knows the truth and can purify all. Let go. Have no fear. Your mind can go no further. Your healing draws from deeper wells than any evil can know.'

Hawklan met the enigmatic black eyes for a long moment. Gavor nodded slowly. Then, closing his eyes and turning away from the voices, Hawklan felt them vanish like smoke in the wind. He reached out and laid his hand on Isloman's head. For an instant he heard the rock song and felt its appalling defilement. 'I'm here, Isloman,' he said quietly. 'I hear your song, rock blind though I am. Listen to me. Can any defilement be beyond the aid of the maker of this, old friend?' And, unclipping the scabbard of the Black Sword, he lifted it in his left hand and held the hilt out towards Isloman.

As he did so, a nearby torch flared gently and its light caught the hilt's inner pattern making the stars there shimmer and dance like a myriad tiny universes.

Isloman stared at the hilt distantly for what seemed an

interminable time then, as if returning from a long journey, recognition came into his eyes, and his right hand slowly reached out and took hold of it. He closed his eyes and clenched his teeth as if moving some massive weight, then his left hand joined his right in clutching the black stone hilt. Tears began to run down his face, but he was not sobbing. 'How could I have forgotten?' he said, very softly. 'How could I?' Then he opened his eyes.

Hawklan reached back unsteadily and regained his chair. Holding out his hands he found they were trembling. Isloman's recovery had been as sudden and startling as his deterioration had been slow.

A faint smile appeared on Isloman's face. He shifted in the chair, and then looking at the carving, nodded admiringly. 'These Fyordyn have a way with wood,' he said irrelevantly. Then he looked at the sword intently and, apparently satisfied, held it out to Hawklan. Hawklan laid it on a nearby table. The cold thought returned to him – this recovery is fortuitous, Isloman's too good a fighter to lose – but he pushed it lightly to one side, realising that his own violent reaction to it before was because Isloman's pain had become his own as the healer in him had reached out to help. Such thoughts had their place, he knew, for all their harshness. Only when they dominated did they destroy.

'I feel as if I've been dropped over a cliff,' Isloman said.

Gavor floated down and landed on his shoulder.

'Can you tell me what happened?' Hawklan asked.

'There are no words, Hawklan. You understand that.' Isloman said. 'Those valleys ring with a great groaning scream that pervades the whole area. The rocks are being tortured, defiled. Deep, deep down. It's unbelievable. There's no way I can describe it. I've never heard the like before and I didn't recognise it at first. Then, when I did, I was trapped. I couldn't ignore its plea and I couldn't do anything about it. Nothing. Except stand there and listen. I've no control over my rock knowledge, Hawklan. I can't shut it out. The sound tore into me and clung like a terrified animal. Imagine you'd been at that castle and seen those men being killed infinitely slowly, and known you could do nothing about it – nothing.'

He looked at Hawklan who lowered his eyes at the thought of this comparison. Then Isloman held out his huge hand and slowly curled the fingers round into a powerful fist.

'I've seen stone damaged by nature, Hawklan. Just as you've seen people laid low by accidents. It's not pleasant, but it has its own strange harmony, its own rightness. But this had no rightness. This was wilful desecration, torture, blasphemy. It was the work of a consciously malevolent force. I learned that in the darkness. A force that feeds on such horror and will grow stronger and faster, the more it defiles.'

Momentarily he looked a little sheepish. 'To be honest, I've taken all this talk about Sumeral and the Guardians with a large pinch of rock dust, for all Gulda and Eldric and the like have to say about it. It seemed too . . . unlikely.' He fixed Hawklan with a grim stare. 'But I *know* now, Hawklan. Whatever name you want to give it, there's a monumental evil abroad. It's powerful and it's growing. A corruption beyond our imagining. I doubt there's any place we could hide from it, and I know there's no place I could hide from myself if I let it destroy the things I love unhindered. It may well destroy us if we turn to face it, but it will certainly destroy us if we don't.'

A silence fell between the two men. Isloman nodded his craggy head towards the Black Sword. 'Maybe one day, you'll understand that sword of yours, Hawklan,' he said. 'But its perfection shone through to me like a beacon. It reminded me in my torment that harmony still existed and told me why it had to be.'

Hawklan nodded, but found no words to answer this affirmation except, 'You'll not be alone. There'll always be two of us.'

'Three, dear boy,' came Gavor's voice. 'Three. The two of you on your own show a great propensity for solemnity. What you really need at a time like this are my bird impressions. They'll chirp you up.'

Hawklan eyed his friend narrowly. 'No, Gavor,' he said. 'Not now. Isloman needs rest, as do I. We have Yatsu's Council tomorrow. It wouldn't do for us to retire in too excited a state, would it?' He smiled hypocritically.

Gavor hissed at him.

Chapter 47

As a deliberate act of policy on arriving at Eldric's stronghold Yatsu asked Commander Varak to restrain all questions until Hawklan and his party returned. 'It's an imposition, I know, Commander. But much has to be said and, as some of it will take a great deal of accepting, I'd prefer it to be said in one place at one time. I want no half truths and gossip cluttering up the proceedings. Besides, we're all very tired and in need of some rest, if you could oblige us.'

Faced with this elite corps and the three Lords, Varak had little choice, but he chewed on his curiosity with a good grace. Even when a distressed Ordan appeared carrying a strange armour he confined himself only to giving Yatsu a significant look.

Thus the atmosphere in the Council of Officers was alive with enquiry. It was not lessened by the entrance of Hawklan with Gavor sitting on his shoulder and the powerful figure of Isloman walking beside him. Both Lorac and Tel-Odrel rose in surprise to see Isloman so suddenly recovered and they greeted him warmly.

The Council was held in a hall with large rectangular windows through which the summer sun flooded. It was obviously a hall designed for meetings, as the light was dispersed evenly all round the large circular wooden table that formed its centrepiece.

Apart from the Lords and the Goraidin, the senior officers of Eldric's High Guard were present, together with Hrostir, Arinndier's son, and various officers from the High Guards of the Lords Darek and Hreldar who had remained at Eldric's castle after the quartet had set off on their ill-fated journey to Vakloss.

Darek spoke first, telling of the Lords' trip to Vakloss and their subsequent arrest and escape. Then Yatsu told of his plan to rescue the Lords with his erstwhile companions from the Goraidin, and of the dreadful use that had been made of the diversionary riots and fire they had started. He told also of the decision by Lord Eldric to return to the Palace to demand an Accounting of Dan-Tor in the hope of saving his son's life, and of his orders that the High Guards be levied to oppose Dan-Tor.

The tension in the room grew markedly as these tellings proceeded but, true to the Fyordyn tradition, no one interrupted.

Next, Tel-Odrel told of the massacre of Lord Evison and his men, and of the journey into the mountains and the discovery of the mines and quarries there. At Yatsu's prior request, he made no mention of the ominous character of Evison's message, nor of the nature of the enemy that had so ruthlessly pursued and destroyed him.

Despite their discipline, the shock of this news showed itself all too clearly on the assembled officers, though Hawklan noted that among the older men, there was almost as much reaction to the mention of the mines as to that of the massacre. Unhindered by Fyordyn tradition, he spoke. 'Tell me about the mines,' he said.

There was an awkward silence, then Arinndier answered. 'The mines are a rather . . . difficult matter for us, Hawklan,' he began. 'They're old workings that were reopened three or four generations ago, but had to be sealed again within a few years.' He hesitated and Hreldar cut through his patent embarrassment.'They were sealed because they were dangerous, Hawklan. The topic's a sensitive one for us because the last use of the mines was as a prison colony.'

Hawklan nodded. 'I understand,' he said.

'No, you don't,' said Hreldar. 'The dangers were not just the normal dangers of mining – rock falls, dust, gas and the like. There was something . . . in the air, or in the rock. Over the years it affected both prisoners and guards. Men just began to . . . waste away. And even when they were taken away from the mines, the wasting continued until . . .'

'They died.' It was Isloman. 'Some rocks sing a dire song,' he said, his face lined with distress. 'A song of warning. I understand your pain, Lords, albeit the blame was not yours.' His face became thoughtful, anxious, as the memory of his recent darkness returned briefly. 'They're so vast. And so deep,' he said, half to himself. 'And so old. Almost as old as the rock itself.'

Arinndier looked at him sharply.

'Still,' Isloman said. 'That's a deed and a tragedy of the past. We must look to the problems of the present. What does it mean now that the mines have been reopened, and their bounty goes north?'

'North,' said Arinndier softly. 'Into Narsindal.' He looked uncertainly at Darek and Hreldar, then turned to Hawklan. 'There's a legend that during the First Coming, Sumeral opened great mine workings to provide materials for His war machines. They were worked by slaves who are said to have died in their tens of thousands. They say the shafts ran so deep that they released things that were older and more evil than Sumeral Himself. Things that the Cadwanol spent generations hunting down and sealing back in the mountains after the Last Battle.'

Irritated by this seeming digression, some of the High Guards were becoming restless. One or two exchanged glances and discreetly pulled wry faces at one another at this example of whimsy by a Lord of the Geadrol.

Hawklan rounded on them. 'Save your irony for another time, gentlemen,' he said ferociously. 'For a time when your own sanity has been well tested. Mock when you have your heel on your enemy's throat, not while your companions are rotting in the mud but a few days' ride away.'

No one spoke and the offending guards sat very still under the force of Hawklan's onslaught. He looked at Yatsu, who nodded to him to continue.

Easing his chair back, he stood up and looked round at the faces of the High Guards. The power of his presence, together with the news they had received, precluded indifference, though their expressions were, for the most part, uncertain.

'Gentlemen,' he said, 'as you've been told, when we met Commander Ordan he was carrying a message from the Lord Evison. A simple and brief message given by a Lord whose High

Guard had just been routed and who was preparing to face what he must have known might be his last battle. The message was a small carved figure taken from one of your Festival Shrines. The fourth figure. The figure of Ethriss.'

Involuntarily, some of the men made a brief circular movement with their hands over their hearts.

Hawklan continued. 'That message confirmed what I already knew and what your Lords here were coming to know. We have been born into the age of the Second Coming. Sumeral is risen again in Narsindal and you will be among the first to feel the strength He is putting forth.'

Their impatience at last overriding their discipline, several of the men signalled to Yatsu for permission to speak, but Hawklan overrode them. 'Gentlemen. This isn't a debate. The Lord Eldric's last order was unequivocal, and it alone commands your obedience. Its confirmation by these other Lords and the Goraidin makes that command absolute. I tell you what I tell you because it is the truth and because you need to know it to understand those orders.' He leaned forward resting his weight on the table. 'Sumeral *is* risen, and the Lord Dan-Tor is His agent. Through Dan-Tor His corruption has reached into Orthlund and into Riddin, and has riddled your own society. We have no proof but, if your heart can't feel it, then let your heads ask why the Watch has been abandoned, why your Geadrol has been suspended, why your Lords arrested. Ask why the High Guards have been disbanded and replaced by liveried thugs. Ask why your society seems to be crumbling at the least touch. And if the answers to these questions don't convince you that a great evil is abroad, then ask how an entire troop of your own kind came to be slaughtered.' He paused. 'Slaughtered by . . . Mandrocs.'

The word hung in the air but, before anyone could react, Hawklan bent down and took hold of the armour that had been retrieved from Lord Evison's. Straightening up he threw it on to the table. 'Mandrocs, equipped thus,' he finished. The heavy, metal-clad jerkin, torn and bloodstained, together with the iron cap and a short vicious-looking sword, lay on the plain polished wood like a scar, ugly and ominous.

The Lords and the Goraidin sat virtually unmoved at this

demonstration. Both had already come to accept the new reality that was dawning. Their traditional image of Sumeral as a storybook ogre had faded and was being replaced by an image of an all too solid and powerful leader who could order troops out to battle and who could build great roads and instigate the opening of vast mine workings for His needs. The massacre of Evison and his men had, ironically, proved to be a reassurance, for all its unexpectedness and the power and ruthlessness that it represented. The menace offered by some ancient, intangible demon had the quality of a poisonous mist that corroded the will, but soldiers were soldiers, and be they Mandrocs or men, soldiers could be fought.

Before anyone else could respond, a distant trumpet call sounded, winding its way through the castle. Varak cocked his head on one side. 'Rider coming, Commander,' he said to Yatsu. 'Alone. And fast.'

The rider was Yengar. Yatsu ran down the broad stone steps from the meeting hall to greet him as he clattered into the courtyard. Slithering down from his horse, he kept hold of his saddle for support. The horse was foaming and steam was rising from it profusely.

Hawklan followed the example of the other Goraidin and Varak, and remained at the top of the steps to watch the conversation between the two men. Yengar was exhausted, but he had the same driving momentum that had propelled Ordan in his charge against far superior odds, and it apparently surged on in his speech as Yatsu had to spend a little time coaxing him into greater coherence.

Hawklan watched as Yengar gradually recovered himself. Relinquishing his hold on his saddle, he straightened up and began talking in a manner that had Yatsu listening attentively.

After a moment, Yatsu raised a hand to stop him briefly and turned to look up the steps. 'Commander Varak,' he called. 'May I ask your help?'

Varak cleared his throat and left Hawklan's side to join the two men. Hawklan put his foot on a balustrade and, leaning on his knee, watched as the conversation became more business-like. Yengar was talking and pointing, and Varak was nodding.

Then Yatsu and Varak spoke a little and abruptly Varak saluted and called out to a group of men who were standing discreetly in attendance nearby. Yatsu made a slight hand movement, and two of the Goraidin by Hawklan moved down to join him.

Almost immediately, Yengar seemed to relax, and both he and Yatsu turned to mount the steps as the courtyard broke into a flurry of running men and shouted commands.

'Is Olvric in serious trouble?' Hawklan asked as the two men reached him.

Yatsu gave him a long look. 'Have you mastered our Battle Language so easily, Hawklan?' he said.

Hawklan shook his head. 'No,' he said.

Yatsu took him by the elbow and ushered him to the door. 'Come. Tell,' he said bluntly.

In spite of the tension that the day had brought so far, Hawklan smiled; he liked Yatsu's manner. He put his arms around the shoulders of the two men, the hand resting on Yengar instinctively reading signs of tension and fatigue.

'You left Yengar and Olvric to observe Lord Eldric, didn't you?' he said. 'Against his express orders, I might remind you.' Yatsu ignored the remark. 'Now Yengar comes back alone and exhausted, his horse nearly dead. Obviously desperate. He tells his tale and relaxes only when a patrol is mustered for his friend's relief.' Yatsu raised his eyebrows, but Hawklan ploughed on. 'Now, the patrol's not too big, so any pursuing force is itself not big, but it *is* being mustered quickly, so Olvric *is* in some danger. I'd say he's out there acting as rearguard or diversion.'

Yatsu smiled slightly and nodded appreciatively. 'Indeed, Hawklan, indeed. A fair Gathering from very little. So much for our Goraidin inconspicuousness.' He accented each syllable of the word.

'It's a Mathidrin patrol, Hawklan,' said Yengar. 'Only a small one, but good. They've stuck with us all the way. It's been a bad journey. We daren't lead them any nearer so Olvric's got them pinned down in a valley a few hours away.'

Hawklan looked concerned. 'Pinned down,' he said. 'One man? A few hours away? He'll be long out of arrows by now.'

Yatsu did not share Hawklan's concern. 'No,' he said.

'Olvric's as good a slinger as he is an archer and he'll have ammunition aplenty where he is. The main problem is that he's liable to be outflanked. It's not all that good ambush country.'

The distant clatter of galloping horses leaving the castle reached them as they walked down the long corridor. Hawklan was pensive. He inclined his head towards the sound. 'Those men know not to take any unnecessary risks, don't they?' he said. 'And to make sure that none of that patrol get back to Vakloss? Preferably by taking them all prisoner.'

A faint hint of irritation showed briefly on Yatsu's face. 'Of course,' he replied, managing to keep it from his voice. 'Two of them are Goraidin. Our main function is to gather information, and where possible confuse the enemy's information. And we *never* take risks without a deal of calculation.'

Hawklan nodded apologetically.

When they entered the meeting hall they were met by a barrage of questions.

'Gentlemen.' Yatsu's voice filled the room, as he strode purposefully back to his seat. 'Yengar is fresh from Vakloss. We'll hear his news, then we'll talk. Not before. Be silent. This is not a Festival Feast.'

A rather shamefaced silence descended on the room and Yengar, still breathing heavily, told of Eldric's Accounting and his subsequent seizure by the Mathidrin together with Lord Oremson.

When he had finished Yatsu leaned forward, frowning sadly. 'And there was nothing you could do, Yengar?' he asked.

Yengar shook his head. 'No, Commander. Nothing. They moved in, in force, very quickly and very quietly. We barely got away as it was. What we managed to see was from a nearby hill. Vakloss is full of Mathidrin and ringed tight. We couldn't even estimate their numbers, there were so many and we had to move so fast. Ethriss knows where Dan-Tor's been keeping them. Besides, you know Oremson's place. It couldn't be defended by a battalion.'

Hawklan felt the man's pain. Yengar knew that he and Olvric had had no alternative but to flee, but that knowledge was a poor antidote to a poison as potent as abandonment of an ally.

'What happened to the people who were in the grounds?' he asked. Yengar grimaced. 'Those who were unlucky enough to wake quickly and offer resistance were cut down. The rest were rounded up and marched away.'

Hawklan leaned back and looked at the grim faces around the table. Oddly, the mood of the meeting had changed abruptly and a heavy silence had descended on the hall as each individual began to search for his own way to face the implications of what he had heard that day. The Goraidin and the Lords had made their own peace already, but for Varak and the High Guards it was a considerable ordeal.

Under other circumstances, the normal momentum of their ordered lives would have made them dismiss such tales out of hand as nonsense, but the presence of the elite Goraidin and three grim-faced and respected Lords stood against this momentum like a cliff face looming over the sea. Then there was Isloman; one of the two Orthlundyn who had served with the Goraidin in the Morlider War, the only outlanders ever to do so, a figure almost of legend. And, finally, the tall gaunt figure of Hawklan, whose green-eyed presence seemed to dominate both Lords and Goraidin alike.

The testimony of these people could not be doubted, nor the accuracy of their observation. Terrible changes were afoot and, while each would have preferred to turn and flee into the comfort of his past routines and tasks, that was effectively forbidden. Of the several ways that lay before them, none led back to the relief of the familiar.

Hawklan felt the pain pervading the hall. Standing up, he spoke again. 'Speak out *now*, gentlemen. Your questions and doubts; your anger and fear. Speak now. Root out your uncertainties and see them in the light, or they'll destroy you from the inside and you'll yield at some future, more critical time, like a rotten-hearted tree. We've little time. Many more than you have to be convinced, and those present here will be the spreaders of the word. If you fail, you condemn yourself and countless others to who knows what dreadful tyranny.'

The room went suddenly dark as a cloud obscured the sun. The torches, touched by the unexpected gloom, bloomed gently into life and lent an unseasonal evening quality to the scene.

Hawklan pointed towards the windows. 'This shadow will pass,' he said. 'But the darkness that's coming is blacker by far. Out of the past comes your worst fear. A nightmare so awful that it's been relegated to the tales of children has come alive and is seeking you out. You, and all you hold dear.'

He leaned forward and seemed to stare into the heart of each man there. 'You cannot flee,' he said slowly. 'Accept that. Arm yourself with your fear and the light that truth sheds, and prepare to face the enemy.'

The room seemed to go darker still, as if some presence were oppressing even the glow of the torches. 'No man will be burdened with more than he can carry,' Hawklan said. 'You hold between you the wisdom of long-gone days if you'll but search for it. You're stronger than you know and your very doubts prove it. But speak them *now*.'

As if at Hawklan's bidding, the cloud moved from the sun and the bright summer light swept through the hall like a far-flung wave rolling and spreading over a waiting shoreline. Like the clatter of stones and pebbles buffeted by such a wave, a babble of voices rose up, sweeping aside the leaden uneasiness that had permeated the gathering.

It was some time before the stream of questions petered out, but as it did, Arinndier rose to his feet and called for silence.

'Gentlemen,' he said. 'We have spoken of this as much as we can, and each of us alone must make his own peace with what he has learned. Now we must turn our minds to how we can implement the order that the Lord Eldric gave us. However, another matter has to be decided first.' He paused and looked down at his hands. When he looked up again, his face was pained. 'We've no Geadrol now, so I'll give you, High Guard and Goraidin, my Accounting. I speak also for the Lords Darek and Hreldar.'

Hawklan and Isloman exchanged glances in the uneasy silence that followed this remark.

Arinndier continued. 'We admit to failing in our duty as Lords of Fyorlund and Lords of the Geadrol. We have not maintained the vigilance that was expected of us. We should have enquired into the origins of our King's "saviour" many years ago. We should not have allowed the Watch on Narsindal to fail. We should not have allowed the decay of our High Guards into foppish shadows of their forebears. In short, we should have looked properly to our duty. Had we done this, then what has happened might never have come to be, or at least we might have been better able to contain it. Now we face an enemy who has infiltrated the very heart of our country and beyond, and who has armed forces at his command that we can't begin to measure.'

He pointed to the Mandroc armour lying on the table. 'The Mandrocs are a savage, nomadic race. But I don't need to tell you that this is from a heavy infantryman. One whose companions defeated a High Guard troop fighting to defend its very home. That betokens either great numbers, or great discipline. Perhaps even both.' He paused to judge the response to the harsh reality of the sunlit armour lying before his audience. 'Its presence in Fyorlund, the fate of Lord Evison, the destruction of our ancient ways all lie at the feet of our negligence. That same negligence may yet bring death to you.'

Hawklan could not forbear to interrupt. 'Lord Arinndier, you're too harsh on yourself,' he said. 'This is no ordinary foe you're facing. His treachery and cunning are . . .'

Arinndier raised a hand to silence him. 'This is our way, Hawklan,' he said firmly. 'We . . .' he indicated Darek and Hreldar, 'are nothing without the judgement of our men.'

Isloman laid a hand on Hawklan's arm. 'Leave them,' he said. 'They know their own kind best. They need a reaffirmation.'

Hawklan's protest died on his lips, and he sat back, frowning slightly.

Arinndier moved away from the table. Head bowed, he knelt on the wooden floor. Hreldar and Darek joined him. There was a long silence in the room until Yatsu rose and moved to confront the three men.

'Lords, we've discussed this amongst ourselves already. Your guilt is indisputable.' Hawklan started, but the Lords remained unmoved. 'As also is ours,' he continued. 'We saw the wrongs and knew them, but did nothing. To look to the leadership of the Lords does not absolve any of us from our duty to each other. Blame and judgement, however, are matters for another time, another place. Too few of us are here and too little is known for a true Gathering. Commander Varak and his men may choose otherwise, but we Goraidin offer you our loyalty unchanged. To yourselves, the King, the Law, the Geadrol and the people, until the day when an Accounting can be called of us all.' Then he drew his sword and offered it, hilt first, to the kneeling Lords. Each in turn laid his hand on it and bowed his head.

Varak, a little disconcerted at being brought to this debate between Lords and the elite Goraidin, spruced his uniform and walked stiffly forward to join Yatsu. He cleared his throat awkwardly. 'Lords,' he began uncertainly, 'I'm a simple soldier. It's my experience that rights and wrongs usually spread themselves fairly evenly when all's been said and done. None of us escape without blame. All I know is that the country's been going the wrong way for a long while, and matters had to come to a head sooner or later. This is no time for changing horses, especially when the ones we have are tried and trusted.' Drawing his sword, he offered it to the Lords, as Yatsu had then, turning to his men, he spoke in a surprisingly gentle voice. 'If any of you disagree, then go now. Go freely and with my blessing. I want no reluctant swords guarding my back.'

'None of the officers moved.

'Tell your men the same,' he continued. Then, raising an admonishing finger, 'No reproaches *of any kind*. No debates. Let those who wish to go, go.' And in a pragmatic echo of Hawklan's words, 'Their doubts will get your throats cut one day.'

The atmosphere in the hall was almost tangible. Looking round at the standing men, Hawklan knew that he could be looking into the eyes of Sumeral Himself, so much did His teachings pervade the group. He knew that in time the hideous reality of mutilated and torn flesh stinking in the churned earth would be lost in the glow of the storytellers' ringing phrases, and the terror and agony would simply be forgotten, as glory and heroism raised their treacherous standards. And yet, such false inspiration would carry young men and women through the training they would need to face the enemy who would surely confront them in time. He put his hand to his head.

Yatsu noted the gesture. 'Are you all right?' he said.

Hawklan nodded. Just a touch of conscience, he thought.

Chapter 48

The group in the hall talked for a long time, provoking more than a few wry asides from Isloman about the seemingly endless ability of the Fyordyn to talk and talk.

'And listen,' Hawklan offered by way of defence. 'They need to shake their thoughts loose. They can come to only one conclusion, but they'll need to come to it their own way.'

And they did. Inexorably, the consensus formed round Eldric's last order like a pearl around a tiny irritation, solid and purposeful. Around it in turn would grow an even greater mass. An army of Lords and High Guards and ordinary people who would stand against Dan-Tor's baleful influence, because his actions had taken him beyond the realm of reasoned dispute. He offered them now only his tyranny, using the King's name as its sole disguise. It was not possible to mount a small operation to rescue Eldric, if indeed he was still alive, so the tyrant himself had to be assailed. With the great web of lies and deceit that Dan-Tor would spread, this could mean civil war. Kin would fight kin, and kin would slay kin. And all with that peculiar viciousness that the righteous possess when fighting for the truth that they alone possess. It was a grim conclusion, but the Fyordyn reached it and faced it.

'Perhaps this time we'll be able to prevent Sumeral spreading from His fastness in Narsindal,' said Yatsu afterwards to Hawklan. 'Stop Him reaching the world beyond.'

It was the first time Hawklan had heard Sumeral spoken of as a mortal enemy. 'Perhaps,' he replied.

His hope lay in Yatsu's remark, but a deeper voice told him he might not have glimpsed the strategy of the Great Corrupter. There were marks of impatience and haste in Dan-Tor's actions which sang a false note to him. The thought nagged at him that, with the Fyordyn being so subtly lured from their old watchfulness and discipline, the knowledge of His awakening could have been hidden for aeons yet. His strength could have been marshalled in the mists of Narsindal, unseen and unknown, while His poisons leached ever outwards to corrupt and weaken His old enemies. A harsh voice rose inside him. Perhaps they already have, it said.

The next day, Hawklan stood with Arinndier on the battlements of Eldric's stronghold. Resting his arm on the edge of one of the great merlons he leaned forward and stared out across the mountainous ramparts that separated the castle from the plains of Fyorlund.

'An admirably placed fortress,' he said. 'Well stocked, defensible food lines, own water supply, almost impregnable at the rear, and flanked by those mountains, needing very little defence. You'd need sleepy guards indeed to be taken by surprise.' He paused as if lost in an old memory. 'Or treachery,' he added quietly. Then he pointed down the long valley and the wide twisting road that led from the castle. 'It's very similar to my own castle in its layout. Very similar. Though the workmanship's different and it's not so old.'

Arinndier shrugged slightly. 'No one knows how old any of the Fyorlund castles are,' he said. 'Or who built them. They're said to be from the Golden Age, after the Last Battle.'

Hawklan nodded. 'It could be,' he said absently. 'They weren't here . . . before.'

Arinndier stared at him wide-eyed and uncertain, but Hawklan seemed oblivious to what he had just said, and before Arinndier could speak, he turned round and met his gaze directly, sweeping the moment away. 'But you didn't join us out here to discuss ancient architecture did you, Arin?'

'No, no,' Arinndier stuttered. 'Of course not. I came to try and persuade you to stay and help us. You're needed here. You could convince and persuade more in an hour than we could in a week. The Fyordyn are very conservative; not given to rapid change. They're not all as flexible as the Goraidin by any means.'

Hawklan looked out along the valley again, resting his head on his hand and frowning slightly. Then he turned and, taking Arinndier's arm, started walking slowly along the wide parapet.

'I understand,' he said. 'I know I could be of service to you. But I see other things as well. Besides, I can offer little more than you yourself. You, the Goraidin and, if I'm any judge of Eldric and Varak, a tough crowd of High Guards, together form a powerful nucleus. Many armies have started with much less.'

Arinndier made to protest, but Hawklan raised a hand and fixed him again with a piercing gaze. 'Sumeral's a force beyond human understanding, Arinndier, for all His human form. He needs sway over all mortal peoples and their lands to corrupt the Great Harmony beyond recovery, and He could achieve this with His Will alone if He so chose. Only one thing restrains Him, if He and His Uhriel are awake, then could not the Guardians also be awake, or awakening? The Guardians? His equals in the older, greater, Power. If He expends His Power on controlling humanity then He'll not be able to face the Power of the Guardians. And even if they're not yet awake, the exertion of His will in such a deed would surely awaken them. So He must raise mortal agents and mortal armies to achieve this.'

A sudden chilling knowledge swept over him. Sumeral would be more cunning, more patient than before, and the Guardians must surely be weaker. But less innocent, he thought, in rebuttal, less innocent, and goaded by a terrible guilt.

Arinndier stared at him almost fearfully.

Hawklan's gaze was unrelenting. 'We must draw on our every ally, and use them where they are most strong. In the end the balance may lie in the thickness of a hair.' He held up his hand, thumb and finger lightly touching. 'So finely balanced,' he said distantly.

'Hawklan, you speak so strangely at times,' Arinndier said, his face anxious. 'What do you know of these things? I don't understand you. You make us sound as if we'll be mere skirmishers in someone else's battle.'

Hawklan's look softened into a smile. 'We *are* skirmishers,' he said. 'But the mortal battle is ours in its entirety, and if we lose *everything* will be lost.'

Arinndier still looked fretful.

Hawklan slapped his arm. 'Gather all your forces, Arin. Look to your own estates and those of such other Lords as you can reach. Then send to Orthlund. To Loman at Anderras

Darion.' A brief look of sadness passed over his face. 'I fear you may have powerful allies there soon.'

'You fear?' Arinndier said. Hawklan waved a dismissive hand, and did not pursue the question in Arinndier's voice. 'Take heart,' he said. 'While you face mortal armies, however foul, however numerous, the war can be won. Gather every resource together and use them well.'

Arinndier seized the straw and reverted back to his concern of the moment. 'But you won't stay and help us,' he said. Hawklan laughed. 'Remind me in future never to engage a Fyordyn in debate will you?' Then, more seriously, 'I don't have the words for this, Arin, but I'm drawn elsewhere – drawn more powerfully than ever. I *have* to go to the source of this ill. My heart leads me. It brought me here to see the massacre of Evison's men and for Isloman to show me the desecration of the mountains. Now it leads me back to Vakloss. Back to my original path. I must find your Lord Dan-Tor . . .'

Arinndier bridled a little. 'He's no Lord of mine, Hawklan,' he said.

Hawklan gestured an apology.

'Could your heart not be leading you into a trap?' tried Arinndier.

'Possibly,' Hawklan said thoughtfully after a brief silence. 'Possibly. But it may be a trap to yield to my inclination and remain here to help you with your army. Dan-Tor holds the answers to my needs. I've no alternative but to seek him out.' Then his face brightened. 'Besides I've got Isloman and Gavor to watch my back. Take this solace, Arin – he'll find me no easy game to hold, no matter what his trap. And time spent pursuing me can't be spent working against you. I may be of greater service in gaining time for you than in helping to organise and train your army. I've told you, you've plenty of good men for that, but none can distract Dan-Tor as I can.'

Arinndier lifted his hands in submission.

'One thing though,' Hawklan continued. Arinndier leaned forward, a faint glimmer of hope in his eyes. 'Let me have two Goraidin to go back to Vakloss with. I'd value their skills and they can report back to you whatever happens there.'

* * *

Both Hreldar and Darek assaulted Hawklan's resolution, following Arinndier's capitulation, but with as much success. Darek was prompted to a wry smile. 'See how easily we fall without your leadership,' he said.

Hawklan smiled broadly and placed an arm around his shoulder. 'Come now, Lord,' he said. 'Would you make me an oath-breaker? Lord Arinndier is witness that I've forsworn debating with Fyordyn. And besides I can tell a fall from a feint.'

But it was Yatsu who struck home, sitting silent in an evening alcove. 'I want none of this, Hawklan,' he said, his face passive but pained. 'All the action recently has kept my mind busy, but there are quiet places in this old castle that bring thoughts crashing down on top of me. Old, long-forgotten memories, Hawklan. Terrible memories. I want none of it.' He looked up, and Hawklan saw his eyes were glistening with tears in the soft torchlight.

He sat down by the man and leaned back against the cool stone wall. The air was very still and a low bright moon dominated the sky silvering the surrounding peaks. It was an evening for celebrating life in quiet joy, but the aura around Yatsu forbade any such ease. Hawklan thought back to the return of Olvric.

When Varak's patrol had reached Olvric, they had expected to find him dead or at least sorely pressed. As it was, it was the Mathidrin who were in difficulties. Of the six, two had died moving to outflank Olvric, one was unconscious with a serious head injury and another had a broken arm.

Olvric himself had moved to ensure that the patrol could neither advance nor retreat without coming under the lethal fire of his sling, and he was waiting silent and unmoving when Varak's men arrived.

'They'll provide useful information,' Yatsu had said, apparently satisfied after Olvric had reported, but Hawklan had caught the subtle, almost unconscious signs that had flickered between some of the Goraidin.

'You mistrust Olvric,' Hawklan said into the cool evening. Yatsu did not seem surprised at this remark, but just nodded slightly.

'Olvric knows his trade better than average,' he said non-committally.

'But?' said Hawklan.

Yatsu breathed out a long breath. 'It's complicated, Hawklan,' he said. 'I'd trust Olvric's loyalty without question. I'd trust him with my life without a moment's qualm . . .'

'But?' Hawklan repeated.

There was a long silence.

'Our training was harsh – brutal, even. It was intended to make us self-reliant under almost any conditions, and to weld us into a single fighting unit – bound by loyalty – and by common suffering.' Yatsu smiled ironically, though the smile faded almost immediately. 'But what really binds us, binds us beyond any release, isn't our training – even though that runs deep. What binds us is a shared horror of the things we saw . . .' His voice faltered. 'And the things we did – had to do,' he added softly in reluctant self-justification. 'We're a unit now because only we understand one another. Only we know what it's like to hunt without mercy, and the terror of being hunted the same way. Know what it's like to chose between killing and abandoning your own.'

Hawklan watched the man intensely, remembering vividly his conversation with Isloman as they had ridden north through Orthlund with Jaldaric.

'But Olvric and some of the others relished the life too much,' Yatsu continued. 'When we came back from Riddin, it took most of us months to adjust to peacetime living. For some it took years. Some wandered off into the mountains to find themselves . . . or just disappeared. Some killed themselves. But Olvric . . . he just carried on waiting. Peacetime was just a long wait, a long interval, until the next time. Somehow, he only lived when he was fighting. Stalking a prey – killing it. Did you see those Mathidrin when they came in?'

Hawklan nodded.

'Terrified,' Yatsu continued. 'Not nervous or apprehensive – terrified. That's what Olvric and his kind do to people – enemies. And he didn't have to kill three of them.'

'Two,' corrected Hawklan.

Yatsu shook his head. 'Come now, Hawklan. I don't need to

be a healer to know that that head injury's fatal. It's three dead, without a doubt.'

'What else could he have done?' asked Hawklan. 'He was heavily outnumbered.'

'He knows that wounded men present a greater problem than dead ones,' said Yatsu. 'He had the initiative. They wouldn't have been expecting an ambush. He's a first-rate slinger. He could have immobilised almost all of them and scattered their horses. The killings were superfluous.'

'But you'll use the terror that Olvric's induced to obtain more information than you would otherwise, won't you?' Hawklan said searchingly.

Yatsu's eyes glinted and he grimaced. 'Yes,' he said bitterly. 'I told you I wanted none of it. I'm too old, seen too much.' He took Hawklan's arm. 'That spirit, that worm that wriggles inside Olvric, wriggles in us all. It's in me, I know. I want it far away – away in the shadows – away from the treacherous old skills for killing and betraying that it feeds on.'

Yatsu's voice was calm and steady. It held no emotional tremor, and its very control chilled Hawklan. The truth is to be faced, however terrible, he thought again, and here was a man facing it at its worst.

'I've no answer for you, Yatsu,' he said eventually. 'You see the truth of what you say, and it's immutable. But just to see it is to be armoured against many things. Every step we take is a step into darkness, you know that, even for Dan-Tor. He knows the future no more than any of us. Travel with a good heart, Yatsu, don't cloud the present with the unknowable future, and don't be frightened of this worm inside you. Your conscience and your judgement will keep it in hand, have no fear.'

Yatsu did not reply.

Hawklan spoke again. 'We may be pawns in some great game played by powers beyond us. But if we can't feel the strings that control us, then we're free. We must use what faculties we have to the full and celebrate the gift of life as best we can. To do otherwise is to do the enemy's work for him.'

'I know that,' said Yatsu quietly. 'I'm not a starry-eyed cadet.' He shrugged apologetically. 'I was just giving my thoughts to the evening, to get rid of them. I'll do what I have to do. Like you, I'm a right piece in the right place, and my real avenues of movement are heavily circumscribed.'

In spite of himself and his protestations to the Lords, Hawklan said, 'Do you need any help?'

Yatsu gazed up into the moonlight. 'Of course I do, Hawklan. But I'll manage without it. And you belong elsewhere – I know that.' He smiled. 'You carry more weight on the playing board than I do, you're nearer the player. Dan-Tor's your quarry.'

Then, abruptly, his face became angry and gripping Hawklan's arm powerfully he spoke through clenched teeth. 'Bring him down, Hawklan. Destroy him as soon as you can – and whatever's behind him. You're the healer – cut out the root of the disease. We'll attend to the body's defences – it's not that enfeebled yet.'

Then he stood up and, without any word of parting, moved off silently into the darkness.

Hawklan looked up at the moon and wrapped his arms about himself. He remembered the sinister chair at the Gretmearc; the strange destruction of the pavilion by Andawyr; the bird that sprang hideously to life; and Andawyr's mysterious tent that disappeared into an eerie distance. Then Gulda, so knowledgeable and yet so enigmatic; the Mandrocs chanting and charging in close order; and the Viladrien dominating the singing sky over the Riddin. Powers and mysteries far beyond his understanding.

Nearer the player, he thought ruefully. No idea who I am, pushed and pulled by forces I know nothing of, a healer inside the body of a warrior that attracts the service and loyalty of others as if of right.

A great wave of fear broke over him, and he sat in the shade of the alcove for a long time.

So, like a sad echo of their departure from Anderras Darion, Hawklan and Isloman left the Lord Eldric's mountain stronghold, accompanied by Lorac and Tel-Odrel. There were few words spoken as they left, although everyone in the castle braved a squalling rainstorm to see them leave.

Some way down the road, Hawklan turned and looked back

at the castle. It was almost totally hidden by the blowing rain and for a moment he could not distinguish it from the crags behind. Some of the watching people, cloaked and hooded against the weather, huddled round its base, while others on the walls broke the sharp lines of its crenellations. It looked like an old cliff face with boulders fringing its feet.

Hawklan raised his arm as a last salute, and a few voices floated down to him. His action opened his cloak and an indignant Gavor peered out. 'Steady on, dear boy,' he said. 'It's raining in here.'

Hawklan gave him a narrow look, then pulled his cloak about himself again. Slowly the four figures merged into the dull grey rain and disappeared from view.

Chapter 49

Light filtered through to Eldric's brain slowly and vaguely, and his mind snatched at it fitfully as it rambled past on its way from nightmare to nightmare. Nightmares of prisons and roof-tops and a smoke-shrouded City filled with shapeless horrors from some distant time; of an eternity in a saddle and an endless argument the threads of which slipped ever away from him each time he reached his clinching point. Occasionally a sound joined the light, and light and sound and pain rose and fell together in an unholy harmony. With infinite reluctance, the light slowly formed itself into a single image which his mind, with equal reluctance, strove to identify. It was a torch. An old torch. Very old, said something in the background.

He could not have said how long he stared at it, seeing it clearly, before he finally identified it. 'Torch,' he said, and his voice sounded like a child's. He screwed his face up irritably. A figure came between him and the light, and he waved it aside crossly. He needed to explain. 'Torch,' he repeated. 'Old – in a book when I was a child. A book of old legends – with great big beautiful pictures. Full of colours.'

He felt his awareness returning, and the pain in his head diffused itself throughout his whole body in a general discom-fort. The figure moved again, and was now by his side. He took its arm, and continued to explain. 'It's incredible,' he said. 'I've never seen one like it. It's strange how childhood memories impress themselves so deeply, isn't it? It was in a picture of a Prince in a dungeon – during the Wars of the First Coming.'

A chill struck him and dispelled the childlike aura protecting him. He struggled to sit up. The figure put an arm around his shoulders and helped him. 'Gently, Father,' it said. 'Gently. I don't think you've any bones broken, but you were badly knocked about when they threw you in here, and you cracked your head on the floor.'

The words disorientated Eldric for a moment and for a while he mouthed them to himself. Then he turned and looked at the figure for confirmation.

Fair hair matted, round flat face with its innocence scarred by lines of care and neglect, and fringed with an unfamiliar beard.

'Jaldaric,' he said. 'Jaldaric. Is it really you, or am I dreaming again?' He closed his eyes as if he expected to find the mirage gone when he opened them again.

'Yes, Father,' replied his son. 'It's me, and you're not dreaming. I wish you were. Rest a moment until you're fully awake.' Unexpectedly, Eldric's face crumpled and he dropped his head into his hands to hide his tears. Jaldaric looked at him awkwardly, uncertain what to do.

Then, wiping his eyes with his hands, Eldric took his son in an embrace and held him still and close like a small child. 'I thought you were dead,' he said after a while. 'When Hawklan told me about the Mandrocs I hardly dared to think about it, it was so horrible. I just . . . pushed the thoughts away. It was all I could do. I'm sorry.'

Jaldaric did not reply but returned his father's embrace and for a long time the two sat leaning against the cold dungeon wall taking solace from each other until the tide of euphoria ebbed a little and left them alone and lost on a strange shore.

Eldric found his memories of recent events returning sporadically, and he winced as a hesitant exploration of his skull discovered a large lump. He recalled being dragged with Lord Oremson from the house and through the City. He remembered the frightened faces of his followers, and did he remember bodies lying in Oremson's gardens, in the moon shadow?

Jaldaric spoke. 'What's happening, Father?' he asked. 'I remember being in Orthlund. And arguing with some . . . thug. And a patrol of Mandrocs . . . and a journey.' He shuddered. 'Then all of a sudden I'm here. The Lord Dan-Tor's asking me question and telling me not to worry.' He shrugged bitterly. 'Now I don't know whether these are memories or whether I've gone mad. I feel as if I've been here all my life. Are you here, Father, or have I truly gone mad?'

Eldric held his son tighter. 'No, son, you're not mad, though the world seems to be. If you've a memory of two Orthlundyn called Hawklan and Isloman, then you're sane enough and so am I.'

Jaldaric started up. 'Yes,' he said. 'The Lord Dan-Tor asked me about him. Green-eyed and . . .' He stopped. 'My friends. What happened to my friends?'

Eldric looked down and then back up at his son. He saw the knowledge in his son's face before he spoke, and his voice seemed to echo through the years, back to the many times he had spoken such words to such faces in the Morlider War. They were always inadequate, but there were no others. His stomach turned over. 'I'm sorry, Jal, they're all dead. Hawklan said they took quite a toll of the Mandrocs, but . . .'

Jaldaric clenched his teeth and standing up, turned away. But he did not weep. So long tormented by his isolation, the certainty gave him as much comfort as it did grief. When he turned round, his face was almost petulant. 'What's happening, Father?' he said again. 'Why am I here? What crime have I committed? Where's the Law? And where were you?' His tone became reproachful. 'Every time there was a footstep outside, I'd think, Here he is, come to set me free and tell me it's all been some terrible mistake. But you didn't come. Day after day you didn't come.'

Eldric struggled to his feet and faced his son. 'I'm sorry,' he said. 'I didn't know at first, and when I did know, I couldn't do anything. I'm sorry.'

The two looked at one another in silence for some time, then Eldric laid his hand on his son's arm. 'Come,' he said. 'That bunk looks none too sweet, but it'll be more comfortable than the floor. Let's sit down and I'll tell you what's been happening.'

Jaldaric listened to his father intently and in silence. 'I can't believe this, Father,' he said when at last Eldric had finished. 'All these dreadful things.'

Eldric nodded. 'I understand,' he said. 'My mind's done some scurrying over the past weeks. Waiting to wake up. But it's all true, believe me. It's all brutally true. It's as if some poison has leached into the people and corroded their spirits so that they just crumble helpless before Dan-Tor's will.'

There was a long silence.

'And you think this is the . . . Second Coming?' Jaldaric said awkwardly. 'That . . . Sumeral has risen in Narsindal and that this is His first step out into the world?'

Eldric held his son's gaze, aware of his fearful uncertainty. 'Yes,' he said unequivocally. 'Beyond all doubt now. But our immediate problem is Dan-Tor. He's foe enough for us and whether he's master or servant is irrelevant. Suffice it that he has all the advantages.' Looking at the doubt still written on Jaldaric's face, he smiled. 'Don't worry,' he said. 'I don't mind you thinking your old father's gone peculiar, I'm sure I would have in similar circumstances, but you'll be able to form your own conclusion when we're out of here.'

Despite himself, Jaldaric smiled in response. Then he rubbed his face. 'How strange,' he said. 'I haven't smiled in months. It's made my face ache.'

Eldric put his arm around his son's shoulder. 'You've passed your lowest point, son,' he said 'From now on we go upwards and out of here. Dan-Tor's probably put us together because he thinks he has nothing to fear from us. Judging from the number of Mathidrin I saw when I was brought here I'd say he's taken the City by force. But he can't take the whole country by force, and I doubt he can hold even the City for long.'

Jaldaric's face clouded as he moved away from Eldric. 'I'm glad of your optimism, Father,' he said. 'But how can we get away from here? They open that door twice a day – at least I think it's twice a day – I haven't seen the sky since Orthlund. There's always two of them, and I don't even know where we are.'

Eldric, however, refused to be downed. He had found his son again. The son he had believed cruelly dead at the hands of Mandrocs. He had good and powerful friends outside, and surely the people weren't all beyond redemption?

'We're in the Westerclave,' he said enthusiastically. 'I watched where I was going this time, for all I was groggy.' Abruptly he clenched his fists. 'We've been no more than a flight of stairs apart all this time.' He pointed towards the door. 'Just out there is a flight of stairs that I shouted down when we tricked our way out of our cell.' His face creased in distress. 'If only I'd known. The Goraidin could've . . .' His voice tailed off. 'Still. That's talk through the rafters now. No recalling it.'

He looked thoughtfully round the cell, and his eyes lit on the torch that he had seen when he recovered consciousness. He stood up and walked over to examine it. Running his fingers around its ornate, fluted body, he said, 'This is old. Very old. I've never seen the like except in an old storybook.' Then his hand moved to the wall by it. 'And look at these.' He gestured to Jaldaric and pointed out some faint scratches in the wall by the torch. Taking hold of the torch he shook it violently. It did not move. 'You try,' he said brusquely. 'You're stronger than I am.' Jaldaric frowned but took hold of the torch and strained at it until his pale face became red. Still it did not move. 'It's well made,' he said offhandedly.

'It's more than well made,' said Eldric, examining the faint scratches again. 'This was made by craftsmen the like of which don't exist any more, nor have for generations.' He became excited. 'I'll wager they've tried to remove that to put in one of Dan-Tor's stinking globes to illuminate his treachery. But this wall's turned their best chisels. And this torch has withstood everything they've hit it with.' He began walking up and down. 'They say that the Westerclave was built during the Wars of the First Coming. Some kind of an outpost that changed hands repeatedly as the war swept to and fro.' He came to a conclusion. 'This room's held prisoners who could exert a power that's beyond us and it was built accordingly.'

Jaldaric could not share his father's enthusiasm. He sat down again and leaned back against the wall. 'I'm sorry, Father,' he said 'I've seen nothing but these walls and that torch for months. Ancient it might be – magic even – but it holds little charm for me. I'll be glad when I don't have to see it again.'

Eldric nodded understandingly. 'Of course,' he said. 'But just think what that torch means, Jal.' He sat down beside his son. 'Outside that door there's a passage, a long passage, torchlit like this, and lined with exactly similar doors. Who knows how many cells there are down there? And I had no idea it even existed. This place probably hasn't been used in centuries, but what happens when someone opens it up? That torch,' he pointed to it emphatically, 'that torch – like any good old reliable torch would – bursts into life. After all this time. An unimaginable span of years and darkness. It lit when it was needed. And they couldn't put it out or destroy it.'

He paused thoughtfully. 'There might be an ancient evil waking again in the world, Jal, but there'll be other ancient forces stirring as well. Bringing light into the darkness. Even if Fyorlund falls and Riddin, and then Orthlund. Each step will take its toll and the world will know Sumeral for what He is sooner this time. Eventually it'll be He who finds Himself surrounded by an iron ring. One that will close on Him and seal Him away forever.'

Jaldaric gently mocked his father's unexpected rhetoric. 'Father, you sound like an old storyteller . . . a Keeper of the Festivals.' But his brief jauntiness vanished abruptly and he wrapped his arms around himself as if for protection. 'And if you're right. You talk about the fall of countries as if it were nothing. Whole populations swept aside for the sake of some greater future.' There was a question mark in the word greater. 'What are people? Just so many dust motes?'

Eldric reached out to his son. 'I don't know, Jal,' he said. 'Maybe we are motes floating through this world at the behest of others, but we have our own wills.'

'But we've no freedom to exercise them in action, Father,' Jaldaric replied. 'No freedom. What can we do here?'

Eldric chuckled and, as if in response, the torch turned to the colour of spring sunshine. Eldric looked at it and threw it a salute. 'Thank you, old craftsman, wherever you are. Your gift continues unalloyed.' Then, turning to his son, 'What we can do, Jaldaric, Eldric's son – as motes – is get in Dan-Tor's eyes.'

Chapter 50

The Mathidrin trooper quailed under Sylvriss's baleful stare. 'Brown eyes a man would drown in,' he had once heard a lustful compatriot wax in a more lyrical moment, but the gaze that held him now took all the moisture from his mouth and throat.

'Release my bridle,' she said but, though the words were slow and soft, they held such menace that the hand did as it was bid without any conscious effort on its owner's part. Two fears met inside him like clashing waves, and from somewhere he found a voice. It was hoarse and nervous, but it would have to do.

'Majesty,' he said. 'It's the Ffyrst's orders. You're not to be allowed out into the City without a full escort. It's too dangerous.'

It was not in Sylvriss's nature to confront when she could walk around, nor did she often use the authority which her position allowed and the people bestowed. But she was a Muster woman, and to obstruct the way of a Muster rider was to invoke responses which transcended normal social restraints. She swung her riding crop round and placed it accurately under the trooper's chin. Then, bending forward, her gaze still relentlessly steady, she said, '*I* am not to be allowed?' in a soft echo of the man's words. 'Even the King would not order me thus. Now stand aside or this horse may kill you before I can stop it.'

The man took a hesitant step to one side. 'Majesty, please,' he said piteously, 'I'll be punished if I allow you through.'

Exuding fear, and drained of the arrogance and disdain that was the hallmark of the Mathidrin, the man became more human, and Sylvriss relented slightly. 'Find a senior officer immediately,' she said. 'I'll give you two minutes.'

It did not help, however. The man swallowed. 'I may not leave my post, Majesty,' he said.

Some materials, when stressed, yield and move, giving outward signs of their condition. Others hold the stress within themselves, allowing it to build unseen, until one last increment bursts the fabric suddenly and catastrophically. So it was now with Sylvriss.

Fretful at the news of repression her contacts were bringing to her, and fearful for their safety as Dan-Tor swept aside the ancient Law and replaced it with the even more ancient law of superior force; fearful also for the safety of Dilrap, daily playing aide and would-be confidante to Dan-Tor; and above all, fearful for her husband, steadily improving in health away from the pernicious influence of his Chief Physician, and becoming increasingly anxious to take to himself some of the reins of government he had so long relinquished, Sylvriss needed her riding to be able to retain some inner peace and outward semblance of calm and composure.

Thundering through the City's great parks, and sometimes beyond the City itself, the wind blowing in her face and at one with the powerful animal under her, she could find again the spirit of the Riddinvolk, and renew her courage and sense of purpose to sustain her when she returned to the claustrophobic atmosphere of the Palace.

Now this was threatened and the many fears came together like sharp-pointed chisels to destroy her. Her mind knew that the guard was only doing as he had been bidden and that she was placing him in an intolerable position, but it was a small cry against the roar of her heart and spirit, and while it did not yield its right, it saw its defeat.

The Mathidrin saw it also, so acute had his fears made him, and he stepped back hastily even before the Queen urged her great horse forward and galloped through the gate regardless of him.

As the hoofbeats echoed into the distance, he recovered himself and, running over to an alarm bell hanging by the side of the gate, he rang out a clamorous carillon in celebration of the passing of his dilemma. He'd done everything he could, cried the bell, let the officers deal with her.

But Sylvriss and her mount were out of earshot before the first resonating vibrations left the bell. At full gallop she cascaded through the streets of the City heedless of direction and destination. What was important was to ride, to ride, to ride. To set aside the endless complexities and ambiguities of her life, and just be, just exist for a little while. She could not be constrained by guards and escorts any more than could the horses of Riddin be penned; free spirits both, they would either die or kill if pinioned.

How long she rode she could not have said, nor through what streets and by-ways, but gradually her passion ebbed and the mind's voice became louder. She had been hasty with that guard. There had been a great deal of trouble in the City following the arrest of Eldric and Oremson, and she knew huge contingents of Mathidrin had been brought in from somewhere to contend with it. Her action had not been wise from any point of view except insofar as it eased her own inner pains. However, she could make amends and at least ensure the trooper was not punished. No great hurt need come of it.

Then, as her spirit quieted, she became aware of the sound of the horse's hooves on the stone street as, reading her mood, it slowed down to a gentle canter. They echoed.

She reined to a halt and looked around. A deep silence pervaded everywhere and rang almost deafeningly in her ears. Only the familiar sound of creaking harness and the easy breathing of her horse told her she had not become suddenly deaf. The street was deserted. And from the silence it seemed as if the whole City was deserted.

She looked up at the surrounding buildings and identified where she was. Not one of the busier parts of the City but, even so, it was late morning and a great many people should have been about. She walked the horse forward, curiosity pushing all other concerns from her mind. For several minutes she moved quietly from street to street. All deserted. Unease began to temper her curiosity.

Glancing up, she saw a curtain flicker. She stared at it pensively for some time, then dismounted and went over to the small flight of stone steps which led up to the door of the house. The strangeness of her behaviour made her feel slightly disorientated but, following her impulse, she walked up the steps and took hold of the large heavy door knocker.

She found its cold contact reassuring, and she brought her face close to it as if to hide from the rest of the world. The striker was a traditional iron ring with a radiant star at its centre, while the striking plate was a simple boss known colloquially as Sumeral's pate. She brought the striker down purposefully.

The sound ruptured the silence and echoed up and down the street before it escaped out over the rooftops. It seemed to breed a myriad tiny whispers all pointing accusingly at her. It also brought her a little more to herself. She struck again, and the answering whispers became terrified.

But no answer came from within. Her jaw stiffened and she beat a powerful tattoo on the door that seemed to raise dust whirls in the street. As the hissing echoes faded, she became aware of a presence behind the door.

'Majesty,' came a faint voice. 'Majesty. What do you want?' The voice was fearful, and the request peremptory.

Its tone dispelled her brief anger. 'Open the door,' she said. 'Tell me what's happening. Where is everyone? Why are the streets empty?'

'Majesty, how can you not know?' came the reply. 'I beg of you, go away.'

Again anger fluttered inside Sylvriss, but she contained it. She knew that no one would speak to her thus except under some dire provocation. 'Are you going to leave your Queen standing at your threshold like some pedlar?' she said gently.

There was a long silence, then some scuffling and whispering from behind the door. Her horse whinnied softly, but she ignored it.

Then a woman's voice. 'Majesty, please, I beg you, leave now, for all our sakes.'

She began to protest, but the words died on her lips, such was the fear in the whispered voice. Baffled she turned and walked back to her horse.

'You, there, stop!'

A raucous command shattered her reverie and brought her harshly back to the street. She turned to see a Mathidrin foot patrol approaching. Patting her horse's neck she whispered, 'I'm sorry. I didn't listen to you properly.'

Scanning the patrol she saw one or two familiar faces, but the Sirshiant at its head was unfamiliar. He was tall and well built, and carried himself with an attitude that set Sylvriss's teeth on edge.

Leaving the patrol he strode towards her purposefully. Sylvriss drew herself up and met his gaze coldly, but his stride did not falter and knots of fear began to tangle in her stomach.

'You're aware of the punishment for being on the streets, wench,' he said coldly, starting to draw his sword. There was a visible tremor in the ranks of the patrol behind him, and a disbelieving hiss of voices filled the air from no apparent source.

The Sirshiant faltered and then stopped. 'Who was that?' he said quietly and ominously. A trooper ran forward and spoke to him softly. Slowly he released his sword, tightening and untightening his grip on the hilt angrily. Then he slammed it back into its sheath and there was an undisguised snicker from someone in the patrol. His face became livid, but he turned again to the Queen.

'Majesty,' he said, as if the words were choking him. 'Forgive me. I didn't know who you were. We've very strict orders about how to deal with people disobeying the Ffyrst's edicts.'

Sylvriss could see a fury bubbling within the man, but it seemed to be disproportionate to the humiliation he had just brought on himself. She felt her horse tremble slightly, instinctively preparing itself for battle, and realised suddenly that the man was demented and barely in control. Then she noticed that his hands were bloodstained.

Abruptly the man's anger meshed with and unleashed her own, and swinging up into her saddle she glared down at him. 'Sirshiant,' she said, 'you need lessons in discretion I think. Have your Captain and his Commander report to me when you return to barracks.'

The man's control slipped a little further, but he managed a restrained salute. Sylvriss swung the horse round, making him jump clear, then urged it forward at a slow walk.

She had gone barely ten paces when she heard, 'Break that door down and execute the occupants for violation of the Edict.'

She spun round in disbelief. Several of the patrol were

running towards the door she had been knocking on, and the Sirshiant was drawing his sword again. It, too, was blood-stained.

'No,' she cried and turning her horse she drove it at the advancing men. Those who knew her retreated immediately while the remainder hesitated only to be scattered as she swung the horse round and placed it firmly across the foot of the small stairway.

The Sirshiant strode forward and took hold of the horse's bridle in a white-knuckled grip. The horse tore it free and sent the man staggering. He raised his sword furiously.

'Sirshiant,' thundered Sylvriss. 'Are you insane? Raising your sword to me. You're under arrest. Hand me that sword and return immediately to your barracks.'

The man hesitated, then turned and walked away from her for a little way. Then he stopped and his shoulders hunched up as if he were pushing against a great weight.

'Sirshiant,' said the Queen, 'lay down your sword. That's an order.' But as he turned, she saw the last vestige of control slip away from him and knew that her words would be no more effective than autumn leaves in restraining him.

Some of the patrol saw it too and, breaking ranks, dashed forward. He struck the first to reach him with a single back-handed blow that laid him out along the street, blood streaming down his face, then turning towards the others he held out his left hand, inviting them forward, while his right hand brandished the sword menacingly. The patrol spread out in a wide, uncertain circle.

When he turned again, the Sirshiant's intent was hideously clear. Battle-fever. Bloodlust. The words burst into Sylvriss's mind. A lesser person would have faltered, disbelieving such a thing possible in this quiet City street. But, Muster-trained, Sylvriss saw it for what it was. Somehow, perhaps intentionally, she had released this demon. Now she must face it, with its dreadful hamstringing sword. There was no retreat. Her stomach was hard and hollow with a dreadful fear, but her only ally was her horse, and to allow fear to dominate would be to infect the animal and betray it. She leaned forward and whispered words of release to it; killing words. It was ready. Its eyes shone whitely and it pranced a little as with its rider it changed its fear to anger.

Hooves clattering on the hard stone street, and forelegs dancing high, the horse moved around the Sirshiant. With trembling hands, Sylvriss seized the handle of the staff that was part of every Muster rider's tackle. It stuck in its loop and her father's angry voice rushed in on her. 'Look after your equipment properly, girl. The dangerous attacks are those you're not expecting.'

The horse skittered to one side and lashed out a foot as the Sirshiant aimed a wild whistling sword cut at its head. The man moved with surprising speed, however, and the hoof barely touched him.

Then, at last, the staff came free, but with such suddenness that it slipped from Sylvriss's grasp. Instinctively, she flicked the elusive end and caught the staff boldly as it spun round. The movement looked calculated and confident and the Sirshiant stepped back into a low, crouching stance. Then, taking the sword in both hands, he lifted it above his head and charged forward with a great roar.

Sylvriss watched the attack coming. Judgement in her too was now the prisoner of battle-fever. She could still flee, it said faintly, but her rage was locked with the Sirshiant's madness in an ancient mutuality of purpose as intense as that of two passionate lovers. They would not part without catharthis.

The horse stepped backwards and sideways abruptly and the blow missed by a hairbreadth. Unbalanced by the unexpected lack of impact, the Sirshiant staggered round in the direction of his swing, and the horse ran into him. At the same time Sylvriss brought her staff down on to his head. His iron helmet protected him from injury, but the loud and incongruous clang was ringing in his ears as he hit the ground.

Curling up into a tight, protective knot, the Sirshiant rolled clear of the horse's hooves as it ran over him. To her horror, Sylvriss saw the man rise a little unsteady, but with the sword still in his hand and his madness rampant. She charged straight at him before he could recover fully and swung the staff at his head again. He jumped to one side and swung his sword to parry the blow.

The steel sliced effortlessly through the descending wood, and Sylvriss saw her staff shortened to half its length as the weighted end clattered across the echoing stones of the street.

Something deep inside her told her the end was near and a peculiar calmness flowed through her. She felt the swinging momentum of her horse as it turned, and, without thinking, she leaned forward towards her staggering attacker and drove the severed end of the staff at his throat.

The Sirshiant shied away from the blow but the weapon he had just forged drove into his cheek, and he felt its impact smashing teeth and tissue.

The demon in the man burst out in a blood-spewing cry and he drew back the sword for a blow that would have felled both horse and rider. But it was too late. The horse lashed out its hoof and caught him squarely under the chin, breaking his neck and lifting him clear off the ground, to fall spreadeagled on the ringing stones. The broken staff bounced out of his damaged face like a final act of disdain.

The horse reared, and let out a great scream of triumph, and Sylvriss heard her own voice, too, ringing with the Muster's battle cry. She felt her heart pounding and her breath gasping, and for a moment she almost lost consciousness under the conflicting torrents of elation and shame that flooded her.

As she watched the troopers, wide-eyed and fearful, gather up their erstwhile leader, and turn to her for their next orders, Sylvriss realised that the whole incident had taken only seconds. But she knew her life had been irrevocably changed. All things were changed now.

Chapter 51

Dan-Tor set little store by the Queen's escapade. With the Mathidrin tightening his grip on the bodies of the people, and with spies and rumours tightening his grip on their hearts and minds, such antics could not disturb his growing sense of satisfaction. In fact, he was quite pleased in some ways. He had seen the Queen returning, magnificent as ever on her great horse, but with fever-flushed cheeks and strange haunted eyes instead of the glowing vigour she normally returned with to pollute the whole Palace.

I'll hedge you in, he thought, make you fret and fume until your passions consume you. For your own good I'll curb you and watch you choke on the invisible leash. It would be a small piece of personal indulgence to heighten his pleasure at the change in circumstances.

As for that dolt of a Sirshiant who'd got himself killed, even that had been useful, not to say amusing. It would teach the newcomers to the City that they weren't dealing with Mandrocs now and they'd have to curb their bloodthirsty ways. More subtly, it would teach them not to underestimate the opposition they might face.

'Remind them that the penalty for that kind of stupidity is death,' he told his Commanders. 'In executing the sentence, the Queen merely saved me the trouble. Channel their resentment and loud talk into harder training.'

The need for those words, however, highlighted the doubts that occasionally rippled the surface of his contentment. The people crumbled, torn by doubt and ignorance, just as he had planned over the years. His assumption of the title of Ffyrst had freed him from many of the petty restraints that had so long irritated him, and since the seizure of Vakloss after Eldric's Accounting, he had begun to feel his progress in measurable strides.

But every now and then, when least expected, there would be a jolt of opposition, like a plough striking a hidden rock. The damage wrought to the Mandrocs by Jaldaric and his patrol, the rescue of the Lords, then Eldric returning to demand an Accounting. That had worked for the best in the end in that it precipitated the seizure of Vakloss, but it had been perilously dangerous, and Hawklan's hand could be felt there, surely? Hawklan? Where are you, you demon? Was Eldric's return but a feint within a feint?

But these were thoughts for darker moments. Already many of the Lords had fallen victim to his wide-strewn lies and some had even joined him in condemning Eldric and the others as traitors. Now he could concentrate on swaying the less gullible to his side. Then, as necessary, he could crush all other opposition by force of arms. But always he must remember that Hawklan too would be laying his traps.

You lose each time we meet, Hawklan. And you'll not tempt me to the Old Power now. Not now. No slip on my part will awaken you. I'll bind you yet, for when the Lords are crushed, the game will have slipped from you forever. When they're exhausted with slaying their own turncoat kin, and their hearts are dead at what they've had to do, then I'll launch my real armies against them.

The thought was comforting. It would be pleasant to see these creatures slaughtering one another again. A fitting atonement for the years their ancestors had made him spend in dark bondage.

'Patience, patience, patience,' he said to Dilrap. 'While we control the knowledge given to the people, events must surely move our way. Ignorance is a vital flux. Melting down the resistance of the people and making them more amenable to our suggestions.'

He stared at Dilrap thoughtfully. Why should I speak thus to this lackey? Why do I even keep him about me now? He's very useful, but no longer indispensable. Surely not gratitude? it had been Dilrap who engineered the details that gave a gloss of legality to his becoming Ffyrst. Dilrap had diligently rendered himself unnecessary and totally vulnerable. Dan-Tor narrowed his eyes, and Dilrap, catching the look, cringed visibly.

It came to him suddenly that Dilrap understood him, insofar as any of these creatures could understand him. Dilrap appreciated the subtleties of what he, Dan-Tor, was doing, independent of whether he approved of them or not, independent of whether he realised the ultimate outcome. He understood and marvelled. And envied. Worshipped, even?

That the pleasure he gained from this thought was simply the despised human trait of vanity, did not occur to Dan-Tor. It was an awe to which he was entitled. A faint, distant whisper asked 'Is he a danger?' but it could hardly be heard above the clamour of self-praise. No, no. Danger lies only in Hawklan and impatience. There's no danger in this scurrying bladder. He's just another human clutching gratefully at the knees of his executioner, in mortal fear for his mayfly life.

And, in part, he was right. Dilrap was in fear of his life, and he did understand the Ffyrst's machinations. But he neither envied nor worshipped. Just as the years of Dan-Tor's influence and 'improvement' to the Fyordyn way of life had accumulated to lead them disastrously from their ancient roots and leave them bewildered and lost, so years of scorn and derision had accumulated and festered in Dilrap to make him a man very different from the plump youth who had trailed after his stern and haughty father, and subsequently gone on to be the butt of every Palace wag. His trembling nature was shored by two great props: his love of the Queen and his deep and growing hatred of Dan-Tor.

But in understanding Dan-Tor, so he knew his own vulnerability, and, like Dan-Tor, he too wondered why he was still privy to the Ffyrst's musings. The uncertainty, and his sense of Dan-Tor's own uncertainty did little to calm him. His nights became fretful and nightmare-haunted, where once they had been a solace and a retreat from the torments of his waking hours.

'Majesty, I'm afraid,' he blurted out inadvertently to the Queen one day.

Sylvriss felt the weight of his burden added to her own. Strangely heavier to bear since her confrontation with the Sirshiant; having gained a deeper insight into the ancient ties between the Riddinvolk and their horses, part of her almost snarled, We're all afraid, Dilrap. Do what you have to do. Don't come bleating to me. But that same insight helped her set this savage shade aside and she laid her hand on his shoulder.

'I understand, Dilrap,' she said. 'Has anything happened to make you especially alarmed?'

Dilrap shook his head and then poured out his complex mixture of doubts and fears. Sylvriss let the words flow unhindered into the scented air of her chamber, until he fell silent. She stared at herself in a small mirror on her table, watching as a hand reached up and fingered a worried line etching itself permanently into her face.

'I've no answers, Dilrap,' she said eventually. 'Who can say what motivates the man?'

Of late she had been trying to pursue Dan-Tor's actions to their logical end, but had given up in despair. They seemed to lead to some form of Kingship. Not the cautious, thoughtful Kingship of Rgoric and his predecessors, but some appalling, unfettered authority over everyone and everything. But why? Why should anyone want such authority? And it could only be over a cowed and damaged people, for damaged they would be. The people of Vakloss were already too afraid to speak publicly in opposition to Dan-Tor, and sooner or later he would have to face the Lords in battle. Lords who would probably fight to a bitter end. The man's mind was beyond her.

She turned away from the mirror, with its wretched intimations of her own mortality. She too was afraid. The fear and mistrust that soaked the City had seeped into the Palace. Her many contacts were dwindling, and she had no way of knowing whether this was through increased caution or whether they had been arrested and had revealed their secrets to their interrogators.

She clung to what she knew and what she could reasonably infer; conjecture was infinite. Certainly, none of the Lords still in the City could be safely trusted. Those with whom she had made discreet contact had quietly slipped away, and those who were left kept an uncertain neutrality or sided openly with Dan-Tor, for a variety of reasons.

It came to her gradually that whether or not Dan-Tor discovered her covert opposition to him was irrelevant. She was effectively imprisoned in the Palace, guarded as she was on the increasingly rare occasions she was allowed into the City. Her ability to influence affairs or even to know of them was diminishing rapidly. He doesn't need to expose any of my deeds, she thought. Save one. His every action stifles opposition and isolates me.

But her one massive act of defiance was gathering a momentum of its own, and slipping beyond her control. It was a blessing turned fearful bane. As Dan-Tor had moved forwards more openly to greater power, his need for the King had declined, and consequently so had the attention lavished on him. However, as an iron ring of warriors had once guarded Ethriss, so Sylvriss had encompassed her husband with a silken ring of trusted attendants, herself its jewelled clasp, affecting the role of demure nursewife. Slowly she had continued weaning him from Dan-Tor's potions and slowly, uncertainly, the King had gained strength and well-being.

She glanced at her face in the mirror again and smoothed out the offending line. Her eyes shone wet for a moment as she knew that the concerns impressed on her face had not been primarily for herself, but for the King, and the constant worry about what he could and could not safely be told of outside events, and how he could be restrained from interfering without too much lying.

It had always been difficult, but now he was improving daily and all her decisions caused her torment. Was he or was he not strong enough to hear the full truth of what had happened? Would her very deceit destroy him and his love for her? Would he be pitched back into his black dependence on Dan-Tor? Or would he be prompted to some dire action against the man, here, with his own Palace infested with alien guards, and with his loyal Lords so far away?

Abruptly, she said, 'We must escape.'

Dilrap looked up, eyes wide. 'Escape, Majesty?' he echoed.

'Yes,' she said slowly. The words had slipped out almost unnoticed while she was preoccupied, but hanging in the air they crystallised her thoughts. 'Dan-Tor may tire of you soon, Dilrap. He may discover our schemes to hinder him. He'll surely find out about the King's health soon, and when that happens, where are we?' She swept her arm around the room, soft and comforting, a haven amidst the turmoil. 'We're already imprisoned. Trussed like market chickens. Helpless and impotent.'

Dilrap fluttered. Sylvriss's remarks had brutally summarised their predicament. He clutched at a straw. 'If the King is stronger, Majesty, cannot he help us?'

Sylvriss shook her head, but offered no other comment.

Dilrap fell silent. This was a domain that he knew the Queen kept even from him, for his own sake. 'But where could we go, Majesty?' he said eventually. 'And what of the King? And all the people who've helped us?' There was a hint of reproach in his voice.

The Queen replied without hesitation. 'We go to the Lords in the east,' she said. 'And the King goes with us. As for our helpers, we do them no great service in receiving their loyalty in this way. Not now. From now on they must watch and wait. Keep the old ways alive quietly, against the coming of happier times.'

Dilrap's eye flickered restlessly around the room as he tried to free Sylvriss's sudden determination from images of shining blades and hard, indifferent faces approaching him purposefully at the behest of some trivial signal from Dan-Tor. 'But how, Majesty? And when?' he said.

'The how should present no serious problem,' Sylvriss replied. 'You're allowed to move freely in and out of the Palace and I'm still allowed to move freely inside. A rendezvous and a small cache of supplies can be arranged inconspicuously enough, then it'll just be a matter of surprise and speed when a suitable opportunity presents itself.'

Dilrap's hands butterflied up in spite of himself. Sylvriss looked at him. 'Majesty . . .' he began awkwardly, 'I . . . can't ride.'

Sylvriss could not prevent a smile. 'I've held more inept than you on a saddle at a full gallop, Dilrap,' she said, with a soft laugh. 'You won't enjoy it, but you'll survive.'

Dilrap bowed his head. 'I'm a poor support to you, Majesty. In constant need of encouragement and courage.'

Sylvriss's hands took his and she looked directly at him, all humour gone. 'No, Dilrap,' she said, 'you work daily by the side of that man, deceiving him, lying to his evil, cracked face, delaying and gently hindering him. And you do this in the face of your own fear. Your courage and strength have sustained me over all these dark months. You belong among the very greatest who've ever held your office.'

Dilrap stood. No courtier, he was at a loss what to say. He bowed deeply to hide his face.

Sylvriss stood up also. 'There is one thing, however, that I must ask of you,' she said. Dilrap's eyes remained downcast. 'If the King and I are thwarted in this, you must keep yourself clear of all blame. Speak against us if you must.'

Dilrap looked up sharply.

Sylvriss raised her hand to prevent his protest. 'This is my order, Honoured Secretary,' she said. 'My Royal Command. I leave you no discretion. If all goes against us, it's imperative that you stay by Dan-Tor as long as you can and work for a time when you can make links with the Lords in the east. You understand?'

Dilrap bowed again.

When he had gone, Sylvriss reached out and extinguished the torches that illuminated her room. The darkness was restful. For a long time she sat on the broad sill of the window and stared up at the stars.

Now she would have to tell the King.

Chapter 52

Although Dan-Tor now controlled Vakloss and various other towns and villages, he was not sanguine about the Lords gathering their forces in the east. He knew that, quite rightly, Arinndier and the other Lords would never trust him to honour any treaty he might offer, so armed conflict seemed inevitable.

He had little doubt that his forces would ultimately be victorious. But while the prospect of these creatures slaughtering one another was not without its appeal, he would have preferred a quieter, more subtle approach. Chance rampaged too wildly through the ranks of war no matter what powers were ranged, and it was a way chosen by Him only as a last extremity.

Nor was his mind eased by the paucity of information that reached him from the east. With the birds bound he had, reluctantly, to rely on human spies, and these either never returned or brought him vague and contradictory information, thanks to the watchfulness and diligent deceit of the Goraidin.

Urssain fretted noisily. 'We've men enough, Ffyrst,' he said. 'Trained, disciplined and willing. More than enough. We should move now and overwhelm the Lords before they can build up their strength further.'

'Commander,' said Dan-Tor benignly, 'you must learn patience. Consider the consequences of such a venture. How many men would you need to keep this City subdued? There's little point winning a great victory against the Lords to find your back assailed by a rebellious Vakloss. And how many would you need to protect our flanks as you moved through increasingly debatable areas of the country?' Urssain looked inclined to answer, but Dan-Tor continued, his tone becoming more severe. 'And who do you think you'll be facing? It won't be their ornamental regiments. It'll be the kindred of those you saw fight in Orthlund. And they were youths led by a youth.

You'll be facing skilled fighters on their own ground, led by battle-hardened veterans from the Morlider War.' Dan-Tor brought his face close to Urssain's. 'But, say you break them, what then? They'll scatter into the mountains before they're damaged beyond repair, and we'll never be rid of them.'

Urssain bridled. This was defeatist talk. He would have killed any other man for less. The given word was that the Mathidrin were the new hope. They had brought peace back to the streets, and would now sustain a New Order that would make Fyorlund great again. The old High Guards had fled before them – unequivocal proof of the guilty part they had played in the decay of the country, and an unequivocal demonstration of the invincibility of the Mathidrin. With difficulty he swallowed his reply.

Dan-Tor noted the conflict in his protégé, and permitted himself a white-lined smile which made Urssain offer up a prayer to whatever spirit had bidden him keep his tongue still.

'Surely we can't leave them alone, Ffyrst?' he risked.

Dan-Tor turned and walked away from him. 'Can't we?' he said casually. Then, 'We'll see what your fellows think, Urssain. Arrange a meeting of all the City Commanders. It's time we discussed the matter. Perhaps it would be appropriate to call it a Council of War.'

Urssain spent the time waiting for the meeting pacing his room or sitting sprawled in his chair rapt in thought. He still couldn't read the brown devil. What had he missed? Why had Dan-Tor so mocked the idea of attacking the Lords, and why had he answered so enigmatically when he had suggested they shouldn't be left there unhindered?

He had still reached no conclusion when he accompanied Dan-Tor into the sparse, cold room where the Commanders were gathered, but he had determined to play a very cautious hand. This would be another time for watching and learning. He might not be able to read the man completely, but he could read him a damn sight better than any of the others.

He was disconcerted, however, to find that several of the waiting men were completely unknown to him, and he was only a little reassured when a quick glance at their faces showed that everyone, strangers included, seem to be unsettled to find themselves amongst unfamiliar faces.

As Dan-Tor entered, they rose as one, coming smartly to attention to greet their Lord. Like Urssain, they were all immaculate in dress uniform.

'Sit down, gentlemen,' said Dan-Tor affably, seating himself at the head of the long rectangular table, and motioning Urssain to sit at his right-hand side. 'I've asked you here because I wish to have your ideas about our problem in the east.'

Straight in, thought Urssain. No introductions. What's he doing? Who are these people? The questions thrust themselves into Urssain's mind, but he dismissed them for later consideration. Now he must watch and listen.

'Our discussion will be informal,' continued Dan-Tor. 'I'm expecting no great strategy to emerge, but with the City and much of the countryside reasonably under control we must begin to bend our minds to this problem, and we have to start somewhere.'

Urssain kept his own face neutral as he watched those now turned to focus on the presence beside him. Only Aelang understood. The others were relaxing. They were taking their Ffyrst's affability at its face value.

The immediate consensus accorded with Urssain's initial view. Attack now. Hard. Before they grow too strong. Dan-Tor listened with nodding interest as various company prides and promises were paraded before him. Urssain said nothing.

Then, as he had with Urssain, Dan-Tor dropped in the occasional comment about troop strengths, supply problems, lack of reliable intelligence, debatable loyalties etc, and slowly, his own strategy appeared. The Lords should be left, he suggested.

The idea was dismissed out of hand. With respect, Ffyrst – allow your enemy to build up his strength? The talk bubbled on again.

But in gathering his strength would he not also gather more mouths to feed, more bodies to shelter, more minds to keep busy? Dan-Tor offered tentatively.

Again the idea was dismissed without consideration. Urssain

continued to say nothing, and began to sit very still. He noticed that Aelang was doing the same.

Inexorably, however, tangled in the snares and traps that Dan-Tor had strewn, the meeting drifted into repetition. The Lords must be attacked. But that would be very dangerous. They couldn't be left because they would build up their strength and . . .

'And?' asked Dan-Tor.

And they'll attack us, obviously.

Dan-Tor spoke very quietly. Who then would have the long supply lines to maintain? Who then would have the odium of living off the land they passed over – local disaffection ever threatening their flanks? Who then would have to assault fresh troops in entrenched positions after a long journey? Aren't these the very reasons why it's too dangerous for us to attack them?

A silence descended on the room. One of the globes spluttered fitfully.

Dan-Tor stood up. 'Gentlemen, ponder this before we meet again: the consolidation and cautious expansion of the territory we hold and the building up of a conscript army to defend it. Will not this, together with the pressure of maintaining their own growing army, eventually force the Lords to leave their mountain strongholds and attack us? And when they arrive, tired and extended, should we not offer them first our con-scripts, whose destruction will tire them further and rack their consciences with its pointless horror? Will that then not leave us with the simple task of holding our ground until they are so weakened and demoralised that we can destroy them utterly at little cost to ourselves?'

No one spoke.

Dan-Tor continued, his voice icy. 'Ponder this also, gentle-men. If I can defeat your strategy with mere words, have no illusions what the Lords and their High Guards will do to you. There is enough uncertainty in combat without adding mind-less folly to it. For your future guidance, do not speak at these meetings unless you have something pertinent to say. And save your barrack-room bravado for the youth corps.'

Then, suddenly and terribly, his presence filled the room.

'You are the Commanders of my Mathidrin. Faithful servants who will be rewarded as my power grows; grows beyond limits you can imagine. But you are bound to me and by me. You can be expunged at my whim. Serve me well.'

Urssain stood outside the Westerclave watching his fellow Commanders leave. He was glad of the overcast sky and the failing light which made it easier for him to keep his eyes in the shade. What a massacre! Lessons within lessons there. He would need to think about what had happened very carefully. Those strange faces? Faces themselves surprised to be among strangers. I alone know my resources, was Urssain's reading of the message. You are all dispensable – there are others who can replace you.

'Weather's a little more like home, eh Urss?' The voice was unmistakable and brought Urssain very sharply to the present. There was one lesson for a start. He'd been too long at the Palace. Too long away from the treacherous and dangerous in-fighting that was the stock-in-trade of ambitious Mathidrin. That was a serious mistake.

He turned to look at Aelang, his erstwhile sponsor and Commander at Narsindalvak. Feared throughout the ranks of the Mathidrin, Aelang's vicious cruelty and ruthless scheming were almost legendary. It had come as no surprise to Urssain when he learnt that the Sirshiant the Queen had killed had belonged to one of Aelang's companies.

'Indeed,' said Urssain, trying to focus on Aelang's eyes. However, like his own, they were shaded in the poor light by his helmet. Standing watchfully behind Aelang were two aides. Urssain knew well enough the trail of disappearances and accidents that had marked the rise of Aelang, and the presence of the two men reminded him that he too must be more careful in dark and lonely places with so many high-ranking Mathidrin now in the City. His nearness to Dan-Tor was as much a provocation as it was a protection. 'Indeed,' he repeated. It was some measure of Aelang that he thought of Narsindal as home. 'But I'm afraid I've grown used to the mellower climes of Fyorlund.'

Aelang smiled, revealing an array of discoloured teeth with

prominent canines. Urssain remembered that in their bolder moods, and well out of earshot, the troopers used to call him Mandrocsson.

'Ah. You always had your eye to softer billets, Urss,' Aelang growled jovially. 'Always anxious to rise above us humble foot soldiers.'

Part jibe, part congratulation, part threat, part calling in of old debts, thought Urssain. Don't turn your back.

'It's not quite as soft as it looks, Aelang,' he replied with equal joviality. 'As you'll find out now you've managed to find your way about here.'

Aelang laughed knowingly. 'Well you've not changed, I'll say that. I should've known better than to bandy words with a courtier.' He stepped closer and spoke softly, confidentially. 'Things are happening that we'd hardly dared to imagine, Urss. Our . . . beloved Ffyrst has used the King's folly to considerable effect. Plenty of opportunities now for those who can see them . . . and more to come if I'm any judge.' Urssain did not reply. Aelang continued, his voice even lower. 'You're the Ffyrst's man in Vakloss.' Thanks to me, said his eyes. 'I'm his man at Narsindalvak. But there were strange faces amongst us today, Urss? The Ffyrst looks only for the most . . . capable, does he not? I think that with all these changes going on, you and I should protect one another's backs, don't you?'

Urssain scrutinised Aelang's shaded face. He must be feeling insecure, he thought, to suggest that. Or was it a threat? Join me, or else. Urssain's eyes turned to the departing Commanders. Either way, it made sense. He and Aelang were well placed, but they would indeed be targets for any ambitious sparks looking to improve their lots. And he did know Aelang for what he was. It could do little harm to have him . . . in partnership, as it were. At least he'd be able to keep an eye on him.

Slowly he nodded. 'I'd be only too happy to give you any assistance that you might expect from a brother officer, Commander,' he said with a smile.

Aelang chuckled. 'Brother officer,' he said approvingly. 'You *have* been here a long time. Still, as I said, you've not changed. It's been good seeing you again.' And, slapping

Urssain's arm affectionately, he strode off towards his waiting carriage, followed by his two companions.

Urssain cursed silently and placing his left hand casually behind his back flexed his fingers frantically. Aelang had struck a nerve with his heavy gold ring and Urssain knew the arm would be dead for over a minute. It had been Aelang's signature on their agreement.

That could have been poison, it said. Or I could have disembowelled you while you groped for feeling in that arm. So look to me. These things happen so easily. Urssain cursed again.

Aelang, reaching his carriage, turned and threw a jaunty acknowledgement to him with a flick of his hand. Urssain let his sleeve knife fall into his right hand and returned the same friendly gesture making sure that the light caught its blade as he let it slip back into his sleeve again. Aelang's Mandroc grin and his grim laugh reached him, then the carriage was driving away, merging into the failing light.

Urssain turned and strode briskly through the maw of the Westerclave. His left arm was easier, but Aelang's message had shaken him. Fear of Dan-Tor was one thing. That was deep and abiding, the fear of the rabbit for the lion. There was no question of resistance, so superior was the one over the other. But fear of Aelang – the old barrack-room fear – that was insupportable.

You're right, Aelang, he thought, as his heels beat a relentless tattoo along the Westerclave's corridors. I've grown too lax and easy away from Narsindalvak. But I'll not risk everything I've gained out of carelessness. Not now. I've hacked my way through the ranks and now I hold the high ground. Your reminder is most timely. It could also be your death warrant in due course.

Chapter 53

A strong, ill-tempered wind blew the rain in gusty squalls across the fields, bending and shaking the trees and bushes, and confining most living things to the warmth of their nests and burrows. It rattled branches against windows, like urgent messengers, and whispered through cracks and crannies the draughty news that soon the weather would turn its face from light and warmth and start its journey into the cold Fyorlund winter.

Wrapped and huddled against its raucous jostling, four horsemen moved greyly through the countryside by quiet and little-used paths. For a moment they paused and then they faded into the gloom of a small copse. Within minutes they had rigged and camouflaged the small shelter that had housed them each night since they had left Eldric's stronghold.

Sitting on the torch-dried earth, they ate a frugal meal in companionable silence as the wind buffeted their shelter peevishly and showers of raindrops cascaded intermittently from the wind-shaken trees to drum over their heads like horses galloping suddenly by.

Gavor eyed a spider struggling to climb its slender swinging thread, but settled ungraciously for the bread that Hawklan gave him.

'We've been lucky so far,' said Tel-Odrel. 'The weather's been very helpful. But we'll not get much further by stealth; we're nearly at Vakloss.'

Hawklan looked at the Goraidin and nodded. 'We'll have to separate soon, then,' he said. 'Having us around might jeopardise your mission.'

The two Goraidin exchanged glances.

Tel-Odrel shrugged apologetically. 'Yes,' he said. 'I'm afraid so.' He looked a little embarrassed. 'Establishing contacts in and around Vakloss is vital. You realise that. Given that that must come first, we'll help you all we can, but you don't even know what you're going to do, do you?' There was a barely controlled exasperation in his voice.

'I know exactly what I'm going to do, Tel,' said Hawklan lightheartedly. 'I'm going to meet Dan-Tor and ask him why he's done what he's done.' But his affected levity merely darkened the mood that Tel-Odrel's words had created.

Both the Goraidin frowned. They had both stopped trying to dissuade the two Orthlundyn from what they saw as a suicidal mission, but its apparent futility still distressed them.

Hawklan continued, more seriously. 'You're a soldier, Tel, and you've a clear-cut task before you. I'm not and I haven't. But we both know that when logic and reason end, we have to follow our intuition. I'm a healer. I have to go to the heart of the sickness, whatever it costs me.'

'I know, I know,' said Tel-Odrel quickly. 'But . . .'

Hawklan waved him to silence. He leaned forward and looked into the Goraidin's eyes. 'Tel,' he said. 'As we near the City, every living thing is beginning to cry out to me. It's as if there's something in the very air round here. What Isloman heard in those mountains, I feel all around. A terrible purposeful corruption. It wasn't there when we left the City . . . or . . . at least I didn't feel it.' He paused, momentarily shaken by the realisation that he too was probably changing. 'But in any case I'm scarcely master of myself because of it. It's certainly beyond me to walk away from such pain. And I'm drawn inexorably to its centre. Only there will I know what to do.'

Tel-Odrel gave up his last attempt with a sigh. 'Well, at least make yourselves . . . less conspicuous. Cover up your weapons, don't talk too much . . .' His voice tailed off.

Outside, the blustering wind rattled the little shelter as it continued its relentless buffeting journey across the countryside.

Over the months since the arrest of the Lords, Sylvriss had pursued her resolve to free her husband from Dan-Tor's influence and restore him to health. She had worked painstakingly and heartbreakingly, knowing that Dan-Tor could at any time, either on an inadvertent whim or as an act of malicious political necessity if he discovered the truth, undo her work with effortless ease.

She had long believed that Rgoric's recurring illness was due in no small part to the medication that Dan-Tor plied him with. However, more subtle causes became apparent to her as she built up the silken wall of dutiful and acquiescent behaviour that kept the King from Dan-Tor's sight.

She began to realise that the very presence of the man was important, with his treacherous words that undermined where they purported to support, and increased the King's burdens when he was at his most weary, so that he would more readily relinquish them. It was a task of joy to replace these sinister blandishments with her own love and tenderness, and she frequently wondered what self-deception in Dan-Tor was preventing him from realising the effects of his absence from the King. The man puzzled her increasingly. For all his perceptive ruthlessness he had the strangest blind spots in his vision. However, as she watched the man she married fight through to some semblance of health and well-being, Sylvriss's hate for Dan-Tor grew apace.

The deceit she practised on Dan-Tor was a matter only of deep satisfaction to her, but she had also to practise a deceit upon her husband to keep from him learning of the true state of his country, and that was a matter of increasing grief to her.

At first her lies had been matters of minor expedience to quiet the restless monarch's temporarily fevered mind. Then had developed a strange, idyllic period of mutual self-deception in which both had lost themselves passionately in their old affections new-found.

Sylvriss entered this world against her judgement, but it was as if the life they could have had, without the baleful influence of Dan-Tor, was allowed to them in those few months. Although in her darker moments Sylvriss saw its ultimate futility, she suffered no real regrets for what she was doing, but drew great strength and resolve from her husband's happiness, albeit that it was illusory.

But just as their marriage would have changed over undisturbed years, so now it changed over the undisturbed months as

Rgoric became stronger. More and more he began to enquire about matters of State, and more and more Sylvriss had to weave an elaborate web of deception to protect him from a direct confrontation with Dan-Tor. That this loathsome gossamer hung from an arbour of trust gave Sylvriss nothing but pain, and she longed for its passing even as she strengthened it under the dictates of necessity. Now the tide of circumstances had swept the moment upon her and she stood alone and frightened in her chamber.

'Go to your room,' Rgoric had said quietly and distantly. 'Go there and wait for me. I'll be some time.'

Around her beautiful Fyorlund pictures decorated the walls, and elaborate carvings fringed the ceiling, while the furniture and carpetings were unmistakably the work of Riddin craftsmen. Sylvriss had blended the two cultures into an elegant and harmonious whole, but she saw little of it now. Her mind was blank with fear and dismay.

For long hours in the past she had rehearsed how she might best tell her husband the truth, but no convincing accounting had ever come to her. That morning, however, advised by Dilrap that their simple escape plans had been laid, she had told him.

Ironically, her very restlessness during the previous night had prompted a worried enquiry from Rgoric which she had stilled only with a promise to explain her concerns to him the following day.

As they breakfasted, Rgoric seemed preoccupied. Eventually he raised an affectionate and enquiring eyebrow, and Sylvriss pushed her chair back and stood up. 'Just excuse me for a few minutes,' she said.

Rgoric took her hand and looked at her earnestly. 'Just a few minutes,' he said, part entreaty, part demand. She looked down at him. Older now than his years, by dint of his lined face and greying hair, he was still weak and a shadow of his former self. But he was no longer the bent, haunted creation that Dan-Tor had made. He was the man she had married. Straight and upright, with a steady hand and clear eye.

She bent down and kissed him. 'Just a few,' she confirmed.

When she returned, he stood up and stared at her. 'Your

Muster uniform,' he said, smiling delightedly. 'The one you insisted on wearing when we rode home from Riddin. I remember. Everyone in their fancy clothes and you in your simple tunic and cloak. And you outshone them all.'

'Not too difficult, the way you Fyordyn ride,' Sylvriss replied nervously.

Rgoric smiled again and looked at her proprietorially. 'I'd no idea you still had it. And it fits too.'

Sylvriss patted her stomach and blushed. 'Just about,' she said. Then Rgoric's expression changed, and he put a concerned arm around her shoulder. 'You need to feel the strength of the Muster and your family behind you before you can tell me whatever it is that's been tormenting you?' he said.

Sylvriss returned his embrace and led him to a long couch. She had hoped that the inspiration of the moment would aid her, but nothing came. Where could she start on this hideous saga that would not risk plummeting her husband down into the darkness from which he had been so agonisingly lifted.

Eventually she spoke the problem out loud. 'I don't know where to start,' she said.

'Then start anywhere,' said Rgoric, simply. He reached up and ran his hand through her hair. As she looked up, their eyes met and an overwhelming poignancy tightened her chest and throat.

What followed next she barely recalled. The whole tale flowed out of her; not hysterically, but with an almost unstoppable force as if that would support Rgoric as much as it might inundate him.

Alone now, she clenched her hands in regret and concern as she went over the subtleties and nuances, the complexities of events that she had brushed aside in her haste. And yet, she began to console herself, he had not fallen screaming into dementia, or raged, or reproached her for her perfidy. Just a simple 'Go to your room. Go there and wait for me. I'll be some time.'

But how long ago was that? She took a deep breath to quieten her heart. She must find him. 'Wait for me,' he had said, but what was a modicum of defiance when added to the total of the months of deception?

Total. The word brought an image to her. An image which she had had at times in the early years of her marriage – an image of a cornucopia rich with many-coloured gifts. Suddenly her guilt fell from her like an ill-fastened cloak. They were each the total of one another's making. They would be together now, whether the moment was one of joy or horror. They were irrevocably joined for this span of their lives. Even though he might at this very moment be rejecting her, he would still be her support, he would still be half her life, and she his.

She straightened her uniform and looked in the mirror. The face gazing back at her was flushed, and radiated a mixture of defiance and triumph. Years of habit took her hands to those small flaws in her appearance that no one else would see, and the face smiled as she saw their practised concern.

Before she reached the door, it opened and Rgoric entered. He was dressed in a simple field uniform of the kind that he had worn to complement his bride when they had returned from Riddin. Around his head was the simple iron ring that was the ancient crown of the Kings of Fyorlund.

Chapter 54

Dan-Tor shifted uneasily on his chair.

Dilrap, sitting at a nearby table and immersed in papers, echoed the movement with a twitch of his own. For all his apparent oblivion, he was in fact watching Dan-Tor closely. The Ffyrst's moods were beginning to alarm him.

There was an increasing restlessness in him that was wholly uncharacteristic, and some of his recent decisions seemed to have been whimsical and arbitrary – as though made in irritated haste.

But why? Dilrap asked himself repeatedly as his unseeing eye scanned the documents in front of him. Why? Dan-Tor, meticulous and endlessly patient in his cunning, usually became more so in the face of opposition. So what was amiss?

What indeed? Dan-Tor was occupied with the same question. Nothing in his schemes seemed to be awry. True, the City was bubbling with anger at his treacherous rearrest of Eldric, and rumours of the attack on the Queen, but that would pass. In general, opponents were becoming doubters; doubters, allies. The young flocked to the newly formed Youth Corps which, with its uniform and parades and raucous, pounding music, provided a mixture of carnival and memories of ancient martial glory.

The old, too, turned increasingly to him to be treated with the ingenious salves he had prepared for the myriad tiny ills that he had so assiduously infected the country with. Indeed it would have been difficult for anyone to analyse or locate the source of the miasma of discontent that pervaded Fyorlund, so long and subtle had been its spreading. Dan-Tor, however, offered the way with a clear light. The fault lay with the Lords who had taken advantage of a sick and ailing King to gratify their own desires for power and self-aggrandisement. Only he had stood against them and thwarted their schemes. And now they were preparing armies in the east to seize by force what he, using Fyorlund's most ancient and precious institution, the Law, had denied them.

The mindless, unthinking roar of the mob and their mounting intolerance were the opening notes of the great symphony he had been so long preparing. Those who thought and saw nearer the truth hid their heads increasingly for fear of losing them. And yet? He banged the arms of his chair with clenched fists.

Dilrap looked up. 'Ffyrst?' he ventured hesitantly. An angry flick of those long bony hands bade him be silent. Dilrap dropped his eyes hastily. A tiny insect crawled painstakingly across the unread page he was staring at. He moved his hand to crush it, then paused and cast a glance at Dan-Tor. Suddenly his intention and its arbitrariness flooded him with shame. Go on your way, he thought. Go on your way. Who am I to take your life for a mere whim? Who am I to divine your purpose? The insect continued its laborious journey undisturbed and Dilrap watched it protectively until it disappeared into a sheaf of papers.

Dan-Tor stood up and turned his head from side to side as if looking for a sound that was annoying him. A narrow band of streaming sunlight cut across him like a bright sash. Dilrap willed himself into absolute stillness, and for an interminable chain of minutes he felt the very air around him was dancing to the beat of his pulse.

The chain was snapped with a deafening abruptness by the opening of a door and the seemingly thunderous footsteps of a servant running across the hall. Without speaking, the man bowed low to Dan-Tor and held out a small decorated gold plate bearing a white card.

Scowling, Dan-Tor picked up the card and studied it. Then with a curt nod he dismissed the servant. Dilrap turned to look at him directly. The man's eyes were like pinpoints of red fire, but the voice was like ice.

'The King requires that we attend him immediately,' he said.

*　　*　　*

The wind was still blowing quite strongly, and the weather seemed uncertain whether it should continue to celebrate summer or warn of impending winter, when Hawklan and Isloman mingled with the morning crowds filling the streets of Vakloss.

Both were glad of the opportunity to wrap their cloaks about them, as there was also a strange tension in the City. Faces among the crowds were for the most part grim and downcast; at odds with the streets of decorated and colourful buildings. Hawklan remembered Lorac's parting advice. 'Don't skulk and don't look anyone directly in the eye if you don't want to be seen.'

Hawklan still had no clear idea how to reach Dan-Tor other than by walking directly to the Palace and asking for him. He looked discreetly at Isloman. That he should voluntarily walk into the hands of the man who had tried twice to capture him was one matter; taking with him his faithful friend was another entirely. But even as he considered this he heard in his mind Isloman's voice. 'I've questions of my own for this man.' Then came the memory of Aynthinn laughing gently and telling him that no Orthlundyn would follow anyone blindly. The memory was reassuring. At least this time he knew he was walking into danger. This time he would be lulled by no strange power, nor bound by fear for a hostaged innocent. This time he would be armed in every way, and with someone to guard his back. He might yet be taken, but not easily.

His thoughts were interrupted by the sound of breaking glass and angry voices. Looking round, he saw a group of Mathidrin smashing down the door of a nearby house. Two of them pushed past the remains of the broken door and reappeared within seconds dragging an old man, blood streaming down his face. Instinctively, Hawklan moved towards the group, shaking off Isloman's hesitant, restraining hand. He found, however, that he was just part of a larger movement, as people rushed out of neighbouring houses, and other passersby converged on the scene.

The old man was struggling violently, and angry shouts began to rise from the crowd as the Mathidrin started to beat him. It looked for a moment as though the crowd would turn on the men but Hawklan sensed that their anger was counterweighted by an equal fear. Eventually, to resolve the situation, one of the Mathidrin raised a baton to strike the old man.

Hawklan could not restrain himself. 'No,' he cried, his voice commanding and clear, even over the noise of the crowd. The trooper stopped, his baton still raised, and Hawklan found himself looking at the man down an aisle of watching faces, as the crowd opened before him spontaneously. The crowd's anger seemed to possess him.

'Leave him alone,' he said and, striding forward, he snatched the hovering baton from the trooper, now open-mouthed at the sight of this approaching green-eyed apparition. Even as he strode towards the man, Hawklan felt the will of the waiting crowd changing, urging him on, and as he snatched the baton, a great roar, angry and defiant, filled the small square.

The globes in the Throne Room had been extinguished, but the room was alive with sunlight bursting in through the single large window. The old torches had been re-struck and complemented the sunlight by illuminating the arched corridors and the upper balcony so that they seemed to be open and spacious, instead of lowering and forbidding as though they harboured night predators in their shadows. Under the caress of this lighting, the stone throne shone and glittered as it had not been seen for decades.

Rgoric looked down at his hand resting on the arm of the throne. There was no movement in the torches, only the occasional dimming of the natural light as a cloud obscured the sun, but the polished stone seemed to dance patterns of light around his hand, like revellers in a Festival Round Dance.

The effect of Sylvriss's tale had been like someone shaking him brutally out of a long and fitful sleep tormented by frightening and elusive images. He had lurched away from it, but Sylvriss had held him with her unremitting telling as she would a headstrong mount. Inexorably, fragmented pieces of memory tumbled into place to form a grim mosaic of truth. A mosaic bound hard in the matrix of his wife's long and faithful love.

Perhaps, he realised, he had been felled by an opponent whose skill and cunning were beyond any man's ability to fathom. But that was of no concern. The weakness still pervading his body tore at him to return to his oblivion, but Sylvriss's love and courage had reached through to the long-dormant King she had married, and he saw only that, as his wife had done, he must pick up the battle flag he had dropped and hold it high again at whatever cost and against whatever foe.

His reverie was disturbed by the opening of the hall's great double doors, to reveal the lank frame of his Chief Physician and adviser.

Dan-Tor started as he entered the Throne Room, and a tremor passed through him such as he had not known since he was awakened from the darkness. The work of the craftsmen of the Great Alliance flooded through the hall, opening its dark crevices into airy openness, and decking the stern figure on the throne with a powerful radiance.

For an instant, the fear gripped him that this light might penetrate even into his own black soul and lay him open to the sight of the man he had worked so diligently to destroy.

That horse witch! he thought. I'll roast her in the belly of her favourite horse when my Mandrocs have finished with her . . .

'Majesty.' An awe-stricken voice interrupted his proposed vengeance, as Dilrap dropped to his knees involuntarily.

Dan-Tor walked slowly forward to greet his King. Stopping at the foot of the steps, he bowed slowly and respectfully. 'Majesty,' he said, allowing his voice to fill with genuine surprise and delight. 'To see you so recovered is as welcome as it is unexpected.'

The King nodded, but his face was unreadable. 'Lord Dan-Tor,' he said. 'The time we've both sought for has arrived. I must now shoulder again those burdens of office that you've faithfully borne for me these many years. And, as the Law requires, I must ask you formally to Account for your Stewardship.'

Dan-Tor dropped his head to hide the red anger in his eyes. 'You shame me, Majesty,' he said regretfully. 'Had I known you were so near recovery after the many years of failure I'd have devoted myself more diligently to your well-being. Perhaps then you'd have sat here many months ago. As for an Accounting . . . sadly, Majesty, I've been so occupied with matters of State that I'm ill-prepared to give one of even the most recent happenings, so grim have they been.'

I'm sure you've done nothing that you could reproach yourself for, Lord,' said the King. 'And I require no stringent rendering immediately. That we can do at our leisure together with the Lords of the Geadrol. Just tell me briefly what has passed in my land since my illness deluded me into arresting four of my good and faithful Lords. Such a telling will satisfy the requirements of the Law, will it not, Honoured Secretary?'

Dilrap started at being dragged into this improvisation of the King's, but after a protracted stammer and a cadenza of flourishes and twitches, he managed to say, 'Yes, Majesty.'

How many years' work has that hag undone? Dan-Tor thought, but when he looked up at the King his face was concerned. 'Majesty, are you sure that you're fully recovered? We've had these flashes of sunlight in the past, only to fall into darkness again.'

The King smiled slightly. 'I'm not the man I was, Lord Dan-Tor,' he said. 'But I'm recovered sufficiently, rest assured.'

An echoing silence filled the hall as Dan-Tor fought back an urge to strike down this usurping clown. There were too many unknown factors at work here. What other schemes had been prepared in secret? Had Hawklan's hand reached into his Palace yet again to wreck this havoc? A rash stroke could destroy not only the spectacular progress of the last few months, but the work of years. The shadow of his Master's wrath almost froze his tongue to his palate. He must play this farce through until a pattern or an opportunity emerged.

'Majesty,' he said, with a helpless gesture, 'you must forgive my hesitation. I'm still overcome by the suddenness of your recovery. However, perhaps I should begin by explaining about . . .'

Seeing his opponent regaining his balance, the King raised his hand. 'Forgive me, Lord Dan-Tor,' he said pleasantly. 'Before you begin, there's an important matter I must attend to so that you'll be spared the embarrassment of retailing my folly to my face. Guards.'

The power in the command startled Dan-Tor. He turned

hastily, half expecting to see an escort of High Guards approaching him purposefully. Even the appearance of the two Mathidrin door guards did not totally reassure him. The Mathidrin were by nature corruptible. Or were they High Guards in disguise again? A voice deep inside counselled patience, but its tone was shrill.

'Fetch me the Lord Eldric and his son Jaldaric immediately,' said the King. The two men hesitated, blinking at the sight of the King, powerful and whole, on his throne, while their Lord stood stark and alone like a lightning-blasted tree.

'Immediately,' thundered the King unequivocally, and the two men disappeared hastily.

Dan-Tor spun round and stared at the King, as the sound of the retreating guards faded into the distance. 'Majesty,' he cried. 'The Lord Eldric and his son are dangerous traitors. They and their co-conspirators have plunged the City, the whole country, into anarchy and turmoil. Even now . . .'

A sharp gesture from the King cut him short. 'I'm aware of recent happenings, Lord. And due reparation will be sought from the offenders, sooner than they imagine.' He turned and looked Dan-Tor fully in the face. 'Have no fear. Our Law is only a reflection of natural justice. It can no more be set aside by man than the tides can be stopped.'

'Majesty, I implore you. Beware these men.'

'Enough, Lord,' said the King firmly. 'Illness may have marred the greater part of my reign, but nothing shall mar what remains. I'll interrogate these men and end this horror that threatens to destroy our land.'

'But Majesty, the matter's complex . . .'

The King's tone became menacingly soft. 'Lord Dan-Tor. This is a matter which I must attend to before I come to your Accounting and my reward to you for your trials. It irks me to be thus badgered.'

Dilrap stepped back a pace as he felt the two personalities clash. Dan-Tor tightened his fist behind his back with such force that Dilrap heard the bones cracking. He felt as though the grip was choking the life out of him.

Enough of this, screamed part of Dan-Tor's mind; caution, whispered another. There's deep treachery here. It had been an error to move so precipitately at the King's unexpected bidding. He must find a way out of the hall . . . contact Urssain.

He slumped slightly and raised his hands apologetically. 'Forgive me, Majesty,' he said, in a tone that rang alien to his own ears, 'I'm still concerned for your welfare . . . as always.'

The King nodded, but did not speak.

'It'll be some time before the guards can bring the prisoners to you, Majesty,' Dan-Tor continued. 'May I take the opportunity to gather some documents which will summarise present conditions for you admirably?'

The King waved him silent. 'That won't be necessary, Lord. I'm not interested in niceties at the moment. As I said, a simple telling will be sufficient.' He smiled broadly. 'However, I'll admit that I'm looking forward to examining your Stewardship in detail in due course. I'm sure there's much to be learnt from the way you've handled things during this period of unrest. But for now, stay by my side, as you've done for so many years.'

Dan-Tor bowed a silent acknowledgement, and stepping to one side, turned to face the door through which Eldric and his son must enter. As he did so, his eyes skimmed the balconies and archways searching for strange shadows. He saw none, but the openness of the place in the torchlight made him uneasy.

The King leaned back in the stone throne and, to his surprise, he found it oddly comfortable. He rested his hands on the brilliant polished arms and felt a great relaxation pass through him. His wife's tale, his own memories, his observations of Dan-Tor, all came together in a vivid whole and he saw what lay before him.

Strange, he thought, to be so at ease in the face of such a testing.

The silence hung, sun-filled and peaceful in the hall, like the quiet of an ocean poised at the turn of the tide when the great forces that determine its destiny are balanced equally. Then, like the first swell of new waves, came the distant sound of marching feet. As they approached, so the deep peace he felt faded like a glowing memory.

Presently, four figures appeared in the doorway.

The King dismissed the guards and ordered Eldric and Jaldaric forward. For a moment Eldric hesitated as if unable to believe either his eyes or his ears. He caught hold of his son's arm.

'Eldric,' said the King. 'You were not wont to be so sluggish.'

'Majesty,' whispered Eldric, 'forgive me.' Then instinctively straightening his soiled uniform, he marched forward to the foot of the throne. Jaldaric followed him, his face set, but his eyes uncertain.

For a long moment the two men looked at one another. The King felt some of Eldric's ordeal and was sickened, while Eldric felt the King's new health and was heartened. Tiny glimmers of hope began to flicker tentatively into life.

'My Lord Eldric,' said the King, 'we've been born into a time of great change, it would seem. Darkness and strife stalk Fyorlund. Ancient ways fade into memory, institutions crumble, kin takes arms against kin as your fellow Lords arm themselves in the east. Is it their intention to move against this City?'

'Quite probably, Majesty,' replied Eldric without hesitation.

Damn these people and their loathsome openness, thought Dan-Tor.

The King showed no surprise at Eldric's response. 'War is not a matter overburdened by logical considerations, Lord Eldric,' he said. 'But someone somewhere usually has a semblance of a reason for it. As you seem to be the first mover in this unhappiness, perhaps you'd tell me what demands you'd make of me.'

Eldric searched the face of the King again, fearfully aware of his last interview in this hall when he had been swept away in a grim black tide. There was tiredness in the King's face, but strength also. And his eyes, those traitors to the inner self, betrayed no instability.

He bowed. 'Majesty, I make no demands of you. I'm one of your Lords. A servant to you, the Law, the Geadrol and the people. I would make only a request.' He paused, but the King gestured to him to continue. 'I would request an Accounting, Majesty. An Accounting before yourself and the Lords of the Geadrol.'

Before the King could reply, there was a clamour outside the hall and, abruptly, a Mathidrin officer burst in. Eldric and

Jaldaric turned round to examine this intruder, while the King folded his arms and discreetly laid his hand on his sword hilt. Dan-Tor, however, almost staggered. The unease that had been increasingly tormenting him over the past days suddenly burst upon him like a raging flood. For a moment he felt as though his mind was like a boat torn from its moorings and tossed to and fro at the whim of some unregarding storm.

'Your request is granted, Lord Eldric.' The King's voice was soft, but it filled the hall and cut through Dan-Tor's whirling thoughts.

He spun round to face the King. 'Majesty,' he said, starting forward. His hands were opening and closing as if to grasp the reins of power he could feel slipping away. 'No . . .' He stopped, mouth agape, paralysed by indecision. He must strike the King down now before it was too late. But this Mathidrin was no ordinary harbinger. He was riding on an evil tide.

Unbidden, the man spoke. 'Ffyrst,' he said, 'a great crowd surrounds the Palace. A man at their head seeks audience with you.'

'What manner of man?' Dan-Tor said, his face rigid.

The Mathidrin was trembling, and seemed unable to speak.

Dan-Tor repeated his question, slowly and menacingly.

The man found his tongue. 'A warrior, Ffyrst. An Orthlundyn.'

The words blurred in Dan-Tor's hearing and a great roaring filled his ears. With a dreadful inhuman cry he strode from the hall.

Chapter 55

Wearily the King stood up and walked down the steps to face Eldric. The noise of Dan-Tor's leaving was echoing round and round the hall like a tormented spirit, and it weighed heavily on him.

'Eldric,' he said. 'My old friend and comrade-in-arms. Today, I've been either very wise or very foolish.'

Eldric barely heard the remark. 'Majesty,' he said in a mixture of awe and disbelief. 'Rgoric. You're your old self again?' He gazed into the King's face and nodded. 'Recovered,' he said. 'It's a miracle.'

'No miracle, Eldric,' the King replied. 'Only some strange fate and the single-minded devotion of my Queen. But she'll tell you all in due course. Right now we must consider your next course of action.'

Eldric frowned. 'Consider, Majesty? Consider? There's nothing to consider. We'll remain by your side and begin the undoing of all these ills.'

The King shook his head. 'You were not wont to be so rash, Eldric, you must realise that's not possible. We're effectively alone in the Palace. Certainly we've no armed friends to aid us. We could be slain within the next few minutes.'

Eldric's eyes opened in disbelief. 'Majesty, this can't be. You're the King. No one would dare . . .' His words faded, strangled by his own knowledge. Then came a little flare of optimism. 'But you held Dan-Tor here, in thrall, at your feet.'

The King shook his head again. 'The only chain that bound Dan-Tor was surprise and caution.' He smiled ruefully. 'We were both playing the same game. He was waiting to see what I intended and I was waiting for some measure of him. Now I fear we both have the measure of one another, and I'm the loser by it.'

'I don't understand, Majesty,' said Eldric, waving his arms vaguely.

'It doesn't matter,' retorted the King. 'Suffice it that I've managed to have you released. You must flee the City and head for your stronghold. Horses have been arranged for you.' He silence an impending interruption with a wave of his hand. 'On my express command, you'll levy the High Guards of *all* the Lords, and drive Dan-Tor and his Mathidrin from Vakloss and all Fyorlund.'

'Majesty.' Eldric almost shouted as he attempted to stem the King's flow. The King fumbled with a ring on his finger.

'Eldric, as you care for me, be silent and listen. Take this.' He thrust the Iron Ring of the Kings forcibly into Eldric's hand. 'We haven't the time for courtesies and explanations. That ring is my authority for what you must do.' He paused. 'You're aware of Dilrap's part in this affair?' he asked softly.

Eldric looked at the Secretary. 'The Queen told the Goraidin Yatsu he's to be trusted,' he said.

The King nodded. 'When circumstances permit, he's to be greatly honoured for the courage he's shown and the aid he's rendered our country. You must see to that, but now, go with him. Horses have been prepared for you but all relies on speed and surprise. Go now.'

Eldric swung from side to side in indecision. 'But, Majesty,' he said, 'what are you going to do? . . . And the Queen?'

The King straightened up. 'The Queen has gone already,' he said. 'I prevailed upon her when I realised what our position was here.'

'Alone, Majesty?' Eldric said softly.

A twinge of doubt showed on the King's face. 'You forget who and what she is, Eldric,' he replied. 'She's a Muster woman on a Muster horse. She'll reach your estates long before you and warn them of your coming. Besides, she's much loved by the people. There are many reasons why no one will stand in her way.'

Eldric shrugged resignedly. 'Well, if she's gone, she's gone. *We'll* never catch her, that's certain. But why are you here?'

Rgoric stared into the old Lord's face. Truth, he thought. Truth was what had kept Fyorlund whole for so long, and truth alone could restore it now. He took Eldric's arm and led him to one side. 'Eldric. I've no plan this day. No scheme. Nothing. To plan implies to know, and I know nothing of Dan-Tor . . . or,' he looked significantly at Eldric, 'the force that moves him.' The two men looked at one another in silence for a long moment, then the King continued. 'I knew only that I'd have one chance to learn and act. It was my hope, no more, that I could effect your release and escape, but beyond that, nothing.'

'I understand, Majesty,' Eldric said urgently. 'But you can flee now.'

Rgoric shook his head. 'No, Eldric, I can't,' he said. 'Dan-Tor's poisons have injured me irreparably, despite the efforts of Sylvriss and my appearance of well-being. It's only a matter of time before I succumb to illness again, and I see no future other than as a whingeing dotard.'

Eldric winced at the force of the King's momentary bitterness. 'Rgoric, how can you be sure of this?' he said anxiously. 'There's a great healer in the land, from Orthlund . . .'

The King waved him silent. 'I'm sure, Eldric,' he said. 'An inner sight has come with my recovery. I can't turn my feet from the path it has shown me. Be assured, what you see now is an unseasonal flowering before a cruel frost.'

Eldric was silent, head bowed.

'It's not what I'd wished for, Eldric,' the King continued. 'But it *is* the truth. Time works against us on all fronts of the battle. If you escape, then I'll have redeemed some of the failures of my poor reign. Next, I'll kill His servant here or perish in the attempt.'

Eldric stared at him. The words rang in his head – *His* servant – but before he could speak, Rgoric led him further from Jaldaric and Dilrap. 'Eldric. Sylvriss thinks I'm following on with you,' he said, very softly. 'When you meet, ask her to forgive me this last small deceit.' He hesitated and looked down at his hands. 'Tell her . . . tell her . . . we've had two lives together, one at the beginning and one at the end . . . tell her, greater joy could never have been.' Then a little more heartily, though his eyes were shining damp in the torchlight, 'As you love me, Eldric, do as I've asked – for all our sakes. Leave me to . . . to attend to my Royal duties.'

Impulsively, Eldric reached out and embraced the King. As they parted, wordlessly, the King nodded towards the door and Eldric, signalling to Dilrap and Jaldaric, marched quickly from the hall without looking back.

Rgoric listened to their receding footsteps, then slowly climbed back up on to the ancient throne of the Fyordyn Kings.

Dan-Tor strode through the corridors of the Palace, his mind in a turmoil. That the King was opposing him and perhaps even now might be wreaking havoc with his plans dwindled into insignificance against the awesome force that was drawing him inexorably towards its heart. His thoughts whirled in imitation of this maelstrom, but as he neared it, words of caution floated increasingly to the surface.

Then came the memory of his Master's terrible cold anger, and gradually his pace eased and his mind became clearer, even though the alien power was ringing like a mocking challenge through his entire body.

A warrior. An Orthlundyn. That green-eyed demon had come to confront him in his own lair! He shuddered at the memory of Orthlund and Anderras Darion and briefly his old reproach returned. Why had he done what he had done there? He brushed it aside, but the fear that came in its wake halted him as he reached the main entrance hall.

For a moment he stood, feeling the powerful presence waiting for him. It was a power such as he had not met since his return from the darkness – but it was not the Power of Ethriss awakened. Slowly, hope began to mingle with fear. With soft words and cunning, he might yet lure Hawklan into subtle captivity. It wouldn't be easy. Hawklan's distrust would be deep and profound. None the less, it was possible. The man might yet be bound and delivered to His care in Derras Ustramel.

He moved forward and the group of people gathered around the main doorway parted silently to allow him through. A harassed Urssain met him.

'Commander,' Dan-Tor said coldly. 'I'm called away from an audience with the King like some scullery-maid . . .' The look on Urssain's face stopped him.

'Ffyrst, I don't know what's happened. There's been unrest since Eldric was taken from Oremson's, and that business with the Queen didn't help, but we've had no indication of anything like this.' Urssain's voice fell to a whisper. 'The crowd's enormous. I daren't set the men on them.'

'Daren't, Commander?' said Dan-Tor, his voice heavy with contempt. 'The Mathidrin, who were prepared to face the High Guards in open battle? Daren't deal with a rabble led by a bumpkin of a healer?'

Urssain made no answer.

Hawklan had found the latter part of his journey torturingly difficult. The chorus of tiny cries that emanated from all the living things around the City had grown appallingly as he had drawn nearer. A myriad spirits sensed him for a healer and reached out to him. Their pleas hung about him like a damp cloth, impeding his movements and distracting his thoughts.

'I can't help you,' he cried out finally. 'I must find the heart of the ill that afflicts you all.'

And it's here, he thought, as the lank figure of Dan-Tor appeared at the head of the steps leading to the main doors of the Palace. It seemed to Hawklan, however, that the figure in front of him was only part of a whole, a projection into this time and place of something unbelievably wrong. Dan-Tor's very frame seemed to tear its way through the very daylight, so wrong was it.

It came to Hawklan suddenly that he had been preposterously foolish in searching so diligently for this confrontation. Perhaps indeed all his journeyings had been but the following of a carefully laid bait. Perhaps he was destined to be caught and bound by this creature. But then another voice spoke to him: told him he had had no alternative. Other things were waking than Sumeral's creatures and he must play the part he saw before him, no matter what the cost. Less would be a betrayal.

The figure rent its way further through the daylight as it moved down the steps towards him, but it stopped part way as if it had walked into some unseen barrier. A white scimitar smile split its face, but illuminated nothing.

'My Lord Hawklan,' a kindly voice floated across the court-yard. 'I can understand that you might wish to twit me for my unusual visit to your fair village, but this . . .' A long arm swept over the crowd at Hawklan's back, now watchful and silent.

The voice was amused, but nothing in Hawklan's sight radiated humour. The crowd had grown rapidly and spontaneously around him, as if his single act of defiance had crystallised the City's brooding tensions.

Before he could reply, Dan-Tor spoke again. 'I fancy we've much to talk over, you and I. Mistakes and misunderstandings to be rectified.'

Hawklan neither moved or replied, Dan-Tor's words and his awful presence belied each other so starkly.

Dan-Tor's smile broadened reassuringly. 'I'm unfamiliar with the ways of Orthlund, but if you've been any time in Fyorlund, then you must know by now that it's our way to talk. To talk endlessly, in fact. It's an old and trusted way.'

Hawklan's uncertainty grew. To stand there silent would serve no purpose. To bandy words with the man in public would be hazardous. But to enter his lair . . .?

There was a slight disturbance behind him. 'It's only the horses,' whispered Isloman, and Hawklan turned as Serian and Isloman's horse walked through the surprised crowd.

Dan-Tor quailed as he saw the sword and bow hanging from Serian's saddle. Casually, Hawklan lifted down the sword and fastened it about his waist.

Dan-Tor's smile did not fade, but the aura around him shifted restlessly. 'Lord Hawklan,' he said, 'I offer you speech, in the manner of the Fyordyn, and you arm for violence.'

Hawklan was about to speak when Serian breathed softly to him. 'Take care. The people don't have your sight. They see only his smile and your sword and stony face.'

With difficulty, Hawklan bent his mouth into a smile. 'Isn't it the way of the Fyordyn to be armed for battle when speaking in the Geadrol?'

Dan-Tor bowed slightly but did not answer.

The smile on Hawklan's face faded. It was no use. He couldn't maintain any pretence in the presence of this abomination. He felt himself being overwhelmed by forces he did not understand, and it was taking all his conscious will to restrain them. Like distant thunder, drums and trumpets sounded in his mind, as if presaging a terrible battle.

Dan-Tor felt himself similarly assailed, though he knew too well the nature of the forces he was dealing with. Around Hawklan was an aura such as he had not seen since the time of the First Coming. Every fibre of him strained to leap out and destroy this obscenity; this distortion and obstacle to His plans. But the danger . . .?

Two great and opposite forces lowered over one another like black storm clouds, held back by who knew what restraints until some tiny stirring would unleash their lightning. Each grew with the other.

Serian whinnied nervously and stepped back.

Hawklan watched, impotent, as the vague ill-formed hopes he had carried with him died at the sight of the pitiless reality he was facing. Visions of ills cured, problems solved, wrongs righted through debate and reason, laughed at him distantly for his naivety, scorned him for a fool.

The few words that he and Dan-Tor had exchanged lay between them like dead leaves: a pitiful rustling futility echoing in the awesome silence. Both pondered the featureless terrain of doubt. Neither could leave the object of his long search. Neither could seize it. The people watched, silent and uncomprehending.

Then from high above came a raucous cry. A cry that had sounded over the Mandrocs as they marched on the High Guards in Orthlund. Dan-Tor started violently. His smile vanished and he looked up at the circling Gavor. Hawklan felt the spirit around the man darken and writhe. Then abruptly he was gazing in Dan-Tor's hate-filled eyes.

'I'll not be mocked by your death bird, Orthlundyn,' came a grim and terrible voice, that seemed to fill the very sky, and Hawklan felt a great blow being gathered for the destruction of his friend.

His vision cleared. He had been drawn from Orthlund on a search for the source of a great evil. Now it lay before him, strong, vigorous and purposeful. The world would crumble before it if it were not struck down.

The healer in him said: 'Excise this diseased tissue.' The warrior roared: 'Kill it before it kills you.' And all the living things about Vakloss cried out for release and vengeance. Words would avail nothing here. The first stroke must now be his, no matter what it seemed in the eyes of the watchers.

With a movement as natural as the swaying of rushes in the wind, Hawklan swung round and lifted the Black Bow and a single arrow from his waiting horse. Dan-Tor's blow for Gavor gathered in strength then faltered, distracted by this sinister harmony at the edge of his vision. As he turned, Hawklan nocked the arrow and drew back Ethriss's Black Bow. It creaked like the mast of a tall ship then, without pause, Hawklan released Loman's arrow towards the very heart of the terrible creation that stood before him.

Dan-Tor heard its ancient song but, for all he despised humanity, it was his human frame that saved him, not his vaunted Power. Reflexes that were ancient even before he was born turned him from the path of the approaching doom, and though the arrow tore through flesh and smashed bones before it tore out through flesh again, it struck no vital organ.

The impact drove him backwards and he stumbled on the steps. Both crowd and Mathidrin stood paralysed by the suddenness of the assault and, seeing its failure, Hawklan reached for a second arrow. But the wound to Dan-Tor was to more than his mortal form. Loman had not the skills of the craftsmen of the Great Alliance, but he was a fine apprentice to them, and the arrow was as perfect in its making as any could be in that time.

Delivered from the Black Bow of Ethriss by a great warrior-healer, it rent not only Dan-Tor's flesh, but his black spirit also. His eyes widened and blazed a baleful red, and his mouth cracked open, his brown face like the crater of an angry volcano. From its depths, rising interminably from the faintest whisper was unleashed a sound that became so loud it seemed solid in the air, and so inhuman that all who heard it, save Hawklan, staggered and fell to the ground in terror.

Far to the north, a dark and brooding form heard the cry of His servant, and in cold anger reached out over the mountains and plains to deny its will.

Unnoticed, an enfeebled form slipped from His thrall.

Hawklan recognised now the creature that writhed on Loman's arrow and stood paralysed with horror. He felt no stirring within him. No resurrection of the Guardian Ethriss or any other spirit to save him from the fate that was to be his – he who had released Oklar, the earth corrupter, First among the Uhriel of Sumeral.

Images of desolated, war-sacked lands, of Tirilen, Loman, Gulda and countless others rose up to reproach him for his failure. Then in the uttermost darkness of his fear a faint familiar voice spoke to him. 'The sword, Hawklan. Ethriss's sword.' The voice was Andawyr's: pained, weak, and distant.

Unthinking, Hawklan drew the sword and held it in front of himself with trembling hands as Oklar unleashed the Old Power at him.

The ground at his feet started to rage and heave as if it were a wind-lashed ocean. Great fissures opened and closed about him like the mouths of predatory animals. A terrible rumbling seemed to fill the very universe and a million tiny barbs entered his body as if to rend and tear his every cell. Somewhere in the distance was the faint noise of falling masonry and a screaming crowd crushing itself in panic.

Hawklan knew only the sword. He poured out his spirit into its perfection and strength, hoping in some way to save those around him. But even as he did so, he knew he could not use the sword as it should be used, and he felt his own strength ebbing as the tumult grew louder and louder.

Slowly he sank to his knees and, as his mind slid into oblivion, he felt a cold presence passing near him. Sweetly spoken words of appalling malevolence formed like ice burns in his heart: '. . . Keeper . . . Ethriss's lair . . .'

Then it was gone, and darkness took him.

Chapter 56

The King sat motionless and stunned as the awesome rumbling and shaking faded and gave way to the more prosaic, identifiable sounds of panic and disorder spreading through the Palace. The torches which had flared up and filled the Throne Room with a dazzling brightness, as if to protect him from some terrible assault, now returned to normal, and Rgoric found himself tremblingly aware that some great evil was near.

Dilrap staggered into the room, wide-eyed and bewildered.

'What's happened?' the King demanded. 'That noise. And the whole Palace shaking?'

Dilrap gesticulated aimlessly. 'I don't know, Majesty,' he said fearfully. 'I was helping the Lord Eldric and his son. People are running everywhere in panic. I came straight back here.'

The King put his hand to his head in despair, then almost angrily, 'And what are you doing here anyway? You were to leave with the Lord Eldric.'

Dilrap looked at the King with unexpected resolution. 'I'm no rider, Majesty,' he said. 'Still less a warrior. It's my duty as your Secretary to stay by your side. A duty determined by the Law . . .'

'Never mind the Law,' shouted the King, his eyes widening in disbelief, 'do as I order you – get after them.'

Dilrap looked apologetic. 'Majesty, you're not above the Law. You're at once sustained and constrained by it. You can't break it without due penalty.'

Rgoric clenched his fists, but Dilrap moved forward urgently. 'Majesty, if you kill Dan-Tor, then punish me as you see fit. But if he kills you, then I'll be the only person close to Dan-Tor and loyal to the old way. I'll corrode his New Order as he corroded the old one. It may be precious little that I can do, but it's more than I can do anywhere else, and I intend to do it.'

Before the King could recover from the shock of Dilrap's unequivocal statement, a grim cortège made a noisy entrance into the hall, bearing the injured Dan-Tor in a chair.

Briefly Rgoric caught Dilrap's eye. 'Go, Honoured Secretary,' he said, very softly. 'You humble me. This is all the protection I can offer you.' Then loudly he shouted, 'Get out, you treacherous ingrate, I'll deal with you later.'

Dilrap fled.

Turning from the retreating figure, the King started in shock as he looked at his erstwhile minister and jailer. The man was both unchanged and changed beyond recognition. He radiated a force that made the King tremble. Only a black arrow embedded in his side seemed to be wholesome; only the arrow seemed to be restraining this force. All enquiry about what had happened left the King.

I must strike now, he thought. Kill this creature swiftly and have done.

Then the figure's eyes opened: distant, baleful and glowing red. They stared directly at Rgoric and fear swept over the King such as he had never known. His mind touched on the edge of the truth that was Dan-Tor.

But he returned the gaze, and the red eyes themselves became uncertain. 'I see you for what you are,' Rgoric said quietly. 'My battle against your own poisons has given me a truer sight.'

A pained hand was lifted and levelled at the King, but though Rgoric felt a power touch him, he could see the arrow absorbing much of it and, with a soundless cry, the seated figure arched its back and tugged vainly at the shaft.

Swiftly Rgoric drew his sword and strode towards the struggling figure. Fear and hatred burned in its eyes as he neared it.

'You may have some sight, Rgoric,' came a low, cavernous voice. 'But so do these, after their own light, and they're mine.'

Rgoric paused and looked at the Mathidrin standing by the figure. 'Stand aside,' he said, but none of them moved.

The fear in the red eyes faded.

'Your time is finished, Rgoric,' said Urssain. 'A new hand rules Fyorlund now. A hand stronger than yours, even though he's been foully struck down.' He looked at his men. 'Kill him,' he said.

Without hesitation, the Mathidrin moved towards the King, drawing their swords. Rgoric took his own sword in two hands and swinging it upwards cut one of them open with a terrible gaping wound from stomach to shoulder. Then, turning and swinging the sword sideways, he almost severed the head of another.

Turning again under the momentum of this stroke he impaled a third before one of them drove a sword into his back. The King rounded on his attacker and severed his hand, but another struck him from behind. His onslaught would have scattered ordinary men, but the Mathidrin were creatures possessed as they closed on him like a pack of hunting animals, regardless of their own safety.

After a few seconds, Rgoric lay face down in a welter of blood, his back and head torn and gashed with appalling wounds.

'Thus perish all our enemies,' said Urssain, his face exhilarated and his eyes shining with a strange fervour.

But, no sooner had he spoken the words, than he stepped back in alarm. The King's hands moved. With painful slowness, they started to claw at the defiled floor and pull the wrecked and bloody body forward towards the pinioned figure. The circle of Mathidrin widened, horror overcoming their bloodlust.

The King raised his head and stared into the baleful eyes again.

'I see you truly now,' said the King weakly. 'Oklar, Servant of the Great Corruptor.'

'Little may it avail you,' replied the Uhriel, though he pushed himself back in his chair as if to escape this relentless witness.

'And I see more,' said the King. A spasm of pain shook him and he grimaced, but still he crawled forward. He seemed to be looking at some distant scene.

'When you die, Oklar,' he said, 'it will be at the height of your power, when all are set to fall before you.'

The red eyes could not free themselves from Rgoric's dying stare. 'You lie,' rumbled Oklar's voice. 'You ramble in your death throes, King. I am immortal. None can slay me. And none can read the future. Not even He.'

The King laughed faintly and shook his head, scattering a

skein of blood across the Uhriel's feet. 'Ah, Oklar. How have you been deceived? Your death is before me now. Am I not descended from the Lords of the Iron Ring? Your assassin . . .'

He coughed and his body twisted in pain. 'Your assassin will be ancient and insignificant, but you will die as surely as I die now, though you will die in failure, while I die in victory . . . Know that my wife carries my heir.'

The King's voice was failing, but his dying body was all that moved in the hall.

'I see beyond your death, Oklar.' Again pain interrupted him, and his voice was weaker still when he spoke next. 'Know this. And take what solace you can, for it is not what it seems. Nothing shall end the reign of your Master.' Then he laughed strangely and, with a last effort, his bloodied hand clawed forward and gripped the cringing Oklar's foot before he fell dead.

Oklar stared down at the stricken King. His eyes blazed red and terrible, but any who could have met his gaze would have seen also fear and doubt. His boast of immortality had been idle. There was a weapon and a hand for any creature; even Him. The King's words burned inside him. Could it come to pass that he, Oklar, greatest of His Uhriel, would perish at the hands of a mere assassin, while He would reign without end? Was that to be his reward at the end of his interminable journeyings through the ages? A great roar of denial swirled inside him at this blasphemy, but he knew that he was impaled on Rgoric's death vision as surely as he was impaled on Hawklan's Black Arrow.

Slowly, the dead King's hand relaxed and slid from Oklar's foot. The movement seemed to release the Uhriel. 'Get rid of this carrion,' he said grimly.

Almost desperate to be away from the terrible presence of their Lord, several Mathidrin ran forward and, seizing the body, began dragging it across the floor. Oklar looked at the bloodstained path trailing behind the corpse and then struggled to his feet. He grimaced and Urssain stepped forward.

'Ffyrst, your injuries . . .' but his words died on his lips at Oklar's glance.

'Are beyond your aid . . . Commander,' he said. 'Beyond all aid until . . .'

He looked down at his hand. A deep and festering weal ran across it where he had seized the shaft of Hawklan's arrow.

But the pain of that was dwarfed by the threefold pain he still felt. The pain of the arrow smashing into and through him. An arrow forged in the Great Harmony of Orthlund and delivered from Ethriss's Black Bow. Then the pain of the Old Power he had released in his rage and hurt, for Ethriss's Black Sword, ineptly wielded though it had been, had returned much of it upon him. But, worse by far, was the wrath of his Master as His hand had reached out belatedly to tear his very soul in its cold fury.

Only that Ethriss had not been awakened saved Oklar from the eternal black dissolution that He offered him. 'Ethriss still sleeps, Uhriel. Accept, then, this, My benison, lest your folly better you again. Go now and do My Will.'

Then Oklar knew he must bear the arrow until He saw fit to remove it. For only He could, such was the nature of its crafting. It would remain embedded in his side, his blood dripping inexorably from the glittering point of its barbed head, to mark his passing with a carmine trail, in mocking echo of the dead King's departure.

Now he could use the Old Power only to the extent that he could withstand the pain its use would bring as the arrow drew it back upon him.

'Your wisdom and mercy are without bounds, Master,' he had cried in his agony.

Yet for all the price he had paid, all was well. Ethriss slept, and Hawklan, whoever he might have been, must surely have perished in the destruction that had been wrought by the Old Power. The Queen and Eldric were fled. They would serve as scapegoats and, together with the Lords in the east, would act as a focus for the fear and hatred of the people.

And his Mathidrin were ready.

Slowly he closed his long fingers on Urssain's shoulder for support. 'Your wisdom and mercy are indeed without bounds, Master,' he intoned to himself softly.

All was well.

The Third Chronicle Of Hawklan

Will be available from Headline SOON

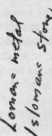

loman = metal
Islomans stone

PETER S BEAGLE

The

Folk of the Air

**"A rare and
heady delight"**
Locus

The last flourish of the pavane set the hands of
the dancers free and the torchlight made their
rings and their jewelled gloves flash fire,
scattering tiny green and violet and silver
flames like largesse to the musicians. Farrell
could not find any faces in that first wonder of
brightness and velvet, cloaks and gold and
brocade – only the beautiful clothes glittering
in a great circle, moving as though they were
inhabited, not by human heaviness, but by
marshlights and the wind. *The folk of the air,* he
thought. *These are surely the folk of the air . . .*

Nothing is quite as it seems in this
modern-day game of medieval romance and
chivalry. The revellers thought they were
playing at time and magic.

No one warned them that Time can be tricky
and Magic dangerous.

Peter Beagle, in his first fantasy novel since the
bestselling *The Last Unicorn,* again proves his
mastery in a glorious tale of magic, illusion
and delusion.

"Highly recommended" *Fantasy Review*

FICTION/FANTASY   0 7472 3138 9   £2.99

RU EMERSON

TO THE
Haunted Mountains

THE FIRST TALE OF NEDAO

Here is the tale of the valorous Ylia, she of the
red-gold hair, daughter of the brave King Brandt and
his witchwife Queen Scythia.

Forced to flee for her life when the barbarian Tehlatt
hordes overwhelm and sack the kingdom of Nedao,
Ylia, sole remaining member of the royal family,
must become swordswoman and sorceress if she is
to claim her throne again.

Accompanied by her magical companion Nisana, the
only Ældran of cat-kind to dwell among the Nedao,
Ylia and her tiny band of survivors must face dark
perils and legendary evils on their journey to
sanctuary through the ominous Haunted Mountains
of Foessa.

The Lady of Nedao must wield her newly-found
powers over an ancient evil and an awesome enemy
if she is to succeed in her quest . . .

The first book in an epic fantasy trilogy in the great
tradition of J R R Tolkien's *The Lord of the Rings*.

FICTION/FANTASY   0 7472 3140 0   £2.99

A selection of bestsellers from Headline

FICTION

BLOOD STOCK	John Francome & James MacGregor	£3.99 □
THE OLD SILENT	Martha Grimes	£4.50 □
ALL THAT GLITTERS	Katherine Stone	£4.50 □
A FAMILY MATTER	Nigel Rees	£4.50 □
EGYPT GREEN	Christopher Hyde	£4.50 □

NON-FICTION

MY MOUNTBATTEN YEARS	William Evans	£4.50 □
WICKED LADY		
Salvador Dali's Muse	Tim McGirk	£4.99 □
THE FOOD OF SPAIN AND PORTUGAL	Elisabeth Lambert Ortiz	£5.99 □

SCIENCE FICTION AND FANTASY

REVENGE OF THE FLUFFY BUNNIES Cineverse Cycle Book 3	Craig Shaw Gardner	£3.50 □
BROTHERS IN ARMS	Lois McMaster Bujold	£4.50 □
THE SEA SWORD	Adrienne Martine-Barnes	£3.50 □
NO HAVEN FOR THE GUILTY	Simon Green	£3.50 □
GREENBRIAR QUEEN	Sheila Gilluly	£4.50 □

All Headline books are available at your local bookshop or newsagent, or can be ordered direct from the publisher. Just tick the titles you want and fill in the form below. Prices and availability subject to change without notice.

Headline Book Publishing PLC, Cash Sales Department, PO Box 11, Falmouth, Cornwall, TR10 9EN, England.

Please enclose a cheque or postal order to the value of the cover price and allow the following for postage and packing:
UK: 80p for the first book and 20p for each additional book ordered up to a maximum charge of £2.00
BFPO: 80p for the first book and 20p for each additional book
OVERSEAS & EIRE: £1.50 for the first book, £1.00 for the second book and 30p for each subsequent book.

Name ....

Address ....

....

....